FOUL LINES

LINES

A Pro Basketball
Novel

JACK MCCALLUM AND **L. JON WERTHEIM**

A Touchstone Book
Published by Simon & Schuster
New York   London   Toronto   Sydney

TOUCHSTONE
Rockefeller Center
1230 Avenue of the Americas
New York, NY 10020

TOUCHSTONE and colophon are registered trademarks
of Simon & Schuster, Inc.

Designed by Jamie Kerner-Scott

Manufactured in the United States of America

1 3 5 7 9 10 8 6 4 2

Library of Congress Cataloging-in-Publication Data

McCallum, Jack, 1949–
Foul lines : a pro basketball novel / Jack McCallum and L. Jon Wertheim.
p. cm.
"A Touchstone book."
ISBN-13: 978-0-7432-8650-3
ISBN-10: 0-7432-8650-2
1. Professional basketball–Fiction. 2. Basketball stories.
I. Wertheim, Jon. II. Title.

PS3613.C34518F68 2006
813'.6—dc22

For information regarding special discounts for bulk purchases,
please contact Simon & Schuster Special Sales at 1-800-456-6798
or business@simonandschuster.com.

FOUL LINES

LOS ANGELES LASERS FRONT OFFICE

President/CEO	Owen Padgett	Pepperdine
GM/Basketball Operations	Manuel Burnett	Ohio State
Director, Media Relations	Henry Shenk	USC
Asst. Director, Media Relations	Evan Peterwicz	Pomona College

LOS ANGELES LASERS ROSTER

NO	PLAYER	POS	HT	WT	SCHOOL	YEARS PRO
00	Litanium Johnson	G	6-2	175	Florida	7
10	Willie Wainwright	G	6-3	192	Hunter	6
11	Wallace Reynolds **	G	5-7	149	Sharpton JC	0
19	James Taylor	F/G	6-5	190	Wyoming	4
21	Ricardo Diaz	F	6-4	171	Puerta de Dios H.S. R	
23	Kwaanzii Parker	F/G	6-6	198	Shabazz (Las Vegas) H.S.	
32	Lorenzen Mayne [C]	F	6-6	210	North Carolina	7
33	Shane Donnelly *	F	6-9	228	UCLA	8
42	Abraham Oka Kobubee	C	6-11	205	Mutombo Prep (Djibouti)	3
44	Clarence Wolff	F	6-8	220	Princeton	6
50	B. D. Lake	C	7-0	255	Liberty	9
55	Charles Reichley	C	7-0	275	Muhlenberg	11

* On Injured List
** No Longer on Squad
[C] Team Captain

COACHES: JOHN WATSON (Indiana, '75)
DOUG CARTER (Butler, '76)

DANCE CAPTAIN: Denise "Cherry Pie" Holstrum (L.A. Chic Beauty College)

CHAPTER 1

The first thing everybody told Kwaanzii Parker was not to blow a hundred grand of his signing money on a ride. Which is precisely what he did. "Gonna get me a phat crib, but the ride's gotta come first, yo," he said. Kwaanzii's selection was a Robitussin-purple Jaguar with plates that read KINGKWAAN! Like most professional athletes, Kwaanzii tooled around in an automobile equipped with a jet engine, two elaborate hood ornaments, neon underbelly, and the vanity plates. But he just hated it when somebody recognized him.

Kwaanzii, a tender eighteen, was eight months removed from his high-school prom—which he attended with rap star Shabeera Slade, an event that rated five minutes on BET—and seven months removed from his high school graduation, which he passed up in favor of Shaq's All-Star Super Jamaica Jam. From the time he was an AAU star in Las Vegas at the wizened age of thirteen, King Kwaan was in the E-ZPass lane to the National Basketball Federation, never a thought that he would spend so much as one night on a college campus, unless, as one recruiter put it, "He was making a weekend booty call."

Kwaanzii had developed a close personal relationship with an older Los Angeles Laser teammate, point guard Litanium "Tribal Cat" Johnson, one based entirely on an overlapping pharmacological aesthetic and a willingness to reach excessive speeds on the highway. Litanium was currently hiding from the public in an orange Lamborghini Gallardo with plates that read YR O DA CAT. Tribal Cat called Kwaanzii a "Jag fag," though secretly he admired the teenager's ride and pondered picking up one himself, though at the moment he was, to paraphrase his accountant, "slightly cash deficient."

The players bonded when, back in early October, they happened to pull out of media day together and begin a friendly race along Figueroa Street in downtown Los Angeles. Kwaanzii won that one, which didn't sit well with Litanium, who the next day kicked it up to 125 mph and nipped Kwaanzii. Litanium christened their competition Drag Club and felt much pride when it spread throughout the team. Litanium had always considered himself a leader. Quoting one of his favorite movies, Litanium often counseled his teammates, "First rule of Drag Club is you do not talk about Drag Club."

Litanium and Kwaanzii were the most avid participants of Drag Club, though. They had raced a dozen times, and Litanium, nothing if not an inveterate competitor, secretly kept a log of the results. Much to his dismay, the rookie had won eight of their showdowns. Litanium considered their races a show of esprit de corps—"closing the generational gap," as he put it—while Lasers coach John Watson, who was almost sideswiped by Litanium as he pulled out of practice one day, called them "brain-dead assholes racing to the morgue."

Having begun as a daylight activity, Drag Club had lately moved to the nocturnal hours. And tonight, as Litanium saw it, seemed ideal for a chapter meeting. Following a 101–83 victory over Seattle, most of the team was scattered about The Vines, a trendy nightclub near Malibu owned by a close friend of Lasers owner Owen Padgett. The occasion was a commemoration of Coach Watson's fiftieth, though the evening's business—a desultory rendering of "Happy Birthday" and the presentation of a laptop to Watson, a confirmed Luddite—was over quickly. Litanium had played well with eighteen points and eleven assists, and Kwaanzii hadn't played at all. (Watson didn't have much faith in rookies.) Litanium figured that Kwaanzii would be angry and distracted.

Litanium wasn't eager to convene a meeting of Drag Club in front of Watson. But he knew he could do it on the sly, since the birthday boy sat alone in a far corner of The Vines, nursing a ginger ale, lost in his own dark thoughts. A former star player, Watson was a recovering addict who missed the halcyon days of cocaine and Jack Daniel's, even though a formidable coupling of the two had on several occasions landed him in the slammer, and, finally, in a thirty-day dryout at the ten-thousand-dollar-a-week Rush Limbaugh Clinic.

He emerged committed to sobriety but, as he saw it, a far less interesting personality; when pressed, friends and family had to agree. The laptop sat unopened at his side. Watson still wrote out his game plans in longhand and his inability to open his e-mails had once caused the Lasers' internal system to crash. The gift was, as Watson saw it, another indication that Padgett didn't really know him, as well as a dead giveaway that the owner was on the board of directors of the computer company and got the damn thing for free.

As for Litanium, he had to weigh the prospect of a race against the prospect of going home with one of the two fine ladies with whom he and Kwaanzii were consorting at the main bar. The women said they were "freelance actresses," though they were vague about their resumes, and Litanium thought that one of them looked suspiciously like an enthusiastic supporting player in one of his pornos. At the moment, Kwaanzii, draining his fourth underage Heineken, was running through his list of favorite shows on the WB and was only up to Tuesday.

Upstairs in the VIP room of The Vines, meanwhile, the mind of Lorenzen Mayne, the Lasers' captain and franchise player, was far from Drag Club. By unwritten edict, the VIP room was off-limits to the team, unless Owen Padgett summoned a particular player for a meeting, which had been the case this evening. The VIP room was stocked (and restocked) daily with Johnny Walker Black, Pellegrino, caviar, and a minimum of two stunning hostesses, and the owner felt quite at home there.

Padgett had bought the Lasers four years earlier, plunking down 425 million of his own dollars, a portion of the billion he had inherited from his father, Preston Padgett, who, before his fifth and final coronary, had been the nation's largest bulk garbage collector. Owen was mortified that his largesse came from the remains of last night's dinner, and, in interviews, tried never to mention his father, subtly selling the angle that he was self-made. When Owen had to mention the old man, Preston was alternately a "refuse magnate" or a "sanitation czar." At any rate, Owen ran hard from his past, carefully cultivating the image of a maverick. At age twenty-five, he had made the cover of *Fortune*, adorned with an ironic Bob Seger and the Silver Bullet Band T-shirt. Owen was on the cover again three years later after he bought the Lasers, posing with an electric guitar around his neck and a sneer on his face. "I'm in the house, and the NBF will never be the same!" read the cover line.

Even more than he considered himself an entrepreneur, Padgett saw himself as a shrewd judge of human nature. Most profiles written about him said that he would've gone for his doctorate in psychology if, as he put it, "the money thing" hadn't gotten in the way. Two things about human nature he knew. First, in a group, particularly a small group such as a basketball team, it is of crucial importance to get the ear of the leader. Second, when you talk to a guy, do it on your turf. The VIP room was his turf and Lorenzen Mayne was clearly the leader of the Lasers.

Tall, broad-shouldered, narrow-hipped, and handsome, Lo Mayne looked every part the leader. He had reached his height (six feet, six inches) by degrees, rather than in one awkward spurt, and he moved with an easy-jointed grace, perfect in every way save the pigeon-toed walk that became more pronounced in competition. Lo hadn't lost any of his hair—in his rookie season he had even worn a throwback Afro in homage to Julius Erving—and he couldn't for the life of him understand why anyone would shave his head. He kept his hair stylishly short. He had worn a mustache (to make him look older) in his first year in the league and tried what Coach Watson called "a starter-set goatee" in the second, but now he was clean-shaven. Lo would've looked comfortable in a white tux coat and black silk pants, singing in a fifties nightclub, like one of the Platters.

Still, in the VIP room, Mayne did feel uncomfortable. Four times he had declined one of the brunettes' invitations to "try the Beluga" and waited for Padgett to tell him why he had been summoned. "You don't like caviar, Lo?" Padgett asked. Apparently, caviar refusal was a capital offense in the VIP room, so he scooped some up with a cracker.

"Now, Lo, here's what I been thinking," said Padgett. "We're going along pretty well. Not the best team in the league but one of them. But we're not real exciting. People don't look at us like must-see hoops."

"Well, I always thought winning was the bottom line," said Lo. "Didn't matter how you did it as long as you did it."

Padgett shook his head. "That's old-school thinking, and I appreciate it," he said. "That's why you were great. That's why you're *still* great. But I gotta look at it from a couple different angles. Like, the angle of putting butts in the seats."

"And?" said Lo.

"And so I been thinking about the kid. Kwaanzii. I wanna tell . . . I wanna *encourage* John to use him more. Maybe even start him."

Lo shrugged.

"What was the biggest story with this franchise last season?" said Padgett. "Making the playoffs and getting beat in the first round? You being named the damn Chic Cologne player of the month a couple times, no offense intended? No, the biggest story was us trading up so we could draft Kwaanzii after the season. The fans were all over it. Now we've gotta get them more of him."

Lo was torn. He didn't believe that a kid who thought setting a pick had something to do with a hairbrush should get much playing time. Lo was no throwback but he was old-school enough to believe that a young man could learn something in college. Lo himself had attended the University of North Carolina for two years and during that time had even shown up at roughly half of his classes, real ones, too, like Introduction to Psychology and Principles of Assistant Coaching. "That college shit rubs off," he often said. On the other hand, Lo felt that coaches were too conservative about breaking in young talent. As a rookie, Lo himself had sat on the bench for a month under the regime of the previous coach, Dean DeShue, and when DeShue finally came to his senses and played him, Lo averaged nineteen points a game and was named Ikea Rookie of the Year.

"Look, think this over," Padgett said. "I'm glad we had this time to talk. Early meeting in Studio City tomorrow, so I gotta get going. I guess you heard about the show?"

Lo spread his hands.

"My reality show," said Padgett, his voice now animated. "Second-season replacement that's gonna start in January. I'm exec-producing and starring."

Man, thought Lorenzen, *they'll put anything on TV.*

CHAPTER 2

After a series of desperate attempts, Harrison Brewster had whiffed with the co-eds at the Anchor Bar. Ushered out after last call, he returned to the dorm, Prescott Hall, for a customary game of "nocturnal solitaire." Prescott, one of the oldest dorms at Yale, has served as the living quarters for three U.S. presidents, eight governors, and countless congressmen. It is a gorgeous, graceful gothic building that plays prominently on most architectural tours of New England.

The interior is considerably less decorous. The halls are perfumed with a mix of pot, incense, and adolescent sweat generated on the intramural fields; the floors are covered with Budweiser-stained carpeting; a marble lobby has been turned into a public computer center, used mostly for illegal downloads and late-night sojourns to porn sites; the walls are festooned with neon-colored fliers calling attention to "A rally of solidarity on behalf of marginalized Ugandan fruit-pickers" and a dorm ski trip to Stowe organized by the Young Republicans.

As Harrison entered his two-room suite overlooking a courtyard, it was illuminated with the fuzzy glow from the computer screen. His roommate, Jamal Kelly, was still up, combing through the late box scores of the NBF's West Coast games. A tall and plainly handsome Will Smith lookalike—albeit with a silly collegiate soul patch—Jamal was technically a senior majoring in political science. But lately he had devoted the bulk of his time to all things related to the National Basketball Federation. He had even spliced the dorm cable and run it to his and Harrison's televisions, enabling him to watch two games at once.

A math whiz with a savantlike gift for statistics, Jamal had created what he called "Sabermetrics for Hoops." It started innocently enough. Early in his junior year, he was watching a game when the announcer described a player with the hoariest cliché: *Jackson is so valuable because he does things that don't show up in the box score.* The cartoon bulb above Jamal's head illuminated. *Well, maybe the box score needs to be changed.*

With a lot of trial and error and a lot of regression analysis, Jamal created a battery of statistics that, he believed, anyway, were more meaningful and revealing than traditional metrics, such as points, rebounds, and assists. Running the numbers through his system, he could determine which players helped their team's average performance and which hurt it—the basketball equivalent of hockey's plus-minus system. He could tell which players ranked highest in retrieving loose balls, which lineups were the most effective, which players were worth their contracts.

What started as a pet exercise evolved into Jamal's final project for his Game Theory course. It earned him an A and, while his bearded, epically halitosised professor was no basketball fan— "How come there are no statistics for Yale's NBF team?" he once asked Jamal—the analysis earned Jamal the Hersch Undergraduate Ingenuity Prize and a story on page one of the *New York Times* sports section.

This year, Jamal had put his statistical model to use in his three fantasy leagues. Though it was early in the season, his teams were in first place by preposterously large margins. Several other "owners" had already said they were quitting if Jamal kept his teams in competition the following season. "It's like getting in a physics game with Einstein," one of them said. Jamal was increasingly confident that he had created a groundbreaking analytical tool, though it also served to intensify a relationship with the NBF that was already close to obsessive. Having spent one too many dinners competing for attention with a game unfolding over her shoulder, Katerina Johansson, Jamal's exchange student girlfriend, had recently dumped him. He had also stopped IMing the sophomore hottie with whom he had reliably trysted for most of last year. He figured those extra few minutes were better spent running his numbers.

"Dude, you're sick," Harrison said, kicking off a pair of cowboy boots Jamal had always assumed his roomie wore to offset his *Mayflower*-sounding name. "It's your senior year and you're a rotisserie geek."

"Yeah, I'd be better off dropping forty bones at the Anchor," Jamal said, "all so I can come back and wrestle the eel."

"Hey, at least I'll be doing it thinking of chicks and not seven-footers who can run the floor."

Jamal shrugged. "Anyway, Lasers won. Beat Seattle 101–83."

"I'll make some calls," said Brewster. "See if I can get a campus celebration together."

Jamal ignored him. "I'm running some Laser numbers. Litanium had a big night. Watson didn't play the kid again."

Jamal had always been a decent basketball player. In middle school he was a backup guard on a Brooklyn AAU team with guys who went on to play in college, though he suspected that his older brother's hoops history had as much to do with it as anything else. Jamal played on his freshman team in high school before getting cut from the junior varsity as a sophomore. Though he never sprouted past six-one, he was one of Yale's better intramural play-ers. As much as playing basketball, he loved watching the game: the ballet, the poetry, the improvisation. While he couldn't afford to go to many NBF games as he was growing up in New York City, he had always known the league the way Huck Finn knew the Mississippi. Between poring over box scores, reading all manner of pro hoops publications, and playing beaucoup NBF games on his Sega Dreamcast, Jamal had a frightening familiarity with every player in the league. Harrison would sometimes flip randomly to a page in the basketball guides stacked against the wall and call out a name. *Montel Mack!* Jamal would dutifully play along, reciting the player's year of birth, college team, height, weight, and scoring average from the previous season. The depth of Jamal's addiction had been laid bare earlier in the semester when he skipped a Comparative Politics class to catch an afternoon Developmental League game between Roanoke and Fayetteville on (spliced) ESPN2.

Jamal knew the pop psychology explanation. As college was drawing to a close, he was wrapping himself up in the familiar—basketball—so he didn't have to deal with so much of the swirling uncertainty in his life. All of his classmates, it seemed, had iron-clad game plans for after graduation. They were lining up jobs and fellowships or landing roster spots in med schools. Jamal was a free agent. When he got the inevitable question that torments all sen-iors—"What are your plans for next year?"—Jamal gave a stock answer about "keeping lots of irons in the fire."

His mother, Betty, was lead vocalist in the nagging chorus. Mostly to soothe her anxiety, Jamal had followed the path of least resistance and taken the LSAT with vague designs of going to law school. The same way other kids in the neighborhood could natu-rally dribble a ball as if it were an extension of their arms, Jamal had a sixth sense for standardized tests. With a little studying and less sleep the night before—after all, Portland was playing Dallas in a critically important November game—Jamal had posted the equivalent of a forty-point, twenty-rebound game on the test. When law schools got wind of an African-American kid from Yale with killer test scores, a solid GPA, and some kind of prize-winning, esoteric statistical system, they all but prostrated themselves before him. Jamal had some sense of what it felt like to be a stud recruit. In the course of a week, unnaturally chipper representatives from law schools at Columbia, Boston College, NYU, and Michigan all called Jamal with a sales pitch, invariably making mention of a "diverse student body." Each made it clear, not just that he would be admitted, but that he needn't worry about tuition. Yet every time he sat down to fill out the applications, he felt a tug at his soul and found a reason to put it off—usually having something to do with a basketball game.

Jamal actually had a small aperture into the front office of the Los Angeles Lasers, his favorite team once the New York Gothams had traded their longtime star center, an act of unforgivable disloyalty in Jamal's eyes. During the fall semester, Jamal's econometrics professor, Matt McQuade, had asked to see him after class. A California transplant in his early forties given to wearing Diesel jeans and shoes without socks, McQuade barely looked up from his computer screen. "Hey, you think Phoenix should have made that trade for Johnson and Woods last night?"

Trick question? "Um, yeah," he said. "They filled a need at the guard spot. Woods plays better in high-scoring games and Johnson plays better against teams in the West—so both should do well in Phoenix. Plus they freed up some cap space for the off-season. Anywhere from five to eight million dollars as I see it." Then came an awkward pause. "Can I ask why?"

McQuade finally looked up. "Someone told me before the semester that you're a boy genius. They called you 'The *Moneyball*

Kid.' Guess you came up with all these amazing metrics for evalu-
ating NBF players. I was talking about it with a buddy of mine
who's big into basketball and I told him this kid in my
Monday–Wednesday is so amped about the NBF that he does his
own statistical analysis and reads over the printouts while I'm lec-
turing."

"Sorry, professor," Jamal said sheepishly.

"No, it's cool. It'd be one thing if you were failing, but you obviously get the material. Anyway, this friend of mine wanted to know
your opinion of the trade. He cares so much because he owns the
Lasers—"

Like a character in a bad sitcom, Jamal came close to performing a spit take with his bottled water. "Owen Padgett?" he said.
"Owen Padgett's your friend?"

"We were in a band together at Pepperdine. Big career mistake
he made not joining me in grad school, huh? Anyway, he asks me
from time to time if there any are bright kids he can hire. Be happy
to pass on your name if you'd ever want to—"

"That would be unbelievable."

"Cool. I'll give him your e-mail. And I'll tell him what you said
about Phoenix."

For the next few days, Jamal could scarcely concentrate during
class or even on the intramural fields, visions of a plum NBF job
dancing in his head. He had even written a small script in anticipation of Padgett's call. But that was more than a month ago and
Jamal hadn't heard anything from the Lasers.

CHAPTER 3

Time to be gettin' on, Kwaanz," said Litanium, tapping his watch. "Curfew and all that."

"I was thinking I'd maybe stick around, Cat," said the rookie. "Talk a little bit more to Leesha here." He leaned over and whispered to Litanium, "I think I can tap this shit."

"I told you before it's A-lee-sha," said the possible actress, who was at least a decade older than Kwaanzii. "Three syllables." Apparently the WB run-through had not been a successful seduction tool.

"Yeah? Well, you been disrespecting me all night, saying my name as Kwan-zee. It's Kwaaaan-Ziiiii. You gotta draw that shit out."

"Young fella has motherfuckin' As and Is all over that first name," said Litanium. "Takes some getting used to."

"Are you leaving too, honey?" asked Litanium's possible actress, whose name was either Kitten or Kristen.

"Yeah, we gotta go," Litanium said. "Kwaanz, you get these two fine ladies' phone numbers and we will definitely be in touch."

"I look like your bitch?" said Kwaanzii.

But Litanium was already gone, looking around for Drag Club

candidates. Shane Donnelly, the Lasers' hulking power forward, who spent much of his time on injured reserve nursing maladies (gastritis, chronic ingrown toenails, impetigo, and soft tissue injuries) that were undetectable by X-ray, had frequently joined Litanium and Kwaanzii in his shamrock-green Porsche 911 Turbo. But, alas, Donnelly had disappeared into the kitchen and, presumably, out the back door with the twenty-one-year-old daughter of The Vines' owner.

Ricardo "Buenos" Diaz had bought himself a little red Corvette when he became Paraguay's first NBF player, and was glad to have been welcomed into Drag Club. Diaz had grown up in Asunción, as most Paraguayans do, and in his section of the city there were no traffic lights. Driving at felonious speeds without the inconvenience of stopping was a natural for him, and he continuously babbled about "mas and mas car races" until Litanium silenced him. But Buenos was otherwise engaged, relaxing with Denise "Cherry Pie" Holstrum, the choreographer of the Laserettes dance team, who had just finished giving him one of her patented backrubs. Cherry Pie used her backrub—her promotional literature touted her as a "licensed massage therapist"—as a way of introducing herself to all the new players, though she had an inviolate policy on fooling around: no sleeping with a Laser until after All-Star Weekend.

"Mañana maybe?" Buenos asked hopefully.

"No mañana," Cherry Pie said good-naturedly.

But Buenos was going to hang in there.

Another enthusiastic Drag Club member was James Taylor, a lightning-quick swingman who was, improbably, a Caucasian and thus inevitably known to the public as Sweet Baby James. Taylor longed desperately to be an African-American, though, and wanted everyone to call him Melvin. He was not successful in this and his teammates mostly called him "Em," short for Eminem. His ride was a coal-black Dodge Viper. Litanium noticed that Sweet Baby James was chatting up two African-American models, the only phylum of female he considered dating, and nothing would deter him from those appointed rounds.

B. D. Lake, the Lasers' starting center, a self-professed Internet-ordained minister and self-proclaimed "born-again virgin," had railed against Drag Club as "an execretious display of automotive amorality." But one day he pulled out of practice in his celestial-blue Lotus Esprit, the one with a vanity bumper sticker that read B.D. IS GOING TO HEAVEN—WHAT ABOUT YOU? and spotted Em's Viper. Next thing B.D. knew, he was in a furious hundred-mile-per-hour duel, which he won. "It's like the devil hisself has his hands on the wheel," said B.D. "I think the Lord is testing me." To date, B.D. had taken a half dozen such tests.

But B.D. was trying desperately to hold the attention of his guest for the evening, a well-groomed, gray-haired man named Wilson Wesley, a best-selling author of religious tomes. B.D. had invited Wesley to The Vines both to explain his concept of "born-again virginity" and to discuss potential coauthorship of an inspirational book entitled *Around the Rim of Righteousness*. Wesley said he would need more time to think about the book deal, and that he would have to "seek God's counsel" on regenerative virginity. Actually, Wesley had been distracted most of the evening by the enthusiastic chiropractic work of Cherry Pie Holstrum.

"My, that dance person is a live wire, isn't she?" Wesley commented to B.D.

"She's a child," said B.D., "of Satan."

Litanium's search continued. He knew not even to ask Abraham Oka Kobubee, a handsome, smooth-skinned backup center from Djibouti. Kobubee, known universally as A-Okay, dared not even urinate unless first granted permission from his wife, a plain-looking American woman named Betty Jo who had met him during an anthropology trip to his godforsaken country just north of Ethiopia. Betty Jo was the only Laser wife who regularly attended team functions, and on this night they sat together in a far corner. Earlier in the evening Betty Jo thought she had detected her husband stealing a glance at one of the Laser cheerleaders and immediately exiled him behind a post.

Nor were Willie Wainwright and Clarence Wolff candidates. Wainwright, a heavily muscled backup guard who grew up in Pittsburgh, had gotten into a bad automobile accident as a senior—his best friend was killed—and he was one of the few athletes on the planet who drove at a sensible speed. And Wolff, a spindly, poetry-writing, macrobiotic-dieting reserve forward out of Princeton, "the unlikeliest black man this side of Al Roker" as Coach Watson called him, didn't even own a car. He got by with a twelve-speed bicycle, public transportation (such as it was in L.A.), and the considerable largesse of friends.

The stalwarts of the Lasers' public relations staff, director Henry Shenk and assistant Evan Peterwicz, sat at the main bar, staring into their respective drinks, Dewar's, neat, for Shenk, Diet Coke for Peterwicz. Over the years they had morphed so dolefully into a single spiritless entity that the reporters covering the Lasers had taken to referring to them as the monolithic "Shenkawicz." Manny Burnett, the Lasers' general manager, insisted that Shenkawicz attend every team affair, even the informal ones. Burnett said it was "in case any news broke out," but, really, it was in case any trouble had to be swept under the bearskin. At a similar function two years ago Litanium had splintered a pool cue over the head of a Laser fan, and last season a near-riot ensued when three of Shane Donnelly's love interests showed up simultaneously. Litanium was desperate for competitors. But not that desperate. Anyway, both drove station wagons.

Litanium had all but concluded it was going to be another two-man duel between him and Kwaanzii when he spotted Lorenzen Mayne coming down the circular stairs from the VIP room. Lo, who piloted a gunmetal Hummer, had indulged in Drag Club only once, finishing second in a three-man scrum with Kwaanzii and Buenos Diaz. Reckless driving actually scared Lo, and he thought about bringing up the dangers of Drag Club at a team meeting. He never did, though, rationalizing that Laser team chemistry was so combustible that anything that brought the players together, including high-risk behavior that didn't contravene the league's drug policy, could be considered beneficial.

"Yo, Lo, you in tonight?" said Litanium. "You looking a little depressed after your meeting. What'd the man tell you?"

Lo shook his head. "Nah, I better be going."

"Well, I guarantee you be home faster if you run with the two dawgs here."

Lo shrugged. The Heinekens did the talking for him. "What the hell," he said. He put one arm around Litanium and the other around Kwaanzii, who had joined them.

"Remember," said Litanium, "first rule of Drag Club is you do not talk about Drag Club."

Kwaanzii looked at him. "Why you always say that?"

"Generation gap," he said to Lo. "You run into it all the motherfuckin' time."

MOST OF THE PATRONS WHO left The Vines turned left and drove down to the Pacific Coast Highway. But if you turned right, Canyon Road continued into the hills, dead-ending after two miles. It was the most deserted area of Los Angeles. Every few years, a hunting dog or a solitary jogger would come upon a body, and the crime-scene squads would show up, and the next day's paper would carry a story headlined "Body Found on Deserted Canyon Road."

Its desolation made it the perfect spot for Drag Club. The road was relatively flat and straight except near the end of the course when it suddenly graded upward, just before it made a slight turn to the right. At speeds of more than one hundred miles per hour, all four tires could leave the ground on that mogul, and it was during those exhilarating seconds when races were won and lost.

Litanium generously offered Lo Mayne and his Hummer the inside position as well as a fifty-yard head start. He was on the far right with Kwaanzii in the middle. As they climbed into their cars, Litanium thought briefly that he should remind Lo and Kwaanzii about the rise in the road, then thought it foolish to squander a competitive edge. He blinked his lights twice and on the third, the prearranged signal, Lo shot forward. Litanium and Kwaanzii waited a second or two, then took off in hot pursuit.

As Lo sped along, all those things he had been worried about—maintaining his status as one of the elite players in the league; losing fifty large on one of his brother-in-law's half-baked schemes (the nation's first "rap-ee-okee bar"); and now Padgett's idea of turning over the team to a child—melted away. *A race is like a basketball game*, he thought. *Focus, determination, competitive instincts.* Peripherally, he saw Kwaanzii gaining on his right and sensed Litanium coming up on Kwaanzii in the far lane. Lo pushed harder on the already depressed pedal, rising off the seat to put all his weight on it, his headlights dancing wildly along the distant horizon. He didn't see the rise in the road until he was about ten yards from it, just as Kwaanzii and Litanium pulled even, then surged ahead. Lo glanced right and by the light of the moon he could see the rookie wearing a malevolent smile. Then he saw that replaced by a look of absolute panic and . . .

What the hell . . .

Lo saw something fly by his left front bumper. For a split second a peculiar thought went through his head: *It looks like a witch on a broom. A witch with a stud in each nostril.* Kwaanzii braked, and his car fishtailed crazily to the left, just as Lo stepped on his brakes and went into his own spin. Lo nailed Kwaanzii's left fender with his right headlight, and they both fought to gain control as the cars broke off. Kwaanzii's car zigged and Lo's zagged and they ended up on opposite sides of the road. Litanium had braked to a stop twenty-five yards ahead. Slowly, Litanium put his Lamborghini into reverse, backed up, and stopped about ten feet in front of Lo's car.

By that time, a panicked Lo was running toward the far side of the road, yanking at the cell phone attached to his belt. *Oh, man, she's gotta be alive,* he prayed. The shoulder was only about two feet wide and the terrain dropped off into a ravine. Lorenzen tightroped along the small, muddy expanse, slushy from recent rains, and saw nothing, no body, and for a moment he could hope it was all a dream. But it was clear that the victim had hit the shoulder and tumbled down the ravine.

"You believe this shit?" said Litanium, who had reached Lo's side. "What the hell is somebody doing walking out here this time of night? I mean, that shit is . . . Lo! Hey! Whassup? Put that phone away!"

"I'm calling 9-1-1," said Lorenzen.

"This ain't the time to be diming anybody, and you sure don't want to be bringing in the cops."

"Cat, there's been an accident and somebody's hurt and that's what you do in these situations," said Lorenzen.

"You gotta chill," said Litanium. "We gotta think this thing through. We got the young fella over in his car, probably in shock and shit."

"Well, when they come, they can take care of him, too," said Lo, resuming his dialing. "But that woman might be alive. We gotta get to her."

Quick as a cat, Litanium, the NBF's steals leader two seasons ago, swiped the phone from Lorenzen's hands and pitched it down the ravine.

"You crazy!" screamed Lorenzen. "Get out your phone and make the call, man! We're talking about somebody's life here!"

"We ain't talking about no such thing," said Litanium. "That woman is dead sure as shit flows downhill. Ain't nobody saving her. Now let's get the young fella out here and we'll put our heads together."

"I'm going down there, Cat," said Lorenzen, rolling up the cuffs of his Lucky jeans.

Litanium grabbed Lorenzen's right arm and pulled him back. At that point Kwaanzii got out of his car and walked slowly toward them, slouching, hands in his pockets.

"Where's he going?" said Kwaanzii.

"Going down to see what kind of mess we're in," said Lorenzen.

"What kind of mess *I'm* in, you mean," said Kwaanzii. "I'm the one who hit her."

"Nobody's in any kind of mess yet," said Litanium. "Let's think this over now. You both sure it was a woman?"

Lo nodded and so did Kwaanzii.

"I saw a young woman's face," said Lo, "with a stud in each nostril."

Kwaanzii nodded assent.

"Ain't no woman surviving that shit," said Litanium, "unless she was Wonder Fuckin' Woman."

Lorenzen began rolling up his trousers again. "One of you two can whip out your cell right now," said Lo, "or I'm going down. Your choice." Neither Litanium nor Kwaanzii moved, and Lo started down the hill, turning his body diagonally to the slope and taking little steps so as not to slip.

"Think what you're doing here, man," said Litanium. "You're

selling this young fella out. You selling the team out. And you might be selling yourself out. Now get your ass back up here."

Lo kept going.

"Wait!" said Kwaanzii. "I got an idea." The rookie ran to his car, popped the trunk, and came back.

"Binoculars," said Kwaanzii proudly, holding out a black case. "Real professional kind. See at night and shit. I keep 'em for special emergencies."

"Young fella can't keep track of his playbook," said Litanium, "but he's got motherfuckin' binoculars in the trunk."

Lo grabbed the case, unzipped it, and trained the glasses on the bottom of the ravine. The binocs, equipped with a powerful ultraviolet light, turned everything a hazy green. The terrain was rough and rocky and Lo could see the outline of a muddy creek bed.

"You see anything, Lo?" Kwaanzii asked, his voice hushed.

Lorenzen moved the glasses back and forth, like a field commander scouting a battle. After a couple of minutes, he froze his glasses on one spot.

"I see her," Lo said in a hoarse whisper.

Litanium moved behind Lo and carefully took the glasses from his hands. It took a couple of seconds but he, too, fixed on the spooky tableau—a woman, apparently young, propped up against a rock as if in some grotesque parody of a nap, her right arm wrapped back around her head at a gruesome angle.

"Damn, like that dude in *Deliverance*," said Litanium. "Kwaanz, have a look."

The rookie recoiled. "I ain't looking, man," he said. "I'm going back in the car."

Lorenzen took the glasses back and stared at the body, hoping for some movement. Then he put both hands on Litanium's shoulders.

"We're making the call, Cat," Lo said. "It's the only right thing to do. Now get your cell out. Or get your ass down there and find mine."

Litanium stepped back and looked Lo square in the eye.

"Now you listen to me, Lo," said Litanium. "The woman is dead. It's a tragedy. We established that. But there ain't no amount of grieving and phone-dialing that's going to change that. You got other things to think about."

"I got her family to think about," said Lo.

"And you got a team to think about," said Litanium. "A team that counts on you. A team that made you the captain. Our go-to guy in the community."

"Cat, you're getting off the main issue," said Lorenzen, "which is that we got a dead woman."

"You also got a young boy in there, eighteen years old," said Litanium. "His whole career about to be ruined by a mistake. A mistake that you were part of, I must add."

"I never said I wasn't," said Lorenzen.

"Man, think of all you achieved," said Litanium. "You were almost MVP a couple times. All that charity work and shit. And how about them two Latrell Sprewell Citizenship Awards you won from the NBF? A man has to think about his Sprees. All that's circling the drain if we make that call."

"Gimme the phone, Cat," said Lo. "I'm making the call."

"You know as well as I do that any woman walking out here at this time of night is probably homeless," said Litanium. "And what I said before—you got other people here to think about. Ain't we your brothers?"

"Sure, you're my brothers. I don't want to mess up . . ."

"Think of the long-range problems if you bring in the po-po. Best player on the team—the captain, the leader, the *Man*—out there car-racing. Our top draft choice, his whole future in front of him, behind bars. We'd collapse, brother."

Kwaanzii had rejoined them. "For real," he said.

"Teammates stick together," said Litanium. "That right, Kwaanz?"

"That's how teammates do," said the rookie.

Litanium moved in for the kill. "Think of how many people are affected by this decision," said Litanium. "How many you supporting right now? How many people gonna go down if you go down? How many mouths being fed by Mr. Mayne? You gotta balance that shit out. Yeah, this ain't good. But that ain't no reason to wreck a dozen other lives."

Lorenzen sat silent. Litanium knew he had seized on the one thing that could make Lorenzen Mayne leave that roadside without calling the police—his sense of responsibility, skewed as it might be.

As if in a trance, Lo went to the front of Kwaanzii's car and studied it. The others followed. "Dented but no blood," Kwaanzii concluded. Looking like three abnormally large insurance adjusters, they walked across the street and studied Lo's car. "Dented," said Litanium. "Nothing that can't be fixed. And I got someone who can do it who won't say shit." Litanium had dented a few cars in his day.

"I'll get mine fixed myself," said Lo.

Litanium shook his head. "Nah, man, have them come to you. That's how I'm gonna set up the young fella here. And whatever you do, don't change rides. It'll look suspicious."

Lo had a sudden thought. "What about my phone, Litanium?"

"Shit, Lo, you'll have a worse mess if you make footprints hiking down there," said Litanium. "They ain't gonna find no three-inch phone in the damn scrub brush."

Lo stared at them blankly, then got into his car and turned on the ignition. Litanium and Kwaanzii stood together, as if awaiting the verdict at a trial. "I'm gonna drive down the road here, turn onto the Pacific Coast Highway, make an anonymous call from a phone booth," said Lo. "It's just not the Christian thing to do, leaving a woman out there."

"You shouldn't make the call, Lo," said Litanium. "You get people out here right away, you're inviting evidence issues and shit."

Lo stared hard at them. "This ain't over," said Mayne. And then he rolled off into the night. Litanium and Kwaanzii watched him go.

"What do you think he'll do?" Kwaanzii asked.

"Hard to say," said Litanium. "I think we're okay, but Lo's a man with a conscience. You ever see what happens when he gets trapped in a mass autograph situation? Motherfucker don't leave till he signs everything. I see him sign a damn dog collar once."

"A dog asked him to sign?" said Kwaanzii.

Litanium gave him a withering look. Together they walked slowly across the street and took a last look down the ravine.

Kwaanzii nodded solemnly. "First rule of Drag Club," he said, proving to be a fast study, "is you do not talk about Drag Club."

"Also the second rule," said Litanium.

LORENZEN DROVE HOME IN a daze, adhering strictly to the speed limit, expecting any minute to hear sirens and see a red bubble light in his rearview. He passed a number of pay phones but kept on going. He turned into his gated community, located between the airport and Long Beach, mustered up a casual wave to Oscar the attendant, and steered the Hummer into the middle berth of his five-car garage. He let himself in and heard the television blaring from his rec room on the first floor. Some old movie. His cousin, Rockford, kept the big screen on Turner Classics. A young Lauren Bacall was on, looking slinky as usual, but it was lost on Rockford, who was snoring loudly.

"Rock, get your ass up," said Lorenzen, shaking his cousin and turning down the volume. "This shit's too loud."

Rockford rose and stretched. "You out late," he said. "For you anyway."

"Team party," said Lorenzen. "I came straight from it. Who's here?"

Rockford thought for a moment. "Wilson's here. R-Dog. And Squeezy. That's all."

Wilson was another cousin, an older one, deep into his thirties. R-Dog was a friend of Wilson's and Squeezy was a friend of R-Dog's. They all had some attenuated connection to Lo's home state of North Carolina.

"Ain't none of them with women in my bed, are they?" said Lo.

"Squeezy got a woman here and he tried," said Rockford, "but I kicked his ass out. I think she left."

"That's good," said Lo. "You know I don't like seeing strangers in the morning."

"Everybody knows that, Lo," said Rockford. "All right, I'm shuttin' it down. You need me to drive you to practice tomorrow?"

Lorenzen remembered the tacitly understood specifics of the cover-up, but he wasn't about to allow a stranger to come to his house to fix his car.

"The Hummer ain't been runnin' right," said Lo, "I'm going to take it in to get looked at."

"Man, I'll take it for you," said Rockford, who looked for any opportunity to drive the Hummer. "You shouldn't have to do that shit."

"It's on my way," said Lo. "If I take it in then I'm sure they ain't gonna be ripping me off. Go on to bed now."

Rockford left and Lorenzen flopped down on his huge leather wraparound couch. With his cell phone lying in a desolate canyon, he picked up his little-used hard line and paged through the Ss. There was a time that Erick Silver, his agent, was number two on speed dial, right behind Jerry Mayne, Lo's father. Now Silver wasn't even in Lo's top ten. And Lo knew that he sure as hell wasn't in Silver's.

But on this night Lo needed someone to call, and Silver had told him he was "available day or night, twenty-four hours a day, even six o'clock on Christmas morning." Of course, he had told that to Lo and Jerry Mayne back when he was seducing him. Silver answered on the fourth ring, his voice raspy with sleep.

"It's Lo, Erick," said Mayne. "I'm in some trouble."

Silver mentally ran through what "trouble" might connote. In order from worst to nearly palatable, what an agent never wanted to hear was "rape," "cocaine," "gambling debt," and "automobile accident." He felt he could rule out the first three with Lo, so he wasn't surprised when he heard "accident." He wasn't even that concerned with the details until he heard "Kwaanzii."

"Kwaanzii was involved?" Silver said, now peering at the green glow of his Rolex, which flashed 4:10.

"Litanium, too," said Lo.

"That psycho's not my problem," said Silver. "Listen, you okay? I mean, you're not in a police station or a hospital? And Kwaanzii? Is he okay?"

"I'm home," said Lo. "Probably Kwaanzii is, too. We're fine. Both of us. So I just wanted to give you the details before . . ."

Silver prided himself on prioritizing. Prioritizing was the key to agenting. And though he deeply respected Lo—no client had ever given him fewer headaches—he wasn't a priority. Kwaanzii, for whom he was in the process of negotiating a giant candy bar deal, was a different story.

"Listen, Lo, I don't want to cut you off, but I gotta call Kwaanzii," said Silver. "You know why, don't you? Because you handle this shit. But Kwaanzii? I mean, he's got trouble wiping his butt properly. So lemme get to him before he does anything crazy, and we'll all talk about it in the morning."

Lorenzen heard the phone go dead. He tried back and it went right to voice mail, and he knew he'd get voice mail the rest of the night. Lo suddenly felt drained. He stared at Bacall for a moment and turned her off. He hated the dark but he sat there, staring into the receding haze of the big-screen TV.

It happened again.

CHAPTER 4

December 18
Los Angeles Lasers Record: 14-8

The Connecticut countryside whipped by—the seven-figure suburban McMansions, the manicured golf courses, the armada of SUVs on I-95—as Jamal Kelly looked out the window of the Metro North train headed from New Haven to New York. When the train hissed to a stop in Grand Central, Jamal dragged his duffel of dirty clothes down an escalator and hopped on the subway headed for Crown Heights. Since his freshman year, this Sunday trip home had been a monthly ritual. In one swoop, he would get his wash done, fill up on a good meal, and tally enough family capital to assuage any guilt from not calling home often enough for his mother's taste.

Betty Kelly, Jamal always thought, was at once the most unique person he'd ever known and a walking cliché, a proud, independent, church-going, single mother of two boys who had plenty of pomp despite modest circumstances. She worked in human resources at Chase headquarters in Midtown Manhattan. And while the family wasn't well off by any stretch, the Kellys were at least on the fringes of middle class. "I've been poor," Betty often said, "and where we are now, I can't even see poor in my rearview mirror."

Betty had raised her two kids, Jamal and his older brother,

Ezekiel, in a row house off Flatbush Avenue. It wasn't sprawling by any definition, but it wasn't oppressively small either. And while it looked pretty much like every other house on the block, Betty did her best to distinguish it, planting daffodils in the front yard and placing a wicker archway over the front steps.

Ezekiel, or Zeke, as everyone not named Betty Kelly called him, was five when Jamal was born. Within two years, Louis Kelly had withered under the strain of supporting a family of four on a bus driver's salary and had hightailed for parts unknown. Birthday cards and Christmas gifts came sporadically, never with the same post-mark, then not at all, and without ever discussing it with each other, both boys essentially hit the equivalent of the "delete" key on his memory.

Until Jamal had left for college nearly three years ago, the broth-ers had always shared a bedroom—at least, when Zeke didn't fall asleep in front of the television and spend the night on the couch, his legs dangling over the edge like clothes hanging out of an over-stuffed hamper. As Jamal dumped his duffel on the floor of his old room, he noticed the posters on the wall hadn't been changed since he left home. He smiled as he saw the images of NBF players wear-ing uniforms that had long been retired, sporting hairstyles that were risibly out of style. (*Whatever happened to the hi-lo fade any-way?* he wondered.) Then he realized there was a certain symbol-ism to it all. Zeke, too, was stuck in an era, his irretrievable glory days having long since passed him by.

He was twenty-eight now, Zeke was, and there was little ac-counting for the last ten years of his life. His hoops career, such as it was, had an all-too-familiar arc. From an early age, Zeke was the star of various AAU teams. In high school, he was a six-five forward with a velveteen jumper and an expansive vocabulary of moves. College recruiters were regulars at Zeke's games and at the Kelly homestead. Jamal, even as a twelve-year-old, was known universally as "Zeke's little brother," a distinction that may have robbed him of his own identity but also conferred on him instant status. Hard as she tried to keep her older son's ego from ballooning, Betty was helpless to stop the fawning peers and back-slapping teachers and shadowy summer coaches who imbued Zeke with this aura of invincibility. The hoops sirens had seduced him with their song, and convinced him that he was destined for the NBF, Zeke simply stopped paying attention in school. So long as he put up his twenty points per game, he passed his classes just fine. Zeke's other passions—notably, high-end automobiles—fell by the wayside, his habit of tracking every new development in the automotive industry replaced by an obsession for tracking his points, rebounds, assists, and recruiting letters.

Zeke was a senior, on the brink of signing to play for St. John's University, when he was undercut by a teammate in practice. Ten years later, Zeke still swore that it was a cheap shot. Whatever, he came down hard on his back, felt a sting and then nothing in both legs. After a few tense hours, he regained feeling, but he was through for the season. And when recruiters heard the phrase "possible spinal injury," they backed off. The same St. John's assistant coaches who had singlehandedly kept the postal service and phone company in business with their pursuit of Zeke no longer returned Betty's calls.

Not digesting the consequences, Jamal was thrilled that the family phone was freed up and that dinners no longer included heavily cologned coaches wearing shiny sweatsuits and talking about "the family atmosphere," "state-of-the-art facilities," and "network of alumni." Zeke barely played that summer, and when he did he resembled an old man, running gingerly, grimacing at the slightest contact. Late in the summer an assistant from a junior college in upstate New York attended a game and approached Zeke afterward. "We don't think you're damaged goods," the coach said, emphasizing "we" enough to imply that others did. He was distracted and depressed and his grades plummeted.

Halfheartedly, Zeke signed with the State University of New York at Oswego in upstate New York. A few days later a friend asked him the name of the Oswego mascot and Zeke told him it was an otter and the friend couldn't stop laughing. "Imagine ballin' for the Otters," he said. Zeke never made it to campus. When he defiantly told his mother that he wasn't going to college, she wavered between wanting to spank his behind and hug her wounded son as though he were a baby. What had the coach called him? *Damaged goods*. What a horrible phrase to describe an eighteen-year-old kid.

The next years were an unending string of false starts, menial jobs, and vague promises. If Jamal had once idolized his brother—not just for his basketball virtuosity but for his bounteous reserves of cool—there had been a definitive role reversal. Zeke both admired and resented his little brother's native smarts and his ability to move easily between circles, as comfortable amid the ivy-swaddled buildings of Yale as he was at Maurice's Barber Shop down on Odessa Avenue. And just as Jamal once desperately craved his big brother's validation, Zeke now wanted his little brother's respect. But, man, he couldn't let him know that.

"WHAT YOU BEEN UP to this week, Z?" Jamal asked as they sat down at the table. On cue, Betty got up to tend to the baked fish in the kitchen.

"Just taking care of my business, little man."

"What does that mean exactly?"

"You know," Zeke said, moving uneasily and averting his glance. "Stickin' and movin' and doing my thing."

"What thing? What are we talking about here?"

"Nah, man. I just don't want to talk about it. Maybe if I was smart like you."

"You *are* smart," Jamal said. "You just gotta stop feeling sorry for yourself for something happened so long—"

"Why you gotta come with that every time?"

When the conversation between her sons took this turn, and it inevitably did, Betty tried to stay on the sidelines. She didn't disagree with Jamal, but she didn't want Zeke to feel double-teamed. This time she couldn't stick to her vow of neutrality. "You're a fine one to talk, Jamal," she shouted, leaning over the baked fish.

Jamal spun toward the kitchen. "What's that supposed to mean, Mom?"

"You're five months from graduating and what exactly are you planning to do?"

"I told you," Jamal said.

"And don't give me that bullshit about lots of irons in the fire," Betty barked. "Have you filled out one law school application?"

It was the first time Jamal had ever recalled his mother swearing. "We've been through this, Mom," Jamal said.

"I haven't gotten a straight answer," said Betty, coming into the dining room with a platter.

"A professor is trying to line up a job for me in the NBF," Jamal said. As soon as the sentence left his mouth, he knew it sounded pathetic. But he also knew that there was a better chance of him joining a convent than of going to law school in the fall. "After the season ends, the jobs open up. Just be patient."

Great, thought Betty. *Every kid in this neighborhood thinks he's achieving deliverance through basketball.* Even she could tell that they had no game, yet she would overhear them talking about the Elysian fields of the "Federation," bragging about the tubes of gold they'd wear, the souped-up wheels they'd drive, the basketball geishas who would service them. It was so delusional. She saw how the false promises of basketball had already claimed one of her children. "My kid is about to graduate from Yale and he wants to make it to the NBF, too?" she hissed. "Nuh-uh."

CHAPTER 5

It had taken Jillian Forrester a month to find the right workout facility after she had arrived in Los Angeles two years earlier. Getting various recommendations from coworkers at the *Los Angeles Times* and sources (CEOs, public relations flacks, vice presidents of this or that, press agents, a B-list actor or two) she had met covering business and entertainment, Jillian had visited palaces of sweat with names like the Vertical Club, the Body Temple, the Feng Shui Studio, and the E Spot.

"I need a treadmill and a mat for stretching," she told a guy at the Whole Body Experience who was showing her where they did the avocado-and-mud facials.

"We have treadmills and mats here," he said.

"What's a membership cost?" Jilly asked.

"Two thousand a month," he said. "And that includes the raw-foods buffet we put out on Fridays."

Finally, Jilly found the perfect spot—the West Hollywood YMCA, an unassuming place where the equipment worked and they didn't know from avocado facials. It cost $150 a month and was only a short drive from her apartment. Jilly was running on the treadmill, working on getting her pace below a seven-minute mile, when her cell phone sounded and up came *Times*. Her caller ID did not distinguish between departments at the *Times*, so it could've been one of her many bosses, her friend Sheila from the "Calendar" section, a guy named Vincent Coles from news side who was hitting on her, or the classified-ad department telling her she had sold her couch.

"Jillian," said the voice. "It's Mary Sue Watkins. Can you hold for David Bechtel?" Just once, when Jilly heard that question, she wanted to answer: Hold what?

David Bechtel, the managing editor at the *Times*, was something of a legend, having distinguished himself as a foreign correspondent in the former Soviet Union, the Middle East, and several other global hot spots. When he tired of chasing shadows and dodging bullets, he returned to the States, where he was installed as a boss, a position that made him feel as comfortable as a mountain goat at a cotillion. He instilled fear in most everyone around the *Times*, though he had well-known weaknesses for forty-year-old Scotch and thirty-year-old women.

"Jilly," he said, "where did I catch you?"

It is part of the journalist's code that he or she is always working. "I'm on my way to Studio City for an interview," she said, projecting into the future. "I'm profiling the new head bean counter at CBS, the guy who came over from United Airlines."

"He runs an airline into the ground, so why not a network," said Bechtel. "Anyway, could you meet me for lunch? Maybe one o'clock or so. I got something to run by you. I'll be at Vera Cruz downtown. You know it?"

"I'll find it," said Jilly.

BECHTEL WAS WORKING ON his third Scotch when Jilly arrived at 1:25, having jogged the final four blocks after stowing her car in a parking garage. "I took Wilshire all the way from Studio City and that was a huge mistake," she said, keeping with the unwritten civil ordinance that every L.A. conversation begin with a personal traffic report.

Jilly raised both arms and hung her jacket on the back of the chair, a move that is possible only for the extremely limber. Bechtel tried to look away but the movement caught his eye.

"I gotta get back for a meeting, so I ordered for us," he said. "Some kind of chicken thing and some kind of shrimp thing. You want a drink?"

"Maybe I'll get a margarita," said Jilly. "I should treat myself after talking to this CFO guy."

"Yeah, well, you'll make the story sing," said Bechtel. "You usually do, which is why I asked you here. I guess you heard about the beat guy who covers the Lasers for us? Quits last week, tells Collins, the sports editor, he's going to become a Buddhist monk." Bechtel favored getting right to the point.

Jilly received her prickly pear margarita and licked some salt off the edge. Bechtel fought back some very evil thoughts.

"Man," said Jilly, "that must be a tough beat."

"Anyway, we got the backup guy on 'em now—they're on a short road trip—but we've begun a national search for a replacement," said Bechtel. "I've talked to a guy from ESPN's magazine, a guy from the *Boston Globe*, and a guy from the *Detroit News*."

The waitress set the shrimp in front of Jilly and the chicken in front of Bechtel. "Sounds like you have a nice problem then," she said, dividing up the plates. "Nice audible on the ordering."

"But I think I want you." There may have been something Freudian in that, but Bechtel assumed it came out sounding professional. He put down his fork and drained his Scotch.

Jilly stopped in midchew. "Me? To cover the Lasers? I'm not even in sports."

"Exactly the point," said Bechtel.

Newspapers, like movie studios, networks, and astronomers, are in constant search of new stars. While scandals involving young reporters who invented material out of whole cloth had made media outlets more cautious about phenoms, there was still nothing that got the blood of a veteran editor pumping more than planting some callow unknown on the national beat and harvesting him once he turned into Woodward or Bernstein. Sportswriters had become the luminaries of the daily paper, always getting interviewed, appearing on panels, pontificating on TV about this player or that executive. *Every time Jilly Forrester opened her mouth,* Bechtel thought, *the* Times *would get credit for putting an intelligent and—not unimportantly—attractive woman on a major beat.*

"I'm just learning this business beat," said Jilly. "I'm sure one of these other guys you're considering is much more qual—"

"You *are* qualified," said Bechtel. "Here's what it takes. Reporting skill. Writing-on-deadline skill. People skill. Period. You've been around—what?—two years. And I think you've shown all those skills. The rest of it you learn."

"Seems like it might be a stiff curve," said Jilly.

Again, Bechtel's thoughts turned impure. He waved his fork at her. "Bull," he said. "That beat you were on taught you how to deal with ego and testosterone in near-lethal doses. And if you can do it with corporations and studios, you can do it with NBF players. Only difference is, these guys are taller and they don't read the trades."

Jilly kept looking for reasons to turn him down. "I never played basketball," she said. "Volleyball and softball were my sports. I'd have to study up to see how many teams are in the league."

Bechtel nibbled at a shrimp. "Nobody knows how many teams are in that fuckin' league, excuse my French. I found out recently that Memphis has a team, though why in the world it would is beyond me. Look, we don't want you to be a coach. Our sports guys—the ones who are any good—don't fill their stories with gobbledygook. You quote somebody on the technical crap and you let it rip."

Jilly stared hard at him and Bechtel flushed. The green eyes were killing him. *A young Naomi Watts*, he thought.

"See, by the time people pick up the paper everyone who cares already knows who won," said Bechtel, while thinking, *Why am I still talking?* "We need someone on the inside who can draw out the players, make us care about them, as well as tell us who's about to be traded and whose mother is sick."

Jilly folded and unfolded her napkin. "There's something else," she said. "All along I've been thinking about going back to grad school. Wharton. I told them that even before they offered me the job in business."

Bechtel waved his hand at her. "That's the thing about journalists—we never know what we want to do, right? I always wanted to review movies, and the next thing I know I'm drinking iced tea in Tel Aviv when a bomb goes off. Then, I come back, want to write about politics, and they give me a bunch of money and stick me behind a desk. Look, maybe you'll go to Wharton. Maybe you won't. But for now do this. Only one thing you have to promise— you have to complete the season. We can't go replacing beat people every two weeks."

Jilly sat silent. She had to admit she was tiring of talking to pretentious, self-important CEOs and "holding one minute" for low-level Hollywood PR flacks. She figured the Lasers beat would give her time off in the summer. It was something new. And her lunk of a fiancé, Robbie, would hate it. All good reasons to take the job.

"I can tell you're ambivalent," said Bechtel, "so maybe this'll help. We bump you five percent, which is maybe a percent or so more than the normal merit raise, right? You do a good job you still get your merit. As long as you stay on until the end of the season. The way the Lasers are going lately you could be just about done in April."

Jilly spread her hands, shrugged, and raised her margarita glass. "Well," she said, "it drove the other guy into being a Buddhist, so who knows what'll happen to me. But why the hell not?"

"Maybe drive you into a nunnery," said Bechtel, feeling exultant all of a sudden.

"A little late for that," she said, killing him again, leaving him thinking about Naomi Watts and ordering a fourth Scotch.

As JILLY SAW IT, THERE were two ways to go at a big issue with Robbie Duckworth. Bring it up right away, then, when he got mad, take him to bed. Or have the sex first, then go at the big issue when he was relaxed. She chose the latter. They were relaxing afterward, propped up on pillows, lights off except for the hazy green of the TV, when Jilly made her move.

"Hey, I'm changing beats," she said, as if she had just remembered a minor detail of the day. *Hey, I got the car washed.*

SportsCenter was on. Jilly wondered if she should sneak a glance at the NBF scores, help her sort out the teams.

"You going strictly on business?" he said. "Maybe give up that Hollywood crap?"

Robbie was a portfolio manager at Goldman Sachs and had majored in finance at Princeton. He wasn't crazy about Jilly even being a journalist, but, to him, a business writer at least served some earthly purpose. And if it helped her get into Wharton, which was a segue to what Robbie considered a real job—the kind that came with an expense account, no matter how socially irredeemable or impossibly stultifying the actual day-to-day work might be—all the better.

Jilly switched off the TV. "No. You better hear this." She pounded her pillow a couple of times and sat up. "They're putting me on the Lasers beat. Like, right away."

In the half light Jilly saw his face slowly morph into a cartoonish fusion of disgust and disbelief.

"The basketball team?" said Robbie. "Why the hell for?"

Robbie didn't much care for the NBF. He was a self-described "NFL guy" who serial-switched channels on Sunday afternoons while wearing a New England Patriots jersey that he genuinely believed brought the team good luck.

"Well, I would hope it's because they think I can do the job," said Jilly. "The guy they had on it quit. And they're looking for—I don't know—somebody different."

Robbie searched for the right words. "No, Jilly, I know you can do the job," he said. "But, I mean, do you even *like* pro basketball? Do you understand it? And half of those guys are criminals. Why you'd want to hang . . ."

Jilly got out of bed and turned on the light. "Look, Robbie, I don't want to *hang* with anyone. That's not what a reporter does. What I want to do is cover the team. And besides, I doubt if there's any more criminals in the NBF than there are in the NFL."

"Statistics show you're wrong on that," he said. "Plus, all these guys are, like, eighteen years old. They're taking 'em right out of grade school for chrissakes, before they know how to dribble. They should make 'em stay in school. Like in football."

"Football players stay in school—and I use the phrase loosely—because the NFL uses it as its training camp," said Jilly. "Half of those guys never graduate. Maybe more. The bowl games end, and then they stop going to class and start working out for that meat market they call the NFL combine."

"So now you're an NFL expert," said Robbie.

"I know more about that than you do about the NBF," she said.

"Look, baseball takes teenagers. Tennis takes teenagers. Golf takes teenagers. Carnegie Hall takes teenagers. Hollywood takes teenagers. And pro basketball takes teenagers. There's only one difference with the NBF." She had her arms folded by this time, staring him down.

"And that is?" he asked.

"Basketball takes *black* teenagers," Jilly said, "and that's what you can't stand. That's what everyone can't stand. They even took one who played at our alma mater."

"Wolff's an exception," said Robbie, switching off the light. "A guy with a brain."

Jilly turned it back on. "And if the New England Patriots found a ten-year-old who could kick fifty-yard field goals," said Jilly, "you'd volunteer to pick him up after school and drive him to practice."

The vehemence of her defense surprised Robbie but surprised Jilly more.

"You're gonna hate covering that fuckin' team," he said softly, a verbal gesture of defeat. "Just hate it."

IT WAS JUST BEFORE MIDNIGHT when D'Angelo Cooper pulled up to the Playa del Rey townhouse where Kwaanzii Parker was living month to month until he closed on a mansion suited to the discriminating tastes he'd cultivated in his 18.7 years of living. Though no one knew precisely how D'Angelo made his living—he spoke alternately of being a record executive, an upscale apparel executive, and a marketing executive—he was a familiar presence around the Lasers, a sort of roaming posse member with a genuine knack for befriending whichever player was hot at the time.

D'Angelo was also an incurable car buff who applied automotive nips and tucks in the players' parking lot. He rewired Buenos Diaz's Bentley so the monitors behind the two front seats could play two movies at once. He added classic, wonderfully incongruous whitewall tires to James Taylor's Mercedes S Class convertible. And at the behest of Litanium, the young executive had paid a visit to Kwaanzii on this night to help him stealthily change the mangled grille on his Jaguar.

Wearing a black Pierre Cardin sweatsuit with nothing underneath save a few leis of gold, Kwaanzii greeted his guest warmly. The two sat on the window ledge of an unfurnished living room, nursing Courvoisier and a joint before they repaired to the garage.

"You believe with what I'm making all I got is a one-car garage?" Kwaanzii asked, genuinely embarrassed.

"But you got a nice ride in there," D'Angelo said reassuringly. "At least you will when I get through."

As the two circled the car, D'Angelo whistled when he saw the smashed grille. The night of the accident, Kwaanzii had spent hours meticulously sponging and drying the car when he returned home. But he was helpless to take care of the dents and scratches that made the car resemble a Kansas trailer park that had gotten the business end of a tornado.

"How'd you fuck this thing up anyway?" D'Angelo asked. "I mean, you gotta *try* to ding a Jag so bad that the hood ornament comes off. Litanium said you hit a tree, but I sure don't see no wood lodged in there."

"Nah, it wasn't like that," he sputtered. "I just lost control a little bit and next thing I knew—*bam!*"

"Guess that's makes sense, young fella," D'Angelo responded. "After all, you only got your license two years ago. Driving is like making love to a sweet young thing. You think you know what you're doing from the start. But it takes time to master the art."

"Think you can fix it?"

"C'mon, man," D'Angelo hissed, already heading out to retrieve the replacement grille and monstrous toolbox from the bed of his Cadillac pickup. "Is the pope Russian?"

Figuring there was no sense looking over D'Angelo's shoulder as he labored into the night fixing a grille—and unknowingly disposing of evidence from a hit-and-run in the process—Kwaanzii retreated upstairs to his den. With two clicks of a stereo remote control, he assured that DMX's throaty voice was audible as far north as Santa Barbara. Then he took another remote and summoned his Madden2000 PlayStation Game—"Old School!"—on his plasma television. With only a tankful of tropical fish looking on, Kwaanzii perfected his safety blitzes and out patterns for the next three hours.

It was around three-thirty when D'Angelo came upstairs. His fingers blackened with grease, his shirt soaked through with sweat, he proudly invited Kwaanzii to check out his handiwork. The rookie flashed an expansive smile as he saw his beloved Jag with a brand-new grille.

"Looks great, bro," he said. "But where's the hood ornament?"

"I don't have an extra one and I don't have the right clips to reattach the old one."

Kwaanzii looked at the old grille leaning against a wall and a silver jaguar talisman—a stray cat, as it were—perched atop. Inspiration struck.

"Could you at least take off that old ornament and give it to me?"

"Sure," D'Angelo Cooper said with a shrug. He disengaged the four-inch chrome jaguar and handed it to Kwaanzii.

"Thanks, bro," Kwaanzii said. "Think I might go for a new look anyway. Maybe put my uniform number on there as the new hood ornament."

"That would be phat, yo," D'Angelo said. "I would do that for you no problem."

Kwaanzii gave D'Angelo a hug. D'Angelo reached down to take the mangled grille back to his truck. It was simply a given that he would clean up the mess, just as it was an article of faith that the work would be performed gratis, the tradeoff for attaching oneself to impending greatness.

Before D'Angelo had gunned the V-6 on his truck, Kwaanzii began removing one of his gold chains so he could affix the Jaguar hood ornament as a medallion. He'd once seen a rapper wearing a Benz figurine around his neck in a video, and Kwaanzii figured that wearing a Jag was going one better.

CHAPTER 6

I n what is either a great asset or an unfortunate side effect, the team charter flight has taken a good twenty nights off the amount of time NBF players spend on the road each season. Time was, a team played a road game, returned to the hotel for a few hours of fitful sleep—or more likely, did some liver-ravaging through the night—and then massed at the airport for the "first flight out." Tired, hung over, besieged by fans for autographs, and then crammed so tightly into seats it looked like they were sitting in wheelbarrows, players needed a full day to recover.

These days, immediately after road games, teams head to airstrips, not airports. As hired hands hoist the bags onto the customized jet, the players unfurl their bodies into leather captain's seats, fire up their DVDs, and either doze off or eat their catered meal. By the time the plane arrives home, the passengers feel like they've spent a few hours at a spa thirty-five thousand feet above sea level.

Still, the road trip is an essential component of life in the NBF. Teams will spend fifty nights a year—minimum—in assorted Ritz-Carltons and Westins. And the bromide still holds true: What's the hardest part about leaving for an NBF road trip? Trying not to bust out laughing when you tell your wife you'll miss her.

If NBF players were polled about their favorite destinations, the results would move in lockstep with the municipalities' hours of nocturnal operation. New York, Los Angeles, and Miami would be at the top. The Calvinist cities such as Salt Lake City, Indianapolis, and Milwaukee would be at the bottom, though even those places have their secret spots where veteran night crawlers can find booze and willing female companionship. (That is particularly true of Salt Lake City; among NBF players it is well known that no one falls harder than a fallen Mormon woman.)

Charlotte is a sprawling collection of strip malls and industrial parks that feels less like a legitimate city than an oversized village, and Bible-thumpers of all kinds, most notably Billy Graham, have taken up residence there. Yet Charlotte is a favorite whistle-stop for most players. Whether it's the congenial weather, the vinegar-based barbecue, the languorous pace, the one celebrated "gentlemen's club," or the soft, lilting southern accents of the waitresses and hotel bellhops, Charlotte has an instant familiarity for most NBF players, none more so than Lorenzen Mayne, whose boyhood home of Spencer, North Carolina, is just forty-five minutes from Charlotte's downtown, such as it is.

Because of the vagaries of the schedule, Western Conference teams pass through each Eastern Conference city only once each season. So for Lo, the Lasers' game against Charlotte took on the dimensions of a pilgrimage, the only time an army of uncles and aunts and cousins and friends could see him play in person. The pressure was not insignificant, but Lo always considered the Charlotte game a forty-second home game. He wasn't just from Carolina; he was *of* Carolina.

The Lasers' team flight touched down at the Mecklenburg County airstrip early Tuesday morning following a narrow win over Memphis. The Lasers had played with uncharacteristic toughness when it mattered most, and Coach Watson had canceled Tuesday's game-day shootaround, giving his players a day to sleep in or catch an afternoon movie. He also signed off on Lo's leaving the team hotel to sleep at home that night. It was an unwritten policy that players can stay with friends and family before games in their hometowns, but Watson appreciated that Lo had asked him first.

Though it was nearly 2:00 a.m. when the players filed off the plane, Jerry Mayne was there to meet his son. A fullback for North Carolina A&T in the seventies, Jerry still looked as if he could bowl over any college linebacker. His torso shaped like a keg, his arms covered by lacy networks of veins, Jerry was a no-bullshit cop for the Spencer Police Department. A crime wave in Spencer meant two DUI arrests in the same night, but Jerry patrolled his beat as though he were working the South Bronx. As a parent, he cut the same stoic figure. He had never been a big talker, but Jerry's wordless praise—an approving slap on the back, a sly wink—was, to Lo, praise of the highest order.

When Lo was drafted out of the University of North Carolina seven years ago, he declared his intention to his dad, then a recent widower, to purchase him a fifty-five-hundred-square-foot home ("the biggest and best in Spencer"). What Lo saw as a rite of passage—a six-bedroom-five-bathroom shout-out for all the love, support, and early-morning wakeup calls—Jerry Mayne saw as an affront. "This home was good enough for me and your mother when she was alive," Jerry told him, clearly wounded. "If you need to give away your money to feel like a bigshot, donate it to a charity." Even though Lo's six siblings had moved out of the house, Jerry continued living in the same unremarkable split-level and gave no indication of ever leaving.

In Jerry Mayne's euphemism, his wife Virginia had "passed" in 1995 from a combination of diabetes and cancer. Lo was a high-school senior during Virginia's last months. He was, at once, devastated yet so wrapped up in his basketball, his burgeoning celebrity, and his college recruitment that he was always able to postpone grieving. Jerry was the epoxy that held the family together during the crisis. Though the Spencer sheriff had told him to take some time off from work, Jerry found comfort in the routine of the job and didn't miss a shift until Virginia's final days. He would come home from work, make dinner for the four kids living at home at the time, help them with their homework, and then head to the hospital. Somehow he also saw to it that the home remained a functioning organism—the grass got cut, the bills got paid, the trash got picked up. Even then, Lo saw the irony. Unlike a thirty–point, twenty-rebound game, Jerry's performance would never get written up in the paper or discussed at the diner the next morning. But his father's grace under the most intense pressure was heroism distilled to its essence.

Lo had always considered himself close to his father, but the two, in keeping with their natures, had never been affectionate. Now, as Jerry climbed out of the driver's seat to greet his son, they half-shook hands, half-hugged, a maneuver they had never managed to make any less awkward with the passing years. "Good to see you, Pop," Lo said. "You look fantastic."

As Jerry silently maneuvered his GMC Jimmy past the familiar signposts—the barns and roadside churches and gnarled palmetto trees—a flood of childhood memories came back to Lo. He had made the drive between Charlotte and Spencer at least a hundred times, first to visit the circus, church retreats, and relatives' homes, later for basketball tournaments, hip-hop concerts, and the office of the oncologist who treated Virginia until the end. He wasn't a millionaire then with his own doge's palace and likeness on a video game. But neither was he fearing that he was a phone call away from having his life come crashing down. On balance, had he been happier as the kid sitting in the same seat, making the same drive ten years earlier? He thought long and hard about that one.

Halfway through the drive, at a red light in Bedford, Jerry broke a long silence. "You hungry, Lo?"

"Nah, Dad. They feed us real good on those team planes. Shrimp and fruit salads and smoothies."

"Smoothies?"

"It's like a milkshake with fruit. This Japanese guy makes them special for us."

"Whew," Jerry said, laughing, "guess that's life in the fast lane."

Lo looked over at his dad, then back at the road. "Sometimes," he said, "the slow lane is the one to be in."

Even in the darkness, the home was just as Lo remembered it, modest in size, dignified in appearance, hemmed by oak trees on the left and Virginia Mayne's garden—"My eighth baby," she called it—on the right. Unlike so many of the homes they passed on the drive from Charlotte, there were neither rusting vehicles nor thatches of weeds blighting the front yard. Jerry pulled in and parked next to the 1993 Ford Escort, once driven by Virginia, that was handed down to Lo's youngest sister, Tiffany, now a sophomore at Furman. (Despite persistent prodding from both the potential purchaser and the potential recipient, Jerry steadfastly refused to let Lo buy a new a car for his kid sister.)

Lo exhaled audibly as he took a long, studied look at the home and walked up the front steps. Growing up, Lo considered his home neither large nor small, just as he had never considered himself either rich or poor. In college and the pros, Lo had teammates who would describe their boyhood homes, usually in Section Eight housing, as "ratty-ass" or "ghetto." Maybe it was another difference between urban poor and the more benign rural poor. But Lo thought it blasphemous to speak ill of your dwelling place.

In previous years—when he was eager to fit in with his teammates, when he wasn't the team's star, when he wasn't harboring

the secret of a hit-and-run accident that could land him in jail—
Lo had invited the Lasers to Chez Mayne for a blowout meal. Jerry
and Lo's oldest sister, Shirelle, had taken the day off from their jobs
and worked to prepare a sclerotic bomb of a soul food dinner:
sweet potato pie, collard greens, fried chicken, and fried okra, to
be chased down with gallons of sweet tea. The players, happy for
the departure from room service, ate like famished beasts.
(Though, Jerry noted, reserve Willie Wainwright and Charles
"Chubby" Monroe, the Lasers' rotund equipment manager, were
the only ones to send him a note of thanks.) Jerry relished the role
of den father, giving these displaced, road-weary kids a sliver of
home, if only for an afternoon. If the members of his son's current
peer group happened to be celebrities making millions, it was lost
on Jerry.

When they got in the door, Lo felt like gripping his dad in a
bear hug but settled for slapping him playfully on those football-
pad shoulders. "Good night, Pop," he said, retreating to his bedroom, which had been bequeathed to Tiffany. With Jared Leto and
Usher smiling down on him, lying on pink sheets, his head on a
pillow that smelled like baby oil, Lo slept more deeply than he had
in months, not even remembering his dreams when he woke at
eleven the next morning.

"Sleep good?" Jerry said when Lo surfaced for breakfast.

"Oh, yeah. Good to be home," Lo responded. "How come
you're not at work?"

"I took the morning off, so we could, you know, just be together. But I didn't want to wake you."

"Sorry," Lo mumbled guiltily between spoonfuls of grits.

His father glanced over his *Charlotte Observer*.

"Lo," Jerry said. "How you doing?"

"Good, Pop."

"Yeah. Right," said his father, returning to his reading.

❦   ❦   ❦

LO KILLED THE DAY in Spencer, hanging out with his oldest brother, Lewis, a drywall installer, and their first cousin, Gabe, whose occupation was a mystery even to those who knew him best. The three shot pool at Smitty's, a gauzy-lit dive bar on the north end of town. With respect to hanging out with Lo, a series of unwritten rules had ossified over the years. Friends and family were expected to treat him as they always had. Sycophancy was the quickest way to be excommunicated from the inner circle. The second fastest was to use the connection as a trump card in any way. Another cardinal rule: Wait for Lo to bring up the topics of basketball, the NBF, or the Lasers.

The three joked about movies they had just seen, CDs they had recently purchased, old classmates, and women in their lives. Betraying the same hand-eye coordination that served him so well on the court, Lo ran three racks. Shortly before four, Lo dropped off Lewis and Gabe.

He then, as usual, made a visit to Spencer's only cemetery and stood silently for a good five minutes over the grave of Virginia Ellen Mayne (1940–95), stifling the instinct to cry before his tear ducts could kick into high gear. Then he looked around and walked stealthily to the grave of another woman who had died too early, this one ever younger. He placed a few pebbles at the foot of the headstone and struggled, as he always did at this spot, to remember the Bible verses his mother had tried to drum into his head. There was a particular one about forgiveness, but it wasn't coming to him.

NBF PLAYERS ARE ALLOTTED two comp tickets for each game, a negotiated perk the Players' Association never fails to bring up when it decides to raise dues. Most of the time, two ducats are plenty. (How many players have more than a pair of friends in Toronto or Minneapolis?) For games held in a player's hometown, however, the ticket situation quickly spirals out of control. No fewer than sixty-two friends and family had hit Lo up for tickets. With the help of Henry Shenk—securing comp tickets, particularly for the star players, is still another unofficial duty of media relations directors— Lo had managed to beg, borrow, and barter twenty-three from Lasers teammates and coaches, sometimes forced to swap with them for a future date at a two-to-one exchange rate. That still left him nearly forty shy. Grudgingly, he gave Shenk a list of the names and a credit card. "Try and get ones that aren't too cheap but don't bankrupt me either," Lo instructed.

"What about the loge seats?" Shenk said, staring at a seating chart. "Not the cheapest, but not the total nosebleeds."

"How much are they?"

"Fifty-five per."

"Damn felony," Lo said, too dispirited to do the grim math. "Yeah, get those."

Lo knew that not everyone on his encyclopedic comp list was there to cheer for him. Their real payoff came when they could strut to the "Will Call" box, give their name, and tell the person on the other side of the Lucite, "Lo Mayne left me two." The comps were an indication that they had ties to celebrity, that however quotidian their lives were, they were a somebody. Who, thought Lo, am I to deny them that? Even at fifty-five dollars a pop.

The game itself was a forty-eight-minute kinetic eyesore. Over the course of an eighty-two-game schedule, there are half a dozen "throwaways" for every team. The league's greatest public relations problem—and there are a lot of them—is that the casual American sports fan believes that *every* NBF game is a throwaway that features minimum effort from uninterested players. Jilly Forrester had thought the same thing until she began covering the Lasers.

"In pro basketball, all you have to do is watch the last two minutes," Robbie had complained to Jilly a few nights earlier, before she left on the road trip. "Another reason why the NFL is king."

"It's a ridiculous comparison," Jilly responded. "The Lasers play five times more games than your beloved Patriots. And there's not thirty seconds of dead time between plays while the clock runs."

"All I know," Robbie huffed, "is that most men would rather watch a preseason NFL game than the NBF finals."

"Whatever," Jilly said dismissively. Jilly's basketball learning curve was steep but she'd already come to realize that, in point of fact, most NBF players try as hard as any athlete in any sport on most nights. That the league's killer schedule—including back-to-back games a time zone apart—assures occasional spells of tired legs and still more tired minds. That as the players vacantly go through the motions on the court, the mood becomes contagious: Refs turn a blind eye to blatant fouls and violations; dance teams botch routines; play-by-play announcers are a second slow with their clichés and banal observations; journalists employ tired leads that allude to the weather and novels ("Thomas Wolfe said you can't go home again, but Lorenzen Mayne proved otherwise as . . ."). But Jilly didn't feel like explaining it to Robbie. Recently, she had reached the irreducible conclusion that the less they communicated, the happier she was.

Charlotte, one of the worst teams in the league, surged to an early lead on the hot shooting of Vernell "The Colonel" Williams. The Lasers put together a run and led at halftime. They then emerged from the locker "colder than the whipping winter wind outside the arena," as Jilly uninspiredly put it, and fell behind by six points. In the third quarter, to the delight of an army of fans from Spencer, Lo made a few jumpers, converted four straight foul shots, and helped the Lasers to a ten-point fourth-quarter lead. The home team made the obligatory comeback, but the Lasers held on to win the dog-ugly game 96–91. As artless as it was, the Lasers had won the second game of a back-to-back series, a rarity in the NBF, and ended the road trip on an encouraging note.

Clad only in a towel, Lo looked contentedly at his stat sheet—twenty-one points, eight rebounds, six assists, and a Lasers win: he could live with that—and dressed quickly. He left the locker room and headed to a rail at the lip of the arena entrance where family and friends ritually waited for him after games. Through the loading dock, he could hear the bus humming. He quickly slapped five with assorted siblings, cousins, and nephews, hugged Jerry, and said good-bye. As the bus eased out of the parking lot and headed to the airstrip where the Lasers' plane would transport him out of Charlotte and back to L.A., for the second time that day Lo felt like crying.

CHAPTER 7

Litanium "Tribal Cat" Johnson thought he had heard the phone ringing, but he couldn't be sure, since his ears had been ringing for the last week, ever since Atlanta's notoriously dirty power forward, Clarence "Postman" Melvin, had elbowed him upside the head.

The phone, in fact, was ringing. Phones were more like it, since Tribal Cat had a couple dozen scattered throughout his twelve-bedroom crib high in the "hills of Beverly," as Litanium always said. Da Cat had a thing for phones, particularly cartoon–character phones. Tweety Bird, Goofy, Mickey Mouse, Bugs Bunny, and Yosemite Sam were all represented. He also had a cordless shaped like a woman's breast, another thing he liked. "The Tweety and the tittie are my favorites," Litanium liked to say. Still, he rarely answered either.

Tribal Cat was a member of a common form of NBF fauna: the lovable, veteran knucklehead. When he left the University of Florida after two years to turn pro, prospective teams administered the standard psychological test that revealed him to have the maturity level of a twelve-year-old. That was a decade ago, and he had now matured into a healthy sixteen-year-old. At least a few times a season, Tribal could be counted on to miss practice, complain vocally about his contract, and injure himself unusually. His 1998 "inner-thigh burn," occasioned while trying to set fire to a fart aboard a team plane, earned him immortality in NBF lore. You could also count on Tribal Cat to hit game-winning shots, have a few unconscious forty-point games, and play through pain. So often in the NBF, immaturity and arrested development translate to a certain inoculation from pressure; the most aware and self-possessed players are often the most susceptible to the yips.

Funny, outgoing, and able to conjure up a joke or bodily excretion for any occasion, Litanium had always been wildly popular among his teammates—and there had been many of them. Fiercely loyal to his friends and family in Baltimore, Litanium had chosen his second cousin, Monty Hook, as his agent. Hook had negotiated Litanium's contracts, each worse than the next, on the theory that "long term means less flexibility." Because of Tribal Cat's relatively low salary, he was often a "throw-in" that enabled teams to make bigger trades that conformed to the league's Byzantine salary cap provisions. In ten seasons, he had played for seven teams and eleven coaches. Cat was, in NBF-speak, a "coach killer," meaning a player who was just good enough and just unreliable enough to get a guy fired. The Lasers' John Watson circled Litanium warily, like an entomologist studying a particularly predatory spider. For his part, Da Cat considered all coaches, all authority figures in fact, to be circumvented whenever possible. Which is why the morning phone call put him in an instant bad mood.

"It's somebody named Coach," a female voice whispered in his ear, holding the breast phone from her as if it were a piece of rancid meat. Tribal Cat smelled a whiff of stale perfume, mixed with Cristal, mixed with a little weed, mixed with sex, and the activities of the previous night started to come back to him, though only in the most general way. He pulled the ends of the pillow tighter around his ears.

"Gimme that phone." Litanium put his hand over the receiver and cleared his throat loudly.

"Coach Watson, it's Cat," he said. "I'm so glad you called 'cause I was about to . . . it's moved back? Till three?"

Litanium looked into the bathroom where his visitor appeared to be messing with his two-hundred-dollar Brookstone hair dryer, which was shaped like a Magnum .457.

"Girl! Don't be messin' with my stuff!" he said in a harsh whisper. "Yes, I'm sorry. I got it. I'll be there. Before three even."

Litanium yanked his boxers up over his hips and stretched out his sinewy six-foot-two-inch point-guard body. He looked to his right and studied himself in a mirror that covered one wall. Objectively, he was terrifically unattractive. When his hairline began to beat a hasty retreat, he shaved his head, revealing a birthmark shaped like Iowa above his left ear. His slitlike eyes made it seem like he was always being blasted by a private sun. Two front teeth dangled from his upper gum like stalactites. Naturally, he believed that when his basketball career ended, he would transition seamlessly into modeling or acting.

Litanium scratched around the covers, located the remote, hit a switch, and down from the ceiling came a giant high-def TV screen that took up most of another wall, the one facing the bed. Cat hit the number for TVLand because at 11:30 *Bewitched* came on. "Honey, come in here," Litanium said.

His visitor shuffled out of the bathroom, covering her upper body with a towel, putting on shy all of a sudden. She walked over to him, pulled away the towel, revealing some sort of spaghetti-strap top, and plopped down on the bed.

"I love *Bewitched*," she said, kissing him on the forehead. "That little thing she does with her nose."

Litanium smiled and put his head back on his pillow, which was covered, like his loins, in black silk. "I'm more interested in that little thing you do with your mouth," he replied.

AT THE EXACT MOMENT Litanium was "getting a Clinton," as the more politically aware Lasers called it, his coach was fulminating in the office of Manuel Leroy Burnett, general manager of the Lasers. Burnett was dressed in what he liked to call the color of the day, which today happened to be "sea foam." Burnett had on a sea foam tie (set off by a deep green shirt), sea foam trousers, and sea foam socks that peeked out from a pair of four-hundred-dollar tan loafers. Manny had been among L.A. Magazine's "Top Ten Clothes Thoroughbreds" three years running, no minor feat in a town with such intense fashion consciousness, and he wasn't about to ease up on the reins now. The Lasers' owner, Owen Padgett, rested one butt cheek on Burnett's desk as he talked on the phone, half-listening to the caller, half-listening to the contretemps.

Watson and Burnett were exchanging verbal shrapnel over Kwaanzii Parker's role on the team. Their fight limned the inherent tension between NBF coaches and NBF general managers, positions that, in theory, work in tandem but, in practice, are completely at odds. Coaches are evaluated on the present. They must win *now* if they want to retain gainful employment. That means fielding the best roster and forsaking the long term. General managers are evaluated on the future. Their draft picks must flourish, their projects must pan out, their trades must bear fruit if they want to keep their jobs. When Kwaanzii Parker, exceptionally talented but exceptionally unseasoned, sat on the bench, Burnett feared for his livelihood. When he played and the team lost, Watson feared for his.

"The kid is not ready, M.L.B., and it's ree-fucking-diculous to think he is," said Watson. (Burnett encouraged friends and associates to call him by his initials; he thought it made him sound like one of those old Hollywood studio honchos.) Watson talked with the passion of a tent preacher, though not with the volume, since his vocal cords had been irreparably damaged by the years of Hoovering coke and gargling Jack Daniel's. "Anyway, we've been through this. I thought we all decided we're doing a disservice to the kid and to the franchise."

"John, you're doing it again," said Manny. "You're tripping on this shit, starting to get all raspy, man."

"Damn right I'm gettin' raspy. I'm the one who's gotta coach this kid. He's eighteen. He's barely old enough to piss standing up and you want me to throw him into the snakepit? It's crazy."

Padgett put one hand over the phone and said: "It's not crazy, John. It's business." Then he went back to talking on the phone, the subject being the looming debut of *Single Rich Dude*, a reality series in which twentysomething women—invariably blonde, silicone-enhanced, and intellectually unimposing—go after heavily bankrolled thirtysomething males. Padgett had sold ABC on the idea, and, when back-to-back sitcoms (one about a New York City policeman who owned an adorable pet monkey, the other about a Milwaukee butcher living with his bitchy mother-in-law) tanked, the show was rushed into production as a January replacement.

Watson had warded off earlier entreaties to start Kwaanzii, but now, as the Lasers sputtered, the subject was surfacing again. Down deep, Watson had to admit that the kid showed flashes. While unable—or unwilling—to grasp the rudiments of Watson's motion offense, Kwaanzii's one-on-one forays did give the Lasers a spark, particularly since Lorenzen Mayne, after a brilliant early start, had been in an inexplicable funk. Watson also knew that the NBF game had undergone a curious transformation in the minds of the fans. Bombarded by special effects, contests during timeouts, giveaways, cheerleaders, music, a whole bread-and-circus presentation, the spectators had come to look upon the games as ancillary, even as a minor annoyance. Watson knew he had lost but pressed on. "The schedule's front-loaded and we've been showing improvement," the coach argued.

Padgett put his hand over the phone. "Special-ed students show improvement. Your job's to win."

Burnett, who had scratched around the league as a player for five years, had some sympathy for Watson's position. He might have even known that Parker wasn't ready. But business was business. "Latelia, get Henry Shenk, please," he said to his secretary.

"I mean, Manny, you're putting me in a bad position here," said Watson. "I been doing nothing but talking about how the kid's not ready, and all of a sudden I put him in the starting lineup? Everybody gonna know it came from up high."

"That's why we want to get a unified position on this, make sure we're on the same . . . come on in, Henry."

The Lasers' director of public relations was a pear-shaped man of sixty, a Los Angeles institution who at one time or another had flacked for the Dodgers, the Rams, UCLA, USC, and a few smaller Hollywood film studios in between. Working for Padgett, however, had presented Henry Shenk with his most formidable challenge, and he had already announced he would be retiring at the end of the season, a move backed by Padgett. Shenk was up to three packs a day and the task of sneaking dozens of cigarettes in a no-smoking culture, to say nothing of playing chaperone to millionaires who were younger than his shoes, had taxed his system to the breaking point. He and Jean, his wife of forty years, had bought a one-bedroom condo on a golf course in Palm Springs, and Shenk thought about little else save his looming escape to that Padgettless paradise.

"Henry, John's been thinking about a lineup change, and we wanted you to be ready for it," said Burnett.

"They been thinking for me," said Watson.

Shenk pulled a small notebook from the pocket of his blue blazer and cast a nervous glance at Padgett, who was still on the phone.

"Kwaanzii?" Shenk asked.

"You got it," said Burnett.

Padgett hung up the phone with a bang, clapped his hands together, and joined the group. He looked excited. There was a nervous silence before Burnett decided it was up to him to speak.

"Owen, we know we're going to get a lot of questions about this Kwaanzii thing, so we wanted Henry here to get some kind of statement together."

Padgett clapped his hands together again, releasing a torrent of dandruff from Shenk's lapel. "Take this down first, Henry," said Padgett. "Las Vegas. The locale for *SRD* has been secret, but it's going to be Vegas. The *L.A. Times* will want it. Been a lot of speculation about it." Padgett extended a balled fist to both Burnett and Watson and they awkwardly fist-bumped him back.

"That's the reality series?" Shenk asked uncertainly.

Padgett clapped him on the shoulder. More dandruff liftoff. "No, it's the PBS documentary."

The condo was on the sixth hole, a tricky par-three of about 185 yards. Whether to hit two-iron or seven-wood—that's what Henry Shenk was thinking about as he dutifully took down the information about *Single Rich Dude*.

CHAPTER 8

Ralph Riley, the Lasers' septuagenarian public address announcer, who, like Henry Shenk, was in his last year with the team, dreaded working in a place called Bokchoy.com Arena. NBF arenas used to have a delicious heterogeneity about them. Yes, they were sometimes misshappen monstrosities with bad ventilation systems, closet-sized locker rooms (especially for the visiting team), and dubious urinals that spilled water out into the hall. But at least they achieved something resembling distinctiveness. They had quaint, even classical names, like the Forum, the Omni, the Mecca, Market Square Arena. To the old-timers, it was fun to walk into a gym—Riley still loved to call a place where basketball was played a gym—that didn't look like every place else, an arena where they might be popping popcorn ten feet from the entrance to the locker room.

In the new NBF, however, everything was up for sale, and thus did Riley's home gym get co-opted by a Chinese Internet company whose austere president, Shung Lien, still thought that basketball had something to do with handicrafts. Riley and Shenk often joked that within ten years individual players would be sponsored by corporations. *Starting at forward for the Lasers, Testron's*

Lorenzen Mayne. Coming off the bench, Buenos Diaz, sponsored by the Mucho Comida Corporation.

The worst part of game day for Riley was the announcement of the national-anthem singers. The names never came with pronunciation guides and it seemed the concept of having "Joe Jones" or "Sharon Wilson" sing the banner had gone the way of the Kareem Abdul-Jabbar sky hook. Riley knew he would be getting himself in trouble with tonight's announcement, but there was no way around it, and, as the lights dimmed, Riley took a deep breath, went into his soothing radio voice, and intoned, "Ladies and gentlemen, here to sing tonight's national anthem, please welcome, uh, please give it up for . . . Lake Temecula recording artists . . . Laneesha and Kaneesha . . . LI-neesa and KI-neesa . . ."

At that point, two lovely young African-American sisters, clothed in red, white, and blue spandex, ass-swirled their way to midcourt. Right behind the Lasers' bench, Manny Burnett checked his watch. He always timed the anthems and put this one at three minutes, thirty seconds, minimum, maybe more depending on how long the sisters dragged out *land of the freeeee.*

The Lasers stood, at varying degrees of attentiveness, along the length of the foul line nearest their bench. Once a year, John Watson gave a halfhearted speech about showing proper respect during the anthem, but it lacked conviction and everyone knew why. Twenty years earlier, during his coked-out phase, Watson had fallen asleep during a particularly protracted rendition of the national anthem and finally keeled over unconscious, banging his head on the court.

Ricardo "Buenos" Diaz, the wiry small forward, was a model of soldierly decorum, standing erect and absolutely still. After the passage of the Patriot Act, he feared he could be deported back to Paraguay if he did not show proper fealty to American institutions. Kwaanzii stood with his hands on his hips; someone had told him that was one way of keeping it real in the "oppressive faux-ciety run by the Man"—the same Man, presumably, who had recently lavished upon him $12 million over three years before he was old enough to drink. Lo Mayne, the captain, stood as straight as Diaz, though his head swiveled from time to time to check which players were not at full attention. Up in his suite, Padgett demonstrated his love of country by enjoying a crustless roast beef sandwich with a fine horseradish mustard while schmoozing a studio exec involved with *Single Rich Dude*.

At home games, the national anthem provided anxious moments for Abraham Oka Kobubee, who, per instructions from his wife, was not supposed to go longer than thirty seconds without glancing over at her, both before and during games. Furthermore, Betty Jo Kobubee had devised a loyalty signal that she and her husband were to flash each other at regular intervals—two fingers held to the heart, then to the lips. How could A-Okay show proper respect for the flag while glancing at his wife and moving his fingers all over the place? He did his best.

Shane Donnelly, dressed in street clothes and on injured reserve owing to what Henry Shenk had told league headquarters was a "lanceable heel boil," seemed to be paying attention, but his concentration was on other stars and stripes. Donnelly, a thirty-year-old blond known around the league as the Gynecologist, considered himself a steadfast Republican and a staunch advocate of national defense, but, for reasons more practical than philosophical, unshakably prochoice. He heard the national anthem a hundred times a year, including playoffs, so Shane figured that he wasn't disrespecting anyone if he used the time—and he was getting three minutes and up from these sisters in the sausage-casing butt-huggers—to line up postgame companionship.

A friend of Shane's in the audio-video biz had rigged up a two-way radio, similar to the one used by Secret Service agents, that allowed Shane to communicate with his bobo in the stands, an unemployed truck driver named Stan. Shane wore the device on his right sleeve, and when he wanted to talk to Stan, he would move that hand to his heart, a gesture taken by the crowd as patriotic. Stan would prowl the lower bleachers within Shane's range of vision (there was never anything wrong with the forward's eyes), and, on a signal from Shane, ask a particular female if she would like to enjoy a postgame repast with a Laser star. The system worked pretty well except for the time Shane ended up with a dominatrix from the San Fernando Valley, who ingeniously affixed electrodes to Shane's nipples, prompting another excursion to injured reserve.

Over on press row, Jillian Forrester, in her second week covering the Lasers, surreptitiously jotted a few words in her notebook as she stood at attention. Or tried to. Next to her, a television reporter named Goodman B. Douglas, a young African-American wearing a monstrous DUKE '98 class ring, kept up a running commentary.

"Yo J-Fo, throw me some digits," he said, offering his palm to Jilly. "Lasers gonna rock da casbah tonight. No'me sayin'?"

"Right on," Jilly mumbled.

"Them's my boys." Goodman B. Douglas smiled.

Back in his two bedroom suite at Yale, Jamal Kelly worked the TV remote with one hand and flipped the pages of *Constitutional Law* with the other. He had an eight o'clock the next morning and these Laser games on the West Coast didn't start until eleven Eastern, but what could he do? From the other bedroom he heard Harrison Brewster and a freshman co-ed he had somehow sweet-talked into coming over for what he called a study session. Jamal turned up the game.

From inside a broom closet near the Lasers' locker room, Henry Shenk listened to the final strains of the interminable national anthem, smoked a cigarette, and pondered his deteriorating state of affairs. As Shenk saw it, he always tried to do the right thing, always endeavored to be a professional. When the team visited the children's hospital and there was good publicity to be had, he buddied up to the writers and cameramen. Days earlier, for example, the Lasers had made their annual visit to the local children's hospital, and Shenk told the same story again and again—"I swear, a ward full of sick kids suddenly had smiles welded on their faces when the players showed up!"—hoping an account would appear in all the papers. The *Times* ran nothing; the story in the L.A. *Daily News* was headlined: "Veteran Donnelly, Rookie Parker No-Shows At Hospital Visit."

When there was controversy, Shenk, acting on directives from on high, guarded information the way Cerberus guarded the river Styx. The specifics changed but the drill was always the same. After importuning the press corps not to "blow things out of proportion," Shenk went to comical lengths to stonewall, spin, and flat-out lie if it meant suppressing information that reflected badly on the team. When he did that, he lost the respect of the reporters (certainly that of the pretty, young newcomer from the *Times*, who treated him kindly but indulgently, as if he were some kind of loveable uncle who put on his boxer shorts over his trousers) without getting concomitant props from ownership.

Shenk was reaching for the ashtray hidden in the corner of the closet when he felt the first stab of pain. Fortunately, he was able to nub out his smoke, his thirty-eighth of the day and last of his life, preventing an embarrassing flare-up in a no-smoking section of a no-smoking state. Then Shenk felt another stab, then another, then a crushing one that knocked him down. He slammed against the half-closed door and fell into the hallway, tripping up Kwaanzii Parker, who was trotting back to the locker room to answer a call from nature. Parker had seen enough *Scrubs* and *ER* to know he should do something, but he wasn't sure which side of Shenk's chest to pound and he sure as hell wasn't going to place his lips on the old man's tobacco-stained mouth. So Parker shouted and alerted a veggieburger vendor, who ran to the bench and fetched Ronald Manley, the Lasers' team doctor.

After a quick examination, Manley pronounced Henry Shenk—"The PR Man of PR Men," as the *L.A. Times* had proclaimed him two decades earlier—dead at sixty.

After the game, which they lost by fifteen points, the Lasers blamed their poor play on the death of their beloved spokesperson, a man whose name eluded most of them. A small circle of reporters surrounded Kwaanzii, who had scored eighteen points in an impressive debut as a starter. Moreover, he had been the first person to see Shenk dead, which seemed more newsworthy than being the last to see him alive. "I come by and, see, I think maybe he's just clownin', you know?" said Parker. "Not that I seen the old man ever doing nothing like that. But, shit, you never know. Then, I think, 'Damn. This for real. Old cat had a heart attack.'"

A reporter from a suburban L.A. paper got the rookie's attention. "Kwaanzii, how did you put the death out of your mind? You hit your first five shots."

"Well, you know, yeah, it's times like this you get perspective on shit. Wait, I'm not supposed to say that word. Times like this you get a reality check on shit. But I'm a professional, too, you know?"

From a nearby locker, a stone-faced B. D. Lake drifted over, put his hand on Jillian Forrester's shoulder, and said somberly, "It wasn't no heart attack. It was a pulmonary symbolism."

They buried Henry Shenk three days later. Willie Wainwright and Clarence Wolff, along with Lorenzen Mayne, who hadn't slept more than three hours a night since the accident on Canyon Road, were the only Laser players who carved out the time to attend the service.

CHAPTER 9

Owen Padgett's secretary, Rhea Moore, could always tell her boss's mood by the amount of pressure he put on the intercom button. Today, the morning after the debut of *Single Rich Dude,* Padgett had already buzzed her six times, the latest lasting at least fifteen seconds. She reached for the Advil in her top drawer and, with a heavy sigh and a roll of the eyes, knocked on his door and went in.

"You try the guy again?" said Padgett, draining the last sip of his caramel macchiato.

"I called three times in an hour, Owen," said Rhea. "You know how these reporters are. They don't come into the office much."

Padgett looked down at that morning's *Los Angeles Times,* which carried a review of *Single Rich Dude* on the first page of the "Calendar" section. Rhea took that as her signal to slink out of the room and wait for the next buzz, as Padgett reread, maybe for the dozenth time, the review.

Money Can't Buy You a Brain

Lasers' Owner Should Be Embarrassed by Witless and Humorless "SRD"... But He Probably Isn't

BY ADAM DEITSCH

Los Angeles Lasers' owner Owen Padgett always said that he wanted to crack the world of prime-time TV in the worst way. And, with "Single Rich Dude," that's exactly how he cracked it. With Padgett himself as the preening, self-indulgent star, a part for which he needed no thespian training, SRD significantly lowers the bar for reality shows—no mean feat—while helping to turn ABC's Monday-night schedule into why watch? TV. Remember Magic Johnson's train wreck of a talk show? Next to "Dude," it looks like a Bill Moyers special on PBS. Padgett got his start in garbage, his father having founded one of the country's largest waste management companies. With "Dude," he most assuredly goes back to his roots...

Padgett bolted from his seat and yanked open his office door. Rhea was halfway through Deitsch's review and was trying to suppress her laughter.

"We got that number for the new *Times* reporter who covers the team, that Jilly?" Padgett asked.

"I have it here," said Rhea. "You want me to get her?"

"No, just give it to me," he said. "I'll call her on my cell."

Padgett got the number, closed his door, then yanked it back open. "You believe that crap he wrote?" Padgett said to Rhea.

"Disgraceful," she said, having committed to memory a particularly tasty line from the review: "One of these unfortunate women will catch Padgett. My question is: Can they throw him back?"

❧   ❧   ❧

Down the hall and around a few corners from Padgett's palatial office, in the section of the Lasers' corporate offices known as "South Central," Evan Peterwicz sat in his airless cubicle paging through the latest copy of *Onward Christian Soldiers* magazine. If Evan stood and craned his neck to the right, he could see the office once occupied by Henry Shenk. Henry's son, a faceless insurance agent, had carted out Henry's belongings, and now the office stood empty, a rebuke (as Evan saw it) to his fifteen years of loyal service. Why wasn't he elevated right away? Manny Burnett told him that they "wanted to let a suitable amount of time pass," but it wasn't like Shenk had much status around the franchise. Hell, JFK got shot and they were swearing in LBJ two minutes later.

Peterwicz was not a subscriber to *Onward Christian Soldiers*. Burnett had come by an hour earlier, dropped the magazine on his desk, and said, "Take care of this shit before it hits the fan." The magazine carried a cover story about B. D. Lake, who, among other things, seemed to endorse the idea of castrating male homosexuals. Evan read from the text: "I'm not saying in all cases that these hell-bound reprobates are deserving of the full wrath of our Lord," B.D. was quoted as saying. "But in moribund cases their transgressions mandate that society's sword fall upon them . . . and upon their family jewels." B.D. further said that homosexuals in sports "should be subject to permanent disinjunction," but doubted that his own team "pavilioned such perverse seed-spillers."

Peterwicz slipped a copy of the magazine into his briefcase and made his way down to the training room, where he found B.D., getting a rubdown from Shenko Kukimoro, the Lasers' massage therapist/herbalist/smoothie maker.

"Listen, B.D., Manny asked me to talk this over with you," said Peterwicz, holding out the magazine.

"I have not seen it yet," said B.D. "Nice picture, right?" B.D.

was shown holding a basketball in one hand and a cross in the other under the cover tagline God's Rebounder. "You like it, Shenko?"

"Is very nice," said the taciturn masseuse, slapping B.D.'s enormous shoulders.

"Anyway, B.D., Manny is worried that we might get some, you know, feedback, from your comments about gays," said Peterwicz, leafing to the castration page.

B.D. sat up on his elbows. "What'd they say I say?" Peterwicz read him a couple of passages.

"Misquoted," said B.D., lying back down. "Taken out of context."

At that moment Peterwicz's cell phone rang. He listened for a minute, then handed the phone to B.D.

"It's the local FOX station," he said. "They read the story and they want to make you their Person of the Week."

B.D. sprang to a sitting position. "Praise Jesus," he said.

LORENZEN WAITED FOR LITANIUM and Kwaanzii in the players' parking lot. He stood by his new car, a gleaming Lucky Charm green Escalade. Since the night of the accident, Lorenzen couldn't help but notice that their bond had grown stronger. A reporter from Riverside had recently written a story describing how Tribal Cat was "mentoring" the young rookie and "imparting valuable veteran secrets." Lorenzen saw John Watson reading the story and shaking his head. "Young fella be better off with Osama bin fuckin' Laden mentorin'," the coach said to Lo.

The repercussions of their union were graver for Lorenzen. He had never been the best of friends with Litanium, and he hardly knew Kwaanzii, but it seemed that they were avoiding him and, moreover, caucusing behind his back. But maybe he was just paranoid. The memory of that horrible night—Kwaanzii's look of panic; the screech of brakes; the thud of chrome against body; the image of that poor mangled young woman in the awkward repose of death—had gotten more painfully vivid for Lo. He still didn't know what to do, but he knew he had to do something, and he wanted to gauge the feelings of his teammates, to see if they, too, had been haunted by the fateful race.

Lorenzen doubted it, though. While his own play had been getting worse, his concentration and energy sapped by thoughts of the dead woman, Litanium's had pretty much stayed the same and Kwaanzii's was a revelation. Litanium and a couple of the other veterans, not to mention Watson, were still bothered by the little things that Kwaanzii didn't do on the court. Kwaanzii didn't set screens to free his teammates. Kwaanzii was slow in his rotations on defense when the Lasers double-teamed. Kwaanzii took too much time off the shot clock backing in his defender, so that when he passed off, another teammate had to take a hurried shot. But those were deficiencies that only coaches, teammates, and aficionados discerned. To the average fan reading a box score or charting a fantasy league, the kid was having a laureled rookie season.

Even Lo had to admit that the teenager had talent. Kwaanzii was scoring about eighteen points a game—Lo had sunk to sixteen—and, worse, had a better shooting percentage than Lo, who had always taken pride in selecting good shots. Kwaanzii was now being mentioned as a legit rookie-of-the-year candidate. Hardly a game went by when some reporter didn't solicit Lo, a former rookie of the year himself, for a comment about Kwaanzii's chances.

Here they came, in hip-hop lockstep. Lo couldn't be sure, but he thought he saw Kwaanzii frown when he spotted him.

"You guys got a minute?" Lo said.

"We're going to get some Chinese at Jimmy Chew's," said

Litanium. "Young fella got a sudden jones for the MSG. They load it on the tangerine beef. You welcome to join us."

"It'll just take a minute," said Lo, looking around.

Litaniuim nodded and rapped two knuckles on Lo's hood. "I'm liking the 'Sclade here, but I thought you got the Hummer fixed. The young fella got his shit all repaired and he's still driving the same thing."

Kwaanzii was draining a Red Bull and had another in the pouch of his hoodie. "I thought we said it might cause suspicion and shit if we changed cars," said Kwaanzii.

Lo saw Puddin' Reichley climb into his Ford pickup. Reichley stared for a moment and waved. He drove away, the sounds of Vince Gill—"that cowboy shit" as Litanium called it—audible from his rolled-down window.

"I mean, I got the Hummer fixed and everything, like we said, but every time I climbed into it I just started thinking about that woman," said Lorenzen. "You noticed what I been driving?"

"And so does everybody else," said Litanium.

Lo tried again. "Look, time has passed and I've been thinking . . . that maybe it's time we said something. To the police."

Litanium and Kwaanzii exchanged glances. Overhead, a plane began its deafening descent into LAX. It muted some of what Litanium said but Lo caught ". . . finger-up-the-ass insane."

Lo regretted that he hadn't planned on how he was going to go at these hardheads; maybe if he had had a strategy . . .

"It don't keep you up nights?" Lo asked. "Not at all? Don't you ever think about it?"

Kwaanzii shook his head forcefully. "You start letting negativity take over and, man, you lost," the rookie said. "My AAU coach taught me that. Negativity's bad. It's all negative and shit."

Litanium put his hand on Lorenzen's shoulder. "I know where you coming from, Lo," he said. "I do. I think about it. But . . ."

Another plane on its way down through the smog, and Lo heard Litanium say ". . . the proportionality of pain." Sometimes Lo couldn't figure out whether Litanium was the dumbest person on earth or some kind of closet genius.

Kwaanzii had grown bored with the conversation and had put his headphones back on, tuning out the world. In a way, the same thing happened on the court. If the game was close, Kwaanzii was a killer. Lorenzen had come to believe that Kwaanzii was maybe the best player in the league either early in the first quarter or, if the game was still close, late in the fourth. He understood 0–0 and he understood 99–99. It was during those indeterminate parts of the game—say, right after halftime when the Lasers were down by eight—when Kwaanzii was most unreliable. He couldn't get his mind around the fact that basketball was a forty-eight minute test of endurance and that games were often won or lost during those pedestrian intervals when the fans were out buying nine-dollar bratwurst and twenty-dollar pennants.

Another plane came in. ". . . the point being that you're not considering the proportionality of pain," Tribal Cat was saying. "You got, on the one hand, the poor woman. You got, on the other, me, you, Kwaanzii, a whole damn team, a whole damn franchise and, in a way, a whole damn city. There's your proportionality of pain."

Is it possible that Litanium's argument made sense? Lorenzen had to consider it. No, it couldn't make sense. No way.

"What you're not figuring, Cat, is that you don't know who else is affected," said Lo. "Did she have a big family? Did she have an important job with . . ."

Litanium waved his hands in the air. "See, now that's where you're not making sense," said Litanium. "The idea that . . ."

They were interrupted by Kwaanzii hollering at them, his voice too loud by half because he was wearing the headphones, blaring

Aisle Nine, a new hip-hop group. "I told you I got an engagement so we gotta get lunch, Cat," shouted Kwaanzii.

"Young fella, keep still," said Cat. "I'm wrapping up here with the captain." Litanium turned back to Lorenzen. "The idea that a woman walking on a damn deserted road where we ain't seen nothing but possums and deer all those times we been out there . . . what? She chairman of IBM?"

Lorenzen put his hands to his temples. He felt a heaviness in his chest. He was back in North Carolina on another day . . . with another young woman . . .

"We're talking about it because I'm making the call!" he shouted. Kwaanzii heard him through his headphones and whipped them off.

Litanium's eyes turned into slits. "Lo, you ain't doing no such thing. I didn't want to bring this up, but this is a two-on-one situation. And Kwaanz and I got the advantage."

Lo's fears had been validated. "What's that supposed to mean?" Lo asked, knowing exactly what it meant.

Litanium clapped Lorenzen on the shoulder and turned to go. "We do not want this shit to get antagonistic," said Litanium. "All I'm saying is for you to look at the situation from a reality perspective."

Lo watched Cat walk away and saw him put both hands in the air as he did. On his right hand he held up two fingers. On his left, one. Two against one.

CHAPTER 10

Jilly Forrester knew today would be the day she would break up with Robbie Duckworth, but she hadn't decided upon a strategy. The engagement announcement that had appeared in the *Providence Journal* six months earlier made it more difficult, having bestowed a kind of permanence on a relationship that she felt was strangling her.

> Robert Charles Duckworth and Jillian Margaret Forrester, both graduates of Princeton University, announce their engagement, with a wedding set for next June in Providence. Mr. Duckworth is a portfolio manager in the Los Angeles office of Goldman Sachs, while Ms. Forrester, who plans to attend Wharton School of Business in the fall, is a business writer at the *Los Angeles Times*.

Jilly's mother, the redoubtable Dorothy Blaine Forrester of the Boston Blaines, had blown up the announcement, laminated it, and sent it to everyone she knew, which was why it was plastered on a wall in the kitchen of Jilly and Robbie's two-bedroom condo in West Hollywood. Jilly always took it down when they had company, which angered Robbie. But a lot of things Robbie had done over the preceding months had angered Jilly, too, not the least of which was his insistence that at age twenty-nine he still be called Robbie. He left "I love you" notes on her pillow when he left for work. He showed up unexpectedly at the *Times* to take her to lunch when it was clear that he was checking up on her. He had brow-furrowing phone conversations with Dorothy about Jilly's unexpected infatuation with journalism. That's what he and her mother called it — an *infatuation*, like a little girl has with a puppy. And that was all before she had taken the Lasers' beat, casting herself, the way Robbie saw it, as the Catholic schoolgirl in skirt and knee socks serving food in the reformatory.

What further irritated Robbie was that she didn't hate the job, as he had predicted. Her stuff was bright and witty and blissfully unencumbered by the Xs and Os of basketball. The only person more dismayed than Robbie by Jilly's new gig was Dorothy Forrester. She took the news that her daughter had exchanged interacting with captains of industry and movie execs for interviewing large, marginally clothed African-Americans by upping her weekly therapist visits — as well as her daily G&T intake — from three to five.

Jilly walked into the kitchen, a blue terrycloth bathrobe tied around her waist, to see if there was a way to ease into a minor argument, which could get them on the road to a major blowup. She went into passive-aggressive mode, unleashing a familiar line, one that she knew would elicit a familiar response.

"You want to shower first or should I?" she asked Robbie, who was waking up the dead with the screeching of the six-hundred-dollar Williams-Sonoma espresso machine he insisted they purchase even though she didn't drink caffeine.

"How about together?" he said, sounding as coy as one could while scanning the Nikkei Index crawling along the bottom of Bloomberg. They'd slept together exactly once since Jilly had taken over the beat two weeks earlier. Whatever Jilly was about to say—and she wasn't exactly sure—was interrupted by the phone. Jilly checked the caller ID and up came Padgett Cell. "This can't be good," she said and ignored it.

"Padgett, that owner, he's got your home number?" said Robbie.

"Evidently," said Jilly.

"How come you didn't answer it?" he asked.

"What? You don't ignore calls?" she said.

"Why you think he's calling?" asked Robbie, sounding increasingly prosecutorial.

Jilly snapped her fingers. "Damn, it must be because I left my shoes in his helicopter last night," she said.

Robbie didn't even smile. "Why don't you check the message while I'm standing here?"

Jilly eyed him steadily. "Why don't you check it?" She punched in the number and gave the phone to Robbie. He smiled as he relayed the message. "Something about his reality show . . . titanic disaster by the way . . . wants you to write an opinion about it . . . TV guy from the *Times* killed it . . ."

Robbie rescreeched himself another demitasse. "How well you know this Padgett?" he said.

Jilly shrugged. "Not real well."

"You know," said Robbie, "every day I go off to work and how the fuck do I know what you're doing. Working in that world with millionaire jerkoff players and billionaire jerkoff owners. You want me to pretend you've got some normal job?"

"It is a normal job, Robbie," said Jilly, turning toward the shower, figuring she could break up tomorrow.

"If you're gonna keep on doing it," said Robbie, "maybe we should talk about where we're going in this relationship."

Jilly sat down on the couch and looked heavenward. Who knew an uncontested layup would come along?

❋   ❋   ❋

AT COCKTAIL PARTIES, WEDDINGS, and college reunions, Erick Silver was a minor celebrity when he told people he was an NBF agent. To the overworked M&A lawyers, IT employees, insurance claims adjusters, and various other members of Cubicle Nation, Silver's line of work had an unmistakable patina of glamour, a melding of sports and money. He didn't disabuse anyone by telling the truth. That his job was that of a glorified babysitter. That he was on twenty-four-hour call to summon a locksmith when one of his players left his house keys at his mistress's apartment or to excoriate a coach when one of his players was spending the bulk of games pinned to the team bench. That his contract negotiations, thanks to the NBF's salary structure, could often be performed by trained monkeys.

Silver had entered the profession on a fluke. He was a star lacrosse player at Bucknell, and what he lacked in native intelligence he made up for with a winning personality. He had vague ambitions of becoming a doctor but a C- in organic chemistry euthanized that plan. The summer after Silver's junior year, his well-connected father arranged for him to receive an internship at OYL, a prominent sports management firm with offices all over the country. By July, Silver knew he had found his calling. The occupational requirements—a head for business, frathouse mannerisms, a love of sports, loads of testosterone, and not least, fungible morality—were tailored to his skill set.

After his graduation, Silver worked for Jay Holmes, an über-agent who was then the vice president of OYL's basketball division. Before long, like all underlings in the business, Silver came to the realization that if he could poach just one client, and siphon 4 percent of a $5-million contract, he would increase his income five-fold. Silver made late-night dates with the company's Xerox machine, copying all manner of confidential agreements, boiler-plate contracts, and internal memos. Then, in the common pas de deux, he ignored the noncompetition clause in his employment contract and wooed Holmes's least-satisfied client, Indianapolis point-guard Sam Carter, with promises of "one-on-one attention" and "getting your calls returned immediately." Carter was seduced; Silver gave notice at OYL, and "Silver Sports" was born. The golden-haired, silver-tongued proprietor was twenty-five and well on his way to earning his first million.

At first, Silver's stock-in-trade was identifying early the players who were going to attend college but would be ready to bolt to the NBF after one or two seasons. That meant following them from the time they were freshmen in high school. He would ingratiate himself with the athlete and the parents—especially the parents—and, unlike a lot of other agents, actually encourage the idea of going to college. Just not for four years. "Your son's the kind of kid who will flourish on campus for a year or two because, see, he's got something between his ears," Silver would tell Mom and Dad. "Then, when he's ready to go to the NBF, he's had maybe a business course or two, maybe something in marketing. And if he ever wants to finish up his degree, by mail or something, he'll have a good start on it."

Lorenzen Mayne was the first player Silver recruited out of college. He flew to North Carolina to meet with Lorenzen and his austere father, Jerry. Silver came armed with talking points and throwaway lines—"I'm a Lo maintenance guy," he said early in the conversation. When he realized that Lo and Jerry were a sophisticated duo, he adjusted his sales pitch accordingly. He referred to his operation as a boutique—a universal business euphemism for "small"—and emphasized that Lo would be his most important client. "Look," he told them. "Am I the biggest agent out there? No. Do I have decades of experience? No. But will I be here around the clock for you? Yes. Will you always be able to reach me? You bet. The guys with twenty-five clients can't promise that."

Lo and Jerry liked the kid's pluck as well as his claim that Lo would be the "cornerstone" of his fledgling agency. They signed with Silver, and for the first few years of Lo's career each side had done right by the other. But after Lo signed his contract extension—and Silver had pocketed a seven-figure commission—the two spoke less and less. Lo's phone calls and e-mails went unreturned for days. When Silver did favor his client with responses, they always seemed to come during games and practices when the agent clearly knew that Lo was unavailable.

Like so many sports agents, Silver had, over time, started to conflate his prominence with that of the athletes he represented. All those floor seats and all those rides on private jets and all those awed admirers at weddings and bogus awards from business schools had inflated his ego beyond healthy proportions. Lo noticed that Erick now perceived himself as players do—as a star.

Kids had been coming out younger and younger and, suddenly, Silver's "one or two years of college" rap became "the jump from high school to the NBF is barely a hop for your son." In fact, Silver's nickname had become "the Babysitter," and he rather liked it. His crowning achievement was landing Kwaanzii Parker, for whom he had procured a lucrative sneaker deal and a few other endorsements that had enabled Kwaanzii to make more money off the court than players who had been around for years. (They didn't know it at the time, but their coupling was a de facto last chapter—shortly after Kwaanzii signed, the NBF passed a rule barring kids from entering the league before their nineteenth birthday.) Silver had sealed the deal by sending the teenager and a special guest to Maui, all expenses paid, along with a note that read "I want to be YOUR asshole."

And so he was. When Silver flew to Los Angeles from his Dallas-based office, he sat with Kwaanzii's retinue during the games and went out to dinner with them afterward. Lo was left with temporal table scraps, forced to review documents with his agent over a quick breakfast the next morning, before Silver high-tailed it to the airport. When Lo confronted Silver about this shift in loyalties, the agent had his script ready. "Lo, you're my man. Kwaanzii is my boy," Silver said. "A man doesn't need to have his ass wiped and the snot wiped out of his nose. A boy does. You know what I'm saying? You're the guy who put Silver Sports on the map, though. I'm never forgetting that. That's a promise."

The explanation didn't completely mollify Lo, but, still, the relationship had spanned nearly a decade, positively Methuselan for an athlete-client marriage. He needed to get on the record about the accident with somebody and Erick seemed like the guy. When Lo finally got him, he knew he didn't have him for long, so he jumped right in.

"We got a problem," said Lo.

"The knee?" asked Silver. "You know it's insured."

"The knee is fine. It's just that night of that auto accident, when I called you . . ."

"Kwaanzii told me about it," said Silver.

"What did he tell you?" asked Lo.

Silver laughed. "Come on, Lo," said Silver. "You know I can't tell you that. Agent-client privilege and all, dude."

"Well, maybe what he told . . ." Lorenzen stopped himself from going further. Silver had made his priorities clear: Kwaanzii and commerce. "I think that's my other line, Erick," Lo mumbled.

"No problem. But call me any time," Silver said. "I'm here for you. You're my boy. You know that, right?"

"I thought I was your man," said Lo, hanging up.

CHAPTER 11

January 23
Los Angeles Lasers Record: 18-19

In an otherwise unmemorable shootaround before a game against Atlanta later that night, the stock of Ricardo Buenos Diaz took a serious tumble on the Coach John Watson Index. Watson was already in a bad mood. He hated the whole idea of shootarounds, the brainchild of an old Boston Celtic fundamentalist named Bill Sharman. "As worthless as a whorehouse to a homo," Watson called these game-day "Practice Lites" that often don't even require players to molt their hoodies.

What's more, the coach, who played back when non-American players were treated as cultural curiosities, hadn't come to terms with pro basketball's foreign invasion. By the late nineties, the National Basketball Federation, like virtually every other sector of the U.S. economy, had collided with the inexorable forces of globalization and technology. As borders and barriers to trade began to recede, NBF owners realized that it was foolish to cull employees only from the United States when the world was their labor pool. But there was a fine line between global village and tower of Babel, and language and cultural barriers were something every coach had to deal with.

Four minutes into the shootaround, as the players were going through the motions of a zone defense that Watson had configured at 3:00 a.m., the horn at the scorer's table locked. An angry AAAAAAAAAAAWWWWWRRRRRR!!!! echoed through the empty arena. "This means we can leave, right?" Litanium shouted in the din.

"Stay the fuck on the court," Watson shot back.

Assistants pressed buttons and kicked the scorer's table in hopes of silencing a horn that sounded like a tornado siren, until a stubby man with a tool belt weighing him down waddled onto the court, bent down near the scorer's table, and unplugged the horn. As Watson moved back to his perch under the basket, out of the corner of his eye he saw something move.

He leaned over to his longtime assistant coach and loyal assistant, Doug Carter. "Doug," Watson said. "Tell me I'm losing my mind, but is that motherfucking sweatshirt moving?" Carter looked to the sidelines and he, too, saw the balled-up fleece move ever so slightly. "Think it's a bomb?" Carter asked.

Watson blew his whistle like Dizzy Gillespie inflating a trumpet. "Bring it in, you motherfuckers!" As the team formed a membrane around him, Watson glared at each of them. "Whoever's sweatshirt that is, better fess up now," Watson barked. "Otherwise, we're going to detonate it. And then I'm going to detonate their ass to the CBA." As the players looked over, the clothing moved another two inches.

In concert, the players jumped back, some of them running to halfcourt. All except Buenos Diaz, who ran toward the garment. "Ees mine, Coach," he said.

Diaz carefully picked up the sweatshirt as delicately as one would hold a sleeping baby. He unfurled one sleeve and slowly pulled out a six-foot snake.

"The fuck is that?" Watson asked, speaking for everyone.

"Now you guys know how I feel when I take a leak," Shane Donnelly cracked.

" 'The serpent was more subtle than any beast of the field which the Lord God had made,' " said B. D. Lake, bringing Genesis into the exodus.

"Ees no serpent," Diaz said proudly. "Ees albino Burmese python. Just got it. Man at pet store sell it to me for fifteen thousand dollars. He call it my impulse purchase. He don't hurt no one. He only eat mice."

"Get that fuckin' eel outta here before I count to *cinco*," Watson screamed, "or you'll be impulse purchasin' back in Uruguay."

"Paraguay, Coach."

"Same difference," said Watson.

As a discouraged Diaz left the court with snake in hand, the players resumed their languid efforts to grasp a rudimentary zone. After a while, Watson looked at his watch. Mercifully, there were only ten minutes left. He blew his whistle, reached into his pocket, and placed a fifty-dollar bill at midcourt. It was the way he always ended practices: The player to win the halfcourt shooting contest kept the dough. "Time for da Cat to hang with Ulysses S.," Litanium announced. "Which one of y'all is playing for second?"

Showing more energy than they had all morning, the players lined up to take turns practicing their range from forty-seven feet. It was the source of unceasing amazement for Watson. The average salary on the team was somewhere around $5 million. Even after Uncle Sam, agents, and assorted other friends, family members, and plenipotentiaries had siphoned their cuts, players were taking home seven figures. Routinely, Watson would find wads of hundred-dollar bills of unknown provenance wedged between the seats of the team's charter plane. Guys would drop ten large on a bar tab. The per diem alone—$110—could feed a family of four for days. Yet he could dangle a fifty and the players would fight for it like it was the last life vest on the *Titanic*.

Watson had two explanations. At some level, the money in the NBF had become an abstraction, contract digits so prodigiously large that players couldn't wrap their brains around them. A crisp fifty, on the other hand, was something they could relate to, recalling from their not-long-ago childhoods just how prized a possession it was. The other explanation: NBF players were incorrigible competition junkies who got a charge from any form of contest, particularly one that featured a reward. It's why they were addicted to video games, why they took bowling and miniature golf so seriously, why they tried so hard to outdo each other's freestyle raps. If you offered a bag of chips as the prize to the player with the largest ovaries, Watson was sure they would line up ready to be examined.

Litanium went first and lofted a high-arcing shot that barely grazed the rim. The other players whooped. "Too much motherfuckin' wind in here," Litanium explained. "Sometimes the physics messes with da Cat's precision."

After the first round, three players had made their shots: Willie Wainwright, James Taylor, and Lo Mayne. As Lo stepped to the line for his second attempt, his approach was interrupted by a high-pitched shriek. Everyone turned around to find Diaz sprinting onto the court, cradling his albino python, now visibly limp, looking like a piece of garden hose. "Eet's my snake! I put him in the training room with all that air-conditioning, and I theenk he's frozen to death!"

"Man, I know from blowing cash money," said Watson, "but that's about the worst-spent fifteen large I've ever seen."

Sweet Baby James finally banked in a prayer, scooped up the fifty, kissed it, and held it aloft. "Yo, represent," he said, and accepted reluctant fist-bumps from Lo and Shane. Lo joined the joyless procession to the locker room, stopping to console Buenos Diaz, still cradling his late herpetological impulse purchase.

Then Lo saw them: Two policemen standing in the corridor next to a Christmas tree no one had bothered to dispose of. While his teammates didn't so much as do a double-take—figuring the cops had flaunted their badges to sneak a glimpse of a Laser practice—Lo went into full panic mode. His breathing shortened and his heart rate resembled a snare drum. Ever since that horrible night when he had allowed himself to be coaxed into the drag race on Canyon Road, Lo had figured it was only a matter of time until he, Litanium, and Kwaanzii would have to face the consequences. A mix of fear and paranoia returned whenever he saw a cruiser on the highway in his rearview mirror. He would lock eyes with a security guard in a mall and figure the guy had just made a positive ID and was about to call for backup. He'd tune into *America's Most Wanted*, fully expecting to see his mug and hear John Walsh, all serious in that leather jacket, detail the horrible crime. That Litanium and Kwaanzii apparently felt no such anxiety made him feel worse.

Now here were two cops right in the Bok. Surely his ration of providence had run out. At the entrance to the locker room, Lo felt his knees buckle when he spotted Watson quietly talking to them, pointing directly at him. *Coach is sellin' me out.*

"Yo, Lo," Watson yelled. "These gentlemen want to ask you a question."

Lo smiled meekly, reminding himself that he had the right to remain silent until an attorney arrived. Lo approached the officers and extended a hand. "Hey there," one said. The good cop, Lo immediately assumed. "I'm Sergeant Archibald and this is Sergeant McIlroy. Look, this is kind of uncomfortable . . ."

"Want to step outside?" Lo suggested.

"No, this is okay. Listen, we just want to ask you a question."

"Sure, what?" Lo said in a steady voice that masked his unalloyed panic.

"We run a Police Athletic League charity basketball game every February and this year it happens to fall on a Thursday when you guys don't have a game."

Lo's earnest expression suddenly changed to one of confusion. Maybe this wasn't a criminal interrogation after all. "Go ahead, officer," he said.

"Well, we were wondering if you wouldn't mind serving as honorary captain. It means throwing up the opening tap, making a halftime presentation, and maybe—"

Lo didn't want to appear too anxious but he could've kissed the men. "Anything you want me to do, I'm there," Lo interrupted.

"Great," the taller officer said. "But we just came to extend the invitation. If you need a few days to check your calendar or whatever, that's cool."

"No, that sounds like it'll be great. Happy to help," Lo said, all but prostrating himself before the cops, who were deeply gratified. "Just tell our public relations department where you need me and I'll be there."

As Lo stepped into the shower, he let the spray sting his face and he felt joyful. Then the bad thoughts returned. *Just postponing the inevitable,* he thought.

CHAPTER 12

Somewhere in the intestine-like tunnels of the Bok, Owen Padgett was deep into a game of Laser Tag. It was a lunchtime ritual he had founded, and any employee bucking for a promotion knew to join him. Plus, Padgett made sure the game was mentioned in every profile written about him. He thought it made him sound like a regular guy who related to his employees, much like the political candidate who throws on a flannel from L.L. Bean and drinks beer with the real people at the feed plant. "Everybody calls me Owen," he would tell reporters. "The guy who sweeps up around the Bok? He calls me Owen. And I call him Jerome." There was no Jerome who swept up around the Bok but that wasn't the point.

On this day Padgett's mind wasn't totally on the game. As he was getting chased by two interns from the marketing department near the entrance to the boiler room, he was seriously irritated. "Shit, Shenk," Padgett yelled. "Couldn't you have died in May and given us time to replace your ass?"

He had barely finished the sentence when a beam of pink neon silhouetted his figure. "You're toast, motherfucker!" yelled one of the interns. Upon seeing it was Padgett, gloating turned to abject embarrassment. "Sorry, sir, didn't realize it was you," he stammered. "Want us to let you escape?"

"No, that's okay," Padgett said. "I got work to do. Nice pursuit. Listen, can you dribble? And call me Owen."

Later that afternoon, the subject of Shenk's successor was high on the agenda at the team's executive meeting, a confab that usually entailed brown-nosing managers from marketing and sales telling Padgett what they assumed he wanted to hear and then breaking down his sentences like Kremlinologists. "Owen, I got a call from the league office asking about the PR director," Manny Burnett reported. "They have a bug up their ass and want to know what the story is."

When Burnett said "league office," he in effect meant the NBF's commissioner, Daniel Drang, a calculating autocrat who took to power the way moths take to light. He was a demanding boss who ran the tightest of ships—even his closest henchmen joked that his life story should be filmed by Leni Riefenstahl. "I wipe my ass," Padgett liked to say, "and I'm worried the toilet paper doesn't conform with Drang's mandated thread count."

But few owners challenged the commissioner. The league's popularity, and thus the owners' return on investment, had skyrocketed on Drang's watch. Beyond that, Drang was pathologically defensive about criticism of the NBF. When players were arrested, he regarded it as a personal affront. When teams had lousy attendance or an owner made an asinine comment or a franchise upholstered its courtside seats in an ugly shade of pink, the commissioner reacted as though it were an assault on his character. The owners, the league employees, and even most of the players grudgingly accepted this, and Drang got his way more often than any other commissioner in sports history.

"What did you tell them?" Padgett asked.

"I told them we'd be making an announcement about Shenk's

successor in the next few days," said Burnett. "They asked if we were just going to promote Peterwicz."

"What did you tell them?" Padgett asked, sounding exasperated this time.

"Probably," said Burnett. "What the hell else are we going to do?"

HENRY SHENK WAS TEN days dead, and, though Evan Peterwicz sincerely hoped the man's smoke-stained soul was resting in peace, he wondered why he had not yet been elevated to the head job. Every time in the past few days that he had encountered Padgett, the owner had slapped him roughly on the back and given him a wink, while Manny Burnett had been even more cryptic, forming a ring with his thumb and middle finger and giving Peterwicz the universal "okay" sign. What the hell did that mean?

So Peterwicz sat in his office, staring at an episode of *ESPN Classic* and pondering still another slight at the hands of the Los Angeles Lasers. For fifteen years, as he saw it, he had propped up the steadily declining Henry Shenk, banging out the daily game notes, reminding Henry about the approach of even the most meaningless team milestone (Litanium Johnson is nearing the one-thousand-career-assist mark!), handling complaints from visiting reporters who were consigned to "Siberia," the press area located in the nosebleed section of the Bok, or found the free popcorn in the press room insufficiently salted.

Peterwicz had been thrilled when he landed the job with the Lasers in 1989. Then twenty-five, he had been the sports information assistant at Pomona College, compiling stats about slow-footed chemistry majors on the basketball team, writing up press releases that went unread, spending weekends chronicling Ultimate Frisbee tournaments, the only sport at which Pomona excelled. His real talent, though, was filmmaking. Even as a kid operating a handheld that weighed in excess of ten pounds, Peterwicz had a knack for telling a story through moving images. At family functions he inevitably took on the role of the Capra of home video. In high school he was the one who pushed the film projectors and Betamax machines through the halls. While at Pomona, he put together a documentary on the Ultimate Frisbee team, called "Floppy Discs," that took third prize at a collegiate film festival.

Anything technical came easily to Peterwicz. His father had been an amateur inventor and world-class tinkerer, one of those distracted geniuses who could take apart washing machines and lawn mowers blindfolded but left the house every morning with his zipper open. Peterwicz had inherited the techno-geek gene. Computers, consumer electronics, iPods—whatever came along, Peterwicz had it mastered within hours. His wife, Lorraine, end-lessly badgered him about getting out of public relations and into something "you've got a real gift for." But his level of risk aversion was such that he preferred a stable if uninteresting job to what he saw as the feast or famine of the movie industry.

After three years at Pomona, Peterwicz applied to work for the Lasers almost as a lark. More than a year after he sent his resume, the team underwent a front-office shuffling and a job opened up as publicity assistant reporting to Henry Shenk. Naturally, Peterwicz quickly became the resident geek around the Laser offices. Something broke down, call Peterwicz. Somebody needed help navigating the Internet, call Peterwicz. The cheerful proclamation of "You're the best!" after he managed to troubleshoot was all the thanks he needed. Shenk was particularly helpless, of course. Peterwicz could never forget the day he was fiddling with a new PDA when Shenk entered and asked him, "Is that one of those Blueberries?" Answering service calls was a small price to pay, at least at first. Besides the twenty-five-hundred-dollar jump in salary,

Peterwicz was suddenly sitting courtside and accompanying the team on road trips throughout the country, calling his college friends from this Ritz Carlton and that Four Seasons.

However, whatever allure there once had been to getting the velvet-rope treatment had long since worn off. Peterwicz had gotten older while the players had gotten younger. His finances had tightened (marriage and the birth of two kids will do that to a man), and the players had steadily gotten wealthier. He couldn't relate to them—Peterwicz wholeheartedly agreed with Gregg Allman's assertion that "rap was short for crap"—and they had little use for him. Peterwicz would seethe when the team members acted like imbeciles. "I'm forty years old and I've managed to get through life without getting arrested, smoking crank from a soda can in public, urinating against the side of a bar, smashing a beer bottle over someone's head, fathering kids with women I barely know," he'd grumble at home. "And you know what? Hasn't even been that hard." Lorraine could always be counted on for nonsupport. "Why don't you stop bitching about it and quit? Couldn't you get a job as one of those key grips? Or what about sports photography?"

But Peterwicz thought Hollywood was for dreamers, and the last thing he wanted to do was work for a newspaper. As much as he didn't understand the players, he also didn't understand journalists and their unceasing cynicism. Hadn't they gotten into the business because they actually liked sports at one time? Why then did they have such obvious contempt for the athletes? Why did they have to amplify everything bad, covering a three-game losing streak or an arrest for marijuana possession as if it were a matter of national importance? And why did they have to be so self-righteous? These profane, thrice-divorced cavemen would lay their minibars to waste and could provide chapter and verse about which dancer gave the most creative, prop-enhanced lap dance at which strip clubs in which NBF market. But when a player missed practice for oversleeping, they would turn into pillars of rectitude and write scathing columns using buzzwords like "incivility" and "amorality."

Plus, he knew the team's press corps had taken to referring to him and Shenk interchangeably, as Shenkawicz. That hurt.

When Shenk died, Peterwicz entertained conflicting thoughts. He was authentically sad: He had always liked Shenk, all the while marveling that the man could even pretend to be so upbeat about the job season after season. But he was excited about the inevitable promotion and the long-awaited move from cubicle to office. But when was it going to happen?

OWEN PADGETT'S MIXED EXPERIENCE on *Single Rich Dude* aside, he had become obsessed by human interaction and interpersonal connections. As Shenk was lying dead in his pathetic smoking closet, the owner couldn't help notice the unfortunate soul's Dockers, his fifteen-dollar Timex, his Rockport walking shoes with built-in orthotics—totems of the middle-aged white man." *This guy was supposed to bond with NBF players? Shenk looked like an extra from* Marcus Welby, M.D., *and now we're going to promote his clone, only with more pent-up resentment? Nice sociology experiment.*

Padgett was thinking of other candidates who might actually relate to the players when he remembered his old college running buddy, Matt McQuade, mentioning a kid he taught at Yale. Jameer? Jermaine? Something like that. Some kind of damn statistical whiz kid. Sharp, African-American. Probably knew R. Kelly from Nelly and could hold his own playing Xbox. Hadn't the Red Sox finally won a World Series because they hired some young genius from Yale named Epstein?

"Yeah, give me a day to make some calls," Padgett said. "I may have another candidate."

"Come on, Owen," Burnett said peevishly. "Drang's politburo will be on my ass. Then Peterwicz is likely to come in here and go postal on all our asses."

"Trust me on this," Padgett said, running a hand through a thatch of prolifically moussed hair. "I got something else for Peterwicz. He'll be taken care of."

WELL, THOUGHT PETERWICZ, *THIS is it. Finally. Took them long enough.* He was knocking on Padgett's door just minutes after the summons came from the owner's secretary.

"Come on in, Ev," said Padgett, "I got this new Italian bottled water, San Gregorgini. Gas or no gas?" Peterwicz went for gas. Every time he entered Padgett's office, which was only a few times a year, his techno-geek soul soared. It was more electronics store than office, the centerpiece a gleaming fifty-five-inch plasma TV that rested majestically on a top-of-the-line Boltz. *The goddamned stand cost more than my TV,* Peterwicz thought. A pair of Japanese Shoji-style rice-paper floor lamps stood on each side of the flat–screen, like vigilant sentries. A popular, though covertly mentioned, topic of conversation among Laser employees was which self-possessed boss spent the most time in his narcissistic obsession: Manny Burnett with his clothes or Padgett with his office toys.

"That's the Sony KDE-55XBR950, right?" said Peterwicz. "Got TruSurround? Two-way passive radiator?"

"I know you're into this stuff," said Padgett. "You got one?"

Yeah, at five grand, I got one. "Little rich for my bank account, Owen," says Peterwicz. "But it's real nice."

"You'll get one," said Padgett. "Maybe sooner than you think."

Padgett looked over at Peterwicz and tried to smile. God, was that the beginning of a damn wart near his left ear? "So, Evan, you know why I called you here?" said Padgett.

"Well, I assume it has something to do with Henry, and—"

"WRONG!" shouted Padgett, jumping out of his seat. He wandered over to his exotic-fish tank and sprinkled a few granules into the water. Peterwicz heard a series of splashes. "These cichlids can be aggressive," said Padgett. "You have fish, Evan?"

I don't have fish and I don't have a goddamned five-grand tube. "I'm sorry, Owen, you said 'wrong'? We've been going along more than a week now without . . ."

Padgett waved his hands in front of his face. "We'll get somebody to take that job," said the owner. "That's beneath you now."

Peterwicz was utterly confused. "Beneath me?" he said. "I was the assistant, so how could being the boss be beneath me?"

"See if this title sounds better than 'director of media relations.'" He paused for effect. "'Assistant executive producer.'"

Peterwicz thought for a moment. "It sounds good," he said, "but of what?"

CHAPTER 13

Harrison Brewster stood in the middle of the Prescott dorm room, his eyes following Jamal, who was ransacking his chest of drawers and the closet and throwing clothes in a suitcase like an evicted spouse.

"So let me get this straight," said Brewster. "This McQuade taps you on the shoulder and tells you a media whatever job with the Lasers falls out of the frickin' sky. That's what you say happened?"

"That's what happened."

Harrison took a long pull on his Bud. "The only comparable thing was sophomore year when those fine young Urban Studies majors from Brandeis came down. Remember? Wanted to do some field work on a legit Brooklyn brother?"

"This is better," said Jamal. "Only catch: They need me right away, so I gotta drop out."

"Your mom'll be thrilled to hear that."

"It's not that big a deal. I checked with the registrar. I've already fulfilled all the requirements in my major. I can do an independent study project to pick up the three credits I need to get the sheepskin."

"Hope they're paying you good money, bro," added Harrison.

"Decent. Plus I get a company car."

"I thought you wanted to be a general manager, doing all your egghead stats. Not a media buttfuck."

"Media relations director."

"Yeah that."

Jamal slammed his suitcase shut and looked around the room. "Hey, you got that sweater vest—that real gay thing—I loaned you last semester?"

Harrison retreated to his room and came back with the black-and-white vest, holding it out in front of him like a wet diaper. "You're not gonna actually wear it, are you?"

"You wore it," said Jamal.

"I had an excuse," said Harrison. "Investment banking interview. Which I didn't get, I might add."

"Well, you'll get one. How the hell is the corporate world going to turn down someone named Harrison Brewster?"

"Shit. Lot easier to land something with the first name of Jamal."

It was a discussion they had often, but now, after the name "Jamal" had in fact helped to fabricate a job, there seemed to be a bite in Harrison's words. They both shrugged away an awkward silence.

"So, how you getting to L.A.?" Harrison asked finally.

Jamal looked embarrassed. "I wasn't even going to tell you that part. They're sending a plane. Not the big thing the team travels around in. A smaller one. They said they need me there fast and a couple of Padgett's other friends are on it anyway. So I'm taking the train home, talk to my mom, and taking off. You believe this shit?"

The friends, roomies since freshmen year, stared at each other, suddenly aware, in a hazy divination, that things would never be the same between them. College friends inevitably come to that point of demarcation, though not generally so soon or so spectacularly. One lands a job before the other, one moves to the opposite coast, one gets into a meaningful relationship, one changes, one stays the same, one gets his ticket punched to paradise, the other goes to his one o'clock in Global Economics. Jamal deeded over the dime bag in his top drawer, most of his CD collection, and a tube sock loaded with laundry quarters. They hugged clumsily. Then Jamal picked up his bags and left. There was nothing more to say.

AS JAMAL CLIMBED THE steps to his row house, he smelled burning tobacco, which meant that his mother was not home and Zeke was stealing a Kool in the living room. Jamal jerked open the door, and sure enough, Zeke almost fell out of the armchair trying to stub it out.

"Freeze, motherfuckah!" Jamal said. "It's the cigarette police!"

Zeke gave him the finger and turned his attention back to the television. He was wearing a brown uniform bearing the logo of the latest delivery service he worked for on a part-time basis. His shoes and socks were off. "Some kind of Yale emergency?" Zeke asked. "Picking up a slide rule for your bitch roomie Poindexter?"

"Something like that," said Jamal. "Where's Mom?"

Zeke took his time. "Shopping. Be back soon. So why you home? Man, you got a lot of shit just for a day trip."

Jamal sat down at the small kitchen table. "I quit school," he said.

Zeke stood up and turned off the TV, the surest indication he was legitimately flabbergasted. "Holy shit," he said. "Holy fucking shit."

"I got a job. With the Lasers. I'm going to L.A. In, like, an hour."

Zeke tried to act uninterested but he couldn't do it. "So, who did you suck off to get that gig?"

Jamal shrugged. "Connections," he said. "Read *The Great Gatsby* sometime. Life is all about connections."

Zeke put on his shoes and socks and started out the door. "Connections," he said, "is something I never had."

AN HOUR LATER, A SULLEN silence had settled over the house on Flatbush. Zeke had not yet returned. Betty had said, "I'm done talking," though Jamal doubted she was. She had presided over the redirection of Jamal's life—washing his clothes, pressing his shirts, approving this article for West Coast transplant, consigning this one to the drawer—while all the time filibustering against it. Her position was threefold: Quitting school so close to graduation was lunacy, even if he had every intention of graduating on time; taking a job he knew nothing about, three thousand miles away from home, was a monumental misstep; and hitching his wagon to such a false god—that was literally her term—could only lead to disaster.

"Mom, you know I dreamed about this," Jamal said, his final defense.

Betty looked at her youngest and saw so much of her husband—the passion, the polish, the intelligence, and the stubborn pride that could trump them all.

"Jamal, this isn't your dream," she said. "Are you telling me you dreamed of being a public relations person? You can't tell me one blessed thing a public relations person does. You dreamed of being in the NBF, just like millions of those other kids on the playground. Only difference is, you were smart enough to know you couldn't make it as a player. So why take the scraps?"

Jamal glanced at his watch. "What do you mean scraps?

They're talking about this as a stepping-stone. You're on Zeke's ass all the time about getting a better job. Then I get one I actually want, with benefits and even a company car, and you're on my ass about that."

Betty stared hard at her son. "I'm on your . . . I'm on your butt because this isn't the job you should have. You graduate, you go to law school, you study, you do well, then you become—I don't know—their general counsel, if that's what you want to be. But don't rush into something just because you know what players are in their starting lineup."

"So you think that's why they hired me? Because I know their starting lineup? You know how many millions of kids know their starting lineup? They read my stat program. They see something in me. They want me."

Betty put her arms on her son's shoulders. "Now, why do you think they want you?" she said. "I know how smart you are, how thoughtful you are, how articulate you are. But they don't know that. They hired you for one reason."

Jamal removed his mother's hands. "What reason is that? Go ahead, tell me. I want to know. I WANT YOU TO TELL ME THE REASON!"

The door opened and Zeke came in, a horrified look on his face. He had never heard his little brother yell at his mother.

"You keep your voice down now, Jamal," said Betty. "You don't leave this house using that tone of voice."

Jamal stared hard at his mother. "Go ahead and say it. Say what you're thinking. I'm a token, right? Your son's a house nigger. That's what you think, isn't it?"

With that, Jamal picked up his bags and left, brushing past Zeke without a word, leaving his mother near tears.

✺   ✺   ✺

WHEN HE EMERGED FROM a cab at the private airstrip on Long Island, Jamal was still equal parts angry and depressed. He was neither the moment he climbed onto Owen Padgett's private jet, a reconfigured Citation II that comfortably fit eight. A comely flight attendant with an even comelier southern accent said, "Hello, Mr. Kelly," when he climbed aboard, and Jamal felt like he had entered the kingdom of heaven. No sooner had his butt touched the leather seats than an Evian was in his hands and a goodie basket was on his tray table. Jamal was sniffing the container of pink-speckled cream cheese when he heard a voice behind him say, "That's lobster-flavored. Owen gets it made special."

Jamal turned around and saw a man in a denim shirt, blue jeans, and cowboy boots extending a hand. He pushed his dark shades onto his forehead and said, "Reid Felker. I'm exec-producing Owen's reality show. *Single Rich Dude*? You've seen it? Asshole critics don't get it. But they'll come around."

Jamal could've kicked himself for not seeing either of the two episodes. *What if Padgett quizzed him on it?*

"This is my companion, Karen Lewis," said Felker. A blonde ten years Felker's junior, which put her at about twenty-five, leaned forward to shake Jamal's hand, giving him an eyeful of manufactured cleavage. She, too, wore jeans and cowboy boots, as if they had just come from some yuppie version of the Calgary Stampede.

"Owen tells me you're going to work for him," said Felker, sipping champagne.

"I'm the new media relations director," said Jamal. "It's quite a sad thing about Mr. Shenk. He had been with the team for a number of years."

"Owen said you're some kind of numbers genius," said Felker. "He also needs you to young-up the franchise. What are you? Twenty-five?"

"Twenty-four," said Jamal. "But I'm willing to lie about it." Which he was already doing, by a year.

"Everybody lies in California," said Karen Lewis.

"I'm sure you'll do just fine," said Felker. "Owen has all the confidence in the world in you. He's a great judge of character."

"Thanks," said Jamal. "I think what helped me, too, was that I got in kind of through a friend."

Felker waved his copy of *Variety* in the air. "That doesn't matter now. You got the gig. And you'll run with it, right?"

Karen adjusted her headrest and added, philosophically, "The important thing is to get the gig," she said. "And anything we can do to be helpful, you just call us." Then she closed her eyes and reclined her seat. She was already being helpful—Jamal hadn't realized the seat went all the way back.

Not many more words were exchanged on the five-hour flight. Jamal divided his time between trying to read his inscrutable employee contract and continuing the to-do list. He scanned it several times to see if his salary was noted but it was not. On his to-do list, he added a couple dozen items, everything from *rent an apartment* to *buy public relations textbook*.

He had just fallen asleep when the flight attendant with the maple-syrup voice shook him gently and said, "Phone call for you. It's Mr. Burnett from the Lasers."

Jamal flicked a few drops of Evian on his face to wake up, cleared his throat a few times, and said, in a voice that he hoped trumpeted confidence, "Mr. Burnett. How are you?"

"It's M.L.B, Mr. Whiz Kid. Owen and I wanted to make sure the flight was going well. I wanted to run through your day tomorrow."

"Well, there's lobster-flavored cream cheese and the seats recline," said Jamal. "What could be better?"

The general manager told Jamal to check in at the airport

Sheraton where he would be staying until he found an apartment. "You're gonna have to hit the ground running," said Manny. "You got a lot to learn and we're at midseason. I want you to meet the players right away, one-on-one, if possible. That's what was missing with Henry, the dead, er, deceased guy you're replacing. Personal contact. I'm going to give you Shane Donnelly's cell. Call him tomorrow morning and set up a meeting after practice. After you finish with him, come on into the office and meet all of us. That sound like a plan?"

After Jamal hung up, he reclined his seat and tried to sleep. He had just taken a business call, in a private airplane, from the general manager of the Lasers, and he was programming Laser numbers into his cell. And, if he wasn't mistaken, here came the flight attendant with another plate of bagels, fruit, and cream cheese flecked with lobster.

CHAPTER 14

J amal had been to a strip club twice before but never at two in the afternoon, which was what he was telling Shane Donnelly, the Lasers' muscular power forward.

"Ain't no strip club," said Donnelly. "It's a gentlemen's club. There's a difference."

A waitress at the Palace of Fur, wearing an abbreviated Catwoman costume, slapped down two L'eggsalad sandwiches on wheat toast, along with a Corona for Shane and cranberry juice for Jamal. Shane picked up one piece of bread and peered inside.

"They got some kind of green shit, maybe ara-goola, on this motherfucker, too," Shane said, placing a meaty hand on the waitress's behind and sticking a twenty into her Catwoman briefs.

"You boys enjoy your lunch," she said. "Or breakfast. Don't know when you woke up."

Following Manny Burnett's orders, Jamal had called Shane earlier that morning—called him six times before he answered—and requested the postpractice lunch. The locale was Shane's choice, which is how they came to be eating while gazing at a woman who had just shed a Girl Scout sash and wrapped her long legs around a gleaming pole.

"Anyway, I appreciate you taking the time, Shane," said Jamal. "I'm new to this and I just thought—"

"You wouldn't think a woman could get herself into that position, would you?" Shane said. "What's your name again? Jabbar? Like Kareem? Is that Muslim? You ain't gonna blow up any buildings on our ass, are ya?"

"It's Jamal. No, I'm cool on that."

Shane stared at the stage, shaking his head contentedly. "You know what I always say, Jamal?" said Shane. "If you ain't thinking about pussy, your mind's wandering."

"Look, Shane, why don't you just tell me what you didn't like and what you did like about the way the late Mr. Shenk did his job. That way I can get a feel—"

"I'd like to get a feel of that," said Shane, pointing to the stage. "I'll tell you this, ol' Henry was heading for a heart attack. A couple seasons ago we had a ghoul pool in training camp about when he'd kick. He beat us that year."

"Anyway, if you could just tell me—"

"Be right back."

Shane rose, stretched, and ambled toward the stage, every pair of eyes in the room following his six feet, nine inches. Jamal knew that he was on injured reserve with what the Associated Press agate referred to as a "rib malfunction," a malady that followed his "lanceable heel boil" and "extreme gastritis." But he appeared to be walking just fine. He tossed a twenty at the stage, now occupied by a dancer who had removed a fireman costume and was gyrating around a large hose in what was announced as a tribute to those brave men who gave their lives on 9/11. Shane continued into a darkened back room. Jamal declined a lap dance from someone named Danielle and waited for Shane. After a while his cell chirped.

"Hi, Mom," Jamal said, reading the caller ID.

"I wanted to see how your first day was going," said Betty. "I'm just leaving work."

"It's going great," he said. "I'm having lunch with one of the players. Sort of."

"You get set up with that luxury company car yet?"

"Not yet. But it's a busy time for the team. I'm sure it will happen soon enough."

"What's that noise?" she said. "You in some sort of discotheque?"

He assumed his mother was the only person in America still using the word *discotheque*. "Something like that, Mom. Listen, I can't talk. I gotta finish up this lunch."

"I understand. And forget what I said last night. Whatever you do, whatever happens, I will support you. You couldn't disappoint me." Her voice started to catch and she hung up before he could say anything.

Jamal finished his sandwich, went to the men's room, left a message for Harrison Brewster ("Guess who I'm having lunch with and where I'm having it . . ."), continued with his to-do list *(memorize Laser bios)*, and finally got up and peaked around the stage.

"You looking for Shane, honey?" said a dancer who had just finished her act and was scooping up the remnants of a nurse's costume. "He won't be back for a while, you can take that to the bank." A long stethoscope swung from her neck, and she lubriciously asked Jamal, "Can I take your blood pressure?"

"Not with that thing," said Jamal.

"Well, honey, I can help you pass the time till he gets back. What's your name?"

"It's Jamal, and I have to get to work. You see Shane, tell him I left."

On the way out, he tipped the waitress ten dollars. Burnett had told him he had five grand to spend on food and entertainment and he figured he might as well start chipping away.

❀   ❀   ❀

TOO EMBARRASSED TO TELL Shane that he didn't have a car, Jamal rode a bus to downtown Los Angeles. The Lasers' corporate offices were located within the Bok and as the bus approached the arena, Jamal's heart rate quickened. Once his car arrived, he envisioned himself driving to work every day—he'd get there as early as they wanted—and playing some noon pickup hoops on the real court. Then maybe he'd catch a quick steam with the players, grab a shower, and be back at his desk by one-thirty. He deboarded the bus and walked through the employee lot just as Lorenzen Mayne got out of a gleaming green Escalade.

"You're Jamal, I bet," said Mayne, slapping him on the back. "We heard you were coming. Welcome."

Jamal couldn't have been struck dumber had one of the twelve apostles stopped to squeegee his windshield. Whenever he shot hoops by himself on the playground, Jamal pretended to be Mayne. *Lo has it, right baseline, he's doubled, he spins . . .*

"Listen, J-Money," Lo Mayne was saying. "We gotta get you a ride. Ask Manny. He gets cars for the club."

"I'll do that, Lorenzen," said Jamal. "I thought I saw on the Internet you were a Hummer guy."

"Yeah, yeah, I was," sputtered Lo. "But I got tired of filling it up every day. Listen, I'm doing this Players' Association thing right now."

Once a year the president of the Players' Association visits teams to discuss general union philosophy and collect general grievances. The players have few philosophical thoughts to offer, though they are generally not lacking in grievances. The main issue on the table this time around was the $110 per diem, which the players found, in the words of B. D. Lake, "Deficiently insecure, particularly in large metropolises." Also, the players were outraged that teams were no longer picking up the tab on hotel incidentals, such as phone calls, minibar damage, and in-room porn.

"I guess maybe I should come in, before the meeting, to say hello to everybody," said Jamal. "I've only met Shane. We just had lunch. Sort of."

"He take you to that strip joint on Manchester?"

"He referred to it as a gentlemen's club."

"You got women, they remove their undies, it's a strip joint," said Lorenzen, holding the door open. "Sure, you come in. I'll introduce you quick. I'm already a little late."

The entrance to the executive offices would've done a sultan proud. The wall-to-wall carpeting was thick and rich, the piped-in music generic. Lionel Ritchie was on.

"Litaniuim refers to it as Lawrence Welk shit," said Lorenzen, pointing to the unseen speakers. "But the club figures the public at large is coming in here, not Snoop Dogg, right?"

Two secretaries, one a luscious, long-legged black woman, the other a luscious long-legged white woman, stood poised behind twin mahogany desks, ready to intimidate supplicants. Jamal glanced at their name tags. The black one was named Barbara Ann and the white one was named Saleeka, as if they had gotten together one day and deviously switched monikers. A large, elegant Victorian case held innumerable trophies, including the seven championships won by the franchise, though none under Padgett's ownership. A Japanese serenity pond bubbled peacefully in the background; it had been Manny's idea "to go a little Eastern."

Behind each of the secretaries, long hallways curved parabolically into the distance. One led to offices, the other to the locker room and, beyond that, to a stairway that led down one floor to an immense practice court. The hallways eventually met at the rear, the whole thing forming a gigantic figure eight. The offices of Padgett, Burnett, and coach John Watson overlooked the practice court. The main court was on the ground floor, two flights below.

"Hello, Lorenzen, everything all right with you today?" said Barbara Ann, speed-blinking her eyelashes.

"Hi, Lo," said Saleeka. "You are looking fine as usual." She smiled professionally and turned to Jamal. "Mr. Kelly, there's somebody waiting for you in your office."

The absurdity of the turn that Jamal's life had taken had struck him many times over the previous twenty-four hours but never more than at that moment—a gorgeous secretary had referred to Lorenzen Mayne by his first name and to him, Jamal, by "Mister."

"You can call me—*should* call me—Jamal."

"Call him J-Money, girls. That's what he goes by."

"I don't go by that," said Jamal quickly. Then he worried that he had offended Lorenzen. "Course it's okay, whatever you want to call me." Everyone seemed to be taking great pleasure at his discomfiture.

"Anyway, J-Money, the reporter's back there from the *L.A. Times*," said Saleeka. "The new girl. Janie maybe? She's in your office."

Lorenzen winced. "Listen, J-Money, her name's Jilly. But, dog, you gotta be cool when you see her. Big old girl with pimples and them short-yardage legs. Looks like she played at a Big Ten school, maybe Northwestern or Purdue. Purdue's still in the Big Ten, right?"

"After you talk to her, you're supposed to see Mr. Burnett," said Barbara Ann. "Your office is down there on the right. And after you see him you're supposed to see Martha Ciccarelli. She's our vice president of marketing. She has a surprise for you."

Jamal started down the hallway to his office, which was second on the right. He passed a cubicle that apparently belonged to Evan Peterwicz; at least, a couple dozen All-Star press passes tacked onto a large pegboard bore that name. A small sign on the door of

Jamal's office said HENRY SHENK, which freaked him out. He was thinking of how to hit up Manny Burnett for his own nameplate when he saw a slender pair of ankles inside his office, nervously dancing up and down beneath a pair of tan Capri slacks. Jamal entered and the ankles sprang up.

"Sorry to make myself at home," said Jilly. "Manny told me it was okay. You're Jamal, I assume. I'm Jilly Forrester. I'm the *Times'* beat writer. And you seem to be laughing at me."

Jamal shook his head. "It's not you. It's something Lorenzen told me. I was expecting somebody else."

"Sorry to disappoint you," said Jilly.

"Not the case," said Jamal, extending his right hand. "It's nice to meet you."

Jilly was about five-foot-six, thin, with athletic shoulders. Her dirty blonde hair was cut short but Jamal had the feeling that she had just cut it. A pair of eyeglasses were pushed up on her forehead, below which a pair of deadly green eyes stared out at him. *Naomi Watts*, he thought. Jamal sat down on the edge of his desk, knocking over a stack of press guides, his first official act as an NBF media relations director.

Jilly pushed her glasses down and studied Jamal. "No offense, but you seem young for this job," said Jilly. "Having you after poor Henry Shenk . . . what's that? A statement? Like they're going with the two ages of man?"

"Couldn't tell you. And you're what, sixty-five?" Jamal tried to keep contact with Jilly's green eyes, but he looked away.

"Twenty-eight. I know you're younger."

"So you were a detective before you were a sportswriter."

"Worse," said Jilly, "I was a business writer. No, they told me about you. Said they got you from Yale and you're some kind of genius with numbers. Not sure what that has to do with this job but good luck."

"I'm not sure either," said Jamal.

They stared at each other until Jilly sprang to her feet. "Well, I just wanted to say hello. And I thought I'd stop by to see if anything came out of the meeting with the Players' Association."

"How'd you know about that?"

Jilly put her hands on her hips. "It's a real NATO summit in there. The lawyer, Avery Short, stops by. He warns them not to use drugs, unless it's marijuana — 'Weed is to the NBF what chewing tobacco is to baseball,' he's been known to joke — or call for hookers, especially if they turn out to be transvestites. He slips in that dues are going up. Then they bitch about the per diem and everybody goes home."

"You know more about it than I do," said Jamal, quicker than he wanted to.

"I have more experience," said Jilly. "Three weeks versus one day. I'm still learning. We'll learn together. I hope we get along."

"Why wouldn't we?" said Jamal.

Jilly looked at him and flashed a killer smile. "Boy," she said, "you are new."

Another voice interrupted. "Jilly, you know you're not supposed to be in here."

Jamal looked up at a middle-aged man who had not yet glanced his way.

"Guilty as charged," said Jilly. "But Manny told me I could come back."

Jamal went to the man's side and stuck out his hand. "Jamal Kelly."

The man glanced briefly at Jamal, turned back to Jilly, and extended a limp hand. "Evan Peterwicz."

"Oh, man, I was just coming over to see you," said Jamal. "You're my lifeline."

Peterwicz put up his hands and forced a wan smile. Heavy-looking shoulder bags rested on both shoulders. "No, not really. I'm pretty much out of public relations."

"Yeah, I heard something about that, Evan," said Jilly. "What's going on? And what's with the bags? You on bivouac?"

Peterwicz put his shoulder bags down on a chair. He tried to look humble but didn't succeed. "Oh, Owen has me doing something for him. Some kind of special assistant thing."

Jilly thought: *Special assistant to program his iPod?*

"Damn," said Jamal. "So you can't even show me some ropes?"

Peterwicz flashed a tepid smile. "Maybe a few ropes," he said. "I'll do most of the stuff for the All-Star Game, which is coming up in a few weeks. But you'll learn. You have plenty of help. They're going to hire an extra intern or two. And Jilly will help you, too." A little Peterwicz humor.

"How can I help him if you're throwing me out?" said Jilly.

Peterwicz hoisted the bags back on his shoulder with a low groan. "I was just kidding. It's up to you guys to work out your rules now." And he left.

Jamal shook his head in wonder at Peterwicz's back. "They hire me, then promote the guy who's supposed to show me everything?" he said.

Jilly picked up her backpack and gave Jamal a slap on the shoulder. "Hey, you went to Yale. You'll be able to figure it out. Let's get down to the locker room."

They left the room, Jamal turning left, Jilly right.

"It's shorter back to the locker room this way," Jilly said as kindly as she could. "They connect back here."

Jamal nodded hopelessly and followed. "I didn't get the tour yet," he said, praying he wouldn't take a header on the carpet before they got to the locker room. There was an uncomfortable silence on the walk, which turned to confusion when they heard shouts and the sound of a slammed door. The Players' Association attorney, Avery Short, rushed by in a huff, followed by Lorenzen Mayne, followed by Charles "Puddin'" Reichley, the Lasers' twelfth man, the oversized center who assisted Mayne on Players' Association matters. Jamal was trying to figure out whether he should follow them when Litanium Johnson stuck his head out of the locker room and shouted after the lawyer, "I don't care what you say, but porn ain't no damn incidental. We're sick of this motherfuckin' oppression from the Man."

Litanium noticed Jamal and Jilly and held the door open for them. "You coming in?" he said.

"You can tell me what happened with the lawyer, right?" said Jilly.

"Yeah, we'll get into that," said Litanium.

"Everybody dressed in there?" said Jamal, suddenly feeling like Jilly's chaperone.

"Yeah, yeah, all dressed," said Litanium.

"I'm Jamal Kelly," said Jamal, extending his hand to Litanium. "They hired me to replace Henry Shenk."

"Yeah, yeah, I heard," said Litanium. "Welcome. Come on in."

The Lasers' practice locker room was a smaller version of the real one downstairs, done up in tasteful blue and white, two rows of soft, velvety movie chairs off to one side where the players could fall asleep when John Watson was drawing up strategy at the chalkboard. A large refrigerated case held Gatorade. Bottled water, fresh fruit, a tub of breath mints, and the remnants of a buffet lunch sat on a large folding table in the middle of the room. In the NBF, every day is a barbecue. Each player had the equivalent of two lockers, except for Kwaanzii Parker, the youngest rookie, who only had one, over in the far corner.

Jilly decided to venture over to Kwaanzii World, collect a comment on his feelings about the newfound stardom to which he appeared to be heading since getting the starting assignment. She approached and he nodded at her to sit down, removing his ear-phones and fingering the monstrous Jaguar hood ornament on a lei of gold he wore around his neck.

"Lemme guess what kind of car you drive," Jilly said, staring at the talisman.

"Righteous, right?" said Kwaanzii. "See, I wanted to put my uniform number on the hood. I got a big '33' riding high up there. So I put this bad boy around my neck. I think of myself as kind of a Jaguar on the court, know what I mean, so it's, like, symbolic and shit."

"I see," said Jilly.

"Anyway, Jill, I was meaning to ask you what you're doing two weeks from next Saturday," Kwaanzii said. "My foundation is having a paintball game. All proceeds go to charities and shit. Ain't that a story?"

Jilly found herself saying, "Could be," revealing the depth of her desperation for off-day stories.

"You're gonna like this part the best," continued Kwaanzii. "Girls play for free."

"I'll put it on my calendar," Jilly said. Sadly, she wasn't kidding.

JAMAL STUCK HIS HEAD into the office of Martha Ciccarelli and was almost blown away by the volume and exuberance of her greeting.

"YOU MUST BE JAMAL!" she said, jumping from her seat and practically leaping into his arms. "I've been waiting for you!"

Martha, a plump woman in her midforties, explained to Jamal that her job was "keeping the Lasers in the news in a positive way" and "expanding the brand of the franchise in a positive way." She talked with a honeyed accent; Jamal guessed Georgia. Her accentuation on the positive was reinforced by the sticker posted on her bulletin board: THINK POSITIVE!

"We're really two heads on the same plant," said Martha, mixing her metaphors, possibly because her office was cluttered with vases of huge sunflowers and pots of small cacti. "You handle the players, I handle just about everything else, always trying to get out that positive message."

"Sure," said Jamal. "I'm glad we had this time. . . ."

"And you're going to be part of the message," she said. "Owen tells me you're some kind of genius."

Jamal shook his head so forcefully that some of the sunflowers began waving. "Absolute exaggeration," said Jamal. "I, mean, with all due respect to Mr. Padgett. I was only a—"

"Anyway, the point is, I got you on this local PBS show," said Martha, wagging her hands back and forth as if she were a referee signaling a traveling violation. "It's called *Math Counts*. It'll be a great opportunity for us to send a *positive* message about this franchise, that we have real brains working here. It's next week. Almost here! Better start studying!"

After a few seconds of muteness, Jamal began to voice his objections, of which there were many. "Martha, I haven't even started this job. I'm going to be incredibly busy and don't have time to study and don't know what I'm studying for anyway. And—"

"Math, silly. You're going to study math." Martha Ciccarelli leaned closer to Jamal. "Tell you the truth, Jamal, we've taken some heat for, well, not having enough adverse people on our staff."

"What do you mean, 'adverse people'?"

"You know," Martha said, "colored people. Or people of color. Whatever they're calling it. Anyway, to have you on there would show 'em. Especially if you won, huh!"

Jamal searched Martha's face for irony and saw none. "I'll probably go on there and mess up," he said, "and then the message will be: The Lasers employ dopes of color."

Martha reached for a huge watering can she kept under her desk and began bathing her sunflowers. "I hear you, Jamal, but it's Owen's orders. Taping's at four p.m. Next week on the eighth."

"There's one problem, though. I don't have any wheels yet," Jamal said, hoping Martha would pick up on the hint and make some inquiries about his phantom company car.

"Don't worry. We'll get somebody to drive you over! It was so nice to meet you!"

As Jamal took a bus back to the Sheraton, he punched up Harrison Brewster on his cell. Brewster answered on the first ring. He and three friends had convened in the suite to watch *Lost*. Jamal wouldn't have thought this possible but he briefly wished he were there.

"Hey! Turn that down," shouted Brewster. "It's Jamal. Bro, how was your first day? Interesting?"

"Well," said Jamal, "that's one word for it."

CHAPTER 15

Hey, Jermaine," an indeterminate voice called from the back of the bus that was transporting the Lasers from the private airfield in Seattle to the team's hotel. "You like hip-hop?"

From his seat maybe two-thirds toward the front, behind the coaches and trainer but far enough from the players so he wouldn't encroach on their space, Jamal turned around. He had been on the job for only a little over one chaotic week and his name had been variously butchered as "Jameer," "Jamar," Jamil," and "Jumaine." So he figured—correctly—that "Jermaine" was intended for him as well.

"Sure, I like hip-hop," he said. "Why?"

"Settle a bet with me and Kwaanzii," Litanium demanded. "If you were going to pick a hip-hop MVP, who'd it be? Jay-Z or Nelly?"

A Gladstone-Disraeli debate it wasn't. But Jamal saw this as another chance to prove his bona fides to the team and distance himself from his late predecessor, Henry Shenk.

"Those my only choices?" Jamal asked, lowering his voice to summon his street. Other players had grown silent, eager to hear

Jamal's analysis. "Jay-Z got the Beyonce factor in his favor. No doubt about that. But he's always playing it safe. What's he done that's even a little bit daring? It's like manufactured, just-add-water hip-hop. Nelly's off to a nice start but he thinks he's a better singer than he is. I don't get the R&B crap he messes in. It's like Snoop Dogg cutting back on his rapping because he thinks he can really act. Nelly still needs a few more good years before he's MVP material. Why not go with Tupac? Ghetto superstar. That's what he was."

It took the players a second to digest the soliloquy. Then Litanium spoke. "Ya all right, Jamal." There was scattered applause. Roughly a year ago to the day, Jamal had been tapped for a secret society at Yale. Somehow this validation on the back of a bus alongside Puget Sound was just as meaningful. "Aiiiight!" came a voice from the chorus in the back. Jamal thought for a second that it might have been Lo, but it wasn't. The team captain, three-hundred-dollar headphones pillowing his ears, looked sullenly out the window.

WHEN THE TEAM RETURNED from Seattle the following day, Jamal mooched a ride home from Watson. "Car trouble," he explained, never bothering to complain that the much-anticipated "luxury company car" he had been promised still hadn't materialized. When Jamal arrived home, he sat and stared at the boxes that consumed most of the living room of his new apartment, a drab one-bedroom in a Santa Monica complex he described as "downmarket Melrose Place." His cable, naturally, was installed—a man needs to take care of the basics—but the television was propped up on a few cinder blocks. Phone service had yet to be activated, as Jamal figured he could economize by using his cell, the bill for which was paid by the Lasers. His refrigerator was vacant save some packets of duck sauce from the Chinese joint on Colorado and a few loose beers he had plucked from the team plane.

As for the job, it wasn't so much baptism by fire as it was baptism by inferno. Part of it was the usual vertical learning curve of a new job: Jamal had to adjust to a PC after years of fealty to a Mac; learn the names of one-hundred-plus coworkers who also had their biweekly checks signed by "Lasers Sports and Entertainment"; find the filing cabinet where he could grab a handful of felt-tip pens.

But Jamal was also figuring out the office politics and the strange alchemy of a professional sports team. Dealing with Burnett—Jamal just couldn't bring himself to call the general manager M.L.B.—was okay, but he was tiring of hearing Burnett call him "Whizzie," short for Whiz Kid. He was sure he heard a touch of sarcasm in it, too. Peterwicz, who wasn't around half the time, showed Jamal nothing about the job. Jamal learned the hard way, for example, that Shane's concubines couldn't be seated within six sections of each other, lest they engage in a full-throated shouting match. "Jameel, you know how much ass you've cost me?" Shane barked at practice one day after a catfight had broken out at the Bok. Jamal learned, too, that he should linger in the general vicinity of B. D. Lake after games, so he could be ready to intercede if the big center started on a tangent about gays, lesbians, abortion, or the evils of evolutionary theory, which on one occasion he had linked to a heartbreaking loss to the Milwaukee Monarchs. He learned that when *Poetry* magazine calls with an interview request, Clarence Wolff actually wants to hear about it. Dealing with the cryptic Padgett was a trip, too. At one practice, the owner pulled Jamal aside, leaned in, and said, "You know Diaz?"

"Buenos Diaz?" Jamal stammered. "Sure, I know him."

"Well, lately, he stinks."

"Maybe you're seeing something I'm not, sir," Jamal, trying to sound confident but deferential at the same time. "But I ran his value rating last night and in the fourth quarter against teams with winning records and he's—"

"No, no, no," Padgett interrupted. "You overthink things too damn much, Jamal. He's been playing great. I mean—literally—he *stinks*. I don't know what they do in Bolivia, but he needs to learn that here in America, we take showers. Part of successful media relations, Jamal, is making sure your players don't go out in public smelling like goats. I need you to get that boy some soap."

"Got it, sir. He's from Paraguay, incidentally."

"Yeah," said Padgett over his shoulder. "Like there's a difference."

Jamal had intended to ask about the status of his missing company car, but decided it wasn't the right time to broach the subject with the boss.

Sometimes it fell upon Jamal to keep track of the Mayne Men, the army of siblings, cousins, friends, former high-school teammates, and various other hangers-on who had affixed themselves to Lo Mayne the way an octopus attaches to a piling. Jamal spent at least half an hour before every home game securing tickets for the Mayne Men. Just when he thought he had learned the roster, one member would abruptly leave town while another would show up, demanding to watch a closed practice. "It's like the friggin' CBA," John Watson complained to Jamal. "One guy comes in on a ten-day, leaves mysteriously, and another comes to take his place. Lo's got to learn to say no."

Jamal was fascinated by the dynamic. Some of these guys were clearly just sponging off Lo, chilling comfortably in the shadow of his celebrity. What sort of an able-bodied twentysomething would fritter away his days playing Nintendo and smoking weed at his Boy's house, then go cheer on his Boy at an NBF game, then let said Boy pick up the four-figure tab for the postgame meal at Morton's? That was exploitation in the worst way. But Jamal was really taken by Lo's loyalty. These were his pals from before he had "blown up" and become an NBF star; now *he* was going to take care of *them*. Sure it was costing him a hell of a lot of money, running a boarding house for half of North Carolina. But in a sense, he was buying a slice of home. These guys spoke the same slang, liked the same food, knew the same people. If this imbued Lo with comfort and made him more relaxed on the court, it was probably a good investment.

Jamal was also troubled by the word "posse," which the press, Jilly included, used (with a tinge of resentment) to describe the Mayne Men. When Hollywood stars ring themselves with a phalanx of handlers, they have an "entourage," a word with a faintly regal ring to it. When tennis players or golfers travel with agents and swing coaches and image consultants and herbalists, and other mood-makers in tow, they are said to have a "support staff." When basketball players or rappers—which is to say: young, black males—travel in a pack, it's a "posse." Jamal brought this up with Lo shortly after they met and the player nodded eagerly. "I wish people would lose the word 'posse' and just call them what are," said Lo. "My friends and family."

On this—an off-day and also the day Jamal felt he was about to humiliate himself on PBS—Lo had agreed to a sit-down with Goodman B. Douglas, the ambitious sports reporter from the Los Angeles CBS affiliate. Jamal had heard Douglas's name before but knew nothing about him. Since part of Jamal's job was getting chummy with the local media, he went on the station's website to read Goodman's bio. Jamal was struck to see that he was a handsome African-American who wore "geek-chic" plastic-framed glasses. He also saw that Douglas graduated from Duke and grew up in Saddle River, a ritzy town in the horsey section of New

Jersey. In high school, Jamal had played a basketball game in Saddle River and still recalled that the student parking lot could have passed for a German sportscar dealership. He figured there would be no shortage of icebreakers.

Jamal waited in the foyer of the practice facility to broker the interview. Douglas arrived first. "You must be Jamal," Douglas said. "You must be Goodman B."

"Whassup, motherfuckaaaah," Goodman B. Douglas said in an exaggeratedly low voice. "How my bizz-oys been treating yahs in the Federation?"

Jamal recalled the scene from *Airplane*—a late-night dorm staple at Yale—when two jeri-curled passengers order their in-flight meal in jive unintelligible to the other passengers, save for Barbara Billingsley.

"Um. Things are going good, man," Jamal said. "Hey, I saw you were from Saddle River. I went to Cardinal Rutherford in Brooklyn and we played a game in—"

"You from Crooklyn and you was kickin' it in the Saddle? Small motherfucking world!" Douglas said. "You fuh real?"

"For real."

"Dat's whack! No'me sayin'?"

"I know," Jamal said, thinking: *This guy is from Saddle River and went to Duke and he makes my dropout brother sound like Noam Chomsky.*

Lo arrived a moment later, apologizing for being ten minutes late. "Car trouble," he volunteered. Jamal had already picked up that "car trouble" was the NBF players' version of the "the dog ate my homework."

Douglas reached out to give Lo an elaborate series of handshakes that ended with Douglas sticking out his pinkie and drinking an imaginary cup of tea. "Whassup, motherfuckaaaah," he said. "How yo portfolio holdin in the Federation?"

"Good, good," Lo said. "What's up with you?"

Jamal led Lo and Douglas to two facing chairs he had arranged on the lip of the practice court. He offered to get a drink for either but both declined. "Let's get started," said Jamal, hoping Lo would appreciate the concern he was showing for his time.

"So," Douglas said, looking pensive. "Dawg, what makes your mad ups so silly mad? I mean, bro, if your ups were madder they'd be *irate* ups."

"Well," Lo responded, trying his best to take the question seriously. "I work hard in the off-season to strengthen my lower body. And I've always been a quick jumper, which helps more than having some outlandish vertical."

"Cool, dawg," Douglas said, nodding in the manner of a bobblehead doll. "Speaking of verticality, what fools on other teams are the worst in trying to front your grille?"

At this point. Lo looked confusedly off-camera to Jamal and then waved his hands. "Hey, can we cut this for a second?"

"Sure," Douglas said, motioning to his cameraman to stop taping.

"Look, man, can you just ask normal questions?" Lo asked. "What's up with that Rick James shit?"

"I'm hearing you," Douglas said, looking down at his three-hundred-dollar Cole Haan loafers. "I'm getting pressure at the station to develop my own style—my own shtick, you know?" Jamal noticed that Douglas's voice and locution had suddenly lapsed outta Compton and straight inta Saddle River. *Shtick?* "They did some focus-group testing shit and I guess people really dig the jive thing. Black audiences are amused by it. White audiences eat it up. *This black dude isn't just giving me six minutes of sports; he's giving me a crash course in urban hip.*"

"Okay," Lo said with a sheepish sigh. "Always trying to help a young brother."

And so the interview continued, Douglas B. going back into character to pose his questions in au courant jive and Lo dutifully playing along, doing his best to decipher phrases like "Hotta than grits in a carburetor" and "Nastier than a naked, fat man with hepatitis B."

When it was over, Douglas again gave Lo an eight-part handshake and leaned into him for a hug. He turned to both Lo and Jamal and, without irony, said, "Thanks for keeping it real, dawgs." As Goodman B. Douglas walked out, Lo and Jamal exchanged glances, bonding over their mutual amusement.

When Douglas was out of earshot, Jamal smiled. "Thanks for doing that interview, Lo. And thanks, especially, for keeping it so, so very real."

Lo shook his head. "Thanks back at you, dawg," said Lo. "Now I gotta go check my portfolio."

CHAPTER 16

Martha had forgotten to send a car, so Jamal, cursing himself for getting goaded into public humiliation, took yet another bus to the local PBS station, located in a dusty part of downtown off Third Street, vowing to put in for twenty bucks on his expense account. Having no idea how to dress for PBS, he had opted for khakis and the sweater vest Harrison Brewster had returned to him the day he left for L.A. "I look like motherfuckin' Willis Drummond on *Diff'rent Strokes*," he concluded as he entered the unimpressive two-story building that also housed L.A.'s NPR station.

Math Counts was a typically bare-bones PBS production—small studio, nondescript backdrop, three stiff-backed chairs, one blackboard, one balding, myopic moderator in a bad blazer-and-tie combo. Jamal was whisked into the studio and directed to a seat between a young man in a turban who introduced himself as Nepir Induri, an engineering major from UCLA, and an older woman who introduced herself as Priscilla Barrett, a high-school math teacher from Pacific Palisades.

"They said you're a professional baseball player?" asked Nepir Induri, his voice impossibly high-pitched. "What position?"

"No, I work for a basketball team," said Jamal. "The Lasers."

"I thought that was the football team," said Priscilla Barrett.

Martha Ciccarelli will pay for this, Jamal thought.

The moderator came over and introduced himself as James Voss, a statistics professor from Cal State–Fullerton. He solemnly shook hands with each of the competitors and said that he would "get to know them" during a "snappy Q&A" that would "break the tension" during what was "sure to be a heated competition."

The format for the show was simple: First player to hit his buzzer got a chance to answer the question. Correct answers were worth ten points, incorrect answers resulted in a penalty of five points. After the first round, Voss took a break to crack up the viewership (of about seventeen, Jamal thought) with his snappy Q&A. After the second round, the contestant with the lowest score was eliminated. The remaining two played a "lightning round" to determine the champion.

At first, Jamal was intimidated by Nepir, who answered the majority of the questions, though some of them inaccurately. Jamal could hear the heavy breathing of Priscilla Barrett, who was visibly sweating and shed her cardigan at one point, accidentally hitting her buzzer and getting penalized five points. After the first round, Nepir Induri had forty-five points, Jamal had thirty-five, and Priscilla had only ten. Voss announced that it was "time to get to know these outstanding competitors."

"Nepir, you're studying engineering?" asked Voss.

"That's right," he said. "I'm a junior at UCLA. Working my way through."

"Tell us something about your family."

"My father is an anesthesiologist," answered Induri. "My mother is an anesthesiologist. My sister is an anesthesiologist, and I have two younger brothers. Both want to be anesthesiologists."

"Well, sounds like you're breaking the mold then. Jamal?

You're next. You work for the—" Voss checked his notes—"the Los Angeles Lasers. That sounds fascinating. They're involved with sports, if I'm not mistaken."

Jamal happened to glance out at the studio audience and saw . . . Jilly? What the hell was she doing here? He saw her shaking with laughter, trying to hide her face behind her small reporter's notebook.

"No, uh, yes. Yes. The Lasers are the professional basketball team out here. As a matter of fact, we're hosting All-Star Weekend and I hope—"

"That sounds fascinating," interrupted Voss. "Ah, Miss Barrett. I see here that you were the California State Math Teacher of the Year in 1991. That is truly something to be proud of. And so let's get back to our game."

The second round went along much as the first. When it ended, Nepir Induri had ninety points, Jamal had seventy-five, and Priscilla had only twenty-five, her fate sealed when she gave the wrong answer to a quadratic equation, then punctuated her frustration with, "Oh, hell, fuck-it-all-to-damn-shit!" As the 1991 California State Math Teacher of the Year rose to leave, Professor Voss said, "We'll be editing that out."

Just before the questions started again, Jamal and Jilly locked eyes and she gave him a little wave. Jamal hated to admit it but her presence served to motivate him. Jamal and Nepir battled it out, both of them jamming their buzzers, spewing out answers immediately. The competition even raised something close to interest in the languid, monotoned Voss. The score was tied at 220 with time for only one more question. "You will need to write out your answer, so the time limit is off," said Voss. "The first one to show me a correct formula is the winner. The question is from the area of statistics." Jamal's heart raced. He tried to keep his eyes from roaming toward Jilly.

"It is known that the IQ scores of workers in a certain company are normally distributed with a standard deviation of ten," intoned Voss. "If 0.13 percent of the workers have IQs in excess of 130, what is the mean?"

The question was a gimme for a stats geek. Jamal could hear Nepir Induri furiously writing, but he took his time and made sure he was correct. After a couple of minutes he rang his buzzer and held out his paper. The moderator walked over, took Jamal's paper, and squinted, trading looks between Jamal's answer and the master answer on an open tablet. "Let's see here," he said. Jamal had written:

$$IQ = N(m, 100)$$

Let $x = F^\wedge\text{-}1\ (0.0013)$ with F the law of the normal distribution $N(0, 1)$

$$P(\ N(m, 100) > 130\ ) = P(\ N(m{\neq}10\ ,\ 1) > 13\ ) =$$
$$P(\ N(m/10\text{-}13\ ,\ 1) > 0\ ) = P(N(0,\ 1){>}1\text{-}x) = P(N(1\text{-}x,\ 1)\ {>}0) =$$
$$0.0013$$

Nepir Induri waited, holding out his own paper, hope in his eyes. Finally, the moderator looked up. "Well," he said, "we have a winner. James . . . Jamal Kelly. Congratulations. Guess you haven't been spending all your time playing baseball, have you, young man?"

JILLY WAS WAITING FOR Jamal in front of the studio. Wearing a black warm-up suit, her blond hair tied into a ponytail, she was smiling as Jamal emerged, bearing the fruits of his victory—a certificate for a one-year subscription to *Algebra Quarterly*, a beige-and-black PBS tote bag, and a CD entitled *The Best of Mantovani*.

"Who's Mantovani?" Jamal asked, holding out the disc.

"I'm not sure," said Jilly, "but my parents listen to him. Not a strong recommendation."

Jamal tossed Mantovani into a sidewalk trashcan.

"Well," said Jamal. "What the hell are you doing here? Let me guess." And they answered together, *off-day story*.

It had already become a running joke between them, though it was less humorous for Jilly, who did indeed have to come up with something almost every day, even when there wasn't a game. There are only twelve players on a pro basketball team, and the public, at most, is interested in four of them. That leaves a lot of scrambling for material.

"Anyway, congratulations," she said. She put two fingers from each hand in the air and sketched a headline. "'Lasers' Boy Genius Brings Home the Hardware.' That whiz-kid stuff I heard was right on."

"I got lucky," said Jamal. "The UCLA student missed too many questions."

"Maybe he was anesthetized. Listen, my first question is this: What's with the sweater?"

"Well," said Jamal, "I figured the only place I could wear it was on PBS, so . . . wait, we're not on the record, are we?"

"No I'm scribbling notes for my diary entry," Jilly said sibilantly. "Rule of thumb: When reporters start writing, it's on the record. Same for when that little red light on the tape recorder is on. But, hey, why would a media relations director know that?"

Over Jilly's shoulder, Jamal saw a man, good-looking guy of about thirty, approach. Jilly followed Jamal's gaze and turned around.

"What are you doing here?" she said.

The man smiled and extended his hand to Jamal. "Since Jillian is being impolite, I'd better introduce myself," he said. "Robbie Duckworth."

"Jamal Kelly," said Jamal, returning the handshake. They both exerted a little pressure, then backed off. Jamal couldn't help but think that he had seen the type many times at Yale. Frat boy, six to eight years out of school, playing hooky from his banking job to come up for the Harvard game, maybe go after a co-ed conquest.

Robbie Duckworth put his hand, familiarly, on Jilly's shoulder. "I called the paper and they said you were down here covering a story," said Robbie. He looked at Jamal and spread his hands. "You're the story?"

"Not much of one," said Jamal, "but, yeah, I'm the story. The off-day story."

The three of them stood uncomfortably, Jamal sensing ancient history in the air. "I gotta get back to the office," Jamal said finally. "Thanks for coming down, Jilly. Gonna be the most boring story in the history of the *Times*, though."

Jilly put her hand on Jamal's arm. "Wait," she said. "I still have some questions." Jilly turned toward Duckworth. "Jamal works for the Lasers," she said. "He just won a quiz show." Then she turned toward Jamal. "Robbie and I used to be . . . involved. We broke up."

Jamal could see Robbie's jaw tighten. "We used to be engaged," said Duckworth.

"I don't think out here, in front of the PBS station, is where we ought to be talking about it," said Jilly. "In front of Fox maybe. But not PBS."

"I don't think so either," said Robbie. "I came down to see if you wanted to get a cup of coffee."

Jamal didn't know Jilly real well, but his best guess was, Robbie D. was going to come up empty on the coffee.

"I have to finish this interview, Robbie, so I can't do it," said Jilly. "Unless Jamal wants to come, too."

Robbie took it all in, looking first at Jamal, then at Jilly, then back again.

"He must be some story, then," said Robbie. "Are you some story, Jamal?"

"Look, man, she said she's got a story to do and I've gotta get back—"

"Whoa," said Robbie. "Now you're calling me 'man.' Do I know you?"

Jilly took a step toward Robbie and put a hand on his shoulder. "Let's not do this here, Robbie," she said. She turned to Jamal. "I'll call you later at the office. Get some quotes for the story. On the record, of course."

Robbie stood for another minute or so, marking his territory. Jamal stared straight at him. Jilly stood between them.

"Your Lasers right now?" said Robbie. "They kind of suck."

"Can't argue with that," said Jamal. "My man."

Robbie stared hard at Jamal, trying to give his best New England Patriots tough-guy look. He leaned down, gave Jilly a quick peck on the cheek, and walked away. Jilly watched him go, breathed heavily, and headed for her car. Too embarrassed to ask for a ride, Jamal started walking toward the bus stop, pausing along the way to throw away the PBS tote bag.

CHAPTER 17

It was supposed to be a typical regular-season road trip for the Lasers, one game in Phoenix and then three in Texas—the "Texas Triangle." The manifest included the players, coaches, Jamal, the massage-smoothie guru (and, lately, an aspiring aromatherapist) Shenko Kukimoro. The team plane was an old 747 that had been gutted and replaced with huge BarcaLoungers for seats, a high-tech kitchen, and plasma-screen TVs, which, depending on the mood of the coaches, were used for breaking down film or deconstructing the *Girls Gone Wild* cinematic anthology.

This was Jamal's third time on the plane, but he still took mental notes, knowing that he would be recalling every detail the next time he spoke to his brother and friends. After twenty minutes on the tarmac, the plane hadn't budged an inch. "Put the key in the ignition, my man, and let's get going!" Watson yelled.

Five minutes later the team pilot, Roger Mitchell, a bearded Air Force veteran who was friends with Padgett's father, fired up the intercom. "We're getting word from Phoenix that there was some sort of security breach at the airstrip and no private planes are being allowed to land. Guess what, gentlemen?" he said, unable to conceal a laugh. "Looks like you guys are flying commercial. Hope you all have government-issued IDs. And remember—beer, wine, and cocktails are four dollars and exact change is always appreciated."

The players unleashed a hail of "fucks" and a few pelted the cockpit door with half-eaten jumbo shrimp and balls of brioche. An hour later, a group rate having been negotiated and expedited by United's special service desk, they were standing in line at security, no more conspicuous than a pride of lions roaming through a supermarket. Jamal did his best to keep the autograph seekers away from the players, but some got through. Everyone was in a collective funk as the entourage snailed toward the security screeners and the confounded machine that squealed every time a grandmother with a pacemaker hobbled through.

"People have to go through this every time they fly?" said Tribal Cat. "I'm gonna remember this shit next time my cousin Monty tells me my share of that Gulfstream is a bad investment." Jamal was right in front of Litanium. He could tell the Cat was losing it.

"Excuse me," Litanium said, buttonholing a security screener on break who was enjoying a snack, "but they must have some special security section? For VIPs?"

The woman took a bite of her Auntie Anne's pretzel, brushing specks of cinnamon from her blue coat. "They only got one section," she said. "Everybody gotta pass through it. Even P-Diddy."

"Yeah," said Litanium, "like Puffy's gonna stand for this shit." A young boy tugged on Litanium's sleeve. "Kwaanee Parker, would you sign an autograph for me?" Litanium stared down hard at the boy. "The player you want is towards the back of the line," said Litanium. "Jug-eared, big-nosed, buck-toothed, cold-sored young mother . . . young-looking fella."

Jamal fell in beside Litanium, hoping to ease his aggravation. When they were about ten feet from the table where everyone had to disrobe, Litanium frantically started patting his pockets.

"Shit, Jamal," he said. "How thorough is this? I mean, it's been a while since I flew commercial."

"Just make sure you take off your jewelry and your shoes," said Jamal. "They like to nail people on shoes. But if you're not carrying any . . . you're not carrying anything else, are you?"

Now Litanium was at the table, disgorging coins, a Motorola pager, and leftover poker chips into the small security bowls. Off to his right, Jamal saw a large, no-nonsense dog—leashed to a large, no-nonsense security guard—turn his attention to the table, and he heard Litanium say, "Oh, shit. Guess the dog don't dig da Cat."

By now the line had stopped and the dog was clearly heading for Litanium. "Down, Kujo!" said Litanium. In keeping with his media guide entry that identified him as an "enthusiastic animal lover," Litanium held his hand playfully near the dog's nose, then upped the ante by trying to put the dog in a playful headlock. The policeman handling the Doberman was slow to respond, and just as Litanium started to walk through the screener, the canine sunk *its* canines into Litanium's thigh, right on the pocket of his cargo pants into which he had stuffed a not insignificant quantity of premium Thai stick earlier in the day.

The policeman corralled the dog and immediately got on his radio. "Gonna need backup." A rivulet of blood ran down Litanium's leg and jeans. Three policemen quickly arrived, first to stanch the bleeding and then to take Litanium into custody.

"Shit," said Tribal Cat. "I loved them pants."

Jamal acted quickly. He threw his jacket over Litanium's head in the event there were photographers around and told authorities that the dog bite needed attention. They guided Litanium to an office near the security station and opened another security line to minimize the delay. Watson called over Lorenzen and assistant coach Doug Carter and told them to make sure the Lasers kept on moving and got on the plane as quickly and as unobtrusively as possible. Lo couldn't help looking on the scene with humor—and with no small amount of schadenfreude. *Well,* he thought, *guess I'm getting five more shot attempts tonight without Litanium in the lineup.*

Watson put his arm around Jamal's shoulder. "Damn fool forgot commercial security's a little more intense," said Watson in a hoarse whisper.

"Apparently the case," said Jamal. "You think I should stay with Litanium and try to clean this up?"

Watson rubbed his eyes. *We gotta trade that motherfucker in the off-season,* he thought. "Well, I got more experience—personal experience—in this area," said the coach.

"Yes, but if you don't show up with the team maybe somebody notices and it's a big deal," said Jamal. "I don't come, nobody misses me. I'll get a later flight, with or without Litanium, and be there by game time."

Thus commenced Jamal's first critical exercise in crisis management. First he called the team travel bureau and made a reservation to Phoenix, landing a seat on a flight in ninety minutes. Then he knocked on the door of the security office and felt instant relief when he saw that Litanium was smiling. "My man here's a homey from Baltimore," said the Cat, pointing to the security chief. "He remembers me from high school." A few minutes of conversation and it was determined that, although Litanium probably wouldn't be charged, he wouldn't be able to get on a flight that day and would have to sign some papers to be released. Jamal called Manny Burnett to tell him what had happened. Manny told Jamal to get on his flight and he would send over a team lawyer to deal with Litanium.

"Yo, J-Dog," said Litanium, as Jamal turned to go. "Don't go lettin' the team fall apart without da Cat there."

Jamal made his flight and, as he munched peanuts in his middle seat, pondered what lay ahead. When the Lasers' beat writers saw that Litanium hadn't made the trip, they were going to ask questions. Was he injured? If so, how come he hadn't mentioned anything at practice? Had there been a personal crisis? The interrogation would continue until they got their answers.

Jamal drew a matrix and, recalling the Game Theory course he had taken as a junior, tried to figure out the best scenario. As soon as the plane landed in Phoenix, Jamal put in a call to the league office. He spoke with Barton Sylvester, a tall, bespectacled PR henchman whom Commissioner Drang had recently hired specifically to help spin the players' criminal conduct and the growing perception that the workforce was composed of spliff-smoking, gun-toting, deadbeat dads. After Sylvester had finished unleashing a string of expletives, he said to Jamal: "Kid, I got one word for you to remember when the buzzards in the media start circling: Stonewall the shit out of them."

Jamal joined the team at the hotel, told Watson what happened, and said, "I got it under control." Watson said, "It's all yours." On the bus ride to the arena, Jamal nervously got the team's attention and said, "Um, if anyone asks about Litanium, it was a dog bite that kept him home. Which isn't, you know, a complete lie."

When the press corps arrived at Phoenix's new, taxpayer-funded venue, Taco.com Palladium, for its pregame session—usually a pointless interval during which they stare at each other in a vacant locker room while the players hide out in the training area—the reporters eventually realized that Litanium was truant.

Jamal had given serious thought to pulling the press corps aside and appealing to their humanity. *Off the record, Litanium was dumb enough to go through airport security with a dime bag in his pants. A trained dog smelled him a mile away, and now he's probably getting bailed out of jail. I'd prefer if you didn't mention his absence*. But that was a fleeting thought. "Weirdest thing," Jamal said to the reporters. "Litanium was bitten by a dog. Right on the thigh. Should be with the team tomorrow."

That seemed to satisfy most of the reporters, especially considering that the celebrated animal lover was known to keep a couple of nasty pit bulls. But Jilly pulled Jamal aside. "You know I'm going to ask to see the dog bite tomorrow," she said. "So, if you're lying, now's the time to give it up."

Jamal hesitated, then smiled. "Jilly, I'm sure Litanium would be more than happy to show you any part of his anatomy. Especially his dog bite."

"You're sure about this, Jamal," said Jilly. "It's a little early to be burning your credibility."

"You think I would lie to Robbie Dickworth's fiancée?"

"Ex-fiancée," said Jilly.

She flashed him a withering glance and joined the other reporters in the media lounge. As they chowed down on Salisbury steak, they toyed around with variations of the same lead sentence: Dog bites Cat.

WHEN OWEN PADGETT HEARD about the problem at the airport, he immediately made a few calls and got hold of the surveillance tape of the incident. Formal charges were indeed not going to be filed—authorities called Litanium a "first-time offender," which Padgett found highly amusing—but he still braced himself when he picked up the *Los Angeles Times* the next morning. When there was no mention of Litanium's bust on the front page, he considered it a small victory. He turned to the sports section and read Jilly's account of the team's eight-point loss to Phoenix. There, in a notes column after the game story, was a boldfaced heading, "Cat gets bitten by dog," followed by three innocuous sentences. *Point guard Litanium "Tribal Cat" Johnson was not with the team last night, having suffered a dog bite, according to Lasers media relations director Jamal Kelly. Efforts to reach Johnson, who has been cited by police in the past for misdemeanors involving his pit bulls, were unsuccessful. He is expected to join the Lasers in Dallas.*

Padgett smiled and dialed the media relations director on his cell. "Suffered a dog bite! No mention of the pot! Good work."

"Thanks."

"Oh, and don't think I've forgotten," said Owen. "Your new car will be waiting for you when you get back."

Litanium did indeed show up the next night in Dallas, all too willingly displaying the teeth marks in his leg, validating Jamal's explanation. Jamal had done a masterly job of spinning a potentially disastrous situation into a game note. And he hadn't even had to lie or burn any credibility. Not yet, anyway.

CHAPTER 18

Newsrooms, old-school journalists agreed, weren't much fun anymore. Time was, they were filled with the smell of stale smoke and stale coffee and the unceasing sounds of phones ringing and editors cursing. Paul Sprague had learned his craft at such places, at a succession of newspapers in Allentown, Milwaukee, Denver, and Houston. But by the time he reached the top, the *Los Angeles Times*, the fun had run out. There was no smoking, the editors paid five bucks to bring back half-caff macchiato lattes, no one used the phone because everybody communicated through e-mail or not at all, and you didn't dare curse at anyone, much less use off-color humor, lest he or she—probably *she*, the way Sprague saw it—file a lawsuit.

Worst of all, reporters never came into the office anymore. They filed their stories via computer and might as well be foreign correspondents on assignment in Marrakech for all the connection they had with the home office. Sprague felt nothing was better than a facial between reporter and editor, which is why he had called in Jilly Forrester. There were two additional reasons: Sprague liked her work, and as he told one of his associates, "She ain't exactly rough on the eyes."

As one of three city editors at the *Times*, Sprague had his own office, though in anticipation that he would be retiring in a year, it was the one without a window. He stole a smoke from time to time — literally sitting under the desk and trying to trap the smoke so he wouldn't get busted — even though his affection for tobacco was an open secret around the *Times*. He was under the desk when Jilly knocked.

"Hello? Mr. Sprague? It's Jilly Forrester."

Sprague smashed his butt into an ashtray and sheepishly emerged from under the desk, bumping his head as he stood up. Sprague could see a few recalcitrant wisps coming up from under the desk.

"You're doing a good job on that beat," he said, stealthily trying to push the smoke down with his palms. "I don't know how you stand it, but your stuff's okay."

"I appreciate that," said Jilly. "I didn't know city side read it."

Sprague waved his hand. "Shit, everybody on this paper reads sports first, except maybe those people over in arts."

Jilly got up and peeked over the desk. "Your pants aren't on fire, are they, Mr. Sprague?" she asked.

Sprague looked at her for a moment and saw she was smiling. "See, an eye for detail. That's why you're good." Sprague suddenly envisioned her as a Manhattan-drinking throwback, wearing a hat and bright red lipstick, chatting up cops and garbagemen and bankers, giving the rewrite guy a few colorful paragraphs on deadline.

"So, how do you like this Lasers thing?" Sprague asked. "Better than business?"

Jilly shrugged. "I basically changed one set of egomaniacs for another. Except these guys have better taste in clothes and cologne."

Now Sprague really had a hard time shaking that Brenda Starr vision. "Anyway, I got this tip," he said. "My brother-in-law, who's a half-drunk pain in the ass but a great mechanic, works at this body shop. One of those shady chop-shop joints near Watts. And he heard that a couple months ago—he thought November, maybe right around Thanksgiving—that Lorenzen Mayne's Hummer came in with a big dent."

He waited. Jilly spread her palms.

"There's a story there?" she said.

"Well, when he came in, he was trying to disguise himself, something that's not easy when you're like nine feet tall and driving a Hummer. Guess he had a crazy cap on with dreadlocks sewn into the back. They said he acted real jittery and uncomfortable, looking over shoulder and mumbling a lot. The guys noticed him immediately and said, 'What's up, Lo?' Know what he said back? 'Nah, it ain't me.' This guy Mario looked at the dent and asked how it happened. Lo said he didn't know. Then, just playing around, Mario said he hoped no one had gotten hurt. They say Lo looked like he was about to cry."

"Did Lo pick it up himself?"

"Nah. Some other guy who he figured was one of Lorenzen's boys. They all got boys, right? They call 'em posses?"

Jilly frowned. "Not their choice of word," she said.

"Well, anyway, here's the chop-shop number and my brother-in-law's number," said Sprague. "And you know how to get ahold of the police."

Jilly stood up and shook Sprague's hand and he reddened. She turned to leave, then turned back again.

"Say, you don't know where a girl might bum a cigarette or two, do you?" Jilly asked, "just for emergencies?"

Sprague reached into his desk drawer. "Didn't know you smoked," he said.

Jilly reached for the Newports and tucked them into her purse. "The NBF'll do that to you," she said.

❖   ❖   ❖

Driving back from the *Times* offices, Jilly did a quick mental inventory. Lorenzen Mayne was, inexplicably, mired in a protracted slump, playing the worst basketball of his otherwise gilded career. His famously genial demeanor had turned sullen. He had recently taken his beloved Hummer to a shadowy chop shop and apparently come close to dissolving into tears when asked about the origin of a dent. Then, one of his aides-de-camp had picked up the Hummer and it was never seen again. The logical conclusion: Lo had gotten into some kind of accident and was desperate to cover his tracks.

Jilly put it all together and . . . well, it wasn't much. But some sort of journalistic sixth sense kicked in and she decided there had to be a connection worth pursuing. Besides, ever since Jilly had dumped Robbie Duckworth—putting him on "irrevocable waivers," as she described it to Jamal when he pestered her about their history—spare time had become a more abundant commodity in her life. Which only meant she devoted more hours to her job. She didn't know where to start except for the car. With these guys, it always seemed to start with the car. Unless it started with a woman. Unless Litanium was involved, in which case it could start with almost anything.

Jilly had wasted most of the afternoon, calling various court clerks around Southern California, when she remembered that Lo had recently spoken of driving cross-country. She rose early the next morning to account for the three-hour time difference and called the DMV in Spencer, North Carolina, just as it was opening. An older woman who spoke in a maddeningly slow southern drawl answered. Trying her best to stifle any hint of impatience, Jilly explained that she was in Los Angeles ("Yes, ma'am, we have very nice beaches"; "No, ma'am, I don't know Brad Pitt") and was requesting to do a record search by phone. Specifically, she was inquiring about whether Lorenzen Mayne held title to any vehicles.

"Lorenzen Mayne," the woman said. "Why you know he's a famous basketball player."

"I do know that," Jilly said, straining to be pleasant.

"He spoke one time at a basketball banquet around here. My brother got an autograph from him." The woman seemed to be waiting for a response. Since she had begun covering sports, Jilly was amazed at the degree to which people would tell her their connections to players, however nebulous they might be.

"That's nice. Now, if you could . . ."

"Hold on, honey."

The woman put the phone down and Jilly could hear the conversations between other attendants and customers. "It's six in the morning and I'm on hold with the Mayberry DMV," she said aloud into the receiver.

Finally, the woman returned. "Well, we have to charge five dollars to give out that information," she said. "You know how local government works."

Jilly hurriedly read off the digits on a credit card.

"Thank you, honey. All right, let's see. Lorenzen Mayne does have title to a Hummer. Registered eight, two, oh-two. August eighth, 2002. License plate number five . . . three . . . 'M' like Mary . . . 'L' like lake . . . 'P' like pumpkin . . . 'X' like X-ray . . . 'C' like chitlins."

Jilly had never before heard the word *chitlins* but she dutifully copied down the plate number. "Thank you, ma'am, for—"

"He also has a Mercedes 500 registered in 2001 and something called a Pathfinder from 2000. And one more. He acquired a Jeep Cherokee in 2001 but it looks like he transferred title the next day to Mavis Robinson. Oh, my."

"What?" said Jilly. "What's 'Oh, my'?"

"I didn't know Mavis even knew Lorenzen Mayne."

"You know Mavis, ma'am?" Jilly asked.

"Oh, since forever. She goes to my church, Mavis does. Uh-huh."

"She's a young woman?" Jilly asked.

"Oh no! Not with that granddaughter she's raising! Mavis is probably sixty, I bet. But listen to me. I shouldn't be talking out of school like this."

"Ma'am," Jilly said, trying to summon some southern charm. "Why do you think Lorenzen Mayne bought a Jeep Cherokee and transferred the title the next day to a grandmother who goes to your church?"

"Honey, I have no earthly idea."

WHEN JAMAL ARRIVED AT the Bok after a particularly hellish bus ride that detoured down Century, Martha Ciccarelli greeted him with—even by her standards—a surfeit of enthusiasm. "Great news, Jamal! Come with me!" He shrugged, dropped his bag behind her desk, and followed her to employee parking lot. As they walked, she fumbled in her pocket for a set of keys. As they reached the back of the lot, where the parking spaces were no longer designated with proper names, but were only stenciled with the impersonal "employee," Martha was so excited she could barely speak.

She stood in front of an avocado-green Prism, midnineties model, Jamal figured, and tossed Jamal the keys. "There you go, sport!" she gushed. "Your first company car! Owen told me be sure it had a full tank of gas! I put air freshener in, too! I picked guavaberry! And get this: There's a cassette deck where you can play your music!"

It was an effective strategy, Jamal thought. Make a man take public transportation in L.A. for weeks, and a 1996 puke-green

Prism passes for the "luxury company car" he was promised. "Thanks, Martha," Jamal mumbled. "I'll shoot Owen an e-mail thanking him, too."

"Oh, I know he would like that," she said in her sing-song voice. "And one more thing I should tell you: Don't drive too far! Owen leased it for you, but you pay twenty cents a mile, I think it is! So don't be a hot rod!"

Jamal drove the Prism home that night and nearly went the wrong way on Sepulveda. He had gotten his phone hooked up and had actually prepared one microwaved meal (Stouffer's mac and cheese). Now, a couple of hours after dawn, he stepped back to scrutinize the rapid-fire paint job ("cornflower blue") he had performed in the bedroom. "It sucks," he concluded.

Worse, he didn't have much to cover up the paint. He had brought along his NBF posters (including one of Lorenzen Mayne) from Yale, but something told him it was terminally uncool to hang up a poster of a fellow employee. So he settled for a photograph of Martin Luther King, Jr., delivering the "I Have a Dream" speech in front of the Washington Monument; an autographed poster of the rapper Q-Tip; the only known photo of his father, who sat on a bench in Central Park wearing sunglasses and a deep frown (Jamal had no idea who had taken the picture, which he kept hidden from his mother); and a framed quotation, crocheted onto a piece of white linen, that his mother had made for him a long time ago. *When I discover who I am, I'll be free.* It was from Ralph Ellison's *Invisible Man.* He stared at it, feeling Betty Kelly's silent rebuke for the job he had taken, when his cell phone jangled and up came "Home" on caller ID.

"You told me to call you early out there because you're too busy once you get to work," said his mother, preemptively apologizing.

"It's fine," said Jamal. "I was just thinking about you."

As Betty listened without comment, Jamal filled her in. He was getting to know the players. He liked most but not all of them. The job was a little overwhelming, but he was handling it. He was now crawling along the expressways in a 1996 green Prism with suspicious brakes. L.A. wasn't as warm as he'd hoped it would be. He ate takeout every night, but there were a lot of choices. His apartment was okay. No, he hadn't had a date, which was true, and, yes, he took his clothes to the laundromat with regularity, which was a lie. He missed her a lot and Zeke a little.

"Did you get your salary straight?" his mother asked him, sounding like a prosecutor.

The question angered him. Like he had a lot of leverage.

"What do you mean by *straight*, Mom?" he said. "I'm getting paid about thirty thousand."

"Which means they're giving you, oh, I'd say twenty-seven. That about right?"

Man, she could be irritating. "That's about right. But I do the job, they kick me up next year by a lot if I produce. Plus I have a company car."

"Is it down on paper? In that twenty-page contract they gave you?"

"It's all in there, Mom." Actually, Jamal still hadn't read the whole thing. Each time he tried his eyes reflexively glazed over—all that jargon about "assignees" and "signators"—a bad omen, he figured, for doing well in law school.

"All in all," said Jamal. "How are things there?"

"Oh, they're just fine," Betty said quickly. Which meant they weren't, and Jamal pulled it out of her: Zeke had stopped communicating almost entirely.

"It's been—what?—a few weeks since you've been out there and it seems like years have passed," said Betty. "I mean, he just sits and stares at that TV and tunes me out. It's terrible. It was bad enough when you were up at Yale, but now you've gone off in a whole other direction. It's hard on him. He's—"

"That's a load of crap, Mom. He's made it hard on himself. What? I'm not supposed to take a job because it makes Zeke feel bad? Why can't he get a job with a dealership or a body shop? He knows more about cars than those two dudes on NPR."

"One thing I never understood about you, Jamal," she said. "You have all this concern and empathy for other people, but you don't have any left over for your own brother. Why is that?"

Jamal took the phone away from his ear and pantomimed throwing it against the wall.

"Because he doesn't deserve my concern and he doesn't deserve yours," said Jamal. "And the day you—"

Jamal heard the phone click, the first time his mother had ever hung up on him. He went to the wall and ripped down the crocheted quotation from Ralph Ellison, replacing it with an old-school poster of Michael Jordan dunking on somebody's sorry ass.

EVAN PETERWICZ'S NEW ASSIGNMENT gave him plenty of time alone, and he had to admit he liked it. Perhaps his wife had been right all along—by temperament and talent, he was suited to working in isolation, just as his father had been.

Peterwicz had taken to eating his lunch on the ground floor of the Bok, near his secret video room just off the main court. He could usually find a workbench that wasn't being used, or he sat on one of those giant rolls of mat they used to cover the floor when the circus was in town. It wasn't nearly as depressing as it seemed. For lunch, Peterwicz liked to buy one of those garlic-loaded lamb sandwiches from an Armenian vendor outside the arena, and the secretaries, particularly that white woman with the black name, teased him about the smell. He got away from the phones. And he wasn't there to help Jamal. He had to admit the whiz kid was a quick learner, but, whenever Peterwicz stopped in his old office, now occupied by three interns who weren't much younger than Jamal, he had to answer questions about game procedures, credentials, or interview requests. Peterwicz sometimes felt sorry for the new media relations director, like he did last week when Jamal had given the managing editor of *Sports Illustrated* a worse press seat than the nineteen-year-old kid with acne who represented a website called Statistical Pinheads. But it wasn't his problem. Not anymore.

Sitting on a bench, Peterwicz was just taking his first bite when an impossibly loud vacuum cleaner split the silence. He dropped his sandwich, and yogurt sauce sprayed onto his Van Heusen shirt. He could hear Lorraine saying, "That's not going to come out. I hope you kept the receipt from T.J. Maxx." Whatever he spilled on his shirt—even if it was water—his wife always told him it's not going to come out. He got up and saw a lone workman aiming the hose of a huge Hoover at swatches of carpeting that hung on a rope. It took him a full minute to get the guy's attention.

"You gotta do that here?" said Peterwicz. "I'm trying to eat."

The guy shut down his giant vacuum and looked around. "If this is the cafeteria," he said, "where's the people and all the food?"

"Very funny," said Peterwicz. "But, seriously, I'll be another fifteen minutes. Twenty tops."

The guy looked at him, nodded, and turned the vacuum back on. "Asshole," said Peterwicz, picking up his sandwich and Nestea.

He walked another twenty-five yards or so along the cavernous curving hallway, turned left at a corridor, and headed for the freight elevators, hoping the Armenian sandwich was staying warm. He didn't like to take food into his new office, so he slurped down the sandwich and the tea. When he was done, he scraped his fingertips along the wall, getting off the grease, and fished around in his pocket for a key. He looked around carefully, looked around again, then opened the door quickly and went inside his video isolation chamber. Alone for four more blessed hours.

CHAPTER 19

The players' parking lot at the Bok was off-limits to civilization at large—that included the press—but Jilly had been careful to develop a relationship with Andy, the octogenarian gatekeeper who swore he was a former Pinkerton "back when that meant something." As Jilly went by on this game night, the final one before the All-Star break, she slipped the guard a couple copies of *People*, major currency in Security Guard Nation.

Jilly waved and ducked behind a post when the coast was clear. It was five o'clock, an early arrival for a seven-thirty tipoff. Fortunately, Lo Mayne, one of the few Lasers with a sense of time and responsibility, was usually early, and he turned into his spot in his green Escalade. He waited for the thunderous bass to settle down and then climbed out of his car, dressed in navy-blue Armani, his eyes hidden under a pair of light-blue shades. *Man, what a good-looking guy*, Jilly thought as she stepped out from the shadows.

"Boo," she said.

"Damn, girl, you out here trick-or-treating?" Lorenzen said, putting his arm around her shoulder. He did that from time to time but never when anyone else was around, and never in a manner that made her feel uncomfortable.

"This looks like an ambush, but I have to ask you something before you get inside," said Jilly.

Lo smiled, raised his sunglasses, and looked at his watch. "Well, the normal interview time starts ninety minutes before tip-off," he said. "But since you sweet-talked your way past ol' Andy to get in here . . . go ahead."

Jilly took a deep breath but tried her best to ask the question casually. "How come you changed rides?" she said. "I mean, you used to drive a Hummer."

Lorenzen felt his heart sink. *Stay cool*, he thought. *Just stay cool.* "Now, why you got a sudden interest in cars, Jilly?" he said. "You a guest correspondent for *Pimp My Ride?*"

Jilly shook her head and smiled. She saw him looking for her notebook and tape recorder. They were inside her purse. She didn't want this to look official.

"Just curious," she said. "Before I got on the beat, I always heard you had this huge Hummer and I haven't seen it."

Lorenzen smiled. "Hey, I got lots of cars and lots of choices. Litanium don't drive the same damn thing twice."

"Yeah, but that's Litanium, and you're you," said Jilly. "You're a creature of habit."

He looked around and leaned close.

"Look," he said. "It's my cousin. One of them. He ran it into a tree one night. Nobody was hurt. He might've been drinking. I don't think that's a story for the *Los Angeles Times*, do you?"

Jilly shook her head. "Of course not. Thanks for your time." She turned away, and then, making like Peter Falk's Columbo, said, "Oh, one more thing, Lo." She hated herself for doing it even as she rather enjoyed the drama. "Do you know a Mavis Robinson?"

Lo cocked his head and put his sunglasses back over his eyes. Veteran police psychologists might call that a "tell."

"I guess you know I do, otherwise you wouldn't be asking," said Lo. "She lives back in North Carolina. In my hometown. I take care of her. Sort of."

"Why would you take care of her?" Jilly asked.

Lorenzen glanced at his watch. "I gotta be getting inside, Jilly, because, in case you forgot, I'm a basketball player and that's why you're here. To cover me playing basketball. But since you're here bothering me before the game, I guess I have to give you this answer. You have any idea how many people I take care of back in North Carolina? And I'd still like to know why it's any of your business who I take care of? Or would that be *whom* I take care of? Now, excuse me. I gotta warm up, see if I can find the jump shot I lost a while back. Maybe with all your snooping around you can find it."

He was either lying or equivocating, Jilly thought, but in either case he did pretty well. The grammatical question had been a great dodge. Jilly watched him go, and, with no small amount of admiration, said to his back: "It's *whom*. I'm pretty sure anyway."

IT WAS THE GAME before All-Star Weekend, the symbolic midpoint of the season. Philadelphia was the opponent. Two years earlier, NBF organizers had chosen to hold the game in Los Angeles, figuring that the league would piggyback on the success of the Lasers and the cross-pollination with the entertainment industry. But now, a few nights before the big game, the mood at the Bok was as mirthless as it had been in years. The Lasers' title ambitions had vanished into the ether weeks ago. Secretly, players were investigating timeshares and fishing trips for late April, assuming their summer vacation would be lengthy ones. The team was two games under .500, and, when NBF writers composed their obligatory "Midterm Grades" column, the "Lazy-ers" topped the list of "Biggest Disappointments."

Things weren't going well for Jamal, either, as Jilly approached him on press row two hours before the game.

"Fuckin' Peterwicz," Jamal said. "He tells me five minutes ago that three ESPN guys are coming to the game. They called him even though he's not in PR anymore. So where the hell do I put them?"

"Not near me," she said. Which irritated Jamal.

"Do you want something?" Jamal asked. "Or do you just enjoy watching me sweat?"

Jilly smiled. "I do enjoy watching you sweat. But I also want something."

Jamal rolled his eyes. "Well?"

Jilly cleared her throat. "I need to know if you know why Lorenzen changed cars."

"Yeah, that's at the top of my priority list right now." Jamal scribbled a name on a seat card and plunked it down, putting an ESPN exec downstairs and exiling a reporter from the *Pasadena Clarion* to Siberia. "That guy'll be pissed at me for life," he said. "Jilly, look, you know how many cars these guys have?"

"Yeah, but I also know you're pretty tight with Lo and you'd know why he changed."

Jamal threw down his marking pen. "Lo's got bigger issues right now, like how he can't throw a basketball in the Pacific from a rowboat. But since you're so interested, his cousin or his nephew or somebody rammed the Hummer into a tree. He told me about it a while back. Is that a story? A player's relative hit a tree?"

Jilly looked both embarrassed and angry. "Keep your voice down. That's it. I asked, you answered. Don't start acting like an ass."

"And you don't start acting like a . . ." Jamal stopped.

"Like a what?" said Jilly.

Jamal shook his head and went back to writing. "Nothing," he said. "And, by the way, I gotta put one of these ESPN guys next to you. Nothing personal. You, him, and Goodman B. Douglas can get a nice three-way rap going."

IN THE LASERS' LOCKER ROOM, Lorenzen, still unnerved by the conversation with Jilly, sat slumped on a bench, rereading a small story in the Metro section of the *Los Angeles Times*. Ever since the accident, he had taken to reading the paper according to a particular routine, scanning first the sections in which he had little interest (arts, society, editorial page), moving to the comics, sports, the front page, and, finally, with fumbling fingers, for the local news. If there were ever to be a missive about a fatal accident on Canyon Road, it would be there. In the two agonizing months since the hit-and-run, there never had been.

And now there was.

Lo carefully turned down the edges of the paper, right corner to the middle, then the left, then the same thing with the bottom corners. Shenko Kukimoro, the Lasers' massage therapist/smoothie maker, peeked out from the trainer's room, caught a glimpse of Lo, and wondered, *Lorenzen does origami?* Lo held the paper, now in the form of a four-point star, in front of him. Then he carefully unfolded it, smoothed it out, and searched for the story on the right-hand side of the page, just below the fold. It was still there.

Ohio Family Sends Plea: Please Find Our Daughter

BY GLEN KIESLEY

An Ohio couple whose 18-year-old daughter left their home in Columbus six months ago with her young child has reported her missing to Los Angeles police. They said she is "emotionally distraught and capable of hurting herself."

In an interview, Elwood and Lucille Denkins said that their daughter, Addie Denkins, left for the West Coast shortly after she gave birth to a boy. They say their unmarried daughter first went to Seattle to live with a cousin, but left there in early October. A few weeks ago they received a postcard from her bearing a Los Angeles postmark.

"Addie had been an honors student who never had any problems until she was 16," said her father, a systems analyst at Ohio State University. "Then she was diagnosed as bipolar. She got pregnant and dropped out of high school. She had loving people around her, but the pressure, we guess, was too much."

Police said the Denkinses gave this description of their daughter: African-American, about five feet, six inches, 120 pounds, brown eyes, braided hair, wears contact lenses, and small studs in each nostril. "She always wears a small gold chain with a unicorn around her neck," said her mother.

Her son's name is Sunstrom. "Addie calls him Sunny," said Mrs. Denkins. "She loves that child, but, considering Addie's problems, we do fear for him. We fear for both of them."

Police encourage anyone with information to call Missing Persons (310-869-7101).

Lo might've passed by the story except for the small photo that accompanied it. Addie Denkins stared back at him in a blue dress with white ruffles, buttoned to the top and slightly out of place with the studs in her nose. She looked proud and nervous. The photo had obviously been cropped from something in a high-school yearbook, maybe from the Spanish Club year-end get-together or something—part of a classmate's hand appeared at Addie's elbow. From the moment he saw the photo, Lo knew.

First, Jilly's questions. Then this. Lo wondered if he could fake a sudden attack of nausea, tell Watson he couldn't play that night. But that would only intensify his feelings of guilt.

Lorenzen smoothed out the paper, placed it on the bench, and planted his butt on it while he laced up his sneakers. At that moment Litanium came out of the trainer's room, wearing his

Lasers' game jersey, a pair of flip-flops, and a white shower cap. Like many players, Litanium showered before games.

"Cat!" Lorenzen said in a hoarse whisper, "you gotta look at this." Lo raised one cheek and handed him the paper, pointing to the story.

"Man, I don't want to read nothing you had your hind quarters on," said Litanium.

"Shh! Man, keep it down," Lo said. "Now check it out. There on the right side."

"I learned a long time ago not to read papers. Only get you pissed off and—"

"This has nothing to do with basketball," said Lo. "It's got to do with Canyon Road."

Litanium rolled his eyes but grabbed the paper. He scanned it for a moment and tossed the paper back to Lo.

"I don't see nothing about Canyon Road in there or nothing to do with anything we should care about," said Cat. "A girl got herself knocked up, then she got herself lost. It's a tragedy, but it happens all the damn time. Shit, don't I know that." He pulled off his shower cap and rubbed his newly shaven pate. "Damn, that shit feels good after you get it all off, Lo," said Litanium. "You should try—"

"I'm talking about the photo, Cat," said Lorenzen, tapping the paper. "Look at the photo."

Litanium rolled his eyes and grabbed the paper again. "So what?" he said. "A high-school girl."

"It's *her*," said Lo. "It's her who Kwaanzii hit. You saw her with the binoculars. You know I'm right."

Lo motioned to Kwaanzii to join the confab. Kwaanzii studied the story uninterestedly. Finally, he said, "Maybe it's her I hit. Maybe it was somebody else I hit. Whatever, it's in the past."

Coach Watson came into the room at that point, signaling the beginning of the pregame meeting. Every player was supposed to be dressed by the time it commenced and being dressed didn't include flip-flops and a shower cap.

"Lo, you trippin' on this shit," said Cat, lowering his voice. "You caught a glimpse of a dead woman down a ravine at night through binoculars. And you're sure this is her. That's fucked up. We ain't talking about it anymore, you got that? There ain't no way . . ."

Watson took a hard look at Litanium. "You figure on playing in a damn shower cap tonight?" said Watson. "'Cause if you are, I'll talk to the refs beforehand, make sure it's not a technical foul."

SITTING COURTSIDE DURING A timeout, Jilly watched Eugene Wyckoff, the Lasers' beat writer for the *Orange County Register*, slip in a pair of ear plugs. Jilly considered Wyckoff, thirty-five, UCLA-educated, meticulous in his grooming and his reporting, her most formidable competition.

"I keep meaning to buy a set of them," Jilly said as "We Will Rock You" blared at ear-bursting levels.

"Wonder what would happen if the NBF tried dead silence for a game or two," said Wyckoff. "None of this bells-and-whistles-at–nine-million-decibels bullshit."

"Never happen, Gene," said Jilly. "They'd be afraid people would actually have to watch the game."

"It'd be bad for the players, too," said Wyckoff. "You ever see Litaniuim and Kwaanzii during a timeout? They bet on that stupid dot race every night."

"I never noticed," said Jilly, wishing she had. "I thought they were too busy checking out the dance team."

"They don't really watch the women," he said. "You know why? Because they get a better show at the strip clubs. Nah, they're all over the other bullshit, just like the fans. Sweet Baby James and Donnelly have a standing wager on Larry the Laser's halfcourt shot. Donnelly gets ten-to-one odds."

Jilly was impressed. "You ever gonna write that?"

"Maybe on a slow off-day," said Wyckoff. "Don't you go using it now."

"I'd never do that to you, Gene," said Jilly.

They both ducked as a T-shirt shot out of an air cannon whizzed by their heads.

"Now, the biggest fan of all this bullshit is Puddin'," said Wyckoff.

"You're kidding," said Jilly.

"Hell, no," said Wyckoff. "What else does he have to do? He never plays."

Indeed, as the reporters deconstructed the timeout activities, Puddin' Reichley, the Lasers' third-string center, was watching a well-endowed woman at midcourt attempt to guess the theme songs to various long-canceled sitcoms. She got the first two but was having trouble on the third. Reichley knew it right away—*Love Boat*—and began to edge his way to midcourt to provide an assist. That was Reichley: an unselfish man, utterly guileless, always looking to help. "*Love Boat!*" he yelled in a hoarse whisper. "Classic show. Isaac the Bartender. Gopher. Doc. Julie McCoy."

The woman saw him but couldn't quite hear what he said. She shrugged her shoulders and the crowd got louder.

Reichley couldn't help himself. He edged closer and closer to midcourt and finally whispered the answer in the contestant's ear. When she repeated, "*Love Boat?*" the crowd erupted.

In the huddle, meanwhile, Watson had called for Reichley to enter the game, an unexpected stratagem necessitated by foul trouble to the entire Laser front line. The coach never noticed that Puddin' was out at midcourt, and Puddin', for his part, never knew he was supposed to be in the game. The ref blew his whistle, Reichley sprinted back to the bench, four Lasers walked onto the court, and the action was ready to begin just as Doug Carter noticed they were one short.

Watson exploded. "GET YOUR FAT ASS INTO THAT GAME, PUDDIN'!" he screamed, veins popping, as he stood in front of the large, chagrined center. The crowd picked up on it, as did the sound effects people, who again began playing the theme from *Love Boat*.

"Look at it this way, John," Carter said to the head coach. "Better to be laughed at than booed, right?"

The coaches got a chance to explore that question in the fourth quarter, when, for the first time all season, boos did indeed echo through the Bok. Not the odd spasm, but, rather, an extended, robust crescendo that left little doubt how the fans felt about the home team. While the Lasers had been playing desultory basketball for weeks, it was a single—if representative—play during this otherwise forgettable game that turned the home fans into an angry mob. Midway through the fourth quarter, Lo Mayne clutched the ball on the left side of the perimeter. Unable to deke his man but unwilling to pass to an open teammate, he unspooled an eighteen-foot jumper that, like so many other shots Lo had attempted recently, smacked the side of the rim and caromed into the hands of an opposing player. As Lo glowered at the rim—as if to say, "What are you doing here?"—Philadelphia sprinted downcourt for an easy, lead-building layup.

After that, the deluge—boos sufficiently voluminous that Jamal couldn't hear Watson shouting plays from a few feet away. What he could discern was that the vitriol was directed at Lo in particular. Lo's twenty points a game were once as reliable as time and tide, but over the past months he had become a shell of his former self. He wasn't injured and he was getting his usual ration of shots. But his average had tailed off precipitously and, more vexing, his passion was seldom in evidence. He played entire games with a hollow look welded on his face. And while Lo held himself appropriately accountable — "I'm just in a bitch of a slump and, as the leader of this team, I gotta snap out of it," he told reporters after every off game — no one had had ever seen him this distracted.

Sherwin Zucker, a notorious Los Angeles defense lawyer whose impeccable wardrobe was at odds with his explosion of curly, unkempt Garfunkelian hair, rose from his seat behind the Lasers' bench. A season-ticket holder since the Lasers had moved west from Pittsburgh in 1969, Zucker had cultivated a reputation as the league's most obnoxious fan to the visiting team and become a minor celebrity in his own right. But lately Zucker had turned on the home team and was particularly disdainful of Lo. While he once brandished a banner reading LO AND BEHOLD! he'd recently replaced it with a new placard: HOW LO CAN IT GO?

Hard-pressed for material on an off-day, Jilly had recently written a small piece about Zucker's sudden switch in loyalties. She quoted him as saying, "I pay $450 a night for my seat — almost what I charge for an hour of work. It would be nice if these guys at least pretended to take pride in their performance, Lo Mayne in particular. What happened to that guy? He's an All-Star? Yeah, right. I just wish my adversaries in court were as passive as that guy."

Jamal confronted Jilly about the story. As he saw it, the social contract that had once existed between fans and athletes had broken down and a certain incivility had taken hold in NBF arenas. Disenchanted by high ticket prices and a system of free agency that turned players into nomads, fans had begun to feel that they were quite literally owed something for all their suffering . . . and felt they were entitled to lash out when they didn't get it. And alcohol, long the catalytic accompaniment for the obnoxious sports fan, had become easier to get than a bag of peanuts. "Why would you glorify a guy like that?" Jamal asked Jilly. "He just wants publicity and you gave it to him."

With some reluctance, Jilly had defended the story as classic off-day material; in truth, she didn't care any more for Zucker than Jamal did. "Besides, Jamal, you should be nice to that guy," Jilly said. "You never know when you might need the best defense lawyer in town."

The cascade of boos continued as the players walked slowly to the locker room after the final horn blared, consecrating a fifteen-point loss. Before they could whip off their sweaty uniforms and shower, Watson stood in the middle of the room and instructed the clubhouse attendants to turn off the Ludacris on the locker-room stereo. By the time the players deigned to turn around, they could practically see the cartoon puffs of steam emanating from Watson's ears.

"That game, gentleman, was pure, USDA prime horseshit," he said, his voice cracking like a teenager in the throes of puberty. "You might think it's okay just to go through the motions and get paid on the first and the fifteenth. But I have more motherfucking dignity than that. I was one embarrassed motherfucker tonight. I may get fired, but not before I make some motherfucking changes around here. When you're on break this weekend, think about whether you play like a man or—"

As if on cue, one of Litanium's cell phones began chirping, the ring tone the upbeat chorus of Outkast's "Hey Ya."

"Give me that motherfuckin' cell!" Watson yelled.

Litanium sheepishly reached into his pocket and pulled out his phone, the one shaped like a breast. Watson had designs of smashing it to smithereens but was gripped by another idea. He turned it on and intoned, "Litanium can't talk now. He and his teammates are reaching between their legs, trying to locate their manhood. So it could be a while, baby."

Then he smashed it to smithereens.

As he retreated to the coaches' dressing room, Watson looked skyward in frustration and noticed several small security cameras placed at odd angles. Watson considered the locker room to be the players' sanctuary and, aside from the pregame strategy session, spent as little time as possible in there. But he didn't recall all those cameras from last season. *It's like I'm in a fucking casino*, he thought. He stared at one of the lenses directly above Buenos Diaz and intoned, "Hey, Owen and Manny, if you're watching, how about getting me some real players. Not these motherfucking Kelly Girls!"

Lo was still sitting in his sweaty game uniform long after the other players had scattered. For the first time in his career, he had declined to be interviewed after the game. One by one, reporters drifted over and Lo held up his hand. "Not tonight," he said. He finally arose and began to pull off his uniform. He reached for the shampoo and conditioner in his locker and there was the *Times* story. Lo looked around, folded the paper into small pieces, and slowly ripped it to shreds, carefully placing the pieces on the bench before gathering them up and depositing them in a giant waste can. Shenko Kukimoro stared at him from behind the training-room door. "Even when Lorenzen Mayne is upset," Shenko said to a high-school student who served as part-time towel boy, "he is very neat man. You could learn much from him."

In his rookie year, Lo had written out a Bible verse and tacked it to the back of his locker. He had found it a few weeks after Tammy Robinson's death; now it seemed to speak to him again. The verse was still there, the paper yellowed with age. It was from Ephesians: "In whom we have redemption through His blood, the forgiveness of offences, according to the riches of His grace." He read it over and over and was still reading it when Shenko Kukimoro turned out the lights.

"I KNOW THIS SOUNDS lame," said Jamal over the phone, "but can I come over and use the washing machine in your apartment? You said . . ."

"What's lame about wanting clean clothes?" said Jilly, vaguely skeptical that laundry was the only motivation for the visit.

"I go to this one Laundromat all the time, but half the machines are broken and it's really kind of a shithole."

"Jamal," Jilly said with a sigh. "I said it's okay."

"You're like the only person I know with a machine, you know, right there upstairs," Jamal said, wondering what the hell he was talking about.

"You want me to send back something engraved, indicating my acceptance of your request?" Jilly said.

"I'll be there in a couple hours," said Jamal. "I'll bring the Tide."

The exchange was the latest in a riot of mixed messages they had been sending each other. In the short time that their professional orbits had intersected, Jilly and Jamal couldn't figure out what they were to each other—understandable, since they were still trying to figure out what they were to themselves. Here, Jamal had decided to make a definitive move—a tentative definitive move, anyway—and felt slightly better about it since he really did find his local Laundromat not only to be loneliness unbound but also in violation of various health department regulations.

Before Jamal's arrival, Jilly began stuffing clothes in her drawers—it was Robbie who'd been the pathological neatnik. She even picked up a feather duster he had left behind and started whacking the tables and lamps. Then she decided it looked too clean, so she took some CDs out of their cases and scattered them around the living room. She jumped into the shower, put on a pair of tight black jeans and a pink sequined tank top—but then decided she looked too nice, so she took them both off, put on a pair of sweat pants and a T-shirt, and was in the process of taking them off, when Jamal rang the doorbell.

"Tide," he said, holding an orange bottle triumphantly aloft, "as promised."

"Some men bring wine," she said, "others bring detergent." *God, had that sounded too forward?*

Jamal immediately wished he had brought along wine.

"Well, I've got my sack here," he said.

"I've actually got to go out," Jilly lied. "So just help yourself. Go nuts. It's right upstairs."

Jamal did his best to hide the disappointment. "Okay, well, I'll get to work, then."

"I don't have to leave right away," Jilly said quickly. "Soon, though."

"I don't want to keep you," said Jamal.

"No, I said I had time," said Jilly.

"No," said Jamal, "you said you had to go out."

"Then I said, not right away. The machine's this way."

Jamal dumped his clothes in a heap, discreetly piling shirts and jeans over his various boxers. "So, where do you have to go, Jilly?" said Jamal. "Shame you can't just kick back and enjoy the rare day off that comes with All-Star Weekend."

"Just some shopping—you know, errands, crap that piles up."

"I know the feeling," said Jamal. "Anyway, you look like you're heading for a touch football game." *Man, was that the wrong thing to say.*

Jilly stiffened. "I didn't realize I needed to dress for the occasion."

"Hey, kidding. Hang around. It's good to see you in sweats. You always look, you know, so professional."

Jilly smiled. "As you can see," she said, "the whole professional thing's only a mirage." She slapped Jamal on the back and grabbed her jacket. "Just make yourself at home, then let yourself out," she said. "I'll be seeing you sometime this weekend. I know Peterwicz is in charge, but I assume you'll be around."

Jamal watched as Jilly headed out the door, waving fingers over her head without looking. He pounded the washer, then loaded the clothes back in his sack. "Fuckin' Laundromat's not that bad," he said aloud to himself.

CHAPTER 20

For most players, All-Star Weekend is a seventy-two-hour furlough. Right after the tongue-lashing Watson gave the team, Litanium had chosen to skip town for Vegas, missing a mandatory morning drug test resulting from the incident with Kujo at the airport. Kwaanzii went with him. They and their cash parted ways at a casino that lured basketball players by shrewdly boasting of having "the longest beds on the Strip." (That it was owned by a family that also held a controlling interest in an NBF team didn't, curiously enough, seem to bother Commissioner Drang.)

Lo was the lone Laser chosen for the All-Star team, his selection less about merit than about throwing a bone to the host franchise. Lo knew as much, warning friends and family not to expect him to see much playing time. The only other Laser who would be part of the festivities was Sweet Baby James. Benefiting from what Watson jokingly called "reverse affirmative action," Taylor was gifted a spot in the dunk contest. "It's gonna be like Slim Shady at the BETs, yo," said Taylor. "I'm gonna shock the world."

In keeping with tradition, the weekend unofficially kicked off on Friday afternoon with Commissioner Drang's "State of the League" address, a chance for him to put on a brave face and trumpet his recent successes. As the media filed into the Magnolia Lounge of the Westin Bonaventure, they were handed a gift bag (consisting of canvas briefcase, cotton T-shirt, and wool ski hat, all adorned with an All-Star Game logo) and ushered to an open bar. It was an implicit quid pro quo: These amenities were the price of a favorable story. Standing on a makeshift podium, a wry smile soldered to his face, Drang spoke for half an hour, offering a particularly passionate explanation about international expansion, his pet project.

"The NBF is the fastest-growing sport throughout the Far East, Africa, Australia, and much of Europe," intoned Drang. "We're sneaking up on soccer."

"And in the United States," Jilly whispered to a reporter from Dallas, "everybody hates your ass."

Drang then fielded questions from the ink-stained wretches and the television hairsprays. Like a seasoned politician, he stayed on message and offered tidy, prepackaged sound bites echoing the theme of the league's manifest destiny. *The Dallas Cowboys want to be America's Team, we want to be the World's League! The Internet is our biggest friend! Our goodwill outreach programs are expanding the NBF brand into sub-Saharan Africa!*

The bonhomie was interrupted by Tom Garfield, an eccentric longtime NBF scribe from San Diego. Wearing his trademark fez and an orange and baby blue sweater that was a keepsake from a 1979 golf tournament sponsored by Howard Johnson's, Garfield stepped forward. "Mr. Commissioner," he said slowly. "One of the league's top players is on trial for sexual assault. A former All-Star is on trial for manslaughter. Over the past year more than five percent of the league has been arrested for crimes ranging from marijuana possession to running a dog-fighting ring to garden-variety domestic violence. How do you account for what is clearly a spike in criminal behavior?"

Drang nervously yanked on his collar and looked off the podium to Barton Sylvester, the public relations henchman hired specifically to address those pesky "character issues," a euphemism for *We're cooked if fans and sponsors continue to harbor the perception that our players are the kind of people you'd cross the street to avoid.* Biding his time, Drang took a swig from his bottle of water. "Well, Tom," the commissioner said. "As with any workforce, there are going to be some bad apples. But I prefer to emphasize the positive. Take Lo Mayne, who's getting a citizenship award as we speak. He's an All-Star player"—Drang paused for maximum dramatic effect—"and an even better person."

At that point, Drang motioned subtly to Sylvester, who took the microphone and said, "Thanks for coming, everyone. Commissioner Drang is due at the Mad Props for Literacy Jam. Hopefully we'll see some of you there, too."

AT TWO IN THE AFTERNOON of All-Star Friday, it fell on Jamal to accompany Lo to the Long Beach Boys Club, where he was going to be honored for his "Integrity and Community Service." There were other Lasers besides Lo who were terrific at public appearances—Willie Wainwright and Clarence Wolff were two of them—but the public wanted superstars and neither fit the bill. Lo was the one the public wanted. Jamal had actually been looking forward to the afternoon, and, so, it seemed to Jamal, had Lo. In the four weeks Jamal had been with the team he and Lo had gravitated toward each other. In Jamal, Lo found a voice of reason, someone able to grasp the politics and demands of being a professional athlete but, at the same time, someone sufficiently detached that he had some perspective. Jamal might badger him to do interviews or shake a CEO's hand, but, unlike everyone else in Lo's life, Jamal didn't want a piece of either his money or his residual stardust. As for Jamal, his fondness for Lo began as a practical exercise. The media relations director who fails to ingratiate himself with the team's best player isn't long for the job. But the more time they spent together, the more Jamal saw Lo as a genuine friend, a man who, unlike most of his teammates, had missed getting his behind whipped with the Hubris Stick.

The ceremony in Long Beach was an exercise in organized chaos. A banner behind the podium fell down persistently. The soft drinks never arrived. Kids approached Lo for autographs even as he was being introduced by the emcee. "My uncle thinks you suck," one nine-year-old said earnestly. "But I told him you were just getting old." As ever, Lo played along, signing everything in sight, shaking hands with the adults, and, finally, walking out to the center of a basketball court, ringed on all sides by young fans, to answer questions.

Jamal took notes, hoping to get something humorous or evocative that he could feed to Jilly or one of the other reporters. (He had asked them to attend but nothing piques a journalist's curiosity less than a canned player appearance.) Most of the questions were predictable, and, to Jamal, even somewhat disheartening. *How much money do you make? Do you live in a big mansion? Do you know Snoop Dogg?* Lo answered them all with a pasted-on grin. (*Not as much as a big movie star; I'm a big guy, so I have to live in a big house; I hook Snoop up with Laser tickets a couple of times a year.*) As the program was wrapping up, one youngster raised his hand and said, earnestly, "Mr. Mayne, what do you like about basketball?"

That was the question Lo wanted to hear. No one had posed it in a while, nor had he asked it of himself lately. He stopped and smiled and took a couple of dribbles, then walked over to the boy and tossed him the ball. "Tell me what *you* like about it," Lorenzen said.

The boy said shyly, "I like when I score a basket." Lo patted him on the head, took the ball out of the boy's hands and returned to center court, talking as he went.

"Scoring baskets is nice," he said. "Scoring baskets is fun. But you know what? It's not about that for me. I'm going to tell you when I fell in love with this game. I was maybe a little older than you guys, maybe my first year in high school . . ."

Jamal noticed that Lo had gone into himself, forgotten about the crowd, forgotten about everything.

". . . and we were playing on the playground in North Carolina in the summer. And the sun was beating down and everybody had their shirts off because that's the best way to play basketball, right? So I had the ball and I was dribbling up the middle, right around midcourt. I went around somebody and, suddenly, it was like I stopped and took a picture . . ."

Jamal looked around. The kids were quiet. Lo's voice was the only sound you could hear.

". . . because I saw everything. I saw one of my teammates coming up on my left and I knew—I just *knew*—when he was going to begin his angle cut toward the basket. I saw another teammate come up on the right, and I knew he probably wouldn't go to the basket because he liked to fade to the corner and shoot three-pointers . . . and I could see the guy guarding me shading a little bit to my left because he figured my best pass was to the guy on that side. And I could see—not really see, but sense—another guy playing defense coming up behind me, maybe thinking about stealing the ball, tapping it away from me . . ."

Jamal saw that Lorenzen was now moving toward the basket, real slow, talking as he dribbled, lost in the memory . . .

". . . and so I moved a little to my right, getting myself in front of the guy who was tailing me. I cut off his angle. No angle, no steal, right? And as I did that—you gotta remember I was seeing all this, *feeling* all this—the defender in front of me moved back in front of me cutting off my path. And I thought: *I got him* . . .

". . . I did, too. One more dribble and a perfect bounce pass to the guy on my left and we had two points. I hadn't scored 'em but it was like I had, you know? They were the two most important points of my life and I didn't score them. Because that's when the game became like poetry to me. That's when I started to *feel* the game, not just play it."

Lorenzen had lost most of them by that point. The kids were getting restless and wanted to charge onto the court and start taking wild shots and the hell with poetry and reverie about plays made on playgrounds a decade ago. Lo's eyes found Jamal's. Jamal knew what he meant. He wasn't as big or as talented and he could never play the game as well as Lorenzen could. But Jamal knew what he meant.

"GOOD SHOW," JAMAL SAID as they sat in the car, staring at the parking lot that was the northbound 405 at rush hour.

"Jamal," Lo said quietly as he turned down Usher on the stereo. "I gotta come clean to you about something."

"Shoot."

"You gotta promise you won't tell anyone."

"Shoot."

A patch of silence descended and Lo inhaled deeply. For a fleeting instant he thought about unloading to Jamal about the car crash. But he couldn't.

"Sometimes I wish I could just quit basketball," said Lo finally. "Just go cold turkey and find another job doing something else."

"Bet we could find room for you on my staff," Jamal said. "We can start you working on some games notes and the media guide. Get you to call back the editor of *South American Basketball* and tell him that Buenos Diaz said *sí* to the interview request but it will have to be after the season."

"I'm being for real, Jamal."

"You're going through a shooting slump. Happens to everyone."

"It's so much deeper than that, you don't know."

"So, seriously, Lo, if you quit tomorrow you could be successful in a million other jobs. Of course, the pay cut . . ."

"Bingo, bro. You know how many people are depending on me? Just this morning I got a call from someone named uncle Lou. I'm like . . . *who?* He says he's the brother of my aunt Linda. I didn't even know I had an aunt Linda, much less that she had a brother. Anyway, the dude asked me for one hundred large in seed money so he could start a combination car wash–cappuccino bar."

"Makes rap-ee-okee sound like a hell of an investment," Jamal responded. "But, see, that's the problem, Lo. You're too nice."

"I wouldn't be if I didn't have to be."

"So join my staff. Or maybe we can switch jobs," Jamal said. "You know Owen is always looking to cut payroll. I'd agree to, like, three or four mil."

"Where am I dropping you off, smartass motherfucker?"

"Just take me back to the Bok. I still have some work to wrap up."

"You're not coming out tonight? It's All-Star Weekend, man. I'll get you into any party you want. Get you more wing than Colonel Sanders."

"I'm saving my stamina for the Pegasus party tomorrow night. You got me on the list for that one, right?"

"You keep smart-assing me," said Lo, smiling, "I'll take your name off."

Lo steered his Escalade off the freeway and toward the arena.

"Seriously, Jamal, think of something we can do together. With my charm and your brains we could be big. Huge, bro."

WHEN PADGETT PUT PETERWICZ on his new clandestine project, the latter had just one demand, which he presented in a halting voice. "Um, Owen, I'd still like to run media relations for the All-Star Game. I already had things started when Henry died." Padgett said that was fine, as long as "my people are taken care of." Peterwicz knew what that meant: Don't mess up the courtside seating for the honchos from *Single Rich Dude* and Padgett's other Hollywood friends.

The media relations duties for the weekend were fairly straight-forward—organizing interview roundtables for the players before the game, compiling a media guide, shuttling requested players to a postgame press conference in a cordoned area near the Bok's main loading dock. But Peterwicz looked forward to it because he could at last be the Man and run the show, even if only for a long weekend. He had designs of dazzling the league personnel and being asked to "run the media" at similar events like the World Championships, maybe even the Olympics. Plus, the two-thousand-dollar stipend he was getting for the extra work was nothing to sneeze at. Not when his last Christmas "bonus" was a hundred-dollar gift certificate to Janko's Croatian Restaurant—a perk the Lasers had negotiated for all employees for giving Janko's premium space on the courtside signage.

Jamal was actually glad Peterwicz was handling it. He was barely keeping his head above water just handling the Lasers' PR, and he didn't need a screwup on a national scale. He was driving home from the Bok after completing his work on Friday night when his cell rang.

"Is this a good time to talk, Jamal?" Betty Kelly asked quietly on the other end. Jamal felt the effects from a shot of adrenaline. "Mom, what's wrong?"

"Nothing's wrong."

"It's after midnight back there. What's up?"

"We have to talk, Jamal," she said, in the calm but earnest voice Jamal knew to take as non-negotiable.

"Sure. I'm just stuck in freeway traffic on my way home."

"Ten at night and there's freeway congestion," Betty said, the easterner's classic one-sentence take on L.A.

"That's the way it is out here. So tell me—what's new?"

So she told him. Zeke had lost another job, "A last-hired, first-fired deal. He rarely leaves the house anymore. He rarely gets off the couch. He sleeps all the time. He barely eats." Betty Kelly took a breath. "I'm scared this time for him, Jamal," she said. "Real scared."

"So give him an ultimatum," said Jamal.

"I'm doing something more drastic than that," said Betty.

Jamal drove on in silence. "I'm waiting," he said. Jamal swore he could hear his mother take a gulp of air.

"I'm moving Zeke out there," said Betty. "To be with you."

Jamal immediately put on his right blinker and cut across two lanes of traffic to an exit ramp, pulling off on the shoulder. He put the car in park and finally found the voice to respond.

"Say that again?"

"He won't get in your way, I promise," she said quickly. "But something had to be done. I just can't bear to see him like this. He won't bother you—"

"What do you mean *you're* moving him out here?" Jamal interrupted. "You can't just throw him in the back of a Ryder truck."

"I floated the idea a few days ago, thinking he would dismiss it the way he dismisses every other idea I have," said Betty. "He didn't say much then. But after this last job disappeared, he said,

'You still thinking about me going out there with Jamal? Maybe it would be a good idea.' For Zeke, that qualifies as wild enthusiasm."

"What about you, Ma?" Jamal asked with genuine solicitude. "Why don't you come, too? Aren't you going to be lonely?" What Jamal meant was: Why don't you come and take care of Zeke? Who's going to provide the kick in the butt to an aging slacker like Zeke? How's he going to get along in a town where UPS delivery-men are hustling movie scripts and dishwashers are negotiating producer credits?

Jamal started up the car again. "You sure about this, Mom?"

"Look, seeing you and Zeke happy means everything to me," she said. "You just don't know how it weighs on a mother's heart when one of her boys is struggling. It's just . . ."

"*One* of your boys," said Jamal. "You said it right. *One* of your boys is struggling. The other isn't."

Actually, that wasn't altogether true. Silence on the other end. Jamal tried to picture what his mother was doing. Fighting back tears? Anger?

"Jamal, Zeke is coming," said Betty Kelly. "That's the way it is. He has to live with you for a while but he understands that he's got to find his own place, got to find his own way, got to find *himself*. California is where people come for a fresh start, right? Well, your brother needs a fresh start more than anybody I know."

Jamal felt the beginnings of a monster headache. "He's sleeping in the living room, Mom," said Jamal finally. "Tell him that. We shared a bedroom for too long. Tell him three words: small apartment. Couch. Make sure he understands that."

CHAPTER 21

There was a time when the Slam Dunk Contest was the tastiest dish on the All-Star Weekend smorgasbord. But ultimately it became a victim of its own success. Even using props, costumery, and other accountrements (one enterprising player jumped over a suite of living-room furniture he was then paid handsomely to endorse) to enhance the moves, there are a finite number of rim-rattling finishes a player can execute. Once fans—living in a culture that overdoses on cinematic special effects—saw a jaw-dropping reverse 360, they expected to see a 720 the following year. Accelerating the decline of the slam-fest, the best players seldom entered anymore. They claimed that they were wary of risking an injury, but, clearly, the dunk contest was no longer an activity for the cool kids in school. And the fifty thousand dollars first-prize loot? They could find that groping for loose bills behind the seats of their SUVs.

Still, the bit players in the league, such as Sweet Baby James Taylor, saw it as a chance to boost their profiles. His own boasting to the contrary, Taylor's "ups" were modest at best and he had few posterizing dunks on his resume. Thus, despite extensive lobbying by his agent, he was only an alternate when the Dunk Contest list was first announced.

"Commissioner Drang had better lawyer up," he said. "'Cuz I'm suing for reverse discrimination!" But after Dallas' Lubricious "Sweet Lou" Mulligan pulled out with a quadriceps injury—several players invariably came up lame right before the contest—Sweet Baby was gifted a spot, the lone Caucasian among eight. Taylor's entry was alluded to carefully in newspaper stories. Even with the European influx, the NBF workforce was 80 percent African-American, and the subtext of race is always the elephant in the arena no one dares pet.

The week before the All-Star festivities, Taylor was a cipher, so nervous that he scarcely spoke. Even as he came off the bench and entered games, his mind was only on Saturday's performance. The other Lasers goaded him. "You know a dunk means your hands actually have to touch the rim," Lo said good-naturedly. "Seriously, Slim Shady, what kind of dunks you got planned?" Taylor stared back at Lo. "All I'm sayin' is I got a trick up my sleeve that will leave the fellas wantin' to hate me and ladies wantin' to mate me."

This year's Dunk Contest, sponsored by Levitra, was scheduled to begin at six on Saturday night at the Bok. But the program was running nearly an hour late after various NBF presentations—including a basketball-themed performance by the Blue Man Group dedicated to "Ballers in the U.S. armed forces stationed all over the world"—exceeded their allotted time. When it finally commenced, the All-Stars, one more nattily attired than the next, sat courtside like dandies in a Parisian salon. The Black Eyed Peas' "Let's Get It Started," blared through the Bok as the contestants took the floor.

Antonio Austin, a reserve for Phoenix best known in basketball circles for shattering a backboard during an NCAA game and then hawking the shards on eBay, went first. As Austin stood dribbling at midcourt, a technician affixed a wireless mic to his jersey. Austin took two dribbles, began a leap at the free-throw line, intoned

"Peace Out and Stop the Violence!" in midair for the crowd to hear over the PA system, and then dunked with two hands before alighting. The crowd went bananas. After the noise had died down, Austin received his score from the judges: Thirty-six out of fifty, numbers that, as usual, seemed as arbitrary as a lottery drawing. "I do a badonka-dunk and at the same time give the kids a message of hope and pi-zece, and all I get is a thirty-six?" Austin told the courtside interviewer. "Them judges should be bitch-slapped."

Seattle's swingman, Scooty ("It was supposed to be Scotty but they misspelled it on my birth certificate and no one bothered to change it") Wiggins, went next. With the crowd already in a lather from the first routine, Wiggins stood outside the three-point arc soaking in the applause. After a casual dribble, Wiggins soared toward the heavens and tossed the ball above his head. While suspended in air, he patted himself on the back with both hands, caught the ball and then attempted to thrust it through the hoop. The ball, alas, lodged between the rim and backboard and bounded toward midcourt. The missed dunk elicited a chorus of "Awwwwww," from the crowd. Wiggins received a score of thirty-four.

The NBF had brought in its own overheated courtside barker— a highly rated member of the "Morning Zoo" team in Encino—to work the PA for All-Star Weekend. "Now," he yelled, "let's give it up and show some love for Los Angeles' own, the pride of the Lasers . . . Sweet! Baby! James! Tayyyyyyyy-lor!" As the cheering in the Bok reached fever pitch, Sweet Baby took the court, clapping his hands above his head. "Yo, check it!" he yelled.

On cue, Nelly's "Ride Wit Me" came thrusting through the speakers. For the first few beats, Sweet Baby stood holding the basketball, rhythmically moving his head like a turtle retreating into and then emerging from his shell. Forty or so seconds into the song, Sweet Baby headed toward the basket, starting his liftoff eight

feet from the basket. At the precise minute Nelly intoned the chorus—"Hey, must be the money"—Sweet Baby extended his left
arm and applied a sticker adorned with a giant $ to the backboard.
With his right hand, he dunked the ball. His feet hadn't touched
terra firma and applause was already echoing. He took a victory lap
courtside while a ball boy, responding to an immediate mandate
from Commissioner Drang, used a mop handle to try to detach the
dollar-sign decal from the backboard. Only NBF-approved decals
were allowed to be pasted onto a backboard. And the U.S. Treasury
was only an unofficial league sponsor.

"Where did you find the inspiration?" the earnest courtside
reporter asked.

"Yo, for this white cat," said Taylor, "it's all about the Ben-
jamins. Respect!"

Clearly affected by the partial crowd, the judges lavished Sweet
Baby with a score of forty-three. Alas, he flubbed his attempt in the
next round and finished fourth. Still, Sweet Baby had done himself proud. "I don't want to make this into too big a deal," he told
Jilly, "but I definitely feel like a pioneer for my race."

IF BOTH THE LEVITRA DUNK Contest and the Depends All-
Star Game were little more than glorified exhibitions, there was
one fiercely contested event over the weekend. The competition
among shoe companies to hold the most obscenely lavish party
had reached the level of blood sport. The end of the Dunk Contest
signaled the beginning of Party Time. Three companies had spent
amounts equal to the GNP of a small country, throwing fetes that
made Caligula's bashes look like Bible study.

There was a business justification to it all: The ability of a company to get the It Players to endorse its shoes means millions in
sales and incalculable amounts in image. And while the brands

can scarcely differentiate their product—most basketball shoes are conceived by a similar corps of twentysomething designers, given similar hip and futuristic nicknames, and manufactured in similar Southeast Asian sweatshops—holding a killer party is an effective way to let the All-Stars know they either are endorsing the superior brand or have pledged their fealty to pretenders.

In Los Angeles, Pegasus won the party derby in a landslide befitting the Malibu hills. The "Pegasus Arty Party," as the invitations called it, was held at the Getty Museum. Sitting confident and well-proportioned high above a freeway north of downtown, the Getty is a stunning edifice that overlooks the ocean, reachable only by tram from a parking lot below. Yet the art collection housed within is average, a stunningly apropos metaphor for L.A.: Even its museums are monuments to style trumping substance.

Predictably, Pegasus had spared no expense in making it the weekend's seminal event. To avoid the snarling L.A. traffic, the company hired a fleet of helicopters to shuttle select guests to the Getty from the five-star hotels where the players and other VIPs stayed. Once there, they were greeted by an ice sculpture in the main foyer depicting a life-sized Salvador Dali balancing basketballs on both tips of his prodigious mustache. Upon entering the party, B. D. Lake eyed the sculpture and identified it confidently to his companion for the evening, a tall woman in a miniskirt who did not appear particularly evangelical, as "the Italian painter P. Casso." Pegasus had hired the hottest deejay in town, L'il Big Dude, a close friend of Litanium's, to spin tunes. The open bar in the Impressionism wing had only premium booze and an Oregon microbrew called Terry Porter, handcrafted solely for the All-Star party. As guests guzzled free liquor like elephants at a water hole, servers theme-clad in Parisian berets adorned with the ubiquitous Pegasus logo served mu-shu lobster and exotic sushi.

It was shortly before midnight when Lo Mayne rolled into the

Getty. When he left the University of North Carolina after his sophomore year and turned pro, Erick Silver had gotten him a contract with Pegasus that paid $6 million a year. Initially, he made more from wearing the right shoes than he did from his playing salary. (And it was a nice piece of change for Erick Silver, too.) Pegasus had sponsored Lo's eleven-and-under All-Star team in Carolina, subsidizing travel and plying the kids with free shoes— and, in turn, an inflated sense of entitlement. So when Lo turned pro, the choice of which brand to endorse was really no choice at all. Silver had never been able to get Lo an Air Jordan–type signature shoe—the ultimate badge of honor for a baller—but Pegasus included him in some of the company's characteristically edgy marketing campaigns. They also FedExed Lo shoes by the gross. One year he wore a different pair every game, handing out his discards to his designated charity for that year, Lo's Down Syndrome Children. By and large, Lo felt Pegasus had "respected" him, the highest praise in the basketball firmament. He now hoped the company would extend his contract—before it caught wind of any vehicular homicide arrests and let him go for violating the "morals clause."

Brian Bunn, an aging frat boy with a heavy arsenal of packaged one-liners and copiously gelled hair, was Lo's contact at Pegasus. ("Call me Lo's liaison, Mayne's middleman," Bunn told Lo the first time they met.) Bunn had told Lo that he had an unlimited guest list for the Pegasus party at the Getty. "You're the King, so why not invite the whole court?" Bunn had told him weeks earlier. Lo obliged, inviting not just his teammates and the full corps of Mayne Men, but also a few non-A-listers, such as Jamal.

Jamal was obviously not among the landed gentry afforded a copter ride to the Getty, and he figured that his Prism would have elicited giggles when he pulled up to the valet, so he had mooched a ride to the party with Dontonio Perkins, a member of the Mayne

Men who had played linebacker at North Carolina State. Just after he made his way through a lobby thick with manufactured fog, Jamal saw Shane Donnelly chatting up an impossibly gorgeous woman with pale white skin and a dress that fit over her curvilinear body as tightly as a shell fits over a hard-boiled egg. As Jamal neared, he heard Shane coo to the woman, "You know what they say: Once you go white, you know that it's right." Jamal didn't break stride.

He was calculating what his first move should be, when a waitress in a micro-mini sidled up and asked if he wanted a "V and Red Bull."

"A what and Red Bull?"

"A V. You know, Viagra."

Levitra may have sponsored the Dunk Contest, Jamal thought, but Viagra was getting the superior product placement this night. "I do okay on my own," he said.

The server had a response at the ready. "You know that commercial that says, 'Consult your physician if your erection lasts longer than six hours'? Let's just say if you take this, you better have Doc on speed dial."

"No, I'm good," Jamal sputtered.

Standing in line in front of a stuffed winged horse that doubled as a champagne fountain, Jamal looked to his left and saw someone he thought was . . . Jilly? She was bopping ever so slightly to the pounding beat, dressed in a leather jacket and skirt that was risqué by her J. Crew standards though downright Amish compared to the attire of the other female guests.

Jilly had wrestled with her decision to attend the bash. When Lo first invited her a few days ago, she was ambivalent. *Did he invite me so I'd back off asking questions about his Hummer and his past?* she wondered. But she also had to admit she was genuinely flattered, because none of the other beat writers had gotten the gilded nod. To varying degrees, journalists who cover teams—even high-school teams—long to belong, to feel some of that locker-room camaraderie that makes sports so great. All in all, though, she felt ambivalent about the whole thing. Attending the party wasn't necessarily a conflict of interest. In fact, she rationalized, if she was going to put together a long story about Lorenzen's past, the party could produce some interesting background material. But even that wasn't clear-cut. Did accepting an invitation, putting on a leather skirt, and downing a few cocktails disqualify her from taking covert notes? Plus, the last thing she wanted to do was give the impression that she was in bed—even figuratively—with her subjects. "You can go to the circus," her old hard-boiled editor in the business section once told her, "but don't fuck the elephants."

On the other hand, she thought, *I do look pretty good in the jacket and skirt.*

Jamal looked over at Lo across the room. He was popping a grape into his mouth and smiling vacantly to a crowd of sycophants. Did Lo invite her? If so, why? Then he looked back at Jilly, who had just finished a drink and was looking for a place to set her glass. *Damn*, thought Jamal, *she does look pretty good in the jacket and skirt.*

On the other side of the room, Lorenzen was debating whether to come over and say hello to Jilly. *Why did I invite her? So she'd back off those questions about the car and Mavis? Could be. But maybe I just want to give a shout-out to the people who cover us once in a while. So why didn't I invite the dudes from the other papers?* Lo contemplated all of this even as a female admirer with a thick accent approached him and asked him to sign her brassiere. Lo smiled and said, "I don't sign undergarments."

"Well," she mewed, "I could take it off."

"I'll sign the palm of your hand," he said, "and we'll talk about the bra later."

Lorenzen took another look at Jilly. Athletes quickly get very good at multitasking while they sign autographs. *Damn*, he thought, *she does look pretty good in the jacket and skirt.*

Jamal had decided to make his move on Jilly, sneaking up behind her. "Thought this was supposed to be an exclusive affair," he said, tapping her on the shoulder.

"Right," Jilly said, recovering quickly. "What, they got some kind of math tournament here?"

"Very funny," he said, straining to be heard over the music. As he leaned in he caught a whiff of her perfume and was transported back to Yale, where innumerable random hookups began with a similar dance. "Can I snag you a drink?"

"No, I'm finding my way to the girls' room."

"Did Lo invite you?" Jamal asked, deciding to get right to it.

"No," said Jilly, "I'm in the same rare-wine club as the president of Pegasus. He asked me personally. Listen, I'll be right back. Girls' room." And then she was gone. She didn't know exactly why, but she felt vaguely uncomfortable seeing Jamal in that setting, as if she had gotten caught performing at an exotic dance club. *I'll get over it*, she thought. *One more drink and I'll be over it.*

For all the exotic trappings, the Pegasus party played out like a middle-school dance. Boys and girls, some of them not comfortable in their own skin, wondering where they fit into the social dynamic. Over the next couple of hours, as the music got louder, the drinks got stronger, and the mu-shu lobster became less important, the three of them—Jamal, Jilly, and Lorenzen—played their parts. They were like boats moored to the same post by long ropes. They drifted toward each other and then away, back and forth. Lo's rope was the longest. He stayed on his side of the room. *Should I come over and say hello?* he wondered. *Or would that be obvious, like I'm trying to be all friendly? Shit, why doesn't Jamal go talk to the girl? The lame ass.*

Jamal stayed in his corner, near Dontonio and some of the other Mayne Men, keeping furtive eye contact with both Lo and Jilly. *I don't want to go hanging with Lo,* he thought. *Some people already think I spend too much time sucking up to him. This is his night. On the other hand, should I at least thank him for inviting me?* Then he glanced over at Jilly, who was politely warding off the entreaties of a tall guy with a buzz cut. Jamal recognized him as Pegasus's vice president of marketing. *I should go talk to Jilly. What? We can't see each other outside of work?*

Then he looked back at Lo. *Why doesn't he look happier? This should be his night. It's his town. It's almost his party.* He decided to broach the subject with Jilly. If nothing else, it was a reason to get closer to her. *Damn, she looks pretty good in that jacket and skirt.*

"Hey," Jamal said. "You having a good time?"

Jilly shrugged. "Depends on your definition of good," she said.

"Just what a party doesn't need," said Jamal. "Somebody getting all existential when they're drinking. But I wanted to ask you something. Why doesn't Lo look happier?"

Jilly looked over at Lorenzen, who was sipping a Heineken and shaking hands with another one of Brian Bunn's cronies. "Isn't it obvious?" said Jilly.

"Apparently not," said Jamal.

Jilly set down her drink and flicked a spot off Jamal's black blazer. "The man has a lot of pride, right?" said Jilly. "But he knows, just like you know and I know, that he shouldn't be on the All-Star team. He got added because we're in L.A. and because of some sort of lifetime achievement award. If he was riding in here all triumphant, it would be another story. But instead he's playing like a buster, and he's embarrassed by that."

"Hey," said Jamal, "that's my man you're talking about."

"Anyway," said Jilly, "I think you came over here just to check up on me. Which I appreciate, but I have to get going. It's three in the a.m., in case you haven't noticed."

Like one of Litanium's pharmaceutical concoctions that kicks in without warning, there inevitably comes a point at which lavish sports parties turn the corner from merely wild to scary, when the components of testosterone and booze and money and entitlement and dark places and pulsating music—none of them dangerous in their own right but lethal in combination—converge. As Jamal and Jilly talked—the former trying to decide if he should make a definitive move on the latter, the latter trying to figure out why she hadn't kept walking away from the former—that point came just as Jilly started to leave the party.

A crowd of players had gathered around a pair of South American women who were, unambiguously, prostitutes. The game was "What color your panties?" and there was no doubt that a decisive answer was forthcoming. After the women bent over in unison, revealing one pink and one white thong, Monty McDaniel, a center for the Cleveland Kings who towered over the masses, bellowed, "Who's next?" A Laserettes cheerleader, breaking about six of Cherry Pie Holstrum's rules on "public comportment," offered up some green micros. Several other women obliged, though the answer in one case was "no color," since she wasn't wearing any. Finally, Litanium, back from a disastrous financial excursion to Vegas and now acting as co-emcee with Monty McDaniel, espied Jilly and Jamal on the edge of the throng.

"What about you, Jill?" said Litanium, motioning with his hands and starting to move toward them. "J-Money, get Jill on up here!"

Pretending not to hear, Jilly walked away from the crowd, which had turned in her direction.

"Don't go away, reporter girl!" McDaniel bellowed. "Come back and let us guess what color your panties is." By now a half dozen or so players were around Jilly.

Lo Mayne was taking in the contest from a far corner of the room, surrounded by two women—"a graduate student from Atlanta" and a "free-form poet from Pasadena"—when he saw what was happening with Jilly. Acting either as principled host or calculating self-preservationist, Lorenzen made his way through the crowd, joining Litanium, Monty McDaniel, Jamal, and Dontonio in a race to grab up Jilly. Smiling like a fool, Litanium got there first and took her elbow. Lorenzen got there second, brushing by Douglas and pushing Litanium's hand off Jilly's left elbow.

"Damn, Lo, why you gotta be such a Melvin!" said Litanium.

Lo locked onto Jilly's right elbow and marched her toward the exit, which was where she was heading anyway. She didn't know who had hold of her. Intent only on getting out of the room, she walked another twenty feet, ripped her arm away from Lo's grip, whirled around, and shouted, "Get the hell off me! I just want to leave!" Jamal had arrived by that time, Dontonio by his side.

"I understand that, Jilly," said Lorenzen. "That's what we want, too."

Shaking with anger and fear, Jilly gathered her leather jacket around her like a shawl. "I never should've come," she said. "Shit."

The three men had no response to that. They stood staring at their feet. From the noise inside, it appeared that Litanium and Monty had found another willing contestant.

"Dontonio, why don't you see that Jilly gets home," said Lorenzen finally, trying to reclaim the role of congenial host. "Tell the helicopter guy she's with me."

"I have my car," said Jilly.

"Copter's quicker," said Jamal, feeling like he should say something. "We'll take care of your car." He didn't know how—it was just something to say.

Jilly stood with her arms folded, trying to figure if she appeared more grateful or stupid. Finally, she tossed Jamal the keys. "Brown Toyota," she said. "Probably the only brown Toyota here."

"I'll find it," said Jamal. "I'll drive it home tonight and take it to the Bok tomorrow. Can you get a ride to the game?"

"No problem," said Jilly. She softened a little as she looked at Jamal. "You sure you're okay to drive? You were hitting it pretty heavy. I don't want my nice brown Toyota coming back all smashed up."

Lorenzen wondered: *Was that for me?*

"I'm fine," said Jamal, "This whole thing sobered me up."

"You should've seen what it did to me," said Jilly. She shifted her glance from Jamal to Lorenzen. "And thanks, Lo," she said. "I should've come over earlier to say thanks for the invitation. And thanks for getting me out of there."

"Sometimes," said Lo, "these parties are more interesting than they should be."

Jilly stepped into the copter and shouted back, "That's true of a lot of things."

The three of them watched her take off. A sign in the chopper's widow, adorned with a Pegasus logo, read: "After two a.m. women fly free!"

CHAPTER 22

When Jamal awoke, his first thought was that he would not attend the All-Star Game. He wanted to stay out of Peterwicz's way and avoid any impression that he was marking territory. Plus, he had a monster hangover and some lingering doubt about how he had acted in *l'affaire Jilly*. Anyway, he could catch up on some reading, maybe tool around on the Internet, studiously avoid the BlackBerry, maybe . . .

"Fuck this," Jamal said suddenly, springing out of bed. He changed into his favorite Joseph Abboud shirt and a pair of slacks. A few months ago, as an NBF-obsessed college kid, he would have considered selling his plasma to buy the worst seat in the house. Now, he had not only a seat near courtside but a credential that afforded him the equivalent of a backstage pass, and he was mulling the possibility of . . . having coffee? Plus, he had Jilly's car to return. He drove it like a madman to the Bok.

By the time Jamal arrived, the All-Stars were already warming up. In front of the Western Conference bench, Lo Mayne and Octavius Clemons, a wiry Sacramento Capitals guard with a buttery jumper, were stretching alongside each other. "Whassup, scrub?" Clemons said to Lo.

"Not much," Lo responded, smiling. "Whassup with you, scrub?"

At the All-Star Game two years ago in Minneapolis, Lo and Clemons had sat at the end of the bench waiting for the coach to call their number. In the end, they played only four minutes apiece. They had joked about it ever since, calling the other "scrub" on every occasion. For Lo, though, that slight was a seminal moment. Sure, a low-tier All-Star is still one of the top two dozen or so basketball players on the planet, a remarkable achievement. But before that game, it was inconceivable to him that he wasn't the best player in the league. True, elite athletes wouldn't be elite without a generous dose of self-belief, but in the NBF it seemed almost always to bleed into self-delusion. Even someone as grounded as Lo at first thought of himself as the second coming of Michael Jordan, and, when the MVP voting hadn't gone his way, he had a laundry list of rationalizations.

As Lo sat at the end of the bench and watched his peers play that day—humiliated and stinging but wearing a brave face—the seeds of self-doubt were planted. *Maybe*, he thought for the first time in his life, *I'm not even* one *of the best*. Many athletes have such doubts. They hide them under a shell of bravado or they say that everything's in God's hands. But they have them.

"For real, Lo," Clemons said. "Seems like you're in your own world—not yourself at all—this weekend."

"No, I'm cool. Just a lot of pressures," Lo responded, upset that his demeanor was that transparent. Or maybe Octavius was just way more perceptive, Lo thought, than any of his Laser teammates. Then again, maybe it was just that Octavius didn't need Lo to pass him the ball.

Lo turned to Octavius and added, "I won't be cool if I only play four minutes tonight. Tell you that right now."

"I hear that," Octavius said, smiling.

The All-Star Game played out like most of them, a defenseless dunkathon that ended with the West winning 169–158. Lo saw respectable playing time in a reserve role—and received a warm, if underwhelming, ovation from the home fans when he checked into the game. He rewarded the coach's faith by drawing a key charging foul on an Eastern Conference opponent and sinking a string of jumpers to finish with eight points. *Where has that been lately?* he asked himself. Deep down he knew the answer: In a game that meant nothing in the standings, with no one depending on him, he could play on instinct. There was an abiding irony to it: At a made-for-TV game that was little more than a self-congratulatory infomercial for the NBF, basketball felt purer to Lo than it had in a long time.

Ditto for Jamal. From his seat in Row H, his credential folded into his back pocket, Jamal spent three hours as a fan, at one point even high-fiving his seatmates after the West ran a perfectly diagrammed three-on-two fast break. Watching all the best players in the world on the court at once rekindled his passion. He saw the plays unfold, the mix of structure and improvisation, the feints and understated maneuvers that no statistician could account for—all the subtle beauty that had made him fall so hard for hoops in the first place.

Late in the third quarter, Clemons checked into the game. Already besotted from a mix of overpriced beer and genuine enthusiasm he had misplaced for weeks, Jamal poked his seatmate, a slender, silver-haired fiftysomething with a Rolex on his left wrist and a camel-hair coat at his feet. "Watch this," Jamal whispered. "First time Clemons gets the ball, he's going to take two dribbles and drive left baseline."

Two possessions later, the West point guard spotted Clemons. Clemons caught the pass on the perimeter, faked a long-range jumper, bounced the ball twice, and promptly drove to the near baseline. He drew a foul and went to the free-throw line. It was a thoroughly unremarkable play—unless you were Jamal's seatmate who had been briefed on the precise sequence ninety seconds before it happened.

"Holy shit," the man said. "What else can you tell me?"

Without Manny Burnett there to cast skepticism on the value of empirical data, the Whiz Kid went nuts. "Any loose ball that comes near Burke, he'll end up retrieving. Anthony will score points but will get eaten alive on defense. As long as Clemons is on the floor, the West will build their lead. If Townsend misses a three-pointer he will try another on the next trip down, no matter how well-defended he is."

Within the next half hour, virtually all of Jamal's soothsaying came true. The genial well-dressed man next to him was in awe. "Amazing," he said. "What do you have, some kind of NBF ESP?"

"Something like that," Jamal said sheepishly.

"No, really," said the man. "I've probably watched a thousand games over the past decade and you're picking up things I've never noticed."

Half conversing, half-paying attention to the action on the floor, Jamal gave a dummied-down version of his quantitative analysis, explaining how points, rebounds, and assists are "only the tip of the statistical iceberg." Hoping he wasn't sounding insufferably patronizing, he added, "If you know how to set up the equations, the right numbers tell you an awful lot about players you'd never know by combing a box score."

When Jamal looked over, sure he had bored his seatmate into submission, the man was shaking his head. "Why can't my guys think like that?"

"Who," Jamal blurted, "are your guys?"

"Oh, I'm Gabe Spielberger," he said. "I'm the Philadelphia owner."

Jamal was mortified. First for failing to recognize one of the league's oldest and most prominent owners, and second for shooting off his mouth and explaining his hoops sabermetrics as though his seatmate were an optometrist from Reseda. Spielberger, though, continued to smile warmly and extended a hand. Unsure what to say, Jamal shook the man's hand and said quietly, "I'm Jamal Kelly. I'm with the Lasers."

"I read something about you in a release," said Spielberger. "But you're just a kid. What do they have you doing?"

"Media relations director," said Jamal. "But the guy under me was hell-bent on working this weekend. And I'm kind of new, so I let him keep the job and I'm off-duty today."

"Nice to meet you, Jamal," Spielberger said, still smiling. "Say, you have a business card on you?"

When the game ended, Jamal was so jacked he didn't want to leave the Bok. He unfurled his locker-room credential, placed it around his neck, and went into the tunnels leading off the court. Jamal tried to look official—like he was actually walking around for some job-related purpose—but in truth he was just a voyeuristic fan doing everything he could to retain a shred of professionalism and refrain from asking for autographs.

After slinking into the locker rooms and watching how the All-Stars interacted with one another—some with a real collegiality, others with icy arrogance—and standing in the back of the postgame press conference to hear the players' bon mots, Jamal departed from his better judgment and stuck his head into the media room. It was packed tight, filled with NBF writers from all over the country sending their dispatches on deadline.

"Damn it, Jamal," came a familiar voice from behind his left shoulder. Oozing stress, Jilly, back wearing J.Crew, had her game face on.

"Goddamn Peterwicz didn't give me a seat and some jerkoff

from Boston who claims I have three extra hours 'cause of the time difference is using my phone jack to file his story. Good thing the L.A. *Times*—which only has a two-million-dollar sponsorship agreement with this arena, I should add—gets second-class status at the L.A. All-Star Game."

"So what do you want me to do?" Jamal said. "I'm not even on the clock today."

"Let me use the phone jack in your office to file my story. Payback for the washing machine." *Best development of the day*, Jamal thought. Jilly grabbed her laptop and followed Jamal into the elevator that led to the executive offices. "Of course, you realize this is the second straight night I've rescued you," he said.

"Yeah, but who's keeping score, right? Anyway, it was Lo who rescued me. You were just my driver."

"Well, I was heading to get you, too," said Jamal. "Lo just has a quicker first step. Here's the car keys. Copter get you home safe?"

"Only way to travel," said Jilly. "He let me out at a heliport on Century, and I cabbed it from there. Anyway, it was an interesting evening."

Jamal opened his office door and Jilly flopped down on the only chair, leaving Jamal to sit on his desk.

"Hey, Mr. Media Relations Guru-slash-Whiz Kid," she said, unzippering her laptop case. "I have a question."

"Shoot."

"Is it some sort of league rule that when they get into the league, every player has to get a tattoo with Mandarin characters?" said Jilly. "I go into a locker room before the game, I see so much Chinese I feel an MSG headache coming on. The only player in the whole goddamn league who doesn't have a Chinese tattoo is Ming Li."

Jamal had often wondered the same thing and warmed to the subject. "You know what the funny thing is? Half the time the characters don't mean a damn thing," he said.

"Come on."

"For real. Kwaanzii got this ink job when we were in Denver and he explained that it meant Honor, Pride, Warrior. When we played in New York, I had a college friend of mine, an East Asian Studies major, check it out. Turns out the symbols mean Metal Tongs, Yak, and Ashtray."

"Tats have become like the Hard Rock Café: You'd never have guessed it was once cool. I wish I never got mine."

Jamal paused, wondering if he had heard correctly. "Did you say you got—"

"I didn't say anything," said Jilly. "Listen, I gotta file this story by—"

"You? Tattoo?" said Jamal, rising off his seat, a big smile on his face. "We're talking about the same thing here, right? Body art? Needles? Pain? Doesn't come off in the shower?"

"What's that phrase you love to use when I ask you questions on the job?" said Jilly. "Hmm. It's not 'None of your Fucking Business,' but it's a little more wholesome and means the same thing. What it is again?" Jilly smiled. "Oh, that's right: No comment."

"Jilly's got a tat," Jamal said, letting the word hang in the air. "Let me guess: It's a rendering of the Forrester family crest? The yacht? No, I got it: the name of your first show pony!"

"Not even close."

"So I give up. What is it?"

Jilly had every intention of ending the conversation, filing her story, and getting out of the Bok. Then, from some dark place in her mind, inspiration struck. "If I show you, it will cost you some down-low down the road."

"Deal," said Jamal.

With that Jilly stood up, walked over toward Jamal at his desk, untucked her shirt, pulled the belt of her jeans down ever so slightly, and there, on her lower abdomen, just above the peach-colored trim of her panties, was a green cobra making its way south.

Jamal spent a few seconds digesting the tableau—the tat, the peach trim, the tat, the peach trim. "Um," he said chomping his lower lip. "Isn't that the kind of thing that gets rich girls disinherited?"

"You think my parents know about this?" she said, laughing, still holding her jeans down. "Everybody's got secrets." She put one arm around Jamal's shoulder.

"Well, let me ask you one of yours," said Jamal, moving closer. "Did you ever—"

Jilly put her index finger to his lips. "Shhh," she said. "I know exactly what you want to ask me. You want to know if I ever fooled around with a guy who got an eight hundred on his math boards."

"That's close," said Jamal. "How about Robbie Dickworth? What did he think of your tat?"

"He didn't particularly like it," Jilly said, "and I didn't particularly care."

"How come you two still aren't together?" asked Jamal.

Jilly smiled. "That's a long story but basically it came down to this: He bought *Patch Adams* on DVD."

"Good answer," said Jamal, then pulled her into him and kissed her. He felt her lips tighten, then loosen, and he slipped in his tongue and put his arms around her hips, and she moved into him. They kissed ungracefully but passionately, but then Jilly broke away.

"I've just violated about a hundred tenets of the journalistic profession," she said.

"Assume you misplaced the manual," he said, pulling her close again.

She broke away. "Listen, I came up here to file a story and that's what I better do," she said. "This can't be the right thing for you, either."

"Funny," said Jamal, "but that never crossed my mind." He looked into her green eyes and saw that she had gone far enough, for that evening anyway. "All right, let me get out of here and let you file. I'll be sitting in Peterwicz's cubicle, maybe channel some of his vibe."

It took Jilly about ten minutes to send her story; Jamal divided his time between taking a mental cold shower and trying to figure out if he should take one more shot. "I'm done," she called out to Jamal, and he came back in as she was gathering up her things and putting on her coat.

"I know what you wanted to ask me before," she said. "You wanted to know if I ever fooled around with a black guy. Right?"

Jamal smiled and helped her on with her coat. "Actually, that's not it," he said. "I wanted to know if you ever fooled around with a black guy who got an eight hundred on his math boards."

They started at each other and smiled, and then Jilly reached out and kissed him on the cheek and lightly on the lips before turning to leave with a cheery, "So now you know the answer. You and only you."

"Know what?" said Jamal.

"You know what color my panties are," said Jilly. "But don't tell anybody."

CHAPTER 23

Ezekiel Martin Kelly had been waiting on the front steps—surprisingly patient by Jamal's reckoning—when Jamal got home from work. They had stared tensely at each other for a moment, then both softened. The hug had been mutual and spontaneous. And now they were jointly tugging to open an old studio couch. Finally, it landed on the bare floor with a loud thud.

"Seems pretty comfortable," said Jamal, pressing on the mattress with the palm of his right hand.

"Specially since you don't have to sleep on it," said Zeke.

Jamal started to protest but saw that Zeke was smiling.

"No, really, man, it'll be fine," said Zeke. "Look, I just appreciate you doing this. I hope I'm not cramping your, you know, social agenda. As soon as I find . . ."

"Shit, I might as well be studying for the priesthood the way it's been going for me," said Jamal. "As long as you keep the snoring to a minimum. And—listen, man—no smoking. I'm serious about that shit. I don't know anybody who smokes anymore. I don't know anybody smokes in the whole state of California. Tobacco anyway."

Zeke held up both hands. "That was a New York habit," he said. "I left it behind. I left behind *all* my New York habits."

"Like being a lazy ass?" said Jamal, trying to soften it with a smile.

"Especially that," said Zeke.

He turned away and began unpacking the two small bags he had brought from home. Jamal knew players' wives and girlfriends who brought four times that much for a weekend road trip. Zeke was coming to stay . . . for what? A month? Six?

The brothers had once been close and now Zeke was reading Jamal's mind. "In case you're wondering what my plans are," said Zeke, "I stopped on my way over and got an application. Someplace in the Santa Monica mall."

"I wasn't wondering that . . . okay, I was wondering that," said Jamal. "What kind of place?"

Zeke took a deep breath. "Jamba Juice," he said. "They had a sign they needed people. I fill this out without misspelling anything, I probably got the job."

Jamal laughed. He pictured Zeke wearing a green-and-orange Jamba Juice uniform and asking liposuction veterans whether they wanted wheatgrass in their smoothies. "You fill it out in Turkish, you still get the job, Zeke," said Jamal. "But that's great, man. Don't think you got to rush anything for me. You take your time and get settled."

"Listen, man, I thank you for this, I really do," he said. "I just had to get out of that fuckin' city. Find someplace different. Maybe this is it. Maybe this will work for me."

Jamal nodded and slapped him on the back. "That's what brothers are for," he said.

"Sounds like Mom talking," said Zeke.

"It probably is," said Jamal.

AFTER FILING HER OFF-day story on the Lasers' Wives Foundation annual Bowl-a-Thon for Emphysema — most of the members campaigned for the proceeds to go to a children's cause, but Betty Joe Kobubee, whose mother was a pack-a-day smoker, shot them down—Jilly decided it was time to put in a call to Mavis Robinson of Spencer, North Carolina. She tooled around on the Internet and located sixteen listings for "Robinson" in Spencer, all of them, Jilly snootily assumed, blood relatives. There was no "Mavis Robinson" but there was an "M. Robinson" at 143 Ridgewood Dr.

Jilly scribbled down the number and left her apartment in search of a pay phone. It's a cardinal rule of investigative journalism: Never place a call from a personal number, lest the subject see your name on caller ID and either screen the call or pick up anticipating the line of inquiry. But as Jilly walked the concourse, she had visions—elitist ones, she acknowledged—of Mavis Robinson turning down the volume on an episode of *The Price Is Right* and picking up a rotary phone. No need to worry about caller ID.

It was five in the afternoon in California, eight in the guts of North Carolina, when Mavis answered.

"Is this Mavis Robinson?" Jilly practically chirped.

"Who's this?" came the response in a crisp, confident voice garnished by only the slightest southern lilt.

"Hi, ma'am, this is Jilly Forrester and I'm with the *Los Angeles Times*—"

"Not interested. I don't deal with telemarketers."

"I'm not a telemarketer, ma'am," Jilly said hurriedly. "I write about the Los Angeles Lasers for the newspaper and I was hoping to talk to you this evening about one of the players on the team here, Lorenzen Mayne."

A few seconds of silence filled the line.

"How did you find me?"

Whenever Jilly got this question from interview subjects, she felt it was their right to know the truth. Having once been the target of a stalker in college, she had always been sensitive to issues of privacy. "To be honest, I was looking into some records about one of Lo's vehicles. When I called the DMV we came across documentation that he had purchased a Jeep Cherokee and transferred title to your name. This struck me as kind of strange because I cover Lo every day and he's a very open guy, but he had never mentioned your name before."

"Of course he hadn't," Mavis snapped.

"Why's that?"

"Oh, it's a long, long story." Mavis Robinson chuckled, her guard descending a bit. Jilly sensed an opening.

"I have time."

"You sound like a nice girl," Mavis said. "But I don't feel comfortable talking to you about this over the phone."

Another pause. Jilly thought she heard a child in the background, no doubt the granddaughter that the woman at the DMV had mentioned.

"You come to North Carolina so we can talk face-to-face," Mavis Robinson said slowly, "and I'll tell you about a side of Lorenzen Mayne no one has ever written about."

WHEN A PRO HOOPS team is going badly, a shroud of gloom envelops the entire franchise—one that had become more pronounced around the Lasers owing to a sinister smog that had rarely lifted from the Los Angeles basin since All-Star Weekend three weeks earlier. "It's like we're living in London when Jack the Ripper was around," the old public address announcer, Ralph Riley, said to Manny Burnett one day. Manny's response spoke to the franchise's collective psyche. "Why the fuck don't you quit then?"

Ticket sellers snapped at one another; Choshi the gyoza vendor and Sanjay, the concessionaire of Sanjay's Samosas, engaged in turf wars at the game; fans arrived at the Bok with the same sense of glee that they arrived for a proctology exam; the Laserettes were a butt cheek or two slow. Cherry Pie Holstrum had to fire two dancers who got into an on-the-court fistfight during a botched routine. The normally cheery secretaries/sentries who defended the sacred entrance to the Lasers' corporate offices had turned as churlish as a Chaucerian washerwoman.

"An appointment would've been nice," Saleeka snapped to Ronald Tacik, the league's assistant commissioner, when he stopped by unannounced one day to see Padgett and Burnett.

"Girl, that man could get your white ass fired you talk to him like that," scolded Barbara Ann.

"I didn't even know who he was," Saleeka shot back. "These suits from New York should wear nametags or something."

Even the promotions and giveaways went sour. On the afternoon of Free Rain Poncho Night, an intern forgot the ten thousand plastic coats in the back of a groaning station wagon, and, when he returned that hot afternoon, he was horrified to find that the ponchos had grafted together from the humidity. Burnett substituted with free California rolls, then fired the intern.

The team, of course, is the tree from which all despair grows, and the atmosphere of misery was most evident among the coaches and players. A certain tension had even developed between John Watson and his assistant, Doug Carter, allies of long standing.

Watson and Carter could've been separated at birth were the former not black and the latter not white. They both had short hair, thin mustaches, and longish sideburns that their wives harangued them to shave off. Small and compactly built, both moved in quick, sudden bursts, which was how they talked, too. There was one major difference between them: Watson had been a great player brought down by his own vices, while Carter was an overachiever who made it to the NBF only because he devoted himself to the game like a monk to prayer. He had scratched around the league as a backup guard, but he performed his most valued work as Watson's designated 911 call. When Watson had fallen, Doug Carter had been there to pick him up.

There was a quid pro quo. Since Carter was not considered head coach timber, his NBF lifeline was Watson. If Watson were fired, Carter would be scrounging for a job at Wisconsin-Whitewater. But now Watson could sense Carter silently second-guessing his strategems. His instincts were correct. Carter knew that unless there were some kind of miraculous turnaround, the hammer was going to come down on Watson, and the assistant couldn't help but wonder if ownership would at last elevate him to the head job.

In truth, Watson had done everything possible to stem the relentless tide of defeat and pessimism—dissect game films into the wee hours, buttonhole coaching gurus from John Wooden to Bob Knight for advice, drag in players for individual conferences. The last had been by far the worst experience. With a few exceptions, the Lasers shifted blame for their poor play onto their teammates. Watson had tears in his ears when he heard that Willie Wainwright and Clarence Wolff, who collectively played about six minutes a game, threw themselves on the sword, pledging to do anything to help the team. But more common was the dispiriting tête-à-tête with Kwaanzii Parker. The rookie had revealed an astonishing capacity for regurgitating his own stats—"I'm shooting 70 percent on threes in the fourth quarter"; "I'm making 88 percent of my free throws in the second half"; "Lo Mayne is shooting 30 percent in the fourth quarter and I'm at 65, so why ain't I taking all the big shots?"—while failing to comprehend that his propensity for dribbling away twenty-two of the twenty-four seconds on the shot clock, then giving it up to a teammate for a desperation heave,

killed the offense. Kwaanzii wasn't alone. Like bloodhounds sniffing for a scent, players pored over postgame stat sheets and comparative statistical analysis websites, both to build a case about
their importance to the team and, more important, to give them
empirical ammunition during contract talks.

"See, being motherfuckin' Rainman with your numbers, that
ain't what it's about for a basketball player," Watson told Kwaanzii.

The rookie looked genuinely hurt. "You saying I'm a retard?
Like the guy in the movie?"

"I ain't saying nothing like that," said Watson. "Anyway the guy,
Dustin Hoffman, wasn't no retard. He was autistic or some shit."
Watson got up and paced. "Look, you remember that pool movie
with Paul Newman and Tom Cruise? *The Color of Money?* See,
the kid, Cruise, Vincent was his name, he knew everything about
shooting pool but nothing about how to play the game. So Paul
Newman, the old guys, says, 'Vincent, there's a difference between
being excellent at pool and *pool excellence.*' You get what I'm saying now?"

Kwaanzii stole a glance at his BlackBerry. "Didn't see that
flick."

By contrast, Watson's meeting with Lorenzen had been satisfying and, in some curious way, even *significant.* But it was ultimately no more illuminating. Lo was the one player Watson could
always count on, the one player who *got it.* Watson knew he
wouldn't hear excuses and rationalizations and blame-shifting
from Lo.

"This shit is on everybody but mostly it's on me," Lo told him.
"This club needs a leader and I'm that leader and I ain't been leading. I'm looking as bad as a turd in a punch bowl."

"It's not just you," said Watson. "I can't seem to get through
either."

They sat there silent for a while, united in their bewilderment, cognizant of higher truths but unsure of how to get at them. Finally, Watson got up, came to Lo's side, and put his arm around his shoulder.

"So what's wrong exactly, Lo?" Watson said. "I'm just an old broken-down ex-cokehead getting tuned out by teenagers. But what's up with you?"

That's when Watson saw the tears in Lo's eyes. Watson understood, or thought he did. He had cried as a player. He had cried plenty, and not just when the coke and the booze and all his soul's demons came out at night. If you care, Watson always said, you cry.

"It's just . . . it's just . . . Coach, I'm having a hard time divorcing off the court from on the court, you know? I mean, we all got this shit piled on us, but I was always able to unpile the shit when I got out there. But this year . . ." Lo's voice trailed off.

"Any particular shit?" said Watson. "Maybe money shit?" 'Cause, Lo, you know, you got so many people you're taking care of. You getting buried in *their* shit?"

Lo shook his head. "Yeah, well, some, but this is mostly on me. I'll deal with it, too."

Watson decided to lighten the mood. "See, you shoulda done what I did a long time ago. Fuck up so bad that nobody trusts you ever again. The people around me? They're happy when I don't hit the floor during the National Anthem. Your problem is, you never fucked up big."

Lo got up and smiled faintly. "Don't be so sure about that," he said.

Jamal, meanwhile, felt the misery in several ways. Lo, his best friend in L.A. if for no other reason than by default, was ineffective on the court and distraught off it. Then there was his relationship with Jilly, which was no relationship at all. Since their tentative but promising contact during All-Star Weekend, Jilly had pulled away. Jamal understood at some level. It was hard enough for a female journalist to maintain her professionalism amid a roomful of men she was covering, and it would scarcely help if she threw herself into the arms of a team employee (though Jamal would've gladly caught her). Then, too, there was the stress of living with Zeke. He had to admit that his brother seemed to be getting it together, but he couldn't shake the feeling that, one day, the guy would lose it again. Finally, there were his bleak finances. Even a single guy with a barren social life has a hard time stretching twenty-eight grand a year before taxes. Jamal found it profoundly depressing that his unspent meal money figured prominently when he calculated his disposable income.

The descending gloom, his own included, surprised and saddened him. As a fan, Jamal had been able to track wins and losses but not psyches. He had assumed, like most outsiders, that, at root, games were games and that players enjoyed playing them and that the whole organization was one happy family—content in victory, conciliatory in defeat, unfailingly considerate of one another's feelings. Because he had been a rah-rah guy on any team he played, Jamal had assumed the paterfamilias role with the Lasers, pounding players on the butt, shouting encouragement at the smallest things ("Way to move without the ball, A-Okay"), feeding the press meaningless statistical tidbits to accentuate the positive ("That's the sixth straight Western Conference game that Litanium's had more than five assists"). Even the rubes from Statistical Pinheads didn't print it.

Jamal had taken to wearing sweats to practices because he was usually invited to participate in the shooting games. He was good enough to furnish competition but not good enough, except on rare occasions, to actually win. Kwaanzii took great delight in hammering Jamal, which he was doing at a morning practice that followed hard upon a discouraging 92–81 loss to the Portland Jaguars, a team picked well below the Lasers in the preseason.

"You coming with me later, J-Money, right?" asked Kwaanzii.

"I'll be there," said Jamal, who had promised to go crib shopping with the rookie. Though obviously no one had caught Jamal's victory on PBS, the Laser players had some sense that he was intelligent. There had to be some reason that Padgett hired him, and Burnett kept referring to him as some kind of whiz kid. So Kwaanzii assumed Jamal to be a shrewd investment counselor, even though Jamal still hadn't made it through his employment contract, was making a barely liveable wage, and, for all the promises of a "luxury company car," was driving perhaps the most unattractive automobile in all of Los Angeles.

As Kwaanzii closed out Jamal once again by throwing in a shot from behind the backboard, Jamal saw Jilly sitting high in the bleachers. Practices and shootarounds were off-limits to the media, but lately Jilly had taken to wandering in from time to time, staying out of Watson's line of vision. She did it partly because she was angry at herself for being scooped by the *Orange County Register*'s Eugene Wyckoff on the fiasco that was Kwaanzii's Paintball for Charity tournament. The *Register* broke the news that a participant had taken a pellet to the eye and suffered a detached retina. Despite Erick Silver's insistence that "everything was cool," the reporter pulled the tax forms and found that not only was the foundation uninsured but three of Kwaanzii's cousins were on the payroll banking six-figure salaries. Given her skepticism about Erick Silver, and her general feeling that the foundations of most NBF players were scams, she kicked herself for not going after the story.

Back on the court, Watson had divided the Lasers into two teams to run dummy offense at both ends. Shane Donnelly had recently—not to mention reluctantly—come off the injured list, and Watson wanted to refamiliarize him with an offense he was trying to install despite Kwaanzii's predilection for lapsing into one-on-one mode. Though the NBF is often criticized for being forty-eight minutes of ad-libbing, offensive structure is an absolute prerequisite for good teams. Even if a set offense is quickly scotched in favor of freelancing, good teams need to set up in something basic. Having an established offensive paradigm is of great help in the late stages of a game, when clock management becomes crucial. Still, there are few things that interest pros less than running through plays unopposed by a defense, the stilted choreography bearing, in their minds, no resemblance to actual basketball.

Litanium and Kwaanzii were less interested than most. On the first set play, Tribal Cat threw a pass that bounced off Shane's head. On the second play, Kwaanzii ignored a cutting Lo Mayne and instead threw up a twenty-footer that clanged off the rim. "You got eye trouble, rookie?" Lo said. On the third, B. D. Lake and Shane bumped into each other trying to set a screen on the same side of the floor. On the fourth, Litanium lackadaisically dribbled around a high pick set by B.D. and bounced the ball off his own right foot and out of bounds. Then he giggled and never made a move toward the ball. Lo walked over to get the ball and threw it back to Litanium, hard and high. Litanium, who was tying his laces at the time, looked up too late and the ball whapped off his temple.

"Motherfucker!" he screamed, starting toward Lo Mayne.

"You want it, come get it!" said Mayne, starting toward Litanium.

Assistant Coach Carter started toward the players, but Watson held him back. "Maybe a rumble will wake these guys up," he said. Up in the bleachers, Jilly put down her James Ellroy novel and picked up her notebook.

Litanium threw a wild haymaker at Lo, who ducked and began bobbing and weaving. "That's weak shit, Cat," said Lo. "You got anything else?"

Litanium moved in again. "Yeah, I got something else," he said, "but I don't want to use it. Unfair fight. 'Cause if you throw hands like you been shooting lately, I could stand here all night and not get hit."

Newly infuriated, Lo rushed in and threw a barrage of lefts and rights at Litanium. Kwaanzii, protecting his boy, jumped in on Lo, and it was on. Sweet Baby James, having nursed an intense jealousy of Kwaanzii, resenting his talents and most of all his complexion, pulled Kwaanzii off Lo, and Kwaanzii turned around and took a swing at him. Buenos Diaz, tired of hearing Litanium make chicken-clucking noises to insult his Paraguayan heritage, crept up behind the Cat and applied a chokehold. "Motherfuckin' spick!" Litanium yelled, forcing Diaz's hands off his throat. B. D. Lake, frustrated at both his play and his failure to sell his preacher friend on *Around the Rim of Righteousness*, leaped on the whole pile, screaming, "Blessed be the Lord my strength, which teacheth my hands to war and my fingers to fight." Happiest of all to rumble was Shane Donnelly, who figured he could work the edges of the scrum yet still emerge with an injury sufficient to return to the injured list. So he half-grabbed, half-tackled Puddin' Reichley, who, acting as peacemaker, was pulling Sweet Baby James away from Kwaanzii.

Over on the sideline, John Watson sat with his head in his hands. "Bad idea, that letting them rumble thing," he said.

"Yeah, well," said Carter, "wasn't like you were getting coach of the year anyway."

Jamal found himself in the pile, ducking under punches and trying to get to Lo, whom he finally succeeded in pulling away from the pack. Lo put up his hands and shouted for order. He held his hands up, palms out, in a gesture of conciliation. "Look, man, we gotta get our shit together," he said. "Myself included."

Abraham Oka Kobubee, who had stayed out of the fracas, made himself heard. "Lorenzen is a sagacious man," he said. "Only when we are united will we find strength."

The players gathered that in for a moment before Shane spoke. "Your wife give you the A-Okay to say that, A-Okay?" he said. Oka Kobubee lunged at Shane, whom he hated for his philandering American ways, and they began trading punches until Shane fell to the floor, gripping his right arm around the area of the shoulder and wincing in agony. B. D. Lake knelt beside him and pronounced, "It could be a torn triceratops."

Litanium nodded. "That," he said, "has got to motherfuckin' hurt."

CHAPTER 24

An hour or so after the donnybrook, which led to Watson's calling off practice and doling out five grand in fines, Jamal stood against a wall outside, listening to some Run-D.M.C., trying to get his head on straight. He had hastily prepared a press release announcing that Shane Donnelly had strained his triceps muscle and shoulder during a "battle for a rebound at a spirited intrasquad scrimmage" and was waiting for Kwaanzii to finish showering so they could go crib shopping.

Jilly emerged, heading for her car, and they saw each other at the same time. She smiled and walked over. "Not your usual morning practice, huh?" said Jilly. "Seemed like maybe there was some subtext to all the fighting?"

"Subtext?" said Jamal. "You mean outside of us being frustrated? No. I think it was all text. No subtext."

"Maybe," said Jilly. She decided to try the nice approach one more time. "Hey, I saw you in there fighting," she said playfully. "They gonna fine you?"

Jamal grunted. "I don't make enough money to get fined," he said.

"Those fines are such bullshit," she said. "You take a guy making eight million, like Litanium, and you fine him two grand, that's like a parking ticket for—"

"How did you hear about the fines?" asked Jamal.

Jilly sensed the conversation had taken a turn. "The guy sweeping up inside told me about them," she said, trying to keep it light. "I asked Watson and confirmed it with Manny. How you think?"

"Yeah, well, that might be, but you can't write it."

Jilly lifted her glasses and squinted at Jamal. "I miss something here? You turn into the sports editor at the *Times*?"

"I'm not your boss, but I am the guy saying you shouldn't have been at practice," said Jamal. "And since you shouldn't have been at practice, then anything you saw doesn't count."

Jilly burst into laughter. "Doesn't count?" she said. "What's that mean? *Doesn't count.* That some kind of Yale stat thing? A don't-count?"

Jamal's jaw tightened. Jilly turned and walked away.

"When did you turn into such a . . . such a . . . pain in the ass?" he said to her back.

Jilly turned around slowly. "Go ahead and say it. You didn't say it last time. At the game. What you really want to say. 'When did you turn into such a *cunt*?' Right? Does that cover it?"

"Hey, your words, girl, not mine," said Jamal.

Jilly stared at him hard. "And let me ask you something. When did you turn into a *playah*, wearing your sweats to practice and bopping around with your headphones on? Your salary count against the cap?"

Jamal put his headphones back on, then whipped them off again. "Why don't you say what you want to say? Call me what you want to call me? A poseur? A wannabe? A fuckin' groupie?"

Jilly walked away, then stopped and turned around. "I don't want to call you anything," she said. "I came over to tell you that I won't be at the next game. Richie O'Brien's covering for me."

Jamal nodded. He didn't want to ask why, but he couldn't stop himself. "You got personal business?" he said.

"Well, if it was personal business that would mean I wouldn't tell you what it is," said Jilly. "But since you ask, I have to go to North Carolina for a story."

Jamal took that in. "You suddenly start covering Charlotte? They're worse than we are, you know."

Jilly turned and began to walk away again, hollering back over her shoulder, "I have your press release here. The one about Shane's injury. I was reading James Ellroy, but this fiction is much better."

TWO HOURS LATER, JAMAL and Kwaanzii were heading north on the 405, an hour late for Kwaanzii's appointment with an agent from Elite Realtors, which was actually ahead of schedule for Kwaanzii, who was typically two hours late for his appointments. Jamal was driving the Prism, which was Kwaanzii's idea. "They see us pull up in your ride, they won't try to rip me off," reasoned the rookie.

"Kwaanz, your salary's in the paper every other day and you're looking into buying a seven-million-dollar house, and you think you're going to lowball them?" said Jamal.

"List is seven-three," said Kwaanzii, "but I ain't paying a dime over six-six. That's my height. So that's my price."

Jamal exited on Sunset and headed west toward the ocean. The property was on Burlingame, one of the most exclusive addresses in Brentwood, itself one of the most exclusive areas of Los Angeles. As they drove, Usher pounding on Jamal's bargain-basement stereo, Kwaanzii read from the property sheet. "Heated pool; don't say what the depth is. Four covered parking spaces; I was looking for six. Guest crib; don't say how big. Fireplace in the master suite;

that shit sounds good. Got eight-point-five bathrooms in this motherfucker." Kwaanzii looked up. "I was hoping at least one would
have a urinal. You think the point-five means it's a urinal?"

"I don't know," said Jamal, "but do the math. You never have to
use the same bathroom more than one day a week."

Jamal pulled into a driveway wide enough for three cars. He
was only a ten-minute drive west from his modest digs in Santa
Monica, but he might as well have been in another kingdom. An
anxious thirtysomething bottle blonde rose from a wrought-iron
chair on the front porch as they pulled up, offering a freeze-dried
smile as Jamal and Kwaanzii climbed out. The Prism had thrown
her, no doubt about that.

"Lauren Villanueva," she said to Jamal, offering her hand.
"And you must be . . ."

"I must be the one not buying this place," said Jamal.

So the Realtor turned her attention to Kwaanzii. Cutting
through the small talk to matters of profound substance, Lauren
locked her eyes on the ornament that looked to be pawing
Kwaanzii's sternum.

"Nice puma," said Lauren.

"Nah, man," said Kwaanzii. "That's a Jaguar."

Jamal took the tour with Kwaanzii and Lauren Villanueva, fascinated with both the sideways motion of Lauren's hips, nicely presented in a short leather skirt, and Kwaanzii's frightening knowledge of Italian marble. "See, the best stuff was made by a Jap,
Noguchi," said Kwaanzii, as he ran his long fingers over the marble countertops in the giant kitchen. "He set up shop in
Pietrasanta and worked there. Sometimes, see, he left some of his
pieces rough, didn't work him much, so they stayed authentic.
This finish here? Kind of overly smooth."

Here was an eighteen-year-old who couldn't come up with the
capital of California if you spotted him the "Sac" and the "to" ser-

monizing on Botticino and Carrara marble. When Lauren suggested they see the "marble statuary" in the Italian-style garden, Jamal decided to wait in the library, where the hip-swiveling Realtor had boasted about a large collection of "Harold Robbins signed first editions." About twenty minutes later Kwaanzii came in and told Jamal he was free to go. "Lauren said she'll give me a lift home," said Kwaanzii with a wink. "She got the same last name as that college in Philadelphia. Those dudes recruited me, too."

Jamal got up and slapped him on the back. "Small world, Kwaanz," he said. "Listen, you buying this place?"

Kwaanzii leaned down and whispered conspiratorially, "No way. They got only two hot tubs in this motherfucker. I ain't paying all that money to go ghetto."

AN HOUR LATER, AS Kwaanzii was finishing his tour of both the mansion on Burlingame and Lauren Villanueva, Jamal was finishing up a bowl of Chunky soup, which he ate just about every night he was home, and feeling restless. He had left work at the office when he went off to scout cribs with Kwaanzii, so he climbed into his Prism and drove to the Bok. Most everyone had left, and Jamal worked undisturbed for a few hours, updating his sabermetrics (he had thoughts about expanding it into a book), sending missives to the league office, even completing a preliminary seating chart for the next home games against Denver (it saddened him to pencil in "O'Brien" instead of "Forrester") and Miami. It was almost 9:00 p.m. when he heard a soft knock on the door and a cheery, "Hey, Mr. Midnight Oil, can I come in?"

"Sure, Denise," said Jamal. "Glad for the company."

Cherry Pie Holstrum wore a blue belly shirt, tight navy-blue stretch pants, and a pair of Reebok aerobic specials. Her hair was up and her makeup was fresh. Jamal put her at thirty-five or so, maybe older, but a gold-plated, hard-bodied certified MILF, as they called it at Yale—an acronym for Mother I'd Like to Fuck. No doubt about that. She had just finished the once-a-week cheerleading clinic she ran in the catacombs of the Bok and was heading out for a margarita at Los Consuelos, a nearby Mexican restaurant. Jamal declined an invitation to join her. "I already dined," said Jamal. "An exquisite carbo-heavy soup from Los Cambelles."

"You poor thing," said Cherry Pie. "Don't you have a girlfriend or a mother or somebody to cook for you?"

"It's just me and Zeke," said Jamal.

Jamal saw her tilt her head in surprise.

"I'm not gay," he said quickly. "Zeke's my brother."

They looked at each other, smiled, and said together, *Not that there's anything wrong with that.*

"But, listen," said Jamal, "what's your story?"

So Cherry Pie gave him the condensed version. Came to L.A. to act but only got work in shampoo and tampon commercials and gave it up. Took up dancing and massage therapy and got good at both of them. Twice married, twice divorced. One an ex–pro football player with a gambling problem, the other a well-known orthodontist with a drug problem. "I collect problem males the way my mother collected Hummels," she told Jamal.

Jamal ran through the basics, too, right up to how he felt a little lost in his job at the present time. Denise came behind him and began rubbing his neck, using all her licensed massage therapist skills. "You poor thing," she cooed. "You feel so tight." The rubbing went on for a couple of minutes. "They say there's some kind of reverse connection between smart people and massage," said Cherry Pie. "They don't take to it real well. But you seem relaxed, like you're enjoying it."

"Maybe I'm not as smart as everybody thinks," said Jamal. "Or you're just real, real good."

After another minute or so, Denise went to close the door. She came behind Jamal again and he turned and put his face on her belly shirt, and then he lifted it up and put his lips to one breast, then the other. He heard her gasp.

He had to concentrate hard so as not to whisper *Jilly*, and did everything possible to get that tattoo out of his mind.

"Contrary to what you may have heard," Cherry Pie said, moving away and kicking off her Reeboks, "I don't do this with everybody."

"Haven't heard anything of the kind," said Jamal, taking her hand so she could keep her balance.

"Yes, you have," she said, now lifting off her shirt, as Jamal put both hands on her aerobically taut ass and pulled her into him.

CHAPTER 25

L ike most members of the Fourth Estate, Jilly seldom let a gripe go unexpressed. Chief among the full complement of annoyances was the travel, the endless constellation of sterile hotel rooms, the low-grade colds she contracted in the steerage of coach class, the traffic-prolonged cab rides to and from LAX, the nutritionally bankrupt meals that originated in deep fryers, the interminable waits at rental car counters while the Des Moines advertising "executive" ahead of her whipped out his cell phone and deliberated with the home office about whether to take supplemental insurance—it was all enough to drive her out of the business and off to grad school.

Still, when she boarded her flight from Los Angeles to Charlotte on this rainy Tuesday, her sprits were at least approaching buoyant. She had no idea what Mavis Robinson was going to reveal, but Jilly's journalistic instincts told her she would return to L.A. a lot closer to solving the enigma of Lorenzen Mayne. As the flight took off, she grabbed a notepad and tried to map out a line of inquiry for Mavis, but it quickly became a futile exercise, since Jilly had so little idea where the conversation was headed. She traded the pad for a copy of Pat Conroy's *Prince of Tides*, figuring the southern atmospherics would get her in the right frame of mind.

Accustomed to the vastness of LAX, Jilly thought that the Charlotte airport, so small and navigable, seemed to have been constructed by Fisher-Price. Within twenty minutes of landing, she had picked up her rental car and was headed down the single-lane state road to Mavis Robinson's home in Edgewood, the next town beyond Spencer—"a suburb of Spencer," Mavis said without irony. The sun was starting to slink beneath the horizon, various agricultural aromas lingered in the air, and Jilly had her favorite Talking Heads CD on full blast. When Jilly traveled to Lasers road games, she drove from the airport to the hotel and then to the arena. But never through the countryside. On this day, she passed barbecue pits and roadside churches and convenience stores selling bait—real America! When she finally passed a wooden road sign welcoming her to Spencer ("Where Freedom Rings!") Jilly turned down the volume on the stereo and paid close attention to Lorenzen Mayne's hometown.

The component of her job that entailed investigative journalism—attacking potentially explosive stories and publicizing facts the subjects would prefer concealed—had always given her a charge. As David Byrne sang of "Burnin' Down the House," and Jilly made a mockery of the speed limit, driving to what she just knew was going to be a watershed interview, she felt as though her job wasn't so bad after all. A few minutes later, as Spencer entered her rearview mirror, she pulled out the crumpled paper on which she had scribbled down the directions Mavis had given her over the phone two nights earlier. She made a right onto McCartney Lane and drove another mile or so. At 148 McCartney, she maneuvered into the driveway and parked directly alongside a black Jeep Cherokee—the very vehicle that had prompted this odyssey.

A simple but tasteful brown clapboard with a satellite dish on the roof, the home more or less conformed to what Jilly had envisioned. Mavis Robinson, on the other hand, did not. A full-figured woman with skin paler than Jilly's and a head of curly hair more salt than pepper answered the door. "Glad you got here okay," Mavis said warmly. "You must be Jilly."

"You must be Mavis," Jilly said, extending her hand while scolding herself for having assumed that Mavis would be African-American. "You give awesome directions."

"Nice to put a face with a voice," said Mavis. "You must be hungry. What can I get you?"

"No, I'm all messed up because it's only two-thirty my time. But if you had a cold drink, a Diet Coke or something, that would be great."

"I make world-class ice tea," Mavis said. "How about that instead?"

As Mavis retreated to the kitchen, Jilly stared at the living room and hallway walls, furtively taking notes. Mavis was, without question, a woman of faith. There were five images of Jesus in plain view as well as an open Bible on the coffee table. On one wall was a framed program from a memorial service; though Jilly couldn't make out the name, she saw the face of a blonde, attractive teenager under the words "We Will Never Forget You." Mavis emerged from the kitchen to catch Jilly staring at a collection of dolls and their component parts strewn in front of the television in the living room.

"Those are Maya's," she said. "She and her friend Taylor do gymnastics on Tuesday, but she should be back soon."

Jilly and Mavis sat perpendicular to each other, each with a couch to herself. It was an awkward arrangement. For some reason, Jilly couldn't get Coach Watson's raspy practice voice out of her head. *It's all about positioning and spacing. Positioning and spacing.*

"Mind if I come sit next you?" Jilly asked.

"Not at all," said Mavis, disarmed. "Sit over here."

The women made easy small talk. There was a pro forma comparison of the weather in California to the weather in North Carolina. Jilly and Mavis discovered that they both had a thing for *Law & Order* reruns. When Mavis realized that she had been sitting on one of her granddaughter's PlayStation cartridges, it triggered a riff about video games. "If Maya played loud music or spoke on the phone too much or watched too much television, I could understand it," said Mavis. "I wouldn't approve, but at least I could relate. These video games, I just don't get it. Beep-beep-beep. It seems so stupid and mindless to me, but she can sit there for hours, transfixed. I want to take these dumb games away, but then she'll be an outcast at school since all the kids play them. Either that or she'll just go to her friends' houses after school to play. And no one will want to come here. So what am I supposed to do? But personally I don't get it. That and the reality television all the kids watch. Totally beyond me."

"I'm with you, Mavis," Jilly said.

Much as Jilly was enjoying a pleasant rapport—and a damn good glass of ice tea—with this guileless woman, she was growing impatient. It had been more than an hour and the conversation hadn't detoured anywhere near Lorenzen Mayne, the reason she had traversed three time zones. The late-afternoon sun threw shadows around the living room, obscuring the images of Jesus as well as the memorial service program. The languorous southern pace needed a jump start.

As Jilly was deciding how to get to the point of the her visit, a car pulled up. "That must be Maya getting dropped off," Mavis said excitedly, getting up. Jilly walked to the window and watched a minivan full of girls in leotards tumble out. A ten-year-old with a dark-blue backpack climbed out, waved good-bye, and gamboled up the front steps. She was beautiful, graceful, and obviously biracial. *Something tells me,* Jilly thought, *this is my segue.*

"This is the friend from Los Angeles I was telling you about, Maya," Mavis said. Maya gently shook Jilly's hand and then repaired downstairs to do her homework and—in keeping with the compromise she and her grandmother had carved out—watch *The O.C.* when she was done. As the two women walked back to the sofa, Jilly put a felicitous hand on Mavis's shoulder. "Your granddaughter," Jilly practically whispered, "is gorgeous."

"So was her mom," Mavis said, her voice also barely audible. After a pause and a sigh, Mavis looked up at Jilly. "I guess I'll start from the beginning."

With that, Mavis Robinson launched into a story that soon reduced both narrator and listener to tears. "In 1995, Tammy was seventeen and a junior at Edgewood, the rival high school of Spencer. She was a gymnast and captain of the Pompette squad that danced during Edgewood football and basketball games."

Like a low-tech PowerPoint presentation, Mavis reached under the coffee table and opened a photo album, turning to a page with shots of Tammy—lithe and blonde and the proprietor of an unflawed body—on the balance beam and posing in her maroon Pompette uniform.

"In the fall of Tammy's junior year," Mavis continued, "she had, um, *relations* with the star basketball player for Spencer, Lorenzen Mayne. Those two had barely known each other, but they had been at a party near Lake Spencer, they struck up a conversation, went for a moonlit walk together, and ended up in this abandoned boathouse. What can I say? They acted the way teenagers with raging hormones act. Lorenzen never mentioned his serious girlfriend, but it almost didn't matter. I think they both knew it was a one-night-stand thing. They were at different schools so there wouldn't be any awkwardness in the halls come Monday.

It was—what do they call it?—a no-harm-no-foul-type of deal.

"For a few months, anyway. Lo went back to his girlfriend, and Tammy began dating a wrestler. But she missed one period and then another and a trip to her doctor revealed she was ten weeks pregnant."

"A familiar story," said Jilly, "but that never makes it easier for the girl."

"She called Lo and he flipped out," Mavis went on. "First he made her swear she wouldn't tell anyone. Then he asked her to get an abortion. Well, Tammy had already told me she was pregnant. And I told her dad. We told her it was her choice to get an abortion—and her choice only. And we would support her no matter what. But my husband, he wasn't a racist or anything, but he wasn't comfortable having a half-black grandchild. Well, Tammy wasn't sure what to do but when she went back to the doctor for the ultrasound and heard the baby's heartbeat, that was it. She was having the baby.

"She called Lo to tell him her choice and he flipped out again. He said he was under a lot of pressure. All those colleges were recruiting him, and he worried that it would scare them off if they knew he was a father. His mother had just been diagnosed with terminal cancer, and he didn't want to put any more stress on the family. His dad is a real stiff-upper-lip type, and Lo said he would have disowned him for doing something he considered to be so embarrassing."

"So what happened?" Jilly asked, all the while scribbling notes.

"Lo couldn't talk Tammy out of having the baby. Finally, Lo said, 'If you have that baby, I'm telling you now, I won't be there for it. I'll support the child financially when I get some money in my pocket. But I won't have a relationship with that child. It's more than I can handle right now.' That was the last conversation they had. Tammy gave birth to the baby on June 18, 1995. She

named her Maya Ann. She didn't even name Lo on the birth certificate."

Mavis then flipped album pages and found Maya's baby pictures, a clump of baby hair, and the obligatory shot of Tammy
beaming as she held her daughter in the maternity ward.

"When the baby was born biracial," said Jilly, "didn't people
kinda wonder who the father was?"

"Well, they wondered but they never found out. Lo, remember,
went to a different high school, so no one really suspected him. And
Tammy had dated other black guys. Color never mattered to her.
Even when her best friends asked her about the dad, she didn't tell
them. She wasn't covering for Lo. She just felt that if he was running away from Maya, he didn't even deserve credit as the dad."

Jilly couldn't square the story with the Lo she knew, the one
who was the lone adult on his team, the one whose moral compass
seemed to point him in the direction of the high road. On the
other hand, sixteen-year-old kids, especially ones whose heads are
turned by the promise of fame, are prone to panic. And she could
envision Lorenzen panicking under the circumstances, especially
if the truth would have brought shame to his parents. Now that she
thought about it, Jilly had never met an athlete so concerned about
image. She looked at the wall and saw the framed program from
the memorial service.

"Maya brought Tammy so much joy," Mavis continued.
"Tammy was only seventeen, when she had Maya. But she was
always mature for her age and she was a great mom. But we had
money stresses and that's—"

Mavis quivered and her voice started to catch. Jilly reached
over to grab her hand.

"No, I'm okay, Jilly. We had money stresses and Tammy
thought she needed to get a part-time job to help pay for diapers
and formula and baby clothes. She worked at the Blockbuster in

Spencer a few nights a week. Mind you, she was also a full-time high-school senior trying to get her diploma and a full-time mom. But Tammy insisted on working for the money. That's what kind of person she was. 'My baby isn't going to be deprived of anything,' she would say.

"Well, one night before Christmas she went to work her shift. Everything was fine, but she was going on three hours of sleep. She drove home, probably fell asleep at the wheel of her car, and hit a tree. She died on impact."

Tears rolling down her face, Mavis turned a few pages in the album and pointed to the obituaries in the *Spencer Herald Times* and the *Charlotte Observer*. "We had a memorial service and more than two thousand people showed up."

"Including Lorenzen Mayne?" asked Jilly.

"Sort of," said Mavis. "Toward the end, when almost everybody was gone, he came up to me. You could tell he was worried about being seen, but I guess I gave him some credit for showing up at all. He shook my hand and said how sorry he was. But he couldn't look me in the eye—outta shame, I guess—and I couldn't look him in the eye, either. The way I saw it, if he had been more of a man and accepted responsibility for his daughter, Tammy wouldn't have felt like she had to get that job at Blockbuster in the first place. Then he was gone.

"Anyway, my husband and I formally adopted Maya after that. It was a horrible, horrible time. Losing a child is something you don't wish on your worst enemy. But in a way, Maya was the best thing that could have happened to me under the circumstances. You can't pour all your energy into grieving when you have a six-month girl, scraping her knee and crawling around and growing like a weed. I honestly think she saved my life. Not my husband's, though. Tammy's death took the wind out of his sails and he just kind of lost his will to live. He put on weight, got real depressed, and had a heart attack in 1997. So for the past eight years, it's just been me and that angel you just met."

By now Jilly was making her way through a box of tissues. She had come to Charlotte forewarned that she would be exposed to another dimension of Lo Mayne, and, in a way, she was. She saw Lo as she hadn't before—as a sixteen-year-old, heralded but confused, subject to the same hopes and fears as any sixteen-year-old. But her feelings about Lo as an adult had hardened. It is one thing to elude responsibility as a teenager, quite another to do the same as a millionaire in your midtwenties.

"After Tammy's passing, I just wrote him off," continued Mavis, as if she were reading Jilly's mind. "He didn't exist. I'd see a headline about him and turn the page. I'd hear someone say how well he was doing at UNC and change the subject or walk away. My husband and I used to love the Tar Heels, but we couldn't watch their games after Lo started playing there. His name was dirt in this house. Then, right after my husband died, I heard that Lo was going to make millions of dollars playing for the Lasers. Know what I did?"

"What?" Jilly said.

"I called him at his dad's house and left a message. He called me right back. I was ready to read him the riot act. But before I could get going, he said, 'I know why you're calling. We had a deal: I'm not ready to be a father, but I'll support your granddaughter in any way. You just tell me what you guys need and I'll take care of it.'

"I'm sure it was a lot of guilt kicking in. I lost a daughter and a husband. And what happened to him? Recruiters never found out, so they weren't scared off and he got his scholarship to UNC. His image wasn't hurt one bit in Spencer where he's a god to this day. His mother died in peace, not knowing that her son had a child out of wedlock while he was in high school. His dad never found out, either. But I give Lorenzen credit for this: When he got in a position to fulfill his part of the bargain, he did it. Whenever I need something for Maya—some money for summer camp, a speech tutor, a new Jeep Cherokee so I can carpool her friends—he's come through, no questions asked."

"But has he ever met Maya?" Jilly asked.

"Never. Maya and I had a long talk a few years ago about me being her grandma and her mom being up in heaven. But she's never expressed much interest in knowing more about her father. At least not yet. And he hasn't expressed interest in getting to know her. That's something I can't understand. He doesn't know what he's missing. Enough time has passed that I can hear the name Lorenzen Mayne without having to leave the room and I can read about him in the newspaper and I can even watch the Lasers—say, they stink this year, don't they? But I still get sick when I hear about him getting this humanitarian award and this Good Samaritan honor. How about being a father to your own daughter first?"

Jilly saw the knob on the door to the basement turn and Maya appeared with an earnest look on her face. "Grandma, I need you to check my homework so I can watch *The O.C.*" Jilly realized that she had been with Mavis for more than three hours.

"Mavis, go spend time with that adorable girl," Jilly said. "I should be checking into my hotel anyway."

"Sorry to dump all this on you but I gotta say, it felt good to unburden myself," Mavis said. "You're a great listener and I really enjoyed speaking with you. I just get so upset by all the Lo Mayne hero worship when people don't know the whole story."

"Thanks for giving me the whole story," Jilly said.

"I gotta ask: Jilly, what are you going to do with all this information I gave you?"

"I have no idea," Jilly said, wrapping Mavis in a tight embrace.

"Honestly, I have no idea. But some of it, I have to be honest, will probably become public."

"Just don't hurt Maya, that's all I ask."

"That's one thing you shouldn't worry about," said Jilly, already wondering how best to fashion a game plan for confronting the Lasers' captain, resident good guy, and the father of Maya Ann Robinson.

CHAPTER

March 18
Los Angeles Lasers Record: 29-33

The Lasers' charter was passing over the guts of America, bound for a three-game swing through Cleveland, Chicago, and Indianapolis. From his seat halfway back, Jamal looked behind him and noticed that every player was asleep save Lorenzen Mayne, who stared glumly out the window. Unconsciousness-on-demand was a gift given to most athletes. Winning teams play cards, exchange MP3 files, and provide running commentary on the video offerings. Losing teams sleep.

Jamal leaned out of his seat and looked to the front of the plane where John Watson was standing in the aisle stretching his back. *Dead man walking,* Jamal thought. He leaned across the aisle and tapped Lorenzen.

"Sorry, man," said Jamal. "I was just wondering. Is Watson a good coach?"

Lo squinted at Jamal.

"If you're thinking about nominating his ass for an award," said Lo, "I don't think this is the year."

"Nothing like that," said Jamal.

Lo sat up straight. "Damn right the man is a good coach," he said. "He knows personnel, he knows matchups, he makes good game adjustments. Anybody would be lucky to play for him."

"But he's going to get shit-canned anyway, right?" asked Jamal.

Lo smiled ruefully. "J., these days you get fired for taking a lame-ass team to the conference finals. The only question is whether John makes it to the end of the year."

"Will he get another job?"

Mayne pondered that for a few seconds. "Well," he said, "he definitely has one of those seats on that coaching merry-go-round. On the other hand, he's—what?—fifty-one or fifty-two. Maybe he doesn't land on his feet this time. Hard to tell."

"Does Carter get the job?"

Lo cocked his head and looked at Jamal. "Doug's a lifetime assistant," he said. "At best they make him interim if Watson walks the plank before the season ends. And interims don't get shit."

Which is exactly what Watson was thinking as he gazed at his sleeping assistant. "They fire my ass, I expect you to go out the door with me," Watson had told Carter a day earlier. Watson figured that his time was drawing nigh, especially since Manny Burnett was along on the charter, and, in fact, plopping into the seat beside him.

"Dumpling?" asked the general manager, holding out a small plate.

"M.L.B., you got any idea how many damn dumplings I ate this season?" Watson said. "Sometimes it's shumai. Other times it's ravioli. Once it was even a kreplach. But they can't fool my ass."

Burnett had hoped to catch Watson in a good mood, but, then, he hadn't seen the coach in a good mood since early December.

Burnett came on a few road trips each year, just to keep his face in front of the team, let everyone know the boss was around. At the same time, he didn't want it to seem overly official, and, in the past, had wandered back to the players' section of the plane and insinuated himself into their card games, talking about how, in his last season before he got out of pro ball, he took two grand playing bid whist off a rookie named Michael Jordan. Burnett had stopped doing that last season when Litanium looked over and said, "Manny, I asked Mike about that, and, shit, he don't remember your ass."

This trip, though, Manny had a purpose beyond face-showing.

"We're making a change," said Burnett, trying to make it sound casual.

Here it comes, thought Watson. *Everybody gets fired in the NBF, but that don't make it any easier. Fired on a damn plane. Wonder if that's ever happened.*

"I just wanna say, M.L.B., that no damn coach in this league — I don't care if it was Red Auerbach incarnated — could've figured this out. Lo's playing like a sack of shit, Donnelly spends more time in the training room than a crate of rubbing alcohol, the rookie —"

"Red Auerbach's not dead," said Burnett, "so he don't have to be incarnated. And you're getting all prematurely frazzled again. We're not firing you."

That caught Watson, pleasantly, by surprise. He knew he was a dead duck at the end of the season but, hell, a lame duck still had life, right? *I coach the shit out of this final month and maybe the Denver job . . .*

" . . . a roster move."

"I'm sorry, M.L.B.," said Watson. "You're thinking about a roster move?"

"No," said Burnett, "I *made* a roster move. Owen's down with it, too."

The trading deadline was past, so it had to be some CBA or Developmental League reject signed for a ten-day. Put somebody (no doubt Donnelly) on the injured list, stick the guy in for garbage time once in a while, and limp to the finish line.

"Whoever it is," said Watson, "I hope he got a perimeter game. We're about dead fuckin' last in three-pointers made. Is it the Skelly kid from that Idaho CBA team? Doug and I kinda like his game."

Burnett flicked some imaginary dust from his lapel. He had dressed down for the charter flight but had given his aqua-colored sweatsuit a quick press before he went to the airport.

"Wallace Reynolds," said Burnett. "He's a guard. He can shoot a little, but penetrating's his strength."

Watson shook his head and frowned. "Don't believe I know him," he said. "He in the Developmental League?"

Burnett tried to sound offhand. "Wallace hasn't been playing much lately, John. But he was a playground legend. Venice Beach. Compton. Oakland. You ask anybody there, they know the Master."

Watson turned his head quizzically. "Now, seeing as how he ain't been playing, how's he the motherfuckin' Master?"

"Actually," said Burnett, "it's Mastah. Mastah Mindya Ps and Qs."

Watson stared at Burnett, burning a hole in the man's forehead. Then he relaxed and smiled widely, maybe for the first time in months.

"You're punking me, M.L.B., right?" said Watson. "'Cause that's the agent-turned-rapper or the rapper-turned-agent or the gangstah-turned-both. I can't remember what. You didn't sign a rapper-agent who ain't been playing anywhere to a ten-day contract? A guy who, as I remember, is practically a midget anyway?"

Burnett called for the flight attendant and asked for some green tea.

"Like I said, John, it ain't like he's some guy off the street. Legit player. Speed. Quickness. Nastier than a pit bull gnawing on a pork chop. Taller than a midget. Much taller."

Watson started drumming his fingers on his seat. Back at the Limbaugh Clinic, he had used it as a technique to forget about how strung out he was. But these days it was nerves. Once in a while, during a tense situation in a game, Watson drummed so loudly on his seat that Doug Carter had to put his hand over Watson's to stop him.

"What you never seem to get, John, is that this is a business," said Burnett. "We're talking about a player who will bring instant buzz to the franchise. It's about crossing over. It's about the marriage between sports and entertainment. It's about that line being crossed. Where is the line these days? Who knows? Do you know?"

Watson stopped drumming and got wearily to his feet. "I don't know, M.L.B., and I don't care where the line is," said Watson. "I'm going to take a piss. And what I might do is stop up there in the cockpit and ask about parachutes. And if you're tellin' me that rapper-midget is on my roster, one of us is going to strap that chute on our back and be outta here before we get to Cleveland."

Jamal watched the scene unfold. Manny had told him of the move before they got on the plane, and Jamal couldn't help himself: He whistled, shook his head, and said, "Oh, Coach is going to love that one." His reaction angered Burnett. "Just get a release together, Whiz Kid," said Burnett, "and leave your opinions out of it."

As Watson rose, Jamal could hear Burnett say: "You are way out of line with that midget shit."

THE RITZ-CARLTON WHERE most NBF teams stay in Cleveland is in a mall, so Jilly got some shopping done while she waited for the team to arrive. She had already checked into her downscale Sheraton a few blocks away. As if to accentuate the economic gap that exists between the athletes and the journalists who cover them, the twain rarely bivouac in the same hotel on the road. Newspaper bean counters won't spring for three-hundred-dollar-a-night rooms, which teams, allowing for the NBF discount, get for less than half of that. But then, Jilly thought, that's how America works: If you can afford to pay for it, you're asked to pay less.

Jilly was in the lobby when the Lasers shuffled through. The check-in procedure is done expeditiously, even clandestinely, thereby adhering to another American rule: If you have large amounts of spare time, you're generally not asked to spend it. Jilly had told Jamal she wanted to talk to Abraham Oka Kobubee for her off-day story, and Jamal had grunted that he would try to arrange it. That had pretty much become their level of discourse: unenthusiastic request; muted grunt.

"A-Okay's waiting for you in the restaurant," Jamal said. "Don't keep him too long."

Jilly turned around and gave him a sarcastic look. "Yeah, okay. I'm sure he's much in demand. The ninth-best player on the nineteenth best team in the league. You should install turnstiles to stem the flow of people trying to get to him."

Jamal couldn't help himself. He smiled slightly. "Eighteenth," he said. "Miami lost last night."

Jilly was finishing her twenty minutes with A-Okay. They were both sipping tea. Kobubee, an unusually intelligent and earnest athlete, was a free agent at the end of the season and had confided to Jilly that he was thinking about quitting basketball and returning to Africa to work as a goodwill ambassador, perhaps even run for high office. As off-day stories go, this one wasn't bad, and Jilly had enjoyed the conversation. She figured she could write and file in an hour and make an 8:00 p.m. movie. When she stood and shook hands with Abraham, she saw Betty Jo Kobubee heading for their table. Given Betty Jo's reputation for pathological jealousy, not to mention the rugby-player amplitude of her body, Jilly had a split-second of panic. Plus, wives and girlfriends didn't travel much to road games unless they were themselves significant earners—they had to fly commercial. Jilly was relieved, though, when she saw that the full-figured blonde was smiling.

Abraham saw his wife at the same time and jumped to his feet, so flustered that he put two fingers first to his lips, then to his heart, mistakenly reversing the order of the secret signal known to everyone in the NBF. Betty Jo walked to her husband's side, smiled indulgently, and put two fingers softly on his heart, then his lips.

"That's the way we do it, honey," said Betty Jo. "You must be nervous." She smiled even wider and turned to Jilly. "I'm Betty Jo," she said. "Have you been having a nice chat? I thought I'd surprise my honey here."

"It's true," said A-Okay. "I was not expecting you."

"That's obvious," said Betty Jo.

"Anyway," said Jilly. "We were finished. I was just going over Abraham's future plans. I appreciate the time. Nice meeting you, Betty Jo."

Betty Jo put a strong arm on Jilly's shoulder. "Why don't you ask me a few things about it?" she said. "Obviously, I'm involved in his future, right? Maybe you can get—what do you call it?—another angle."

Jilly thought: *There goes the eight o'clock flick.* "Sure, sit down. Both of you." Abraham looked like a little boy watching a horror movie, curious enough to keep one eye on the screen but ready to bolt at the first sign of a chainsaw.

"Oh, no, Abraham is finished. He needs his rest. You go on up, honey. I know what room it is. They told me at the desk." The head of Special Forces couldn't get a player's room number out of a desk clerk, but Betty Jo Kobubee had managed. A-Okay nodded and walked away. Jilly thought she'd get right to the point.

"So, your husband tells me he's thinking about giving up this life? Going back to Africa? That's where you two met, right?"

Betty Jo didn't answer. She folded her arms and stared across the table at Jilly, who suddenly felt like she was in some high-stakes poker game.

"I know what's going on," Betty Jo said finally.

Jilly caught the ice in her voice and remembered reading a bio about her. Betty Jo had been some kind of softball star at Wichita State.

"What's going on with what?" Jilly asked.

Betty Jo got out a small vanity from her purse and did some primping. "With you and my husband," she said finally. "You and everybody else probably. But you and my husband's what I'm concerned about."

Jilly began looking for an escape route. "That is simply ridiculous, Betty Jo."

"I'm not the only one who thinks it, you know," said Betty Jo. "I sit with Topaz, John Watson's wife, at the games and she figures you're doing everyone, too."

Jilly put her purse over her shoulder. "I'm leaving now," she said. "That doesn't dignify a response. Your husband's a sweet guy, and he doesn't deserve you."

Jilly walked straight across the lobby of the hotel into the alcove and pushed the down button on the elevator. She was reaching for the iPod in her purse—a little R.E.M. was all that stood between her and insanity—when Betty Jo Kobubee came up behind her and violently pushed her against the wall. The iPod went flying and Jilly's first thought was, *She's paying if it's broken.*

"Stay away from my husband, you bitch!" Betty Joe screamed. Jilly tried to regain her balance but slipped on the carpet and fell in a heap against the wall between the elevators.

"Goddamn clogs," she grunted. She was trying to regain her footing, but Betty Joe had moved in by then and—the way it seemed to Jilly—was about to stomp on her in a pair of black heels that didn't really coordinate with her green jeans. So Jilly caught hold of the heel of one of Betty Jo's heels, gave a toss upward, and Wichita State's all-time women's softball saves leader fell backward onto her butt. Betty Jo was stunned, but this wasn't her first fight. She was scrambling to her feet, ready to go, when the elevator door opened and there stood Lorenzen Mayne and Jamal Kelly, burger bags in hand, soda straws in mouth, amazement in their eyes.

"Jesus H.," said Jamal.

Two Ritz-Carlton desk attendants, attired in subdued beige, had arrived by that time, one of them holding a walkie-talkie.

"It's okay," Jamal told them. "We've got it. Don't call security. Please." Ritz employees had been briefed on all sorts of contingencies involving NBF teams—everything from persistent autograph hounds to hookers of ambiguous gender—but a female fistfight was something else again.

Jilly was picking up her iPod, checking to make sure it worked. Betty Jo Kobubee stood a few feet away, fuming, staring at Jilly like a bull ready to get busy on the streets of Pamplona. Jamal and Lorenzen stood between them like referees, arms raised slightly, ready to do something if one of them charged.

"All right now," said Lo, "this is over."

"It's over for me," said Jilly. "I never wanted it started, never saw it coming."

"You started it," said Betty Jo. "You started it the day you walked in here, all Miss Innocent, all Miss Blonde Slut covering the team."

Jilly couldn't help it. It sounded like she had walked into a Lindsay Lohan movie and she began laughing. Betty Jo Kobubee took this as a sign of disrespect and charged at Jilly. Lorenzen got hold of her and lifted Betty Jo off her feet, her legs swinging and kicking.

"Jamal, get Jilly outta here NOW!" said Lo, duckwalking

toward the lobby with an armful of Betty Jo Kobubee. He tried to smile at a Ritz attendant, who was no doubt thinking about the new topic to be discussed at the next security meeting.

Mercifully, the elevator bell rang, the door opened, and Jilly jumped on, Jamal behind her.

"Well, we have to rescue you again," said Jamal, lightly. Which he knew immediately was a mistake.

"Why are you riding down with me?" said Jilly. She turned away from him, arms folded across her chest.

"I just want to make sure you're okay," said Jamal. "Sugar Ray. I mean . . . Jilly." He put on a silly smile.

She looked back at him. "Let me tell you something, Jamal. I hear one more word about this, one reference to a fight or calling me Sugar Ray or anything like it, this is going in the paper. This wasn't my fault—I'm guessing you know that—and I'm going to kill you guys. Just *kill* you. The only reason I'm not writing it is because I was involved."

The elevator stopped, the door opened, and the noise from the mall rolled over them.

"You wanna get a four-dollar bottle of water or something?" Jamal said, stepping out. "Talk this over?"

"There's nothing to talk over," said Jilly. "I tell my bosses, this is in the paper, and we'll need another of those lame 'Team spokesman Jamal Kelly said blah, blah, blah.' "

"No reason to take it out on me," said Jamal.

Jilly raised her index finger. "One word, Jamal. I don't want to hear one word." And she left him there in the elevator doorway, getting jostled by shoppers.

IN ROOM 711 AT THE Sheraton, Jilly had decided against the movie. She sat cross-legged on the bed, a room-service tuna salad sandwich at her side, finishing up the story on Abraham Oka Kobubee. She munched on the sandwich as she typed:

> Before making his final decision, A-Okay, as he's known to his teammates, will be talking to his wife, Betty Jo. The pudgy blonde psychopath, who should be made to walk around in manacles and a Hannibal Lechter mask, if allowed to walk around at all, exercises utter mind control over the docile African, a free agent at the end of this season.

Jilly looked it over and smiled. Then she deleted the passage. Her cell phone rang. Someone from the league office in New York.

"It's Francis," said the voice, that of Frank O'Rourke, a long-time public relations man and one of the league's good guys.

"Lemme guess," said Jilly. "Drang abdicated, you sold your soul to the devil for a player to be named later, and they named you commissioner."

"I got a better shot at Archbishop of Canterbury," said O'Rourke. "This is something else. I got a tip for you."

"What's the price tag?" asked Jilly.

"The thanks of a grateful nation," said O'Rourke. "Actually, you might mention to your bosses about that United Way story. Drang's always on my ass about that. Then you can tell me your boss said it has no chance and I can tell Drang I tried."

"I'll try, Frank. Promise. Whatta you got?"

O'Rourke cleared his throat. "Well, it's not that big. But we're about to suspend Litanium Johnson one game for missing one of his mandatory drug tests. I just wanted you to have a day on it to beat everybody else. He can play against Cleveland tomorrow night, but he's missing the Chicago game."

Jilly felt like she was back in school and just found out she got a D in algebra. "Mandatory test?" she said. "Is that in his contract?"

"No, well, I don't think so," said O'Rourke. "Of course, you never know what's in Litanium's contract. But this is recent, from that thing at the airport. When he got caught with the pot."

Jilly's thoughts went back to the Phoenix road trip. *The dog bite. I'm gonna kill Jamal.*

"Sure, okay, got it, Frankie," she said. "I owe you one. I'll just say it came from league sources. That okay?"

O'Rourke said that was okay and hung up. Jilly called the sports editor at the *Times* and told him that she had something better than the Kobubee story and that she'd try to file within the hour. Then she called Jamal's cell.

"Can it wait?" said Jamal. "Lo and I are about to see a movie."

"No, it can't wait," said Jilly. "I hate to interrupt your evening plans to make you actually do your job, but I need a comment on Litanium getting suspended for a game."

Silence on the other end. "Jamal?" said Jilly.

"Yeah, I'm here," he said. "We were going to announce that day after tomorrow. I was going to tell you."

"That may be," said Jilly, "but I'm announcing it in the *Los Angeles Times* tomorrow morning. Anyway, you'll probably say he's been suspended for having an overdue library book."

Jamal let out a long sigh. "Let me talk to Owen or Manny and get back to you. It'll be—"

"No, you're not getting back to me," said Jilly. "You're giving me a statement right here and now without any shit about a dog bite or anything else and then you're going to give me the official team apology for lying to the public. If you get Owen or Manny in the next couple of hours, call me back and I can still get something in. But right now it's 'team spokesman Jamal Kelly' said this."

"You know, Jilly, this is making too much—"

Jilly pushed the disconnect button and began typing.

CHAPTER 27

It was no coincidence. After his brief confab with Jilly Forrester weeks earlier, Paul Sprague had taken to smoking openly, all but daring someone to bust him in his office. He was firing up his fifth Marlboro of the day when Jilly rapped on the door.

"About time we got a designated smoking area," she said.

"Have a seat," Sprague said, smushing his cigarette into an empty Altoids tin. "Another enthralling road trip?"

"Thrilling. One win, two losses," Jilly said. "Could easily have been oh and three."

"That was good work on the drug-suspension thing. See, you're cultivating sources already."

Jilly reddened. "Yeah, well, I should've had the drug thing when it happened. I fell for a dog-bites-man cliché and didn't follow up. Rookie mistake."

"That was months ago," Sprague said, waving his hand. "And then the story on that rapping midget they signed. Couldn't start for a good city league team in Hermosa Beach, but I bet Padgett thinks it will help his team get street cred."

Jilly laughed. "Do you even know what street cred is?"

"I know I don't have it and don't want it," Sprague said. "Any other excitement from the fly-over states?"

"Well, Psycho Betty Jo Kobubee accused me of sleeping with the players, her husband included, and then tried to beat the shit out of me," Jilly said. "Other than that, pretty routine road trip."

"Sounds it," Sprague said, shifting in his seat, trying to look casual while he relieved pressure from his nether regions. "I'm assuming you didn't show up to check on the progress of my lung cancer."

Jilly sat down. "I have a question about a story. Actually, about whether something is a story."

Sprague had a hard time suppressing a smile. He had no illusions that Jilly found him even vaguely attractive, but at some point he had become her Yoda. He could take that into retirement, along with his five-grand-a-month pension and a new set of Pings.

"Why aren't you talking to Sports?" Sprague asked.

Jilly shrugged and took a sip from a bottle of water. "They're my next stop," she said, "but they say everything is a story. They got pages to fill. I fill them. But this is a news-value question. It's either a nonstarter or it's A-one material."

"Shoot," said Sprague.

Jilly recounted the chain of events that had led her to finding Mavis Robinson and Mavis's revelation that Lo was the father of a child he had never seen, the mother of whom was now dead. Clearly, she knew it was a hell of a story. But she also knew that the day it all found its way into print, Lo's life would change ineradicably.

When she finished the soliloquy, Sprague exhaled and leaned back. "What does Lorenzen Mayne say about this?"

"I haven't asked him yet," Jilly replied. "I only want to burn — carpet bomb, more like it — that bridge if it's a real story."

"Well, let's apply a little Socratic method. What do you think: Is it or is it not a story?"

Jilly hesitated. "I'm not sure —"

"*Be* sure, Ms. Forrester," Sprague said.

"I think it's a story," she said quickly.

"Why?" said Sprague.

Jilly had played this out a dozen times since her trip to North Carolina. "Because Lo Mayne is a public figure. Because we cover his heroics so we have to cover his screwups. Because he's been honored time after time for being a good guy and he's living a lie. Because if we let this one go, we put ourselves on a slippery slope and maybe we let the next one go, and soon there's no telling what we let go. Because it's of interest to the public." She stopped and spread her hands. "Should I keep going?"

"But don't a lot of these players have kids out of wedlock?" continued Sprague.

"Probably *most*," said Jilly. "But they don't win citizenship awards and get singled out by the commissioner and celebrated by their own team as paragons of virtue. All that, plus I happen to cover this one."

"You may sit down, Counselor," Sprague said, holding out his pack. Jilly took one and put it behind her ear. "Just for emergencies," she said.

Sprague fell in love all over again. "Go talk to Sports," he said, "but, depending on what Lorenzen has to say for himself, we might want it for A-one."

WHEN A TEAM ISN'T winning, nongame days at the executive office can pass slower than a kidney stone. No mad runs on tickets, no sponsorship deals, no interviews to arrange, no playoff plans to formulate. After a languorous eight hours spent cruising websites that had nothing to do with hoops, Jamal was ready to cut out at 5:00 p.m.

That is also the time that L.A. freeways metamorphose into parking lots. As Jamal once put it in an e-mail to Harrison

Brewster: "If Randy Newman had mentioned the traffic when he wrote that cloying L.A. song, no one would be shouting 'We Love It!'" Instead of facing a three-hour commute to his home fifteen miles from the Bok, Jamal rebooted his computer, ordered dinner, and spent the next three hours running his statistical program.

When the clock struck eight and the roads had thinned (they never empty), Jamal boarded his Prism chariot and made it home in twenty minutes. He walked through the door and felt a minor stab of disappointment when there was no sign of Zeke. Jamal's time in Los Angeles consisted of one surprise after another. But his relationship with Zeke was a pleasant one. The move to L.A. had done his brother a world of good. A shiftless, first-team couch potato in New York, Zeke now rose with the sun and was usually out the door before Jamal woke up. An old laptop Zeke had picked up at a yard sale for fifty dollars became all but surgically attached to his hands. Before Zeke came home, he ran three miles along the Santa Monica pier. When he overheard his big brother telling Betty about the psychic benefits of running, Jamal didn't know what was more shocking: that Zeke was exercising regularly or that he had used the word "psychic."

Jamal was also pleased (and at the same time somewhat stung) that Zeke was jealous of neither his job with the Lasers nor his proximity to celebrity. Zeke hung around the team, but he was never fawning. He interacted with the players he liked, Lo Mayne and Buenos Diaz—"Half the time I don't understand what Buenos is saying but he's still a cool cat"—chief among them. Predictably, Zeke was more interested in the players' souped-up, six-figure cars than anything else about them.

Shortly after nine, Zeke came home, his laptop bag slung over his shoulder.

"Where you been, bro?" Jamal asked, casually but genuinely curious.

"Starbucks. Working on my blog," Zeke said, removing his sweaty shirt.

"That's a good one."

"What?" Zeke said, walking to the bathroom. "Don't believe me?"

"Sure I believe you," said Jamal. "Just like I believe the Lasers will still be playing come June."

"You online?" Zeke yelled from the bathroom. "Go to www.socal-sweetrides.com and click the blog icon."

Jamal followed orders and, to his utter shock, there appeared Zeke's face alongside a headline: "Aston Martin Brings Da Funk (Not to Mention Da Good Gas Mileage)." Under that was five hundred words gushing about how "seamlessly the latest model handles curves and highway alike." Interspersed with text were links to sites devoted to other cars. The entry ended with . . .

> The company's vertical/horizontal platform that will underpin all future models will enable Aston to surpass the Porsche 911 and the Lamborghini Gallardo as the most princely car not in Formula One. If they come up with a convertible as rumored, James Bond will really eat his heart out. Till next time, get out of the left lane if you're not flooring it. Out—Z-man

"Shit, Zeke," Jamal said. "Where'd you learn all that?"

"All what?" said Zeke, who was shirtless on the floor, midway through a set of crunches.

"All that. How to set up a blog. How to create links. All that stuff about cars that cost four times more than I'll make this year."

"I dunno." Zeke said, gasping. "I picked up the web stuff real fast. And Lo was test-driving that Aston Martin so he let me take it for a spin while he was playing a game the other night."

He stopped crunching and looked at his brother with a half smile. "Hey, you think you're the only Kelly boy with a brain?"

"For a long time," said Jamal, "that's exactly what I thought."

CHAPTER 28

The Denver Pinnacles were one of the few teams in the Western Conference mired in deeper futility than the Lasers. Their low finish the previous year had landed them the second pick in the draft, which they used to select a seven-foot center from Moldova with a name like a rare disease—Prpic Vowel. Selecting players from Eastern Europe is a risky proposition. To be sure, there were unmined gems able to make a seamless transition from their club teams to the NBF. But all too often, the talent scouts—seduced by size—failed to consider that the opponent a prospect was going against was a chain-smoking auto worker. Such was the case with Vowel. Just a few games into summer league play, after he had signed a three-year, $10-million deal and transported entire branches of his family tree to Denver, Vowel was exposed as a center with the skills of a marginal Division II college player.

In part because of the wasted pick, Denver brandished a league-worst 19–41 record when it came to the Bok. "Playing these motherfuckers is going to be like going to the health and wellness spa," an upbeat Watson told his minions at practice. "They're going to make us feel a hell of a lot better." His divination looked accurate early on when the Lasers raced to a double-digit lead.

Then, succumbing to pressure from M.L.B., he inserted Mastah Mindya into the game.

There are no official records for the category, but Mindya surely played the most disastrous half minute of basketball in the NBF's annals. With L.A. winning 47–36, Mindya made his appearance late in the second quarter, the usual juncture for scrub substitutions. Immediately, the man he was guarding demanded the ball beyond the arc and threw an exaggerated pump fake. Mindya bounded into the air as if aboard a Pogo stick. Before he landed, his man bumped him, drawing the foul and then hitting an off-balance three-pointer. He nailed his free throw to complete a four-point play. On the bench, Watson smacked his hands together. "Okay, let's play now, Mas—" he looked at Assistant Coach Carter. "Hell, what do I call this guy? Mastah? Or Mindya?"

Carter shrugged. "What about not playing his ass and then you wouldn't have to worry?"

"Not an option," Watson said, looking straight ahead.

At precisely that second, Mastah inbounded the ball after the made free throw but stepped directly on the baseline. While refs generally turn a blind eye to the infraction, the officials this night knew that every second of Mastah's time on the court was going to be replayed on the highlight shows (not to mention MTV) and scrutinized like the Zapruder film. A ref who let a mistake that obvious go uncalled would hear from his supervisor the next day. As Denver took possession, Mastah shook his head and smiled, his gold teeth gleaming in the lights.

"I don't believe this shit," Watson said.

Mastah's man, again, raised his hand, demanding the ball. When it arrived, he didn't bother faking this time. He simply elevated in front of Mastah and drained another three-pointer. In a matter of seconds, L.A.'s eleven-point lead had been whittled to four. Mastah inbounded the ball, this time making damn sure he was behind the line. He passed to Litanium and headed down-court but didn't stop when he reached the perimeter. Instead, he camped underneath alongside Lo Mayne. Seeing the five-eight homunculus standing so close to the basket, Litanium waved madly at Mastah, directing him to move away from the basket.

The Laser's spacing was now awry. Litanium dumped the ball to Lo Mayne, who was promptly double-teamed. With nowhere to turn, Lo slipped the ball to Mastah, who still hadn't vacated his position near the basket. When Mastah caught the pass, he hesitated and then hoisted a shot. By that time, the help defense hovered over him. Denver forward Monty Wilson, towering over Mastah by more than a foot, smote the shot beyond halfcourt. Mastah's man retrieved the ball and cruised in for an uncontested dunk. Suddenly Denver was down just two. Watson called timeout and unleashed a hail of F-bombs. When Mastah returned to the huddle, Watson was waiting for him.

"What the fuck is your five-eight ass doing in the lane?"

Mastah smiled again, nearly blinding those near him with the reflection off his gilded teeth. "When it comes to basketball, I'm agoraphobic," Mastah shot back.

"What?" Watson said, dumbfounded. "What does that even mean?"

"You know, agoraphobic. I only like playing inside."

"Manny Burnett—who's the only fuckin' reason you're on this court—said you was a perimeter player," said Watson, his voice carrying ten rows up into the bleachers.

"See, I was once, but my game kind of transmogrified over the years," said Mastah Mindya.

"Is that right?" said Watson. "Well, how 'bout you transmogrify your ass on that bench and don't get up until you see all zeros on that big scoreboard clock."

Indeed, Mastah wouldn't re-enter the game, inside or outside, but the damage was done. Galvanized by their 9–0 run in the twenty-eight seconds Mastah was on the floor, the Pinnacles went on to win 98–94.

After the game, as members of both teams posed for pictures and spoke obsequiously with Mastah Mindya in hopes he would hear their demos or cast them in an upcoming video, Watson sprinted to M.L.B.'s suite above the court.

"Tough one, coach," M.L.B. said as he saw Watson approaching.

"A tough one, M.L.B.?" Watson said apoplectically. "That gold-toothed midget you told me to play had an epic, thirty-second fuck-up that turned the game around. And you come back with . . . TOUGH ONE?"

"Yeah, but did you see how the crowd reacted?" M.L.B. said. "And when I get home I guarantee Mastah Mindya's NBF debut will be the lead story on *SportsCenter*. Think Lasers-Pinnacles even makes the first half hour otherwise?"

Watson stared at Burnett hard for at least ten seconds. Then the coach got a big smile on his face, turned around, and bent over, placing one hand on each of his butt cheeks.

"Why don't you just get it over with, Manny," said Watson.

"Get what over with, John?" said the GM. "Turn around here and start acting normal."

"You been screwing around with me all season," said Watson, "so just get it over with and FUCK ME IN THE ASS. Right here! Right now!"

Watson remained like that, bent over, staring at his GM upside down, through his legs. He couldn't help but notice the perfect spit-shine on the man's patent-leather blue loafers.

"Damn, Manny," said Watson. "They from that British company, Guat Shoes, something like that?"

"The very same," said Burnett.

FOR A GROUP OF alpha males who would fight to the death to defend their manhood, NBF players have an odd fixation with body lotion. It is the rare player who doesn't have an industrial-sized vat of exotically flavored moisturizer displayed prominently in his locker. Players whose masculinity can be easily affronted think nothing of holding open forums about apricot exfoliants. Lo's product of choice was key lime pie moisturizer he had picked up at the Body Shop in the Cleveland mall. An hour after the Pinnacles game had ended, he stood in front of a mirror in the Lasers' emptying locker room, applying a coat of the green gel to every nook and cranny of his body, a form of self-worship.

From a swivel chair in front of the locker-room television, Jamal watched Lo meticulously apply gunk from head to toe.

"Hey, precious," Jamal said. "Need some nail polish to go with that?"

"Shut up, punk," Lo said. "Shouldn't you be arranging interviews for Mastah Mindya?"

"He doesn't talk on game days."

"I wouldn't talk either if I played like that."

Jamal and Lo laughed and slapped hands. Then Lo's face went taut. "Listen, J., can I talk to you about something?"

"Sure. Zeke is in the hall waiting for me. Let me just tell him that I'll be a second."

"Bring him in. What I got to say, he can hear, too."

Jamal returned with Zeke. They sat on the wooden panels of the lockers on both sides of Lo. The locker room had cleared out, save for a teenage attendant picking up towels and scrubbing moisturizer stains out of a swatch of carpet. "Meeting of the minds," Jamal said, trying break the tension. "It's like a black Yalta."

Lo didn't laugh. He inhaled deeply and exhaled. Jamal tried not to stare at Lo's trembling hands. "I should have gotten this off my chest a long time ago," Lo said in a voice barely audible.

He then gave chapter and verse on the fatal drag race. How he had stupidly let himself get talked into Drag Club. How Kwaanzii had hit the woman alongside the canyon—"right smack in the middle of the hood ornament." How his Hummer was banged up as he screeched to a stop. How he, Litanium, and Kwaanzii made a pact to conceal what'd happened. "Makes me just as guilty," he whispered.

How Litanium and Kwaanzii were clearly unbothered, but how the weight of guilt hung heavily around his neck. How he was sure that every traffic cop and security guard was about to arrest him. How he had barely slept since he saw the story in the *Los Angeles Times* about the Ohio woman. How he had never been in this sort of bone-deep funk, not even when his mother had passed a decade ago. How he felt like "that woman in the play we read in college, Lady Macbeth, whose guilt made her crazy." How, without detouring into specifics, it had been the second time he'd had a connection to a young woman who lost her life in a car crash.

Jamal had two prevailing thoughts. He empathized with Lo and knew it was unfair that such a genuinely good guy, who spent more time on the moral high road than anyone else on the team, was in a hell of a mess. But Jamal also knew that his job was about to get a lot more challenging. If Litanium's bust for marijuana possession was an exercise in crisis management, what do you call it when your team's three best players are involved in vehicular homicide?

When Lo finished his story, timbre had returned to his voice and an inchoate smile had started forming on the edge of his mouth. "You believe this?" he said.

Zeke, who had been staring blankly and shaking his head during the story, spoke up. "What are you going to do now, Lo?"

"I don't even know," Lo said. "But just unloading to you guys, you don't know how good it feels."

It turned out that Lo wasn't the only player in a confessional mood that night. In the executive offices three levels above the court, Shane Donnelly sought out Manny Burnett. As Donnelly knocked, the Lasers' general manager was typing his name into Google, a nightly indulgence triggered by M.L.B.'s hyperactive vanity glands. Reacting as though he been caught in flagrante delicto with a high-school cheerleader, Burnett wheeled around, knocking over his Diet Coke. Greeting the player, Burnett reached behind his back, trying to reboot his computer.

"Hey, Shane, you caught me by surprise."

"Sorry, M.L.B.," Donnelly said. "I just need some, um, financial advice."

"Sure," said M.L.B. "But I'm telling you up front. I'm not renegotiating your contract, Shane."

"I wish that were it," Donnelly said, dropping his head.

Donnelly went on to explain that he had met "an unbelievably hot chick" at the Pegasus party at the Getty Museum over All-Star Weekend. "She was Lithuanian. Or Romanian. One of those -anians. I told her my nickname was the Gynecologist because, well, you know. One thing leads to another and we find a bench in the Renaissance wing. That's where they have the modern shit, right?"

"Sounds right."

"Anyway, when we finished I told her, 'That was the best sex I've ever had without paying for it.' The only problem is that it looks like I'm paying for it now. Big-time."

"How's that?" Burnett wondered, still running mental inventory through his personal greatest hits, wondering if he had ever "laid cable," to use his favorite phrase, in an art museum.

"I get a call from some mobster-sounding guy with an accent, saying the girl got pregnant. And if I didn't come up with a hundred large, they were coming after my ass. These guys are serious. They said if I didn't pay, I wouldn't have to come up with any phony reasons to go on the injured reserve. They'd give me a *real* reason."

"Welcome to the NBF, Shane," Burnett said, chuckling. "That's the oldest sting in the book. When I was playing it was a Nigerian girl. They only hit me for fifty thousand. Inflation is a bitch."

"You pay it?" Donnelly asked, disappointed.

"Hell yeah, I paid it," said Burnett. "But I wrote it off as a cost of doing business. If your agent wants, he can call me and I'll tell him how to set it up as a deduction."

Before Donnelly could leave, Burnett's phone rang. Unsure whether to give the general manager some privacy or wait out the call, Donnelly awkwardly paced the room, pretending not to eavesdrop.

"Well, Watson will be happy," Burnett said when he got off the phone.

"How's that?" Donnelly said.

"That was Padgett. We're announcing tomorrow morning that we're waiving Mastah Mindya."

"Really," said Donnelly. "I'll kind of miss the little midget."

"Oh, he'll still be around," said Burnett. "He's buying a minority interest in the team."

CHAPTER 29

J illy took a deep breath and stepped in front of Lo as he left practice and headed for his car. "I'm sorry to spring this on you, Lo, but we have to talk," said Jilly. "I hope you have the time, but, if you don't, it has to be soon."

This is it, thought Lorenzen. *She found out about the accident. Maybe it's best this way.* Lo put on his best faux smile and directed Jilly to his green Escalade, the very vehicle that had aroused Jilly's suspicions.

"Let's grab something at WhattaBurger," said Lo. "Unless you think I shouldn't be eating when we talk."

"No, that's fine," said Jilly. For a reporter trying to keep a subject on task, seclusion is usually best. But Jilly felt she would have Lo's undivided attention on this matter no matter where they were. Plus, she was hungry and hadn't grazed at WhattaBurger lately. She climbed in for the tense five-minute drive. They acted like a couple driving together to the courthouse to finalize divorce papers. The hum of the air-conditioning and some Stevie Wonder were the only sounds.

"Is this *Talking Book?*" asked Jilly finally.

"*Innervisions,*" said Lo, pulling into a parking spot. "Put it out right after *Talking Book.* They're both solid."

He held the door open for Jilly, and they walked briskly to the counter, where Lo, both a celeb and a regular, was greeted by name. Two burgers, two fries, two Cokes. Jilly whipped out a twenty to pay and Lo didn't object. *Least I can do for taking a man down*, Jilly thought. *Least she could do for taking me down*, Lo thought. They found a seat in the far corner, applied catsup to the necessary surfaces, and Lo said, "Fire away."

Jilly pulled out her tape recorder and pad. "We can talk later, if you want, about why I—we—think this is a story," said Jilly. "But let me get right to it. Do you have a child in North Carolina you've never seen? A daughter?"

Lo was caught off-guard, but for a different reason than Jilly thought. Lo figured the first question would be: Were you present when Kwaanzii killed a woman with his car? Was this better or worse? And what business is it of the newspaper's if he had a kid or not?

"Obviously," said Lo, "you know the answer." He folded up his burger, his appetite abruptly gone.

"I talked to Mavis Robinson," said Jilly. "I went down there. So I assume you would confirm what she said. A young girl. Maya. She's ten. Lives with Mavis in Edgewood. Her mother died in a car accident. You send money from time to time and you gave Mavis a car, but you don't really acknowledge Maya as your own."

Lo looked down at his hands. Not a day went by when he didn't think about Maya, but he always—*always*—pushed her to the back of his thoughts. It wasn't easy at first but then, sadly, it got easier. Send some money, make sure she was doing okay, no fuss, no muss, no image problems back in Spencer or anywhere else. But wait . . . Jilly saw her?

"You went down there?" said Lo. "You were in Mavis's house?" Jilly nodded.

"Can you tell me . . . what does my daughter look . . ." Lo suddenly got up and went over to the condiment table, stuffing a few napkins in his pocket.

"Never mind," he said, sitting back down. "Don't tell me. It's not the way I should find out." He pulled out a napkin and idly wiped away the table in front of him. "She has a good home down there, Jilly," he said finally. "I wouldn't let it be any other way."

Jilly nodded. "I know that, Lo. Maybe you should just give me the story, from your perspective. I have the tape recorder going, so if you want something off the record, you ask me and we'll talk about it. But we're on the record."

Lo's account all but echoed the story Mavis Robinson had given ten days earlier: the mutual attraction between him and Tammy. The one-nighter. His shock when he found out she was pregnant. His desire that she get an abortion, and his fear that the arc of his career was going to flatten if he had a child to support, indeed, if anyone knew he had fathered a child.

"You know what that's like, Jilly, when you're sixteen years old and everybody's telling you you're the greatest?"

"No," said Jilly, "I don't know. But I'm listening."

Lo folded his hands in front of him. "You hear that every day from somebody. You're gonna be great. Your parents are counting on you and your school's counting on you and your state's counting on you, and, shit, one day you wake up and you can't count all the people who are counting on you. And you're a kid. You don't know whether you can pull this off, but all you know is that basketball—*basketball*—is how you're going to do it. Because whatever else don't make sense—like the damn governor of the state sending letters of congratulations, getting free haircuts from the town barber, people treating moms and dads like queens and kings just because their kids can play basketball—the basketball makes sense. I lose that, I become a father at sixteen and lose that special thing I had, man." Lo took a deep breath. "It just seemed like too much to lose."

Jilly had sympathy for his position, but she had to keep pressing.

"Later on, after you had made it, Lo, and Tammy had died in the accident, did you think about acknowledging Maya then? Think about supporting her on a full-time basis?"

Lo looked ashamed for the first time. "Course I did," he said. "But every year it seemed to get further away. Every year it seemed to become more—I don't know—unnecessary. She was doing okay. I was doing okay. Everybody was doing okay without it coming to light. The one night I spent with Tammy—damn—I mean, I didn't do that all that often. Sometimes, sure, like any man. But it was one damn time. After a while, I had trouble remembering what Tammy looked like."

Jilly looked at him and smiled wanly.

"I know," said Lo. "It sounds lame. Truth is, I was a jerk. I thought about my image. I thought about my endorsements. I thought about my dad and what he'd think of me. I thought about all that."

Jilly scribbled a few accompanying notes. What Lo was wearing, the time, the general ambience in WhattaBurger as the two-time Sprewell Citizenship Award winner came clean.

"So, Jilly, what do we do now?" asked Lo.

She snapped off the tape recorder. "I'm going to write the story," said Jilly. "I'll be sensitive to your position. I hear what you say about the pressures that were on you. I won't bury that stuff. But I am writing the story. What you do so far as getting in touch with Maya and Mavis, well, that's your decision. I'll call your cell if I think of anything else, and you do the same if you want to add something. And thanks, seriously, for sitting down with me. You can finish my burger if you want. It's a short walk back to the Bok. I can hoof it."

Lo stood up and followed Jilly to the door. "Jilly, you think after all this time a daughter would want to know who her father is?" asked Lo. "Even if he ignored her for ten years?"

Jilly smiled and patted his shoulder. "Well, I'm a daughter," she said, "and I'd want to know."

Jilly started back to the Bok, then turned around and re-entered WhattaBurger, where Lo was still sitting at the table picking at his cold burger. He looked up and Jilly saw that his eyes were red, and for a moment, just for a moment, she wished the last half hour had never happened.

"I think you'd want to know this, Lo," Jilly whispered. "She's beautiful."

JAMAL HAD A COUPLE of issues to discuss with Owen Padgett.

"He's not in a very good mood," whispered Rhea, Padgett's secretary. "I think the ax officially just fell on *Single Rich Dude.*"

"Damn, I kept forgetting to watch that thing," said Jamal.

"You and the rest of America," said Rhea. "Thus, it is no more."

Jamal liked Rhea, who was at least forty and seemed far too sharp to be answering Padgett's phone calls.

"I'll come back," said Jamal.

"No, no, he's just in there stewing," says Rhea. "He likes you. Anyway, I let you in, he blows off steam in your face, not mine." She turned official as she hit the buzzer, which Owen had wired to sound exactly like the horn at courtside. "Owen, Jamal's out here. Can I send him in?"

Padgett yanked the door open and practically pulled Jamal into the room.

"You heard the news?" Padgett said. "Just as the show was picking up heat, they pull the plug. These people at the networks have no imagination."

"You'll be back," said Jamal, having no idea what that meant. "I mean, with a show. You'll get another one."

Padgett smiled widely and clapped Jamal on the back. "Funny you should say that, Whiz, because I'm pitching them one right now. And they're going to love it. Absolute gold-plated lock."

"Well, I give you credit," said Jamal. "I don't know how you have time to work on all this stuff."

Padgett tapped a little fish food into his tropical tank. "The key is not getting discouraged, Whiz," said Padgett. "Staying positive. Always have new ideas. Have an alternative plan if something fails."

Jamal nodded. He didn't know whether he was supposed to say something. "Alternatives," he echoed and watched the scrimmage in the tank.

WITHIN TEN MINUTES, LORENZEN Mayne made the hardest phone call of his life. Jerry Mayne answered on the third ring. Lo rushed through, telling him first about Tammy Robinson, then, after a series of inhales and exhales, about Maya, and then about Tammy's death. Jerry Mayne listened without comment, silence hanging in the air like long jumpers. At one point the dead air lingered for so long, Lo checked the cell phone to make sure there was still a connection. When Jerry finally spoke, it was first about Tammy.

"I remember reading about the accident," said Jerry. "So sad for that family. She was your year, right?"

Lo said she was. Then he waited for the rest.

"You should've come to your mother and me," said Jerry finally. "You made an error in judgment when you were young and you compounded it as you got older. It's happened to everybody. So now you deal with it. You deal with the consequences. You don't run from them.

"You read history, you discover one constant thing," continued Jerry. "The coverup gets you in as much trouble—sometimes more than the actual crime. Happens all the time."

Lo's answer was a heavy sigh.

"You've been running and now you've gotta stop running. You know what your mother would tell you if she was here. What did she always say?"

Lo could hear his mother's voice. "She'd say, 'The truth will set you free,'" said Lo.

PADGETT HAD NEVER USED the phrase "reality show" in conjunction with the secret video project he had given Peterwicz. But Peterwicz had figured it out pretty quickly. What else could it be? Every Los Angeles dreamer with a Mac and a T-Mobile account at Starbucks was developing a reality show.

What he couldn't figure out in the beginning was how Padgett was going to procure consent from the unwitting cast. This wasn't a fifteen-minute *Candid Camera* or *Punk'd* goof; this was designed as a season-long excavation of their lives. When Peterwicz asked Padgett about it, albeit timidly, the owner flashed a jack-o'-lantern smile, reached into a file drawer, and plopped down a contract. "You ever read that employment contract you signed?" asked the owner. "Of course you didn't. It's twenty-five pages long. Everybody and their agent is too damn lazy to read it all."

"And it says?" Peterwicz asked, starting to thumb through the document.

"Clause twenty-three, subclause A, superscript little I," said Padgett. "It says that you—the signee—'grants permission for franchise to use any and all videotaped material, candid or otherwise, in any way that it sees fit.' Page seventeen, I believe."

And there it was.

In his secret video room, to which only he and the owner had a key, Peterwicz was logging mountains of feed that streamed from hidden cameras into his Avid, a computer with two monitors equipped with special editing software. He had been summoned to Padgett's office at nine that morning. The owner had spent a half hour cussing out the network execs who had canceled *Single Rich Dude* and the next half hour talking about the "all-star hour" he was about to present them with. That struck Peterwicz as a little like complaining about the food at a restaurant, then hiring the chef to cater your wedding. But Padgett moved in mysterious ways, and, as Peterwicz saw it, hitching your wagon to a billionaire was a smart play, especially if that also got you hitched to a producer credit, the coin of the realm in L.A.

Peterwicz had never seen the cameras—hadn't looked for them, in fact—but they were all over the place. At least one in the locker room, a couple that collected action on the court, one in the entryway to the Lasers' offices, several in various individual offices, Manny Burnett's and Jamal's, to name two. There was apparently no camera in Padgett's office. *Padgett might be a shame-deprived egomaniac*, Peterwicz thought, *but he wasn't stupid.*

In his typically meticulous manner, Peterwicz had researched the (lamentably) flourishing logistics of reality shows and knew that he was doing the work of a small battalion. On most reality shows, underpaid loggers sit in a room behind a row of Macs, input time code numbers, and transcribe dialogue for the producers. The drudgery goes on twenty-four/seven in twelve-hour shifts. Padgett hadn't applied that kind of pressure . . . until today. Now, after the cancellation, Peterwicz's instructions were to amp up the workload and present a full report in two weeks.

Owing to his *Single Rich Dude* commitment, and the ancillary work of running a losing basketball team, Padgett hadn't paid much attention to what Peterwicz was doing—which Peterwicz considered a stroke of good fortune. From what he had logged to date, Peterwicz couldn't imagine it was going to turn into televised fare that the public would watch. He had interminable hours of video of Manny changing clothes (sometimes two or three times a day) and Jamal working at his computer and handling media calls. It killed him to admit it but the kid was pretty sharp, handled himself in a casually cool way that made people want to be his friend.

Peterwicz felt guilty that he had rerun a couple of minutes of the secretaries in the outer office, Barbara Ann and Saleeka, crossing and uncrossing their legs. On the other hand, he felt secure that he had sped by, without a second thought, any footage of naked men in the locker room. What was Padgett hoping to do with that kind of stuff? He couldn't run it on network TV, even with clearances. And there was surprisingly little in the way of conflict. True, the cameras near the court had caught, albeit from long range, full video of the team brawl that had occurred after the All-Star break. But the public knew about that. Jilly had reported it in the *Times* and follow-up stories had appeared in every other newspaper.

But Peterwicz figured that he had better pick up the pace and start scanning everything; if the footage turned out to be a dud, Padgett would find a reason to blame him, and the all-important producer credit would be dead and buried. So he sat in front of his machine and went to work. He had watched ten minutes of tedium when he heard two voices and a door open into Jamal's office, activating the camera. The lights came on and, suddenly, there were Jamal and Jilly. The time code read 2/22, 9:43 *p.m.*

"All-Star Sunday," said Peterwicz to himself. "Game's over. Jamal's not working. Hmm, Jilly should be writing." He suddenly remembered that Jilly had thrown a mild fit about seating in the press room.

The audio went in and out and Peterwicz could only hear

snatches. *I give up*, Peterwicz heard Jamal say. *Cost you some down low down the road*, he heard Jilly say, whatever the hell that meant. But the video was as clear as the worry lines on John Watson's face. Peterwicz saw Jilly smile and walk toward Jamal, who was sitting at his desk—the same desk where Henry Shenk sat for all those years, never getting any show like this one—and untucked her shirt and pulled down the belt of her jeans. The camera caught all of it. Peterwicz watched Jamal look over her belt line and stare and then he heard Jamal say *rich girls disinherited* and figured she was showing him a tattoo.

Peterwicz saw Jilly hold the belt of her jeans down and he heard some more conversation, something about college boards and a guy named Dickworth, and then he saw them kiss, tentatively at first, and then he saw Jilly move into him, and then . . .

And then he turned off the machine.

Peterwicz realized that he was hemorraghing sweat. The room was cooled to no more than sixty degrees, but the heat stuck to his shirt and his palms felt greasy. At some level Peterwicz had felt squeamish about this whole project, almost hoping he wouldn't come across anything provocative, but he had always rationalized his way out of it. He was an employee and the boss had given an order. Now, it felt wrong. He logged the tape vaguely as "All-Star Sunday, postgame," and fast-forwarded. When he resumed editing, it was a couple of days later and Jamal was talking to someone from ESPN, apologizing because his press seat had been too far from the action.

Peterwicz had profound doubts about whether he could continue working on the project. But then he remembered the producer credit and—smothering his emotions—went back to work.

LORENZEN HAD TOLD JAMAL about his uncomfortable interview with Jilly, and her uncovering his "fatherhood issues." So when the media relations chief wandered out to press row that night and saw Jilly, he knew what was coming. "We have to talk," she said, and Jamal flopped down on the press table and spread his hands. Jilly looked around and took out her tablet.

"I need some kind of official response from Owen or Manny," she said. "To a few things. I can go right to them, but if you want to run with it, here it is."

"Go ahead," he said.

"You may want to write this down," said Jilly.

"I'm not brain dead from this job, Jilly," said Jamal. "Not yet anyway."

Jilly cleared her throat. "I'm writing a story—it's running tomorrow morning—about Lo fathering a child out of wedlock," said Jilly. "I just want to know if the Lasers have any comment."

"We don't comment on players' personal lives," said Jamal reflexively, momentarily stunned that she wasn't inquiring about the fatal auto accident.

"You *do* comment on players' personal lives," Jilly persisted. "I looked it up. Lo won two Sprewell Citizenship Awards, and Owen and Manny and Martha Ciccarelli and everybody else in the organization stumbled over themselves to say that he was the second coming of Christ. When B. D. Lake was recognized as "Fundamentalist Christian Athlete of the Month" you wrote a release about it. When Willie Wainwright was man of the year in Pittsburgh you wrote a release about it. When Clarence Wolff read his poetry to a grad class at UCLA you . . ."

"You made your point," Jamal snapped.

"By halftime, please, Jamal," said Jilly. "I'm pushing the button on the story then."

CHAPTER **30**

Paul Sprague considered himself a bulwark against the soulless polling data that he thought played too large a role in his newspaper's coverage decisions. In daily edit meetings he advocated the prioritizing of stories based on newsworthiness, not flimsy reader preferences. In particular, he believed that sports stories belonged in the sports section. But even he recognized that Jilly's story on Lorenzen Mayne deserved the prominent placement it received, smack on the front page, alongside dispatches from the Middle East and accounts of a terrorist attack at the hands of Indonesian Islamists.

The headline atop Jilly's story veered toward the sensational: "Lasers Forward, Citizenship Award Winner, Acknowledges Paternity of 10-year-old Girl." But Jilly's lengthy account was an exercise in restrained, professional journalism. Suppressing the urge to tinge it in purple, she stuck to the facts.

The story began with a classic page-one lead, cutting directly to the chase. "The public face of the Los Angeles Lasers, renowned for speaking with area youth groups on 'personal responsibility' is the father of a 10-year-old North Carolina girl whom he has never met." But Jilly, true to her word, did not bury Lo's side of the story.

She devoted ample space to discussing the unnatural pressures that beset a teenager who happens to be adept at tossing a ball into a hoop.

While there was little doubt that the story put Lo's reputation through the wood chipper, the Laser's franchise came out looking worse. Jilly made it clear that Mayne was the player they dispatched to ribbon-cutting ceremonies and hospital visits and meet-and-greet sessions with well-heeled ticket holders. Yet when the captain found himself in a predicament, little support from the franchise was in evidence. In the context of Lo's good deeds on behalf of the Lasers, the official team response—"We don't comment on players' personal lives," said Jamal Kelly, Lasers director of media relations—rang particularly cold.

Jilly had practically memorized her article, but she woke up three times during the night in anticipation of scooping up the copy of the paper on her doorstep. There's something about the tangible evidence, about seeing your work in print rather than on a computer screen, that imbues journalists with a real sense of satisfaction. It completes the cycle that began with reporting the story. When the paper finally arrived at six-forty-five, Jilly read every word, smiled contentedly for a second or two, then took stock of potential backlash.

She was certain that Lo's agent, Erick Silver, would make a pro forma irate call. His motivation would be to cover his ass, not to convey meaningful outrage. Jilly could almost hear him reporting back to Lo: "Yeah, I lit into that bitch. I got your back, bro!" Then there was Jamal, who would surely express displeasure with the way his quotation was used. She could live with that. No doubt Padgett would make a snide remark as well, though as the season progressed he had become much less a presence around the Bok.

But the only response that concerned her was Lo's. The story would change his life—Jilly knew that—and that was on him, not her. Still, in that curious set of circumstances that sometimes turn journalists into beneficent hangmen, she didn't want to see him suffer. When, shortly before noon, Lo's number flashed on Jilly's caller ID, she hesitated. Her first instinct was to start the call with a lighthearted remark—"Image-busters anonymous, may I help you?"—which was always her fallback in awkward situations. But she stopped herself, recognizing that someone exposed to millions as a derelict father was unlikely to be in jocular spirits.

"How ya doin', Lo?" she said.

"I've been better," he responded with a half laugh.

"Listen, Lo, I—"

"No, Jilly, you listen. Just want to say that I read your story. I can't say I appreciated it. I can't say I'm happy I have to deal with this publicly—"

"Look, Lo, you have to realize—"

"Quit interrupting me, girl," he said with mock exasperation. "Listen, a part of me is pissed off at you. I mean, you went into my closet, found a skeleton, and showed it off to everyone. But another part of me accepts that you have a job to do, you did it well, and you were fair. You let me give my side of the story and that's all I can really ask. I just wanted to let you know that."

"Lo, I really appreciate that," she said. "What can I say? You're a big man."

"Maybe not as big as you think."

"What's that mean?"

Lo cleared his throat. "Long as we're being all confessional, I have something else to tell you."

WHEN JILLY WAS A teenager still fine-tuning her identity, she smoked Camels. Aside from the affectation, she could impress her older classmates by showing them the profile of the man with an erect penis on the Camel logo. This subliminal image may have been a curious device for inspiring brand loyalty, but it worked. Ten years later, on the rare occasion she lit up, Camels were Jilly's smokes of choice. Before she left her cubicle at the *Times* to head for Sprague's office, she put two Camels in the back pocket of her flare bottoms.

Emboldened by her hot story—and thus by her rising stock around the *Times* newsroom—she didn't bother knocking when she reached Sprague's door. "I've come armed this time," Jilly said, crossing the doorway and helping herself to the seat across from Sprague's hopelessly cluttered desk. She casually handed him a cigarette and feigned a Mae West accent. "Here you go, big fella."

Sprague knew his circulatory system was about to redirect his blood flow. "As vices go, you could do worse," Sprague said, accepting one of the Camels. "What can I do for you today?"

"Just want to make you aware," Jilly said, oozing confidence. "I have a hot story about Lorenzen Mayne that belongs on A-one."

"No kidding," said Sprague. "Citizenship Award winner is a deadbeat dad. Mother of his daughter died in a car wreck in North Carolina. Blah, blah, blah. I feel like I recently read it in a fine urban daily."

Jilly let the monologue go on a while. "No, I have *another* hot story involving Lo Mayne."

She began by recounting the conversation she'd had with Lo in WhattaBurger, how he had not merely been a stand-up guy but seemed almost relieved that she had stumbled upon the story, since soon he would no longer have to harbor the secret. Then she told Sprague about the phone call she'd received from Lo that morning in response to the story.

"I was sure he was calling to tell me what a wretched human being I was, and how he would sooner quit playing basketball than give me another quote. As soon as his name came up on my caller

ID, I started rehearsing my speech. *I'm sorry this might cause you pain, but I practice journalism, not PR. My loyalty is to truth and newsworthiness, not to upholding your image.* I never have to go there, though, because he starts with another confession."

"About the kid in Carolina?" Sprague interrupted.

Jilly held up her hand, a conversational stop sign. "Lo says, 'You know how you were asking me once about my car?' I said, 'Yeah.' He tells me I was onto something that day. According to Lo, late one night, early in the season, Lo, Litanium Johnson, and Kwaanzii Parker take part in something the Lasers players call Drag Club, where these guys gun their cars around blind curves in the canyon. Their favorite spot is Canyon Road, out there where that club, The Vines, is located."

"So this is leading back to the tip from my pain-in-the-ass brother-in-law, right?"

"Right," said Jilly. "But it's Parker, not Lo, who hits a woman, killing her on impact. Body sails into a canyon . . ."

"It's real isolated up there," said Sprague. "Every three years or so some dog sniffs up a body on that Canyon Road. It's like there's a whole bunch of dead people just waiting to be found by dogs."

". . . so Lo screeches to a halt, dinging his Hummer on the bumper of Kwaanzii's Jaguar. Lo grabs his phone to call the police, but the other two talk him out of it. Too much is at stake. Image, endorsements, contracts, the Lasers' season. The three players decide that they won't say anything—they got each others' backs— and leave the scene."

Jilly took a long drag on her Camel, aware that she was engaging every one of Sprague's journalistic synapses.

"Season goes on. No one says anything. They all get their cars fixed. For Litanium and Kwaanzii, it's business as usual. But Lo starts playing the worst basketball of his career and no one knows why. He can't sleep. He can't concentrate. He is terminally unhappy. The guilt is starting to overwhelm him. He can't even drive his fixed car, has to get a new one. He hates that he's covering for Kwaanzii and Litanium, who are teammates but people he would otherwise have nothing to do with. He hates that he is harboring another lie. So he comes clean. To me."

Sprague sat silent, digesting the story and determining how it would play out journalistically. "This was all on the record?"

"I impressed upon him the rules of engagement," Jilly said.

"What if he denies something?" Sprague asked.

Jilly rifled through her purse and pulled out a black contraption that enabled her to record phone conversations.

"You have it all on tape," Sprague said.

"Cost nine-ninety-nine at Radio Shack," said Jilly. "Best investment a journalist could make."

"You're going to go to Litanium and Kwaanzii for their account?"

"Already put in my interview request with Jamal Kelly," Jilly retorted.

"What did you tell Kelly?"

"I needed to interview them urgently. Independently as in 'not together.' He asked why. I told him it was a real man-bites-dog story, unlike the dog-bites-man story he didn't give me before with Litanium's pot bust. I have the feeling he knows what it's about. He's close to Lo."

"What about the LAPD?" Sprague said. "You have to go to them."

"Verona at the city desk gave me a contact in public affairs. We have an epic game of phone tag going, but I'm supposed to call him tomorrow night."

Satisfied with Jilly's answers, Sprague decided that his feelings about Jilly were no longer based on a raw (albeit hopeless) sexual attraction, but, rather, unalloyed admiration for her journalistic skills. She was a tenacious reporter with unfailing instincts, a first-rate bullshit barometer, and a knack for getting people to feel comfortable speaking to her.

"So let me get this straight," Sprague said, shifting in his chair. "The three best players on the Lasers were involved in a deadly drag race. They covered up the story, but now one is ready to come clean, even if it means ratting out the other two. There's apparently no body and so far no arrests."

"In a nutshell," Jilly said.

"Okay," Sprague said, clapping his hands. "I think we can probably move some things around and find room to get that into at least a regional edition. Now go write it up and win us a prize."

"I got some work before I can start writing, Paul," said Jilly.

Sprague got up and bowed gallantly. As he did so, he thought that he had never done such a thing in his life. "So why are you still standing here?"

CHAPTER 31

April 9
Los Angeles Lasers Record: 37-42

As a lifeless morning practice was breaking up—"At this point, practice is about as pointless as tits on a goat," John Watson had said on more than one occasion—Jamal saw Jilly lurking by the tunnel that leads to the locker room. Lorenzen had told him that he'd confessed everything to Jilly, so he knew exactly what she wanted to talk to Litanium and Kwaanzii about when her interview request came in.

"Litanium and Kwaanzii aren't going to talk to you, Jilly," Jamal said.

"Is that your decision or theirs?" she said.

"It's the team's decision," he said.

"Mind if I ask them myself?" said Jilly.

Jamal tried his hard face, then his soft face, then his I-don't-know face. "I can tell you right now what their answer will be," he said.

"I'll wait for them here," said Jilly.

A few minutes later Jamal watched as Jilly cornered Litanium and Kwaanzii. To his dismay, the conversation seemed to be going pretty well. Jilly nodded and came over.

"I'm seeing them in a half hour or so, after they shower," she said. "Down by the family room. I asked to talk to them separately. Just thought you should know."

Jamal nodded. "When they say a half hour, it's usually more like an hour or ninety minutes," he said.

"Like I don't know that," she said, giving his cheek a little pat. It was the first time anything friendly had passed between them since the All-Star Game.

OWEN PADGETT DIDN'T FIGURE he *should* have to wait, but, then, Warren Colson, *ABC's* head of programming, made everybody wait. If George W. Bush and Fidel Castro walked in with a proposal for a show in which they would Indian wrestle to the death wearing nothing but jock straps and dashikis, one of Colson's army of attractive secretaries would tell them to take a seat and offer them Pellegrino. On the flip side, this was the only waiting room that offered sushi. Padgett nibbled on Toro and cucumber as he waited for an audience with one of the most powerful men in television.

"Nomari, did you see *Single Rich Dude?*" Padgett asked the sylphlike young lady who had brought him his water and sushi tray.

"I saw an episode or two, Mr. Padgett," said the woman, rather icily, Padgett thought.

"Did you enjoy them? The shows you saw?"

Nomari smiled ambivalently. "Well, Mr. Padgett, one of my girlfriends was on there? Allison? She was the dental hygienist with the long blond hair? Very pretty?"

"There were a lot of pretty blondes with long hair," said Padgett. "And, as I recall, more than one dental hygienist."

"Well, she was one of the early ones? Maybe the second week? Anyway, you didn't treat her very well."

Padgett knew she wasn't kidding because she didn't phrase that last statement as a question.

"Somebody had to get eliminated every week, Nomari," said Padgett. "The show was set up that way. Everybody couldn't win."

"But, like, your comments? You told her that when she smiled she looked like a chipmunk? I mean, that isn't, you know, nice? Especially to say it to someone, who's, like, in the dental industry?"

Padgett considered that. "In retrospect, maybe you're right. The show I'm pitching today is going to be different. Much broader appeal. But that is so outstanding, you standing up for your friend like that. I was wondering, maybe, if you'd like to get a drink or an early dinner or something when I'm through with Warren?"

Nomuri smiled. "Mr. Padgett?" she said. "There is, like, so no chance on that."

Padgett was saved further humiliation by the appearance of Kaitlin, the last of Warren Colson's gatekeepers. "Mr. Colson will see you now, Mr. Padgett," she said, and Padgett, already one rejection into the day, went in.

JILLY HAD ASKED TO talk to Kwaanzii first and Litanium second. She considered Litanium the more reliable of the two, which was akin, she acknowledged, to ranking the python and the cobra according to their ability to ride a bicycle. Jilly's spirits sank when she saw Jamal walking alongside Kwaanzii.

"Do you mind if I stay?" Jamal asked. "It might be better to have two sets of ears on this thing."

Jilly smiled indulgently. "We have two sets, Jamal," she said. "Mine and Kwaanzii's. Three sets, if you include his headphones."

"You know what I mean," said Jamal.

"I arranged the interview myself, so that clearly makes it one-on-one," said Jilly. "Unless he asks for something off the record or on background it will be on tape. I'm probably going to have to get back to you and we'll talk. Okay?"

Before Jamal could answer, Kwaanzii took off his headphones. "This about rookie of the year?" he said. "Because my agent, he had some shit prepared on it, like a statement."

"It's not about rookie of the year, Kwaanzii," said Jilly.

Jamal shuffled awkwardly, suddenly the third wheel. "I'll be out in the hall if you need me," he said.

Jilly motioned Kwaanzii to sit down. She removed her tape recorder, and Kwaanzii took his headphones all the way off, set them off to the side, an extraordinary gesture of cooperation. He had never appeared in any school thespian productions—hoops and honeys had occupied most of the young man's time—but Kwaanzii was playing his part to perfection. He and Tribal Cat had realized this moment would be upon them at some point and they had been through a couple of rehearsals. They didn't know whether the questions would come from the police, the NBF, a lawyer, or some other form of the Man, which turned out to be the Woman.

"No use fooling around," said Jilly. "I'm working on a story about the night that you, Litanium, and Lorenzen were road racing. And a woman was hit and killed."

Kwaanzii nodded his head several times. "Terrible thing," he said. "Terrible thing what happened. We should've 'fessed up about it."

Jilly was taken aback by such a quick confession. "Could you just take me through the events?" she said. "All I have is what Lo told me."

He withdrew a missile of Red Bull from his backpack and took a big swig.

"Once in a while we raced cars," began Kwaanzii. "It started as kind of an after-practice thing, but then we'd do it at night, too.

After this one game early in the season—I don't remember the exact date 'cept I remember Watson didn't put me in the game—"

"It was December second," interrupted Jilly. "You beat Seattle."

"Yeah, that was probably it. So we went out to race, me, Cat, and Lo. Me and Cat was a little surprised 'cause Lo didn't really like it much, you know, and he was kind of a whack driver. Not really whack, but, you know, not, like, real secure at high speeds, like me and Cat were. So we took off—we gave Lo a little start 'cause he was driving that Hummer, which really ain't a racing car—and he was ahead at first, and then, just as me and Cat were pulling even, we heard this noise and then we saw—well, I don't know what Cat saw but what I saw—was a body go flying. A woman. I can't remember how clearly I saw the whole thing, but I knew right away it was a woman. She was young, kind of skinny, and had these little studs in her nose. The car lights lit her real good."

Jilly let that sink in. She was impressed by Kwaanzii's comportment. After wrapping up a clinical account of the accident, he smacked his hands together. "That's about the long and short of it, Jilly," he said breezily, as if tidily summing up a twenty-five-point game against Atlanta.

"So, this happens and everybody stops and pulls over, is that right?" asked Jilly.

"Right away," said Kwaanzii.

"So did you think about going down after her?"

"Course we did," said Kwaanzii. "I got a pair of binoculars outta my car—I carry them around to, you know, check up on shit—and we seen that she was dead. That ain't no excuse for us not calling the cops. But she was dead. She was beyond help."

"Did you guys even consider calling the police?"

Kwaanzii looked off into space, as if in deep contemplation.

"As I recall it, Litanium said maybe we oughtta, but Lo didn't want to," said Kwaanzii. "Being the rookie, you know, with the veterans and all, I didn't know what to do. We talked it out maybe five minutes, but Lo won us over about not going to the police. Course he had the most to lose."

Jilly looked quizzically at the rookie. "Why did Lo have the most to lose?"

Kwaanzii spread his hands. "Well, he hit the woman. I mean, me and Cat knew we was in some shit because of the no-reporting-it thing, but, you know, it was on him."

Jilly waved her hands in the air. "Are you saying Lorenzen hit the woman?"

She heard a sound behind her and Litanium, after a knuckle-knock, entered and jumped right in.

"That's what he's saying," said Litanium. "Why? What did Lo say?"

Jilly pulled out her notebook where she had the transcriptions of the cell phone call from Lorenzen. "Here's what Lo said: He was in the inside lane, nearest the ravine, but he said you, Kwaanzii, hit her from the middle lane, and he saw her go flying past his bumper down the hill. Then he slammed on the brakes and Kwaanzii slammed on the brakes and both cars fishtailed and he hit your car in the back." She skipped ahead and added: "Then he said he was the one wanted to call the police."

Litanium and Kwaanzii looked at each other and collectively shook their heads.

"Ain't that some shit, Kwaanz?" said Litanium. "See, we knew this might happen. We shoulda just called the damn police right then and there. Taken our punishment. But what Lo's saying just ain't right."

Jilly didn't know what to ask next. "Are you saying Lo's lying?"

"He told us he was so guilty he couldn't even drive his car no more," said Kwaanzii. "He got a new Escalade and retired the

Hummer. Don't that sound like a guilty man to you? I got my shit fixed, the back end where I caught the fishtail. And I'm still driving it."

"And he admitted he was on the lane near that hill, right?" said Litanium. "I mean, if you're out walking late at night, damn fool that you might be, you ain't walking in the middle of the road."

Jilly considered that. "If you're out walking on that road," said Jilly, "I'm not sure you're thinking straight. So that's not really—"

"Look, Jilly, you know, this could've happened to anybody," interrupted Litanium. "I mean, we shouldn't have been goin' that fast. But Lo, he's got control issues with that big car. Me and Kwaanz are more, what you call it, dexterial with our cars."

Jilly drummed on the table. "Look, fellas, no offense at this, okay? But, Lo has always been, you know, kind of a straight shooter. Won those Sprewell Citizenship Awards. The captain. Your leader, right? And . . ."

"And what, Jilly?" said Litanium. "We're criminals is what you're saying?"

Jilly shrugged. "Well, this doesn't prove one thing or another, Litanium, but you did have that pot bust," she said. "I mean, I write it up as a dog bite and—"

"And a few damn days ago in the paper, you wrote about what a big liar he is," snapped Litanium. "Yeah, I was carting some weed. So what? Lo's a damn father and didn't tell no one. What's that add up to?"

Jilly switched off the tape recorder, gathered up her notebook, and stuffed them in her giant-sized purse. "Conundrum," she said. "It adds up to a conundrum."

CHAPTER **32**

Jilly commandeered a table in the back of one of the endless string of coffee bars that dot Santa Monica Boulevard. Her legs casually crossed, a laptop splayed on the Formica in front of her, and Bose headphones on her ears, she looked like a typical citizen of Frappuccino Nation firing off e-mail while escaping into her music during a coffee break, in her case an iced-tea break.

Jilly was sufficiently self-aware to know that she was playing favorites and hoped to hell Lo was the one telling the truth; she was also sufficiently self-aware to know that Lo was in serious trouble. Unlike Kwaanzii, he had no one who could corroborate his version of the events. There was his twitchy trip to the South Central chop shop and his abrupt replacement of his beloved Hummer with an Escalade. And, thanks to her, Lo's credibility was far from unimpeachable now that the revelations about his unacknowledged child had come to light.

After transcribing her exchanges with the three players, Jilly braved the late-afternoon traffic and drove to Canyon Road. She went, in part, to describe where the accident took place. But, not unlike the Oregon kids in *Stand by Me*, she also had a perverse hope that she would find the body. When she pulled over to the shoulder at the approximate spot of the accident, she immediately understood why a body had yet to be recovered. Only a small guardrail stood between the asphalt ribbon of road and a gaping maw of a ravine. Staring over the precipice, Jilly looked down and couldn't help thinking that, from the standpoint of the victim, there could scarcely be a worse place for a hit-and-run. If the impact didn't kill the woman, falling off the side of the cliff sure did. Feeling physically ill, Jilly got back in her car, took a few mental snapshots, and returned home.

Journalism 101 dictated that she talk to the police before she could even give thought to writing the story. Thinking of the missing woman's family, Jilly also felt a moral obligation to involve law enforcement. A metro editor had given her the name of an LAPD spokesman with a reputation of being "very good to the *Times*." When Jilly called and asked if he had any information he could share about a possible unsolved hit-and-run death, the spokesman was of little assistance. "We do not discuss ongoing investigations."

"What if I have information that might help the ongoing investigation progress?" Jilly asked.

"Let me take your name and number then."

Within five minutes, Sergeant Dennis Archibald called Jilly. "I knew your name right away," he said. "You cover the Lasers, don't you? Crappy season they're having, but you always manage to make the games sound interesting."

"Trust me, they're not. Interesting, that is. They are, however, very crappy."

"And you're calling about a hit-and-run? Maybe you have some information that can help us?"

"Maybe."

"I'm all ears."

"I'm going to need some promises from you first."

"We don't make promises," he said. "We're the police department." Jilly waited and he finally relented, "Okay, let me hear it."

"When you have news to share, you're going to give me an exclusive. You're going to call me up, make your announcement, and call no one else until the following day's *Los Angeles Times* is on every newsstand and every doorstep from Laguna Nigel to Santa Barbara. This is my story and I can't be getting scooped."

"Put it this way," Archibald said. "We can make a good-faith effort."

Jilly took a deep breath and recounted what she knew about the night of December second and the circumstances that followed. On the other end of the line, Archibald scribbled furiously. "*Canyon Road . . . Dec.2 . . . race . . . Hummer . . . Jaguar . . . woman hurtled into ravine . . . players drove off . . . conflicting accounts . . . Lorenzen Mayne knows location of body . . . chop shop in South Central . . .*"

She ended with: "And so they left her there. Like so much roadkill. Even Lo. And Lo's a good guy." Her voice caught.

Archibald gave her some time. "Look," he said, finally, "sometimes people who aren't all bad get caught up in things. I see it all the time. I'll call you as soon as I have something to share. Thanks for the information."

JILLY'S CONCERN OVER LO'S fate intensified when she called Tony Silver the next night for a comment. Including Lorenzen Mayne and Kwaanzii Parker, Silver's stable of NBF clients numbered sixteen—up from eleven since the beginning of the season, thanks to some deft, if ethically bankrupt, poaching. When Jilly reached Silver he was sitting courtside at a game in Dallas, watching Indianapolis forward Dontell Abrams, whom Silver had lured largely by promising the player future romantic liaisons with models also represented by his firm.

"Hey, Jilly F., good to hear that sultry voice of yours, sister," said Silver. "But can I hit you back at halftime? My boy Dontell A. is lighting it up in the Big D!"

"Don't get so excited: They play no D in the Big D," Jilly replied. "Besides, when you hear why I'm calling, I think you'll agree this is more important."

"Shoot, Jilly F. Just bear with me a sec. I'm heading toward the tunnel and this BlackBerry phone gets a bad signal here."

When the background noise from the game had receded, and Silver had assured Jilly that he had "big bars" on his phone, she began rehashing her interview with Lorenzen Mayne. Before she could ask Silver if he wanted to comment on behalf of his client, he cut her off.

"You sure like to stir the pot, don't you?"

"We're not talking about a trade rumor here," Jilly said. "We're talking about a drag race that left a woman dead."

"Well, all I'm going to say is that Kwaanzii Parker did not hit that woman."

"Who said anything about Kwaanzii Parker?" she asked.

"I'm just telling you. Listen closely: Kwaanzii. Parker. Did. Not. Hit. That. Woman."

"I'm asking you about Lorenzen Mayne."

"Next question."

"Is that a 'no comment'?"

"Look, off the record, Lo called me at home close to midnight that night real upset. That's all I know."

"Did you talk about the accident?"

"The conversation didn't get that far."

"You want to add anything else?"

"Nope," he hissed. "Hey, we still off the record?"

"If we have to be."

"You can't take down Kwaanzii. Listen, that kid is the Truth."

"I'm more interested in whether he's *telling* the truth."

"You and I," Silver said, "have different objectives."

Jilly thanked him and hung up. She was trying to digest the impact of her call to Silver—obviously he had been briefed by Kwaanzii—when her cell phone began bleating.

"Jilly, it's Sergeant Archibald. You might want to grab a pen and take this down."

CHAPTER **33**

LASER STARS HELD IN ROAD DEATH

Lorenzen Mayne Charged as Driver; He Points Finger at Rookie Phenom

BY JILLY FORRESTER,
Times STAFF WRITER

Three members of the Los Angeles Lasers, including both the player often considered the face of the franchise and their rookie-of-the-year candidate, were arrested last night in the aftermath of an auto accident three months ago that killed Addie Denkins, 18, a Columbus, Ohio, native whose body was recovered yesterday in a desolate ravine off Canyon Road.

The most serious charge—vehicular manslaughter, a crime that can carry a sentence of up to 25 years in prison—was leveled against team captain and four-time All-Star Lorenzen Mayne, who police say was driving the car that killed Addie Denkins around midnight on Dec. 2. The accident, which happened during a drag race that involved Mayne, rookie Kwaanzii Parker, 18, and seven-year NBF veteran Litanium "Tribal Cat" Johnson, 26, occurred on Canyon Road, a desolate stretch of highway located about one mile east of the PCH. All three players confirmed to the *Times* that the accident occurred, though their accounts of which player's car struck Denkins are at odds. The *Times* has learned that, prior to Denkins's death on Dec. 2, various Lasers players used the road for high-speed car races.

Los Angeles County District Attorney Terrence Bauer said that it is impossible to determine if drugs or alcohol were a factor since too much time had passed to administer toxicology tests to the players. However, the fatal race took place after a team party at The Vines, a Laser hangout. Mayne told police he had "five or six beers." Johnson said that he had "maybe one cocktail" and Parker said he was not drinking "because I ain't even old enough."

A grand jury convened last week found sufficient evidence to charge Mayne, Bauer said. The DA also said that his office is satisfied that Mayne was the driver, which contradicts what Mayne had told the *Times* last week. In an interview that took place before the charges were filed, Mayne said that it was Parker's car that hit Denkins. Under advice of counsel, Mayne declined comment after Bauer filed the charges, which included numerous other violations under the California Vehicle Code, including leaving the scene of an accident, reckless endangerment, and conspiracy. Collectively, Mayne is facing a possible 40 years in prison.

Parker, the odds-on favorite to win the NBF's Aveeno Baby Lotion Rookie of the Year Award, and Johnson, the team's starting point guard, face many of the same charges as Mayne but not the most serious, the vehicular manslaughter. In such cases, the DA has the discretion to charge the nondrivers with manslaughter, but Bauer said that there was not "equitable culpability" among the three players. Bauer said that he depended upon information from

Parker and Johnson to piece together the facts and that their stories "corroborated down to the last detail."

All three men were indicted last night. After posting bail—$500,000 for Mayne and $250,000 for Parker and Johnson—the three were immediately placed on suspension by the Lasers. According to the terms of the NBF's Collective Bargaining Agreement, the players will be paid during their suspensions, though they might have to surrender monies later if found guilty.

Lasers spokesman Jamal Kelly said that the team will have no comment "until the appropriate time." He did not say when that time might be. A spokesman for NBF Commissioner Daniel Drang said the league will take no additional action "until this plays out in a court of law. We don't even have all the facts yet." Drang, who has spoken with both Lasers owner Owen Padgett and general manager Manny Burnett, said he is "disheartened" by the events. "Lorenzen Mayne has been one of the most upstanding citizens of our league for several years," said Drang in a statement faxed to the *Times,* "but, if he is guilty, he must face the full consequences of the law."

Laser officials must be doubly disheartened since, in a season of on-the-court disappointment—the Lasers are 37-42 and have been mathematically eliminated from playoff contention—there has been no shortage of off-court drama. A recent *Times* story revealed that Mayne, who has twice been honored by the NBF with the Latrell Sprewell Citizenship Award, has never seen a 10-year-old daughter he fathered out of wedlock in North Carolina. Days before that, the *Times* discovered that Johnson had been caught, by a drug-sniffing dog who bit him, with marijuana at LAX during a January road trip. The Lasers' Kelly, with the apparent blessing of Padgett and Burnett, told reporters that the dog bite had occurred in Johnson's home. Johnson was not charged in the incident but is required to take spot drug tests, one of which he has

missed. Parker, too, has had his problems. His charitable foundation was found to be uninsured and employing three of his relatives at six-figure salaries. Those revelations came to light after a
participant suffered a detached retina at a paintball event.

In early March, as the season began to disintegrate and the
locker room became increasingly fractious, a routine practice
erupted into fisticuffs. Team members later confirmed that the
fight was provoked by a disagreement between Mayne and Johnson. Power forward Shane Donnelly hurt his right triceps muscle
in the fight.

It's unclear whether the origin of the dustup bore any relation
to the night of Dec. 2. What is clear is that the accident has turned
into a he-said-they-said conflict that has ripped apart the team.
Before going silent at the advice of counsel—Mayne hired as his
attorney Sherwin Zucker, well-known as a leather-lunged Laser
fan—the Lasers' captain had fingered Parker as the one driving the
car and said that he, Mayne, was the one who wanted to call police.
"A couple of different times I tried to get them, to get all of us, to
come clean," Mayne told the *Times*. "But they always made the
vague threat that they would say I was the driver."

Johnson and Parker tell a different story, one that the DA finds
more credible. Sources say that the following factors figured in the
decision to come down harder on Mayne.

—Parker and Johnson gave corroborating accounts of the
events from the night in question.

—A cell phone belonging to Mayne, traced through the SIM
card, was found near Denkin's body, about 50 feet down the side of
a steep hill. According to police, Johnson said that he was going to
use it to call police but Mayne ripped it out of his hands and threw
it down the ravine. Mayne denies that.

—Wallace Brubaker, 30, who works at an unregistered auto
body shop in South Central, told investigators that Mayne was

wearing a disguise when he brought in a gunmetal Hummer to be repaired. Brubaker wasn't sure about the date but said it was in early December. The damage was to the right front, which police said was consistent with a collision with a body.

—Under questioning by police, Erick Silver, the agent who represents both Mayne and Parker, said that on the night of the accident he received a "troubling phone call" from "an obviously agitated Lo" at about 1:00 a.m. Silver told police that Mayne said: "I'm in some trouble." Silver said that he did not get a phone call from Parker.

—The recent revelations about Mayne's paternity cast considerable doubt upon his credibility. "Obviously, the DA can't use that as a reason," said one source, "particularly since Johnson just got busted for pot. But trust me on this: It factored in."

By all accounts, including his own, Mayne was not an avid participant in what Johnson called "Drag Club." Both Johnson and Parker said they were nervous about Mayne joining them on that evening because they didn't trust his driving. The three agree on the general details of the accident up until the point of the collision.

Denkins's parents, Elwood and Lucille Denkins of Columbus, said their daughter was bipolar. She was a single mother, but she had left her child, an 11-month-old boy named Sunstrom, with a friend that evening and disappeared. "Sunny," as Denkins called him, is now living with his grandparents.

"My daughter was a warm and loving child, and it's a tragedy all around," said Elwood Denkins. "No, she shouldn't have been on that road. But those men were engaged in criminal behavior, and now she's dead. Someone should pay."

CHAPTER 34

Special exceptions notwithstanding—calls from Michael Jordan or internationally known swimsuit models—it is a point of honor among athletes that they never answer their phones. Reaching a member of the jockocracy therefore requires repeated telephonic beseeching. So Jamal had worked out a signal with Lorenzen if he really needed to talk to him. He would ring Lo's phone once, hang up, then call back and let it ring twice. Lo would then return the call.

Which is what Jamal did on the dispiriting morning that Jilly Forrester's blockbuster story went out to the 1.1 million subscribers of the *Los Angeles Times* as well as to millions of others through syndication and the Internet. It was also the major item on the infernal "crawl," the condensed news items that scroll nonstop along the bottom of cable news channels. Between phone calls, Jamal was watching a Fox News pundit declare the NBF "a nest of reprobates" when Lo called back.

"How you doing?" asked Jamal.

Lo let out a rueful laugh. "I'm a murderer, a deadbeat dad, and I'm shooting less than forty percent from the field," said Lo. "Other than that I'm doing awesome."

"Don't say that kind of shit, Lo," said Jamal. "You're not up for murder, and there are a lot of people around here who believe you."

Another rueful laugh. "Doesn't much matter what they believe now, does it?"

Jamal waited for a moment. "Listen, the reason I'm bugging you, I just want to check on how you feel about doing interviews," said Jamal. "Obviously, I got every damn TV network here and overseas, every damn newspaper, every damn radio show, every damn everything. You wanna think about doing just one of them and getting it over with? Tell the story once. Or maybe hold a press conference, read a statement, take no questions? That's what Carpaccio Cook did when he had his trouble with that female bell-hop in Utah. And he came out smelling sweeter than baby's breath."

"Hey, Jamal, I tried to tell the story to Jilly once and where the hell did it get me? You listening to this shit on TV? And those ass-wipes on radio? They are killing me. Just killing my ass."

"Turn that stuff off," said Jamal. "Don't listen to it."

"They could drop a bomb on Chicago and this would still be the big story," said Lo.

"Listen, maybe you talk to Trocki and Johnson," suggested Jamal, naming the hosts of a popular ESPN show. "Do five min-utes, say what you want, get it the hell over with."

"What do you think I should do?" Lo asked. Six months ago Jamal was dispensing advice on where to find the cheapest Chinese takeout in New Haven; now a superstar athlete—and the world's most infamous athlete on this day—was asking him for counsel.

"I think you should only do what makes you comfortable, Lo," answered Jamal.

Jamal could hear him breathing. "Then I'm just gonna sit this one out for a while," said Lo. "I've no comment under the advice of my lawyer. Tell them something like that. I'll think about it."

"All right," said Jamal, "you be strong now." But he wondered how that was possible.

JAMES FIORENTELLI WAS A bust in every sport he tried back in Worcester, Mass. Too slow for football, too fat for basketball, too deprived of hand-eye for baseball. In his junior year, he climbed into a wolverine costume and became Worcester High's overly ebullient mascot, and that finally got him on the playing fields. The costume itched like hell and smelled like a storm drain, and a group of basketball jocks peed on him from the top row of the bleachers at the Thanksgiving Day game. But, dammit, he was the Worcester Wolverine!

Fiorentelli parlayed a degree in communications from the University of Connecticut and an encyclopedic knowledge of sports into sports-talk jobs at a passel of radio stations until he reached nirvana—afternoon talk at KJOK in Los Angeles. Fiorentelli had just gotten back from his twentieth high-school reunion, in fact, where he approached a couple of the Thanksgiving Day urinaters and showed them photos of him posing with players from the Dodgers, Lasers, and Kings. "They call me Line Judge Jimmy out there and everybody knows me," he said. Without the benefit of a seven-second delay, he added: "So fuck you."

Line Judge was so relentlessly positive in his first couple of years on the air that the *Times* media critic called him "The Afternoon Suckophant." He eventually discovered, though, that a calculated negativity best fed the sports-talk beast. There was a certain predictability to it all. Slander the underachieving superstars, particularly if they're African-American. Venerate the plucky underachievers, the invariably white gritty second baseman up from Double-A, the goonish defenseman from Moose Jaw. Be kind to those who appear on your show and know your name.

Lo Mayne had always been a favorite, not least because he unfailingly did interviews when requested. But Line Judge Jimmy didn't have to stick his pudgy finger in the air to feel the winds of change. Jilly's first story about Lo's child had triggered a wave of anti-Lo calls, and now this latest one unleashed a tsunami. Line Judge Jimmy had almost fallen off the commode with joy when he read the long page-one story that morning.

"I've got a photo of me and Lo, taken a couple years ago, hanging RIGHT ABOVE MY HEAD IN THIS STUDIO!" Line Judge Jimmy hollered to his listeners.

"You should rip that sucker down," said the caller, Ralph from Bakersfield.

"You know what, Ralph from Bakersfield? That's a great idea. Listen everybody. LISTEN UP. Make sure they can hear me, Barney—I'm talking to the control room now—I'm getting up, I'm reaching for the picture, and LISTEN UP EVERYBODY . . ." Line Judge Jimmy ripped down the photo of him and Lo, taken at a banquet two years ago when Mayne received KJOK's Jock of the Year.

The next caller was a woman, a rarity. Sharon from West Hollywood felt that the blame should fall upon the *Times* reporter, "that woman named Jill or whatever in Sam Hill her name is." Sharon was just getting going on Jilly—"And why in the name of heaven is a girl covering a bunch of men who get naked in the locker room . . ."—when Line Judge cut her off to take another call.

"Speaking of that broad who covers the team," said Roger from Compton, "I think I'm going to take up pro basketball just so I can get covered by her. I don't care what she writes, she can—"

"Hey, out there, everybody, she was just doing her job," said Line Judge. "I know Jilly a little. She does the same thing I do—she tells it like it is. That's all we got in this gig, our credibility."

IN THE SEA OF public opinion, Lorenzen Mayne was chum. Pro basketball is not much of a hot-stove sport—UCLA's spring football game is likely to generate more interest than the Lasers out of season—but everybody loves a story about a tragic fall from grace. And Lorenzen Mayne was about as fallen as fallen gets.

Evan Peterwicz, working in his isolation chamber like a Pegasus sweatshop shoe stitcher in Southeast Asia, smoothed out that morning's copy of the *Los Angeles Times*, perused Jilly's story, and once again praised himself for his superb sense of timing. Upstairs in the corporate offices, poor Jamal Kelly, still damp behind the lobes in the PR game, was fielding calls from all over the known universe, while he, Peterwicz, sat in his air-conditioned video fortress, munching on ham salad and carrot sticks. Still, he thought, it might be nice to be in on the action. Peterwicz had breezed through the corporate floor an hour ago while Jamal was, at once, screaming at a Japanese TV crew that had barged into his office and getting lambasted by Manny Burnett. "You gotta get control of the circus, Whiz," Burnett said. "You gotta ringmaster this shit."

Peterwicz had his own pressures. Conventional wisdom suggested that Padgett would be concerned with other matters on this dark day in Laser Land, but, no, he had called Peterwicz that morning and told him to redouble his video efforts. The owner didn't exactly sound gleeful that his team captain and franchise player had allegedly killed a woman with his automobile, while two of his teammates conspired to keep it quiet. But he didn't exactly sound crushed either.

As Peterwicz contemplated the fates of Lo Mayne and Kwaanzii Parker, his mind jumped to a swatch of conversation he had logged a week or so ago. What had he labeled it . . . ah, there it was. *Mayne, Parker, Johnson, locker room, pregame.* The date said Feb. 18. It was obvious the three players weren't happy with one another but, when Peterwicz had listened the first time, he assumed Kwaanzii was talking about an incident with a female when he had acted badly, which wouldn't exactly be a surprise. Peterwicz performed a search command and queued it up. There it was. Kwaanzii distinctly said: "Maybe it's her I hit. Maybe it was somebody else I hit. Whatever, it's in the past."

Maybe it's her I hit.

Peterwicz thought back to Henry Shenk's funeral, how Lo had been one of the only Laser players to show, how gentlemanly Lo had been toward Shenk's widow, Jean, how he had exaggerated Henry's importance to make Jean feel good. Then he thought about how voyeuristic he felt when the montage of Jamal and Jilly had come on the screen. Then he thought how his wife would take it when he told her that the assistant executive producer credit was probably not going to happen.

"You busy?" he asked when Jamal picked up his extension.

JAMAL KELLY WAS A bit of a techno-geek himself, so his first reaction to seeing Evan Peterwicz's secret video room was awe. "Evan, dude, you must be trippin' down here."

Peterwicz nodded proudly. "It is quite a setup," he said.

Jamal fiddled with a few buttons and put on a set of headphones and tinkered with some volume and then sat down and looked at Peterwicz. "So, you gotta be kidding about this, right? Padgett has this setup to tape his own team? Everybody? Me? You? Himself?"

"Not himself," said Peterwicz. "And I don't seem to be on there much, probably because I'm always down here."

Jamal cocked his head and concentrated. *Let's see, I screwed Cherry Pie Holstrum on my desk. I must've scratched my balls about a thousand times. I once called Manny Burnett a "clothes whore" to one of the reporters on the phone. That should get my ass fired. I cussed at my mother after I hung up the phone . . . I . . . whoa! . . . I came on to Jilly over All-Star Weekend. Or she came on to me. Or . . .*

"You got anything, uh, showing me on there?" asked Jamal, trying to sound casual.

"Look, Jamal, this isn't about what I have on you or anybody else. You may think so, but it isn't. If I have anything to say about it, none of this stuff—except what I'm about to show you that concerns Lo and Kwaanzii—will ever become public."

"So, you have me, um, having fun with Cherry Pie Holstrum?"

That caught Peterwicz by surprise. Apparently, there were more interesting things to come on these tapes, and he briefly regretted having come clean.

"Nothing like that, Jamal," he said. "Look, let me show you what I have." And he queued up the tape. Together they watched the brief exchange among Lo, Litanium, and Kwaanzii. They watched it again and again and again, six times in all. Then they stared at each other for a full minute.

"It doesn't really prove anything, does it?" said Peterwicz.

"Not by itself," said Jamal. "I mean, Kwaanzii could be talking about one of his girlfriends."

"That's what I thought when I first heard it," said Peterwicz.

Jamal shook his head. "Look, one way or the other, Padgett can't get away with this anyway. No tape will ever see the light of day. I'm no lawyer, but, man, there must be a hundred violations of the right to privacy in these tapes. Didn't you think about that?"

Peterwicz took a deep breath. "You ever take a look at that twenty-five-page employment contract you signed?"

WHEN JAMAL GOT BACK to his office, his mind blown by the session in the Peterwicz video room, there were twenty-five telephone messages. Barbara Gordon herself, the queen of morning TV, had called requesting an interview with Lo on the *Today* show. The message said: "Tell Lo that Babs almost never calls personally." One of the messages was from the NBF PR man, Barton Sylvester, the man tasked with smothering off-court conflagrations. Jamal called him back.

"How's this playing back in New York?" asked Jamal.

"It's all over the place. The *Times* teased it. The *Post* and the *Daily News* ran it as the wood on page one. Lot of publicity for a nonplayoff team. Glad you left Yale?"

"Right about now I'd be a second-semester senior playing Frisbee on the quad," said Jamal. "Did you call because you're coming to help sort out the interview requests?"

"Better than that," said Sylvester. "I'm calling with news about Kwaanzii. He won rookie of the year. Congratulations."

"Jesus," said Jamal. "How 'bout that timing?"

"I know," said Sylvester. "Listen, nobody knows this. Nobody. Keep it under your hat and figure out when you want to announce it. We'll keep the lid on it here. Let a week or so go by and maybe this will die down."

Jamal laughed. "Barton, I've got three TV stations from Australia who said they're sending over news crews. That sound like something that's going to die down?"

CHAPTER 35

That Kwaanzii Parker had won rookie-of-the-year honors presented the Lasers' franchise, not to mention the NBF, with a dilemma: How to celebrate the accomplishments of a young man charged with a felony days earlier? The league honchos thought briefly about miscounting the vote and presenting the award to Hierumus "The Toaster" McWilliams, but, since Parker's dominance among the yearlings was so surpassing, the league chieftans figured everyone would smell a rat.

Besides, in the days since Jilly's story had appeared, the public perception of Kwaanzii had, curiously, risen. As opinion hardened against Lo, Litanium had become kind of a third-party nullity, but Kwaanzii was cast in the role of innocent. He was the teenager caught by circumstance, led astray by the philandering, father-in-absentia, reckless-driving veteran who tried to hide his treachery from the police. Plus, there was Kwaanzii's heroic play in the face of considerable internal pressure; while Lo Mayne had gone into the tank, Kwaanzii, the superstar-to-be, had carried the Lasers in this dark season. As a raft of other malefactors can attest, there is no quicker route to expiation in the NBF than a thirty-point game or two. So, eventually, the league office told Jamal that, while the franchise shouldn't organize a ticker-tape parade through down-town L.A., it was free to honor Kwaanzii in any way it saw fit.

How it saw fit, though, was a sticking point. Owen and Jamal agreed on only one thing: The ceremony should take place during the Lasers' last game of the season, two nights hence against Portland. There would be no playoff battles for the Lasers, so why not send the message to the home fans that the future was redolent with promise? Beyond that, owner and PR chief were at odds. Padgett, feeling validated in his season-long insistence that Kwaanzii get more playing time, wanted bells and whistles; Jamal—still distrustful of Kwaanzii's role in the accident, distrust-ful of anything related to Kwaanzii, in fact—wanted a brief and understated pregame ceremony. Ultimately, it didn't matter what Jamal wanted, so he and other Lasers employees planned a half-time observance during which the suspended Kwaanzii would be ushered to center court, in mufti, and panegyrized by Padgett, Manny Burnett, and the president of the Props for Parker Fan Club.

Erick Silver, meanwhile, sensing that the Lasers' public rela-tions machine wasn't exactly gearing up for an all-out effort on behalf of his young client, had contacted the local ABC affiliate about doing a puff piece. In exchange for unfettered access to Kwaanzii during that summer's production of the rookie's debut rap album, *Jes 4 the Folks*, the station would do a five-minute piece about the rookie of the year in which his legal troubles would be minimized.

The reporter was Joannie Carthadge, until recently an unre-markable beat writer for the *L.A. Times* who—like so many ambi-tious, passably attractive twentysomethings in the sports depart-ment—found a refuge on the television airways as a sports "person-ality." Jilly, too, had received a number of offers to decamp to tele-vision but paid the overtures no mind. "You could double your salary in TV," a producer told her. "Maybe," Jilly said. "But no one frames a ninety-second sports desk clip. My passion is writing, not getting recognized at the airport."

Over tasteless Chinese takeout in their Santa Monica apartment, Jamal and Zeke sat down to watch the piece on Kwaanzii. "I'm sure this'll be up for every journalism prize," said Jamal, wrestling with a piece of oversoyed cabbage.

"Every time I see that ride, I get jealous all over again," said Zeke, as the camera and Joannie Carthadge followed Kwaanzii into his garage. With the reporter looking on with a plasticized smile, the rookie picked up a rag and began polishing his Jag.

"Yeah, like Kwaanzii's out there cleaning his own car," said Jamal.

The scene shifted to a closeup of Kwaanzii palming his hood ornament necklace. Jamal watched as his brother stopped in mid-bite, leaned forward, and stared hard and wide-eyed at the screen. "You TiVO-ing this, J.?" asked Zeke.

"Matter of course," said Jamal. "Let me guess. You're going to do a blog on Kwaanzii's Jag."

Zeke was deep in thought. Jamal looked at the screen. They had the sound down low, but Jamal could hear the rookie say, "Kind of my good-luck charm." The piece ended with Kwaanzii in the driveway of his mansion (he had finally found one to his satisfaction high in the Hollywood Hills with the requisite urinal in one of its nine bathrooms) frolicking with his Lhasa Apso, which he had named Spin Move. As with Italian marble, Kwaanzii apparently had a profound if inexplicable knowledge of all things relating to his pet. "The Dalai Lama, see, he used to give Apsos as gifts to the Manchu emperors," Kwaanzii was telling Carthadge, who was aerosoled into a white sweatsuit. "It was considered, like, sacred."

The clip finished with both Kwaanzii and the interviewer playing with the dog. "This is Joannie Carthadge reporting for KABC," she said, "on a lucky young man with an unbelievable spin move on the court . . . and a lovable Spin Move at home."

Zeke sat in silence, replaying over and over the scene in which Kwaanzii showed off his necklace.

"What?" said Jamal, growing impatient.

Finally, Zeke spoke. "You got the number of Lorenzen Mayne's lawyer?" he said. "That Zucker guy? I think you should call him."

JAMAL SHOULD'VE BEEN IN the middle of the postgame pack surrounding Kwaanzii, but the rookie and his designated spokesman for the evening, Erick Silver, seemed to have it covered. Improbably, the Lasers—still playing without Lo, Litanium, and Kwaanzii—had pulled out a season-ending 97–93 victory over the Portland Jaguars, a team in more serious disarray, if that were possible.

Buenos Diaz, playing like a man possessed—which is to say, like a man trying desperately not to be exiled to the Dual Circles of Hell, otherwise known as the CBA and the NBDL—scored a season-high 33 points. B. D. Lake, the righteous force in the middle, grabbed 19 rebounds. Willie Wainwright, always the ready-and-able fireman, directed the team with 10 assists. But since the game didn't mean anything, the big story was still the rookie of the year, who had been honored at halftime. The press peppered him with questions, which Kwaanzii handled, Jamal couldn't help noticing, with a dexterity that had increased as the season went on. And when a question veered too close to a legal matter, Erick Silver, like a valuable utility infielder, was there to field it.

Can you play with Lorenzen if he's here next year?

"Personnel decisions are up to management, but, sure, why not? He's our captain. I don't hold no grudges."

How much did the accident affect you guys as a team this season?

"I'd be lying if I said it helped, but I was able to play through it and I think Litanium was, too. You'd have to ask Lo how he felt about it."

Do you expect to do time for what happened?

"Come on, fellas," interrupted Silver. "You know he can't talk about the specifics of the case."

Jamal looked around. The two other suspended players had been given the option of staying away, which was what Lo had chosen to do. But Litanium was there, basking in the reflected glow of Kwaanzii like a proud midwife. The story line that had Cat as Kwaanzii's mentor had again taken hold, now that they were presented as partners against the disgraced Lo. All the Lasers, it seemed, were united behind their new franchise player. "*And a Child Shall Lead Them,*" the L.A. *Daily News* headline had proclaimed after Parker's rookie prize was announced.

Jamal looked over at Jilly, who had just wrapped up an interview with Buenos Diaz. She sat down wearily on a bench, alone, the crowd over by Kwaanzii, and Jamal caught her eye. He smiled. She smiled back. Jamal came over and plopped down beside her. Together they stared at the pack around Kwaanzii. "I just had to keep my perspective," they heard him say.

They were both stifling a laugh when the locker-room doors banged open and two men in suits entered the room. The men looked around as if to get their bearings, and one pointed to the crowded corner where Kwaanzii was answering questions. They walked over and began "Excuse me-ing" their way to the front of the pack.

"Kwaanzii Parker," said one, "would you come with us, please? You're being recharged in the vehicular death of Addie Denkins."

They whisked him out of the room briskly and efficiently, leaving everyone—teammates and reporters—wondering what the hell had just happened. Erick Silver reached for his cell phone and began punching in numbers so frantically that it flew out of his hands, like a slippery mackerel. The only one who didn't seem surprised, Jilly noticed, was Jamal, who wore a tight little smile.

"What do you know about this?" Jilly whispered to him.

"It's kind of complicated," he said, enjoying the moment.

"I'm on deadline," she said, "so can you do your best to uncomplicate it?" Jilly could see the other reporters, her competition, approaching Jamal like moths to light.

"Go to your office and instant-message me," he said. "I'll hold off everybody else."

CHAPTER 36

——Original Message——
From: Jilly Forrester—<inkstained@aol.com>
Sent: Mon 4/17 9:48 PM
To: Jamal Kelly—<JKHoops44@aol.com>
Subject: WHAT UP????

Okay, Jamal, I'm at the office. I got an hour until deadline. What the hell just happened in there?

——Original Message——
From: Jamal Kelly—<JKHoops44@aol.com>
Sent: Mon 4/17 9:51 PM
To: Jilly Forrester—<inkstained@aol.com>
Subject: RE: WHAT UP????

Not the smartest thing in the world to leave a paper trail. Then again Padgett is probably too busy with his video surveillance to monitor his employees' e-mail as well. Before I tell you anything, you're assuring me that my name's not going anywhere near your story. "Source within the organization" is as close as it's getting. We got a deal, Woodward?

— —Original Message— —
From: Jilly Forrester—<inkstained@aol.com>
Sent: Mon 4/17 9:55 PM
To: Jamal Kelly—<JKHoops44@aol.com>
Subject: RE: WHAT UP????

Have I burned u yet? Your name has pretty much disappeared from my memory bank. Get to the brass tacks. Please.

— —Original Message— —
From: Jamal Kelly—<JKHoops44@aol.com>
Sent: Mon 4/17 10:01 PM
To: Jilly Forrester—<inkstained@aol.com>
Subject: RE: WHAT UP????

Fair enough. Where to begin? Whether everyone—you, your editors, and the DA's office—wanted to believe it or not, there was always something fishy about the way "LoGate" went down. He comes forward and breaks his silence but then lies about the level of his involvement? C'mon now. If you know Lorenzen, you know that's not consistent with the way he is. Lo is a lot of things (not all complimentary), but he is a not a liar. Also, if you know Kwaanz and Tribal Cat, you know that their "corroborated" story still doesn't move the credibility needle. Even before a grand jury. And you also know that a prosecutor looking to make a name for himself will trump up charges against a celebrity—especially a black millionaire, I might suggest in my more cynical moments.

Anyway, my brother Zeke (think u met him a few weeks back) and I are watching the KABC(TV) puff piece on Kwaanz a few night ago. We're only half paying attention but then Zeke says, "Hold Up!" . . . Z knows everything there is to know about cars. He sees

Kwaanz fingering that Jaguar talisman he wears and notices that its hind leg is chipped. Then he remembers that Kwaanz has a different hood ornament on his Jag. Why would he change ornaments, which (not that I'd know firsthand) is apparently a real pain on a Jaguar? And why would his Jaguar medallion be chipped? Then we remember Lo saying that Kwaanz hit that woman smack-dab on the front of his Jag.

See where this is going?

— —Original Message— —
From: Jilly Forrester—<inkstained@aol.com>
Sent: Mon 4/17 10:08 PM
To: Jamal Kelly—<JKHoops44@aol.com>
Subject: RE: WHAT UP????

There's no time for the I-was-only-doing-my-job riff . . . but I WAS ONLY DOING MY JOB!!! I was covering facts. It's not my place to give opinions on guilt or innocence. The DA charged Lo and the folks on the grand jury believed what they heard. Anyway, I see where it's going, I guess, but you wanna flesh it out a bit more? You mean, your brother, the one you told me was an All-American slacker, is going to turn out to be the hero?

— —Original Message— —
From: Jamal Kelly—<JKHoops44@aol.com>
Sent: Mon 4/17 10:11 PM
To: Jilly Forrester—<inkstained@aol.com>
Subject: RE: WHAT UP????

Call Zeke what you want. You're the journalist. I'm just the . . . what was that term of endearment you once laid on me?

Wait, it's coming to me. I'm just the Lasers' Home Boy Friday. But no hard feelings or anything. I'd practically forgotten that.

Where were we? Oh right. Anyway, to answer your question, I suppose Zeke is the (admittedly unlikely) hero in all this. He notices the busted hood ornament. We call Sheldon Zucker—the subject, you'll surely recall, of one of your many memorable off-day masterpieces—who, of course, is representing Lo. We tell him our theory. He calls the DA and says, "You gotta get a warrant for that necklace and you gotta get a forensics team to take that medallion, enter it into evidence, and send it to a crime lab." Usually these things take weeks, but I guess because this is a high-profile case, the DA consents.

Not that you got any of this from me . . .

— —Original Message— —
From: Jilly Forrester—<inkstained@aol.com>
Sent: Mon 4/17 10:20 PM
To: Jamal Kelly—<JKHoops44@aol.com>
Subject: RE: WHAT UP????

Just like that? Zucker snaps his fingers and the next thing you know they're hauling Kwaanzii out of the locker room? Hey, the Zuck doesn't have that much jack with the people getting him drinks at the Bok. Didn't the police get reinvolved? You sure you can get DNA evidence that quick?

— —Original Message— —
From: Jamal Kelly—<JKHoops44@aol.com>
Sent: Mon 4/17 10:30 PM
To: Jilly Forrester—<inkstained@aol.com>
Subject: RE: WHAT UP????

Way this team finished the season, the least the courtside grandees can expect is prompt drink service.

So of course the cops got involved again. As I heard it, investigators go to scene of the crime, comb the grounds and, sure enough, they find the chipped Jaguar leg. Then they head to Kwaanzii's pad and ask for his necklace. (Check out the pictures from tonight's cere-mony—already downloaded on our website, thank you very much—and you'll notice he's not wearing his "great-luck charm" for the first time in memory.)

When the cops were over there, Kwaanz put up a stink but he had a buddy over, that shadowy guy, D'Angelo. You've probably seen him around; all-time fame siphoner; one of the Lasers turns around quick he's liable to whack D'Angelo in the nose. Anyway, D'Angelo convinces Kwaanz to hand over the necklace. But I gath-er adds, "Don't sweat it, Kwaanz, I can get you a new Jaguar hood ornament tomorrow." Oops. Cops realize that D'Angelo has "auto-motive expertise." All starts to make sense.

Cops leave with medallion in a bag. Take it to a crime lab in Long Beach. Forget the name but Sheldon will know it. Results come back three days later and sure enough it's covered with DNA that matches Addie Denkins's. Which means that not only did Kwaanzii hit the woman but he (along with Litanium) lied to the grand jury, lied to the police, and obstructed a police investigation. Which proves one of life's verities: The coverup will be the thing that bites you in the ass.

——Original Message——
From: Jilly Forrester—<inkstained@aol.com>
Sent: Mon 4/17 10:39 PM

To: Jamal Kelly—<JKHoops44@aol.com>
Subject: RE: WHAT UP????

Doesn't Kwaanzii realize the hammer's going to come down when they take his beloved necklace? Also—maybe this is a question for Zucker—does Lo automatically get "uncharged" as soon as they charge Kwaanzii?

— —Original Message— —
From: Jamal Kelly—<JKHoops44@aol.com>
Sent: Mon 4/17 10:45 PM
To: Jilly Forrester—<inkstained@aol.com>
Subject: RE: WHAT UP????

You know how Kwaanz is. Ever since he was a 12-year-old AAU star, he's had an army of enablers and toadies ready to tell him that his shit smells like Aramis. Guy has a level of supreme self-belief that you and I will never know: He's always gonna hit the big shot to win the game. At least that's how he thinks. Investigators come to take away take his Jaguar medallion that chipped when he drove his car 90 mph into an unwitting pedestrian? No problem. It will still work out. Why? Because I am Kwaanzii Parker. That's why.

I doubt he even told his lawyer when they came for his necklace.

As for Lo, I haven't spoken to him tonight. It's not like he's out of the woods. He was there that night, driving his car at a ridiculous speed. He saw what happened. He waited months to report it. We're not in slap-on-the-wrist territory here. But now that it's HIS turn to make a deal with Bauer and get a lesser charge in exchange for testimony against Kwaanzii and Litanium, I don't see him doing any time. It's clear Kwaanz hit and killed the woman. Not

Lo. It's also clear that Kwaanz and Tribal Cat perjured themselves before the grand jury.

— —Original Message— —
From: Jilly Forrester—<inkstained@aol.com>
Sent: Mon 4/17 10:50 PM
To: Jamal Kelly—<JKHoops44@aol.com>
Subject: RE: WHAT UP????

All right, I gotta call Zucker quick. Just give me the sentence or two background on Zeke. Is that his real name? Age? How long's he lived out here? You told me once he had a luxury-car blog? I'll mention that. Probably get him a few hits.

One other thing: Peterwicz, of all people, sez he wants to see me tomorrow. And you're going to be there? Know what that's about?

— —Original Message— —
From: Jamal Kelly—<JKHoops44@aol.com>
Sent: Mon 4/17 11:05 PM
To: Jilly Forrester—<inkstained@aol.com>
Subject: RE: WHAT UP????

I can tell you this right now: Ezekiel (Zeke) Kelly will not be returning calls seeking comment. I suppose that, JUST DOING YOUR JOB and all, you need to note that he is the brother of Lasers' media relations overlord Jamal Kelly. But the less time you dwell on that connection, the better. (Do right by me and I may treat you to WhattaBurger when the dust finally settles.)

Zeke (who has consented to me sharing this with you) is 28, moved out from Brooklyn two months ago. He writes a popular blog for the website: www.socal-sweetrides.com. He also is a Taurus, knows every episode of *Good Times* by heart, snores a lot, and makes a mean three-bean chili, but don't feel compelled to write that.

As for Peterwicz, let's just say he may have yet another interesting tidbit for you. When it rains . . .

——Original Message——
From: Jilly Forrester—<inkstained@aol.com>
Sent: Mon 4/17 11:12 PM
To: Jamal Kelly—<JKHoops44@aol.com>
Subject: RE: WHAT UP????

Now you've given me something else to think (worry?) about. All right, lemme call Zucker and start typing this sucker up. It's been an interesting season to say the least. I'm almost sorry it's . . .

NO I'M NOT.

I'll see you tomorrow. Peterwicz said to meet him down by the court. I hope it's something more interesting than a game of H-O-R-S-E.

——Original Message——
From: Jamal Kelly—<JKHoops44@aol.com>
Sent: Mon 4/17 11:29 PM
To: Jilly Forrester—<inkstained@aol.com>
Subject: RE: WHAT UP????

You can spot him the H-O-R. Dude has no game whatsoever.

But stop by when you're done. I'd be interested in a debriefing. So to speak. And in case your superiors read your e-mails, assure them you're paying me for tonight's intelligence briefing in small, unmarked bills. I'm outta here. Mention me in the Pullitzer speech. JK

From: Jilly Forrester—<inkstained@aol.com>
Sent: Mon 4/17 11:41 PM
To: Jamal Kelly—<JKHoops44@aol.com>
Subject: RE: WHAT UP????

Pulitzer has one L, Whiz Kid. Stick to math. See you tomorrow.

CHAPTER 37

April 18
Final Los Angeles Lasers Record: 38-44

After the last game of the season, the front office has the feel of a beach town the day after Labor Day. There's a palpable realization that it will be months before the masses return and the excitement of high season kicks in. On this unseasonably hot day, that transitory feeling was particularly pronounced at the Bok, for the Lasers were due for more than cosmetic surgery over the summer. No one from Padgett down to the locker-room towel boy would say he was sad it was over, not considering the steady diet of tabloid entrees that had defined the season. But there was a feeling of disappointment, too, of hope lost, opportunity squandered. For a decade, the Lasers had been at or near the top of the league, a standard of excellence that most other teams didn't come close to meeting; not making the playoffs, in a league in which more than half the teams *do*, represented a colossal fall.

The ultimate responsibility rested with the players and coaches, of course, but every Laser employee shared in it. *Could I have answered the phone better?* wondered the secretaries. *Could I have gotten the players in better shape?* wondered the trainers. *Could I have marketed the Lasers any more aggressively?* wondered the marketing people. (Actually, Martha Ciccarelli thought she had made many *positive contributions!*)

Jamal Kelly felt a little blue but didn't have time for self-flagellation. He had to finish the press release detailing the "mutual decision" that John Watson would resign as coach, which was in fact rooted in truth. If there was one thing Watson could decipher—aside from an opposing team's offensive sets—it was handwriting on the wall. The Lasers would not elevate Doug Carter to the position and would immediately begin "an aggressive search for a name coach." That meant that Carter would again play Sancho to Watson's Quixote, waiting, with bags packed, for his master to get another assignment.

Everyone knew that the Lasers would be gutted—"Think Filene's Basement on Labor Day weekend," Manny Burnett told the other GMs. Litanium and Kwaanzii were awaiting trial, and in the face of overwhelming evidence, were in reality awaiting sentencing. They were expected to do time, and would no doubt miss the following season.

One deal was already all but finalized: Lo Mayne would be sent to Charlotte in exchange for Vernell "The Colonel" Williams. It wouldn't be announced for months because "future draft rights and financial considerations" would have to be worked out to make it fit within the Sphinxian salary cap. But The Colonel, who fashioned himself the Hollywood action hero going uncast in actionless Charlotte, would be coming to L.A., and Lorenzen Mayne would be going home.

As Jamal walked down the stairs to floor level, heading for his and Jilly's meeting with Evan Peterwicz, he encountered Cherry Pie Holstrum. In the weeks since their satisfying but somehow sad coupling, Jamal had felt chagrined when he ran into her, sometimes literally, as he always seemed to be rounding a corner when she came bustling by. But Cherry Pie would give Jamal a quick peck on the cheek or a squeeze on the palm.

"Hey, where you going, Whiz Kid?" she said, grabbing his hand. "There's no more games. Haven't you heard?"

"Oh, just checking on something down here," he said. "Hey, I'm sorry about your girls. All that lost revenue. They get paid by the game, right?"

Cherry Pie sighed. "Goes with the territory," she said. "Some'll just go to more auditions. Some'll just work more hours as waitresses or whatever. Me? I can squeeze in another couple weeks of cheerleading camp and get a few more massage clients."

"Ever resourceful," he said. "Listen, I—"

She put an index finger to his lips. "You don't have to say anything," she said. "What happened, happened. I never called you again, did I? I never moved in on your action, did I?"

Jamal laughed. "Denise, there's not a bachelor in L.A. with less action going than me. No, what I wanted to say was thanks. I mean, for acting the way you did. There was at least one adult between us."

Cherry Pie put her hands on her hips. "Hey, you're talking like this is good-bye. I'll see you around. This job doesn't stop just because we lost forty-five games."

"As the head of PR," Jamal said, "I'm obligated to tell you we only lost forty-four. Okay, I'll see you around."

As he walked away, he reached into his pocket and pulled out a piece of paper. *Gabe Spielberger, Philly owner, 215-766-7676.*

No, Jamal thought, *you probably won't be seeing me around.*

PETERWICZ HAD ALREADY APOLOGIZED a dozen times, and he hadn't even switched on the monitor yet.

"Evan, I get the point," said Jilly. "I have the feeling I'm not going to like what I see, but I promise not to take it out on you."

She turned to Jamal. "Do *you* know what we're about to see?"

"Only in a general sense," said Jamal.

"Can I take it out on you then?" she said.

Jilly and Jamal, their hips touching, moved in behind Peterwicz. A date-time stamp flashed on, *Feb. 27, 10:17 p.m.* They watched as Cherry Pie Holstrum massaged Jamal's neck, then moved to shut the door, then . . . and Peterwicz clicked it off.

"Ah," said Jilly, moving away from Jamal, "I have the feeling we missed the best part."

Peterwicz fiddled with his controls. Jamal noticed that Jilly kept her distance from him this time. Another date-time, *Feb. 22, 9:07 p.m.* Jamal could hear Jilly breathe in and out as she watched them in Jamal's office on the night of the All-Star Game.

"This isn't chronological, Evan," said Jilly. "Have you arranged this according to some sort of theme?"

Jilly watched as, on the screen, she reached for the belt line of her jeans. That's when Peterwicz clicked off the image. No one said anything for a full ten seconds.

"Fucking scumbags!" said Jilly finally. "So this is what you've been doing since your midseason MIA? How proud you must be."

"Jilly, it wasn't my idea," stammered Peterwicz. "I had to—"

"Fuckin' save it, Evan," Jilly interrupted. "Somebody's ass is getting sued. Let me guess whose? Owen Padgett's!" She whirled to leave and Peterwicz jumped from his seat.

"Listen," said Peterwicz. "I just want to let you know that a touch of the button and all this is gone."

"How do I know you and Padgett don't have this backed up?" she said.

"Padgett doesn't know how to work this, Jilly," said Peterwicz. "He left that up to me."

Jilly sat down, still seething. "He's trying to do some reality show, right?" said Jilly. "But who's he kidding? Who's going to sign a waiver to appear on this bush-league NBF Real World? Litanium maybe. But that's it."

Jamal took a deep breath. "Believe it or not, we all did," he said. "We just didn't know it. It was some of the small type in the employment contract."

"I didn't sign squat," said Jilly.

"Correct," said Peterwicz. "That's why this is all up to you. You want to write a story, it's yours. You want it to go away, it goes away."

Jilly sat back and put her hands behind her head, running through the options. It was a legit story. *Ego-mad owner tapes his own team.* She'd have to mention her own small part in it. But it *was* a story. On the other hand, if she wrote about it, she'd need the tapes to prove her point, and if the tapes existed, then a lot of people could get hurt. Tapes always get out. That's what tapes do.

She looked at Jamal, then at Peterwicz, then back at Jamal. She smiled and then she started laughing. They loosened up and began laughing, too, though at what they weren't sure. "I was just thinking about the guy before me," said Jilly. "Became a Buddhist monk after a few years of covering this team. And, when I got this gig, I remember thinking, Something must've been wrong with him. It can't be that weird." She smacked both hands against her knees and stood up.

"Zap it, Evan," she said. "Make it all go away."

And he did.

JAMAL CAUGHT UP TO Jilly in the parking lot. She was getting into her car, just as Lo Mayne, now driving a tan Chevy Blazer, was pulling into a spot. Lo got out and stared at them a minute, then put down his bag and motioned for them to come over.

"Is this what they mean by a harmonic convergence?" said Jilly.

"Not sure what that means," said Lo, "but it sounds right."

Jilly said, "I notice you have a new car." She tried to make it sound casual but *car* had become a charged word.

"Better gas mileage," said Lo. "Or so I learned on Brother Zeke's car blog." He picked up his bag.

"Listen, I have something to tell both of you," said Jamal, "so I might as well do it now. I got a job offer. I'm going to Philly. The owner there, I met him during All-Star Weekend, and he went for some of my stats stuff, and asked me to come be his assistant GM. I'm going to take it. Zeke's staying—his blog's going real well—but I figured, Lo, since you weren't going to be here . . ."

"Wait a minute," said Jilly. "Where's Lo going?"

"J., you don't even work here anymore, and you're giving out scoops," said Lo. "I'm getting traded, Jilly. To Charlotte. But nothing's worked out yet so I'd appreciate it if you . . . man, who am I kidding? You're going to write it anyway, so go ahead and write it."

With that, he started walking toward the entrance of the Bok, Jilly and Jamal staring at his retreating form. Then he stopped, turned around slowly, and came back. He put down his bag and threw his long arms around both of them.

"Jamal, shit, man, congratulations," he said. "That's what I should've said."

"Me, too," said Jilly. "Congratulations, Jamal. I mean that."

They stayed like that for a while huddled together, too embarrassed to break apart.

"I'm going to be a father now," said Lo. "That's why I asked to get traded back to Charlotte. I don't know how people are going to accept me. But I'm going to be a father. A good one, too."

"I know you will, Lo," said Jilly.

"Maybe you can go down there sometime, do a follow-up story," said Jamal. He smiled. "Least you could do after fucking up the man's life."

Jilly was the first to break apart. "I'll come down for a visit, Lo," she said, "but I probably won't be doing a story. Like you guys, I'm making a change."

"You getting hitched with Robbie Dickworth after all?" asked Jamal.

Jilly stared him down. "Moving East like you," she said. "The *New York Times.*"

"You get dealt for an op-ed columnist to be named later?" Jamal asked.

"Straight up free-agent deal," said Jilly. She looked at Lo. "Didn't even have to give Erick Silver a cut."

"Seriously," said Jamal, "what are you going to do there? Not sports, I guess."

"It's pretty open," said Jilly. "They're calling me an enterprise reporter. Pretty much chase my own stories, make my own schedule. Too good to pass up."

"New York and Philly," said Lo. "You guys are a ninety-minute train ride away from stayin' in each other's face. What's that you said before, Jilly? Harmonic convergence? Maybe it's another one of those."

Jilly gave them each a peck on the cheek. "Clearly," she said, "that remains to be seen."

DESPERATION HAD CLOSED IN on Owen Padgett like fog off the ocean. He had gotten a bad vibe about his "can't-miss reality show" several weeks earlier when Warren Colson told him "everybody's trending away from reality." But Padgett, nothing if not - self-enchanted, refined his presentation, and, with renewed confidence, had scheduled four meetings for the same day.

At CBS, Padgett excitedly talked up the scene where John Watson bares his ass to the general manager. He was told, "We're skewing hero these days, Owen." At ABC, Padgett animatedly peddled the sexy choreographer making it with the PR guy. He was told, "*Distressed Domestics* does that every week and I guarantee our women look better than her." At Bravo, Padgett passionately promoted the "inside drama about the fatal car accident that's been in all the papers." He was told, "Precisely. It's been in all the papers. So why would we rehash it?"

And here he was at Fox. He didn't want to troll that low on the network food chain, but he found himself pitching like a Fuller brush man to a guy named Gavin, who was balding with a compensatory goatee.

"Gavin, dude, I got the clearances, I'm telling you," he said.

Gavin from Fox shook his head. "Owen, I ran it by legal, man, and they say, 'No go,' he said. "The gestalt is all wrong. Contracts like that have more holes than a block of Jarlsberg. We can't go getting blind-sided by million-dollar lawsuits."

"Gavin, I've watched your network," said Padgett. "Fistfights. Sex. Threats. It virtually defines the Fox ethos."

Gavin was rather enjoying the moment—the deep-pocketed playboy owner of the Los Angeles Lasers in his office, begging like a dog for a biscuit.

"I have one thought, O," said Gavin. "Why don't you repackage it as fiction? Do the whole thing like it's made-up. The viewers will try to figure out who the characters correspond to in real life. It's win-win, O."

Padgett was a broken man, but he couldn't let Gavin from Fox see that. He gathered up his papers, shoved them into his Ferragamo briefcase, and stood up.

"Make it realistic, only change everything around, the names and all that," continued Gavin, following Padgett to the door. "Make the team—I don't know—the Los Angeles Lakers. Something along that line. You get the same crazy stuff, but you don't worry about lawsuits or burning bridges."

"I'm not willing to stoop that low," said Padgett, walking away.

"You kidding me?" shouted Gavin. "Just call it 'reality-based fiction' or some bullshit like that. The eighteen-to-thirty-four demo will eat it up!"

Padgett was down the hall by this time. "What kind of a coward would do that?"

ACKNOWLEDGMENTS

This project never would have gotten off the ground without the diligence of our agent, Scott Waxman. We owe a debt of gratitude to our editor, Brett Valley, both for his assiduous work and for his willingness to let two sports writers try their hands at fiction. Special thanks to a team of readers that included Bill Colson, Hank Hersch, Rich O'Brien, Sam Silverstein, Lester Munson, and Jeff Spielberger. We also appreciate the support of our bosses at *Sports Illustrated* — Terry McDonell, David Bauer, Rob Fleder, and Mike Bevans — gave to this project. Finally, a shout-out to our friends, colleagues, and contacts in the NBA. For the record, we really do love this game.

J.M./L.J.W
10/01/05

ABOUT THE AUTHORS

JACK MCCALLUM has been at *Sports Illustrated* since 1981 and the chief NBA writer since 1985. His work has appeared in the *Best American Sports Writing Anthology*, and last year he won the Basketball Hall of Fame's Curt Gowdy Award for outstanding writing. He lives in Bethlehem, Pennsylvania.

L. JON WERTHEIM, who has been at *Sports Illustrated* since 1997, is the author of *Venus Envy* and *Transition Game: How Hoosiers Went Hip-Hop*. His work has appeared in the *Best American Sports Writing Anthology*. He lives in New York City.